"If I'd gone out right then, maybe it would have gone different."

"Different how?"

Her answer is a dark, bitter grunt. She leans back, and I catch another glimpse of the bright blue fluid. It is bubbling in the well of her damaged ear. Rounded with surface tension, it has the liquid weight of blood.

I've seen this fluid on TV, at the heart of a swarm of deadly alchemized wasps and flowers.

"I went to bed," Astrid says. "I lay there with the kaleidoscope and stared into other people's houses. I spied on my next-door neighbor, who was scrubbing her kitchen floor. She was crying, completely freaking out. I thought about the gold flakes and whether money could help her. Magic, turning lead into gold . . . I could help everyone. . . ."

"Your first thought was helping the neighbor?"

She shrugs: according to the psych profile, Astrid rarely admits to being altruistic. "I wouldn't have wanted to end up like that. Alone, half-crazy. Watching her, I remembered I wanted a real home, a family. Kids, husband—"

"A husband specifically?"

"Anyone," she insists, coloring. "The point is I hoped to use the chantments to pull my budding family together."

"Soon enough I learned what the chantments were, that they had to be a secret."

"But by then you'd already told Sahara and Jacks."

"It was my first big mistake." The bead of blue liquid in her ear seems to strain upward, reaching skyward. Then it sucks back down, out of sight.

"This is an entertaining and terrifying tale. Astrid, Jacks, and Sahara will enchant you, and lead you down unexpected paths of discovery and danger. A great read that will make you look for magic in everyday objects!"
—Toby Bishop, author of *Airs Beneath the Moon*

TOR BOOKS BY A. M. DELLAMONICA

Indigo Springs
Blue Magic (forthcoming)

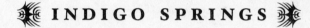

INDIGO SPRINGS

A. M. DELLAMONICA

TOR®

A TOM DOHERTY ASSOCIATES BOOK

NEW YORK

This is a work of fiction. All of the characters, organizations, and events
portrayed in this novel are either products of the author's imagination
or are used fictitiously.

INDIGO SPRINGS

Edited by James Frenkel

A Tor Book
Published by Tom Doherty Associates, LLC
175 Fifth Avenue
New York, NY 10010

www.tor-forge.com

Tor® is a registered trademark of Tom Doherty Associates, LLC.

Library of Congress Cataloging-in-Publication Data

Dellamonica, A. M.
    Indigo Springs / A. M. Dellamonica.—1st ed.
        p.   cm.
    "A Tom Doherty Associates Book."
    ISBN 978-0-7653-1947-0
    1. Young women—Fiction. 2. Magic—Fiction. 3. City and
town life—United States—Fiction. I. Title.
PR9199.4.D448I52   2009
813'.6—dc22
                                                        2009031595

First Edition: November 2009

Printed in the United States of America

0 9 8 7 6 5 4 3 2 1

To Kelly, and the next twenty years of our sleepover

ACKNOWLEDGMENTS

Many people have provided me with advice and assistance since I began writing *Indigo Springs* in 2001, and continued to do so after I completed revisions in mid-2003. I am deeply grateful to my agent, Linn Prentis; my editor, Jim Frenkel; and a host of editors, writers, and supporters who've guided me over the years, especially Wayne Arthurson, Ellen Datlow, Gardner Dozois, Nalo Hopkinson, Doug Lain, Louise Marley, Jessica Reisman, Harry Turtledove, and Peter Watts.

I am blessed in having a loving and supportive family. My wife, Kelly Robson, and my parents—Barb Millar, Brian Millar, William Robson, and Sandra Robson—have always been enthusiastic, clear-eyed, and loyal supporters of my writing. Michelle, Sherelyn, Susan, and Bill have done the same, while providing the much-needed teasing that is the province of siblings. Friends too numerous to name have done everything from reading drafts to providing moral support. In particular, I would like to mention Lisa Cohen, Ming Dinh, Trent Doiron, Denise Garzon, Nicki Hamilton, Liz Hughes, Elaine Mari, Ginger Mullen, Annie Reid, Ramona Roberts, Lealle Ruhl, and Brian Wetton.

You made it possible for me to write this book, and I will always be grateful.

INDIGO SPRINGS

"YOU'RE GOING TO FALL in love today." It is the first thing Astrid Lethewood says to me. A heartbeat later Patience joins us in the foyer and I nearly believe her.

I've seen Patience—on TV, on security feeds—but nothing has prepared me for meeting a demi-goddess. My brain seizes up, my hands get damp, and my mouth dries. I smell popcorn, hear the distant music of a carousel. A tingle of arousal threatens to embarrass me, but that, at least, I am ready for. My jacket, folded over one arm, hangs discreetly over my groin.

Today Patience is curly haired and black, with breasts—I can't help looking—as firm and curvaceous as if they had been sculpted by Rodin. Her lips are full, her teeth straight, and her brown eyes are luminous and warm. Her skin has the seal-fat sleekness of youth, but she does not look young.

Soon she will look utterly different, if just as devastating.

"Who are you?" she asks, voice full of music.

"My name is Will Forest. I'm—"

"Another of Roche's inquisitors? When'll he give up?"

"Don't be naïve," I say.

She pops a candy into her mouth, crunching defiantly. "I got nothing to say to you."

I pull in a breath. The carousel music tinkles on, and my spirits ride along, taking my inner child to the circus. "I'm here to talk to Astrid."

"Great—another therapist type who thinks he can get through to her." She puts a protective hand out to Astrid, who is hiding in her shadow. Proximate invisibility, the doctors call it, as if naming the behavior gives them a measure of control. The everyday world of telecommunications and two-hour commutes is crumbling, so they crouch in the surveillance center, labeling Astrid's every twitch.

Even now she is shrinking against the wall. "Is this when the guards start shooting?"

I glance at the well-armed young women in the corridor. They frown back, probably annoyed that I'm blocking the threshold of the apartment entrance.

Astrid sobs into a clenched fist, and Patience strokes her hair, glaring at me. "Just leave us alone!"

"I'm not here to upset you, but I'm not going away either." To emphasize the point, I step inside and shut the white door. Steel bolts clunk into place behind it: a vault door sealing us inside. This prison is two hundred feet belowground and surrounded by bedrock. To get here, I have been X-rayed, frisked, fingerprinted, and DNA tested. My identity has been confirmed and reconfirmed so completely that I am almost beginning to doubt it.

"As I said, my name is Will Forest." I take care to speak to them both. "I'm here to interview Astrid about—"

"Please, Doc, go away." Patience locks her bewitching eyes on me. "She can't help you."

I want to give in, like the others before me, but I hold her gaze, fighting the spell with thoughts of my missing kids. "I'm not a doctor, Patience, and I'm not leaving."

Astrid stops crying with a hiccup. "Didn't I show him around the place?"

"Show him the door, sweetie."

"Why don't you let her decide?" Opening my suitcase, I bring out a battered, plastic-wrapped paintbrush.

Astrid's breath catches. She looks at me closely, searching my face. "I'm supposed to believe you'd let me have it back?"

"Cooperation is a two-way street. I don't expect something for nothing, Astrid."

She licks her lips. "I need paper. Cards. Playing cards."

"I've brought them."

"Astrid, you're not ready," Patience says.

"How long do you expect us to give her?"

"She's in shock."

"Astrid?" I say.

"It was okay, Patience." She slides to her knees, face raised, eyes locked on the paintbrush.

"Fine." Throwing up her hands, Patience wafts away.

Astrid begins to hyperventilate. "When are we?"

"You said something about showing me around."

"I said that?" Her tone is dubious. "Is that today?"

"Do you know how long you've been here?"

"We were locked up for about twelve weeks. . . ." Her eyelids flutter; she seems to be counting. "Eight in jail, four here. That's twelve."

"That's right. You were moved here a month ago."

"The comfy prison." She shudders.

The apartment is part of an underground military base: a VIP housing unit that got converted to a jail cell when this crisis arose. It comes with false windows, frosted glass alight with phony full-spectrum sunshine.

"You razed your gardens," Astrid says. "Bird blood, right? If you put tulip bulbs in the front, daffodils—"

"I'm not much for the outdoors these days," I say.

"The woods aren't as deep as they seem." She breaks off, eyes wandering. "Have we . . . Sahara—"

"It's all right," I say, because I've watched hundreds of hours of surveillance footage on this pair, and that is what Patience tells her.

Astrid curls away, then bangs her head against the drywall. "Roche sent you down here to screw me over."

"It's not like that." I grasp her shoulders. "You help me, I'll help you."

"Help . . ." She jerks her head again, but I'm holding her away from the wall.

"Let me help you, Astrid."

She flinches, then seems to calm down. "Want to see the rest of the place?"

"Sure."

She listlessly tours me through the apartment. Every counter, shelf, and tabletop is cluttered with baubles and jewelry, offerings from Patience's admiring public. The air smells of paint, and the furniture is inexpensive particleboard, two decades out of date. One piece stands out: an oak cabinet that dominates the living room wall.

"My grandfather is gonna make that," Astrid explains.

"I thought he was an accountant."

"He took up woodworking after he retired. Terrible at it— made Ma a rocking chair that almost killed her. Tips too far, falls, hits her head."

"Ouch." Evelyn Lethewood has mentioned the incident too; it happened when she was a teenager.

Astrid leans a damp cheek against the varnished wood. "Colonel Roach takes this out of Ma's garage for me."

"I asked him to."

"You?"

"Yes." She's mentioned the cabinet in her ramblings, even searching for it in the spot it now occupies.

"You're a regular Santa Claus, aren't you?"

"I meant it as a show of good faith."

"It's all happening." Her hand drifts out, settling on my briefcase. "It's finally Will day, isn't it?"

"It's the sixth of September."

She starts to weep, tugging her hair. "Will day, Jackson day, fire, quake day, cutthroats, boomsday. Blood on the paintings, painted spatters across the walls . . ."

Patience peers through a doorway, arching her brows in challenge. "Making out okay, Santa?"

"I'm fine." I rap my knuckles on Astrid's cabinet, drawing her attention. "Only things my granddad ever made were model airplanes and bad wine."

She sniffles. "Think you can trade with me? I'll bare my soul for treats, like a dog?"

"I thought you'd like to have something familiar around, that's all."

"Thinking of my welfare." Her eyes narrow. "I know about you."

"Do you?"

"You're divorcing, I know that."

"Am I supposed to believe you're psychic? Patience could have gone through my office."

"Right, Patience. I'm small potatoes, right? The side issue. The material witness."

"The accomplice?"

Her mouth tightens. "You have two kids and a pit bull, which is funny because you don't like dogs."

The words bring up gooseflesh on my neck. "My son Carson wanted a puppy. I'm a soft touch."

She scoffs. "You're here to break me open."

"Astrid, all I want is to talk."

"Gull dropping mussels onto rocks, that's you. Cracking shells, getting the meat. Break everything open."

"Astrid, I know you've been through a traumatic—"

"I'm *not* insane."

"Then you've no excuse for not cooperating." I will coax the truth from this raving, damaged woman. I need to learn how Patience became a shape-changing beauty, how she defies locks and assassins by turning to mist and drifting through walls and bullets, rocks and people.

I'm here to find out how Astrid, a landscape gardener who never finished high school, came to possess a collection of objects we can only label as mystical, despite our science and rationality.

Most important, I'm supposed to learn how Astrid's child-hood friend, Sahara Knax, took those mystical items and used them to create an eco-terrorist cult with half a million devoted followers. I need to discover Sahara's weaknesses, anything that will tell my panicked government how to fight as her numbers grow, as she unleashes monsters into the seas and forests, as she forces us to napalm U.S. territory to destroy the infestations. Her actions grow more dangerous daily, and our attempts to locate her have failed. Astrid may be our only hope.

"The grumbles are so loud," Astrid says, "I can't remember when things happen. So much compressed magic . . ."

"You want to make things right, don't you?"

She clutches my arm. "You had an accident last month. A contaminated blue jay attacked your car."

I rasp my tongue over my lips, remembering the eagle-sized bird pecking holes in my windshield.

"That's when you killed off your yard."

Caroline had vanished with our kids just days earlier. I'd shot the bird, then pulled up the garden and, in a rage, burned it. Instead of telling Astrid this, I say: "Lots of people are sterilizing their gardens."

With a defeated sigh, she leads me to the kitchen, where Patience is sorting tea bags. "Santa Claus drinks coffee," Astrid says.

"We don't have coffee."

"It's okay, tea's fine."

Patience holds up a bag of Darjeeling. "You don't look military."

"Are you asking what I do for a living?"

"Yeah," Astrid says. "This is the part where you tell us."

"You don't already know?"

"Patience asked, not me."

"I'm no psychic," Patience says, crunching another candy as she dangles the tea bag. The swing of her wrist is hypnotic; I nod to show Darjeeling is fine.

"I'm a crisis negotiator for the Portland city police," I say.

"Hostage haggler. Same as Roach." Astrid's voice is flat with dislike. I remember anew she has been charged with kidnapping and murder.

"Civilian rather than military, but essentially yes, the same as Colonel Roche. We went to school together."

Patience runs hot tap water into a stoneware teapot to warm it. "So you're a cop *and* a shrink?"

"If you like."

Dreamily, Astrid says: "He was at the sewer outflow before they firebombed it. He got some of Sahara's converts to come out."

"Does that make you uncomfortable, Astrid?"

She eyes me like a stalking cat, ready to pounce. "You don't make me uncomfortable, Santa."

"I'd prefer it if you'd call me Will."

"Would I, won't I, will I?" Another predatory glance. "Okay . . . Will it is."

The kettle shrieks and Patience puts a tray together. Sugar, cream, three cups. "You sure about this, sweetie?"

"Yeah. It's Will day, Patience."

"If you say so. Want to set up by the couch?"

"I think that's what we do." Astrid pushes at her curls, flashing the mangled cartilage of her right ear. "It's hard . . . so much going on. Tuna and bullets and gates of brambles—"

"Let's try, all right?" With that, Patience leads us back the way we came. As she passes me, she whispers a threat: "Don't you mess her up worse than she already is."

The living room's lack of a TV gives it a Victorian aura. Photographs cover the walls—snapshots of Astrid's parents and missing stepbrother. Four couches sit facing one another in a box.

Roche tried to keep the personal touches out of the suite, but Patience kept telling the media that she and Astrid were being kept in a barren subterranean hole. Her fans raised a hue and cry. Finally Roche allowed the bric-a-brac and Patience resumed her public campaign against Sahara. Without her broadcasts, the Alchemite cult would be even larger.

Astrid slumps on a grass-green chaise. I sit on a matching love seat and pull out my digital recorder.

She scowls. "Apartment's bugged."

"It can go out of sight if you like."

"Doesn't matter. The cards?"

"Will these do?" I hand over a bulging manila envelope stuffed with greeting cards, playing cards, and a Tarot.

"Perfect. Are you really going to give me my chantment?"

"Of course." I pass her the paintbrush.

"Oh, thank you, thank you," she murmurs, rolling it between her fingers. I imagine how Roche and the others upstairs in Security must be tensing up. But her gratitude and relief seem sincere.

"Astrid?"

She holds the brush to her cheek, eyes glistening. "You took a chance, bringing it here."

My gut clenches. Roche hadn't wanted to hand over the paintbrush. It's magical, he'd said. What if she uses it to change you into a frog, like the Clumber boy?

I'd brushed the objection aside, producing the transcripts of Astrid's ramblings. "Can't think," she'd said hundreds of times. "Need the brush, Jackson day, fortune cards."

"Will day" too appears repeatedly. Maybe it's arrogance, but I knew she'd been saying my name.

Turn you to a frog, like the Clumber boy. It doesn't seem so funny now.

"Are you going to show me what it does?" I ask.

"Yes." Astrid pulls her hair up, knotting the curls atop her head. She pins them into place with the paintbrush handle. Her hands drop to the table . . . and as they do, they *change*. The fingers become longer and wider, while the nails take on the flat, fibrous texture of paintbrush bristles.

She says, "Relax. Nothing terrible happens today."

"Is that so?" I turn her hand palm-up, running my finger over the bristles of her thumbnail.

She draws back, aloof as a cat, and digs out a ten of hearts. "The cards help me keep track of things . . . things to come?"

"I'd like to talk about the past six months."

Ghosts of dimples dent her cheeks. "Past, future . . . it's all the same."

"Tell me about the magic—when and why things started to change."

"That's two different questions." Patience tosses a couple of high-calorie protein bars onto the tray. Then she serves the tea. "What exactly do you want to know?"

How to change it back. "Let's start with Sahara."

"That's two questions too." Astrid cups her palms above the surface of the ten of hearts. The red ink fades, leaving it blank. Then a bead of brown paint wells from the stiff paper, like a minuscule drop of blood coaxed from a pinpricked finger. It streaks across the card, outlining a dilapidated car. Astrid watches it raptly. Me, I burn my mouth, slurping too-hot tea in a sip that becomes a gasp.

"Not what you expected?" Patience laughs.

"On the fifteenth of April, Mark Clumber told Sahara he'd been cheating on her," Astrid says, eyes locked on the card as if she's reading text. "He confessed, then took off for a few hours—to give her space. Sahara packed her bags the second he was gone. She took his car and cat, half their money, and drove west. She was eighty miles out of Boston before Mark slunk back, looking for forgiveness."

"She just left?"

"When someone hurts Sahara, she cuts them out of her heart forever. Ask Mark."

"Mark's beyond speech," Patience says sharply. The Clumber boy is in one of the compound's other apartments, suffering from severe alchemical contamination.

"Beyond speech," Astrid murmurs. "Sahara would be pleased."

I can believe it. Sahara routinely attacks Alchemites who leave her cult, not to mention police who oppose her and reporters who question her claim to be a goddess.

On the playing card, brown paint colors in the outline of the car. Wispy strokes of black sketch a cat on its rear dashboard. Brushstrokes from an invisible brush; the hairs on my arms stand up.

"So Sahara isn't particularly forgiving?"

Astrid doesn't contradict me. "She called from Billings and asked if she could stay at my house."

She means the home she inherited from her father, I know, on Mascer Lane in Indigo Springs, at the epicenter of the alchemical spill. "And you said yes?"

"I said she could stay forever if she wanted."

"What did she say?"

On the card, dots of green brighten the cat's eyes. "She said I'd have to make life pretty goddamned interesting if I was going to keep her around."

CHAPTER TWO

IF THE HOUSE ASTRID had inherited from her father was in un-expectedly good repair, the yard was in a state of war. The chief aggressor was a blackberry bush that had established squatter's rights along the fence before allying itself with some bindweed vines. These two runaway growths were making a claim for the whole backyard.

The line of defense began at an umbrella-shaped fig tree. In the spring, Astrid could see, hyacinths had flowered under the fig's protection. Now, with summer barely under way, the tree's leaves had unfurled. They blocked the light at ground level, daunting even the blackberries. The hyacinths had yellowed and shriveled in its shadow.

What grass remained was marshy, forlorn, and edged by moss and silverweed.

Once, though, the garden had been loved. It was bordered by hexagonal paving stones, and as she cut back the blackberries, Astrid found sickly perennials—black-eyed Susans, a lone candy-tuft, rust-covered hollyhocks.

She cast a worried eye at the kitchen window. Her stepbrother, Jackson, had stalked off to the grocery an hour ago. He'd barely spoken since they moved in two days before, and her attempts to lighten his mood were hitting a wall. It wasn't like Jacks: he was the most easygoing person she knew.

As for Sahara . . . she was overdue. She could have cracked up on the highway, or gone back to Mark.

Things might be easier if she did go home, she thought un-easily.

As if in response, a filthy brown Toyota wobbled to a stop

behind the house. Its engine died with a surly bang and the horn started up instead. Tripled honks, loud ones, ripped through the neighborhood.

Groping for the water-filled bucket at her knee, Astrid began scrubbing dirt off her hands.

"Hey!" she shouted. "Cut it out!"

Blat blat blat . . . extravagant and noisy.

Heart singing, she heaved the bucket over the fence, water and all. It hit the rear hood, splashing the back window. The honking stopped; the door ratcheted open. Sahara emerged, her hair shorn, arms full of cat, and manic glee written on her face.

"What are you doing?" Astrid shouted.

"Making an entrance!"

"My neighbors are going to call the cops." She wrestled the gate open before Sahara could kick it out of her way. "You said you'd be here days ago."

"Got into an altercation." She leaned in to kiss her cheek. Astrid hastily put her dirt-slimed hands out of reach. The cat squirmed, momentarily squished.

"Altercation?"

"Car got towed. Had to take on the Spokane police with nothing but my trusty slingshot and some thumbtacks."

"You stopped to visit your grandmother."

"Should have called, I know. Did I miss the heavy lifting?"

"Not all." That was Jacks behind them, emerging from the shadows at the rear of the yard, moving with the wiry grace of a natural athlete. A forest-green pack bulged on his back. Smudges of color—paint—decorated his hands.

Years of hiking trips, river rafting, and rock climbing had given Jacks a rugged physique that belied his artistic side, but as his gaze flicked over the two of them, Astrid could hear mental shutters clicking. He often drew, from memory, things he'd seen for just a few seconds. "There's a ton of work waiting in there for you."

"Is that so?" Sahara's voice chilled.

"Fridge needs moving," Jacks said. "And you can unload the boxes we packed and hauled over here."

Sahara peered up into his gray-green eyes. "You martyr. Want me to nail you to a cross while I'm at it?"

He smiled faintly. "How are you, Sahara?"

"Dumped. Miserable. You still the most eligible bachelor in this lousy town?"

Instead of answering, he said: "Do you need a hand?"

"Thanks. Take Henna." She held out the cat. Jacks collected the beast and disappeared indoors.

"Nice of him to help you move in," Sahara said sourly.

"He's living here." Without waiting for an answer, Astrid hefted a suitcase out of the trunk. "His father's lost it. 'My son, my son, you must carry on my name.'"

"Lovely. Old-fashioned *and* maudlin. Who cares if Jacks takes over the family business?"

"Ask the Chief."

"It's a beer-bottle factory, not the crown of Spain."

"Jacks needed some space."

"Then why isn't he leaving town, or at least quitting the Fire Department? Maybe it's not so much about getting away from Dad as getting closer—"

"He did quit the Fire Department," Astrid interrupted.

"So he's homeless and jobless? And you, the woman who helps everyone with everything, all the time—"

"I love you both. You both need a place to stay. For the first time in my life I have room," Astrid said. "Anyway, it's not just the bottle factory. Lee wants Jacks to be Fire Chief too."

"Doesn't Jacks run back to Mommy's place when the two of them start bickering?"

"Olive sold her house when Dad died."

"Why didn't you say Jacks would be living here?"

Because you wouldn't have come. She kept her voice light. "You said you weren't staying."

"I said I probably wasn't staying."

"So you might stay?"

"No." The reply came too fast, and Astrid tried to strangle a burst of hope as she led the way upstairs. "Is he paying rent? You're not going to be a woman of property for long if you don't start exploiting someone."

"He's my brother, Sahara."

"Please. You're barely in-laws. You were eighteen when your father married Olive."

"This is yours." Astrid dumped the suitcase in a bright, white-washed rectangle with west-facing French doors that led to a small deck with an outlook over the Victorian-era houses of Mascer Lane. In the distance, the Blue Mountains were visible above the roofs and trees, darkened peaks backlit by a showy peach and magenta sunset.

Sahara turned slowly into the light, revealing shadowed and teary eyes, a thinness around her mouth and cheekbones. Her hair, once waist-long, was a spiky mass of irregular tufts. Had she cut it off herself?

A night's sleep, a good meal, and she'll change her mind about Jacks, Astrid thought, fighting an urge to wring her hands.

"This is the master bedroom, Astrid. Shouldn't you be living here?"

"I took one in back. It overlooks—"

"The garden. I should have guessed."

"And the ravine."

"Ooh, ravine view. Can you see the infamous Indigo Springs?"

"It's too far, Sahara."

"Indigo my ass. Should've called the town Stinky Algae Swamp."

A streak of drying mud on the back of Astrid's hand cracked. "Um . . . we can get you a different bed. I've got a desk for your laptop."

"Relax. I won't bolt if there's a pea under my mattress." Sahara peered into the closet. "This is nice. Not to bad-mouth the dead, but when you said Albert left you a house . . ."

"You thought it'd be a shack. Bad plumbing, leaky roof, sparks whenever you turned on a light. Me too."

"He never told you about the place?"

"No. Mysterious, huh?"

"Why, Miz Lethewood, is that an attempt to intrigue me?"

"Sorry."

"Don't be—it's nice to be wanted." There was a thump downstairs, then a curse. Sahara flung herself onto the mattress. "Half wanted, anyway."

Astrid sat on the edge of the bed. "I need you two to get along."

"Me and Jacks?" There was another bang, followed by the sound of running water. "If he's making supper, I may have to offer him my body."

"Keep your paws off the kid."

"Meow! He's all yours."

"He's my only other friend."

"I left you with a perfectly good social circle."

Astrid shrugged. She'd always felt as though their gang of friends was tolerating her for Sahara's sake. Instead of explaining, she said: "When I tried going back to high school, Jacks was around. We got close."

"Look, I have no designs on Eligible."

"Anyway, it would be nice if the next person to fall in love around here was me."

"Fall in love?" Sahara scratched her neck. "You don't just want someone to fuck your brains out?"

She felt her cheeks redden. "That too."

"I'll get right on it," Sahara said, yawning.

"I meant—"

"Astrid?"

"Yes?"

"Do I stink?"

"What?" She found herself scowling. "Is that something your ex said?"

"He's still Mark the Unfaithful Prick. You have to stop caring before he's an ex, and I'm still having bawling fits and revenge fantasies. What I meant was: Do I stink from being in the car?"

"Oh." She leaned close to Sahara's fluffed hair, inhaling a reek of vinyl, dust, and sweat. "Yeah, you do. Grab a shower, okay? I'll help Jacks with dinner and you can find someone to take me to bed later."

" 'In love.' 'Take to bed.' Always the euphemisms." She didn't move. "Astrid?"

"Yeah?"

"I fucking love this room."

"It's yours as long as you want it." Closing the door, she slipped downstairs.

She found Jacks making soup, hacking vegetables with grim brutality. Onion fumes scratched the air.

"Your mom's coming by tomorrow," he said, blinking rapidly.

"She called?"

"I'm not psychic. She'll be here at eleven."

"Great, thanks."

"How's the prodigal?"

"Weary. Are you okay—?" She swallowed the question when his head snapped up, eyes sparking with fury. "Do you need any help?"

"Every box I open is full of spices and dish towels."

"What do you want me to find?"

"Bowls and spoons."

"Didn't that box go in the pantry?"

"Only thing in there is a bag of junk."

"Junk?" She ran her thumbs under the flap of an unopened box, revealing four mismatched bowls packed in shredded paper.

"Albert junk—antiques," he said, viciously cleaving a potato.

"Dad left something?" She set the bowls on the counter, abandoning the search for spoons. Opening the pantry door, she groped for the light.

"The usual. Cat dragged it out from under a pile of bolts and wire."

"Bad plumbing, bad wiring, bad electricity," she mumbled. The light flickered, and she saw it—a plastic grocery bag sprinkled with dirt.

"Bad checks," Jacks grumbled.

Shaking off the grime, Astrid opened the bag, picking out its contents. A broken perfume atomizer first, lavender-fragrant, its pewter pieces glistening with a mixture of dirt and bluish oil that clung to her fingers. A lipstick next. A broken pocketknife and a pendant shaped like a mermaid, hung together on a rusty chain. A watch and a pencil sharpener. Last, a cheap red kaleidoscope . . .

Astrid's mouth dropped open as she touched it, struck hard by a long-forgotten memory: herself, sitting on Albert's lap. How old was she then?

She was five. The heat of her father's body through his clothes, his smell of beer and aftershave, had held a delicious sense of comfort. She had held the kaleidoscope to her eye with too-small hands, Dad turning the cap to mix the beads. Then . . .

She frowned.

The kaleidoscope was tiny in her grown-up hand. She peered in, saw colorful beads jumbling, reflecting, and refracting. She turned the cap clockwise, watching the patterns shift and mingle.

"I said the spoons aren't in there," Jacks called.

"Coming." Tingling with an idea that couldn't, shouldn't be possible, she turned the cap the other way.

There was momentary resistance, then a click . . .

. . . and like that, a circular section of ceiling melted away. Impossibly, she was looking through the floor at the bottom of Sahara's bed.

She turned it counterclockwise again, heard the click, and saw through bed and mattress to Sahara's thick cotton shirt. Click again and the shirt vanished, leaving a view of Sahara's back. Another click, and Astrid stared through bed and friend both, up at the ceiling of the room.

Click again. She looked through the attic roof and saw the full moon rising against a darkening sky.

Magic toy, she remembered, blinking against a sudden flicker of headachy pain. I called it a magic toy, but Daddy had another name.

Magic. Sahara will stay for magic.

She felt like she'd been shocked out of sleep by a blast of cold water. Her flesh hummed; her right temple throbbed, her ears rang. Her eyelids blinked and jittered.

Her belly rumbled. She was starving.

Turning, Astrid looked through the closed pantry door and into the kitchen. Jacks was opening a box of oven mitts and potholders. She scanned the boxes, looking through the cardboard and packing materials until she spotted their bundled cooking utensils.

Sliding Dad's "junk" back into its bag, she stepped out into the kitchen and opened the box. The spoons were inside, packed just as she had seen them. She tugged one loose and handed it to Jacks.

"Just in time," he said, stirring the pot. "Sahara, come and eat!"

There was no answer. "You think she's in the shower?"

"She dozed off," Astrid said, and then added, self-consciously, "I bet."

"Great. Let her sleep."

"No, she's hungry." Skirting the boxes, she tiptoed upstairs to her room. She rolled the plastic bag into an old T-shirt and tucked it under her pillow.

"Magic toys," she whispered.

Leaving them reluctantly, she crossed the hall. Sahara was on the bed, eyes shut, a sleepy pout on her lips. Tear tracks marked her cheeks.

"What?" she groaned as Astrid tapped on the doorframe. "Floor show starting already?"

"Chef's got dinner on, milady," Astrid said.

She sat bolt upright, sniffling once before reaching back to sweep aside the long hair that wasn't there anymore. "Tell the opera to hold curtain until I arrive."

"The opening is canceled. The soprano broke her nose playing rugby."

"Hick towns." Sahara leapt up and hugged her, overpowering Astrid with intense joy and clogged body odor. "You shall have to work harder, darling, if you propose to keep me entertained." Then she swept out, head high.

"I'll get to work on that, milady," Astrid murmured, following her friend downstairs.

CHAPTER THREE

ASTRID COUGHS, LIFTING HER hands from the table. She has been leaching the color from one card after another, covering them with images and describing what she sees. Underneath her bristle-nailed fingers, the surface of the current illustration is alive with liquid movement. It is a miniature painting of the house, cut down the middle like a dollhouse to expose the interiors of its rooms.

Inside the second-story shower, a drooping Sahara washes her hair. Two floors below, Jacks brandishes a paintbrush as if it is a dagger. Astrid is cross-legged on her bed. Gold winks on the upper curve of her right ear—an earring.

Here in the underground apartment, the real Astrid is in exactly the same pose, contemplating her tea with shadowed eyes. The flesh of that ear is ragged and scarred.

"You okay?" I ask.

With a grimace of distaste, she reaches for Patience's protein bars. "Haven't talked so much in months. I mean, I babble, but . . . General Roach hated that."

Hated. Her grip on past and present has slipped again. I wonder if she's right, if Arthur will get promoted . . . and when? "You speak with Patience all the time."

"Patience understands I get turned around. And Ma—" She looks around, seeming to search for her mother.

"I'll set up a visit with Ev if you keep cooperating."

She throws her head back, staring upward. A mole on her throat shivers in time to her pulse. "How was she? He?"

I'm not about to lie. "Alchemized. Not as bad as some."

She rubs her wrist, wincing, as though it hurts. "We fix him, you know. With a ten-cent piece."

"Who's we?"

"So if I cooperate, I get a visit? Ma's a carrot?"

"I'm afraid so. But you're doing well, Astrid—"

"You getting what the boss wants?" A challenge glints in her eye. "Do you even care about that? You've got more than a paycheck riding on this."

"That's true of everyone at this facility."

Evacuating Astrid's hometown hasn't contained the alchemical outbreak; nor has firebombing the parts of Oregon where the trees are growing to twice their normal height. Everyone I know has lost something in the past three months. The lucky ones are only out a job, victims of the deepening recession. Others have lost homes in areas destroyed by alchemized plants and animals, or have buried relatives, victims of the earthquakes and riots.

Then there's those of us whose loved ones joined Sahara's cult.

For three months, through upheavals and disasters, Astrid has been incoherent and uninformative. Depressed by day, weeping at night, crying even in her fitful sleep, she has withheld information about magic and Sahara Knax.

If I want to find Caro and my children, I'll need to break down Astrid's walls, draw out more than she plans to say.

"And step one is to make me trust you," she whispers. A thick squirt of something blue rolls through the white of her right eye, breaking blood vessels in its wake. It is gone almost before I register it.

"You talked to Ma." Her voice gurgles, as though she is speaking from deep within a lake.

"Is that so?"

"She's asking for me. She's 'alchemized'—that's what you called it, right?"

"Alchemically contaminated."

"She's changing, scared, and you, Will, *you* told Roche to hold out a little longer."

"Did Patience tell you that?"

She tilts her head. "Wouldn't you know if she was spying on you guys?"

I inhale through my nose, visualize strength coming in with the air—a grounding technique. "What I know is if you keep helping us, I'll happily authorize a visit."

"Like I said, Ma's a carrot."

"Do you want me to apologize for doing my job?"

"Would you?"

"Astrid, I know this is tough for you, but it's time you came clean. You're talking about carrots, but upstairs people are starting to think about sticks."

"People. Roche."

"Sahara and her Primas destroyed an aircraft carrier yesterday."

She nods. "Biggest thing she's done yet. Drawing all that power, rivets popping, ocean freezing as the deck plates buckle . . ."

"Yes. You can appreciate that important people are becoming concerned—"

She smirks. "You mean desperate."

Any reply I might make is interrupted as Patience emerges from the kitchen, dizzying me with a nod as she helps herself to a handful of sugar cubes.

"Want some?" Astrid holds out a cup.

"Thanks, but I'm going out." Popping a sugar cube between her lips, she glides up to one of the false frosted windows. There she fades like fog in sunshine, becoming insubstantial and passing through the wall.

She will drift up to the surface, ignoring bedrock and security both, and when she resolidifies, her appearance will be changed. Her form will be that of a different—but still utterly gorgeous—woman.

Usually on these jaunts aboveground Patience holds court in a park about five miles from the holding facility. News crews wait there to document her appearances. On other occasions she obliges her fans to drive her to a TV studio, homing in on live tapings, preferably talk shows.

Roche hasn't seriously attempted to stop her—assuming he could—because her message suits him. Don't trust Sahara, she says. The Alchemites do not have the answers.

As Patience leaves, I realize Astrid is standing with tea outstretched, offering it to her insubstantial back. When our eyes meet she settles back onto the couch with the wary dignity of a rejected cat.

I am suddenly glad she is so thoroughly locked away. For the first time I see why Roche is worried: she may be a minor player, but I sense she may be dangerous.

Astrid sips tea, pretending to be invisible.

Surveying her wall of photos, I linger over a shot of Evelyn Lethewood dressed in slacks, a postal worker's shirt, and a bow tie. Her hair is parted on the side and slicked down with something greasy. She has a man's watch on her wrist and a bag of letters tucked under one arm.

Is it the prospect of seeing Ev that has secured so much cooperation from Astrid? I have my doubts, but all that matters is that the interview is going well.

Sahara spread footage of the sinking of the *Vigilant* across the Internet, despite every attempt to stop her. The Alchemites rescued the carrier's sailors and pilots, but if anything, that lack of a death toll—the good PR spin—has only made the Navy angrier. Nobody likes to seem helpless.

If we don't catch Sahara soon, Roche, political genius or not, will lose his job.

All I can do about it is keep Astrid talking. I had expected to spend weeks picking scraps of meaning from a madwoman's ravings. Instead . . . I offer her a three of swords from the pile of cards.

"Let's stay on track. Jacks was acting hostile?"

"It was the house," she says as the swords vanish and a picture of Jacks begins painting itself onto the Tarot card. "I didn't realize it, but he was angry about the house."

"Angry?"

"My dad spent his life buying antiques and weird keepsakes

on credit and getting involved in get-rich-quick schemes. He was destitute when he married Jacks's mother. He promised Olive he'd reform, and she bailed him out of the hole. He got them back in. Eight years later, when they happened to be ahead of the bills, he passed away, leaving me a nice house that was totally paid off."

"Put it that way, I'd be angry too."

She nods. Splashes of paint adorn her palms, a pointillist blur.

"When did you tell Sahara and Jacks about the chantments, Astrid? That night?"

"No."

"How could you resist?"

She flips the card, revealing a portrait of herself, head bent in study though the object of her scrutiny is out of the frame. Three gold twists of metal curl high on the arch of her ear—a trio of earrings that together form a dragon twining in and out of the pinna.

"I was all ready to sing," Astrid says. "I just didn't have an audience. At dinner, Sahara told us all about her cross-country road trip. After, Jacks retreated downstairs and started a portrait of his father. He made Lee's firefighting gear look like a Gestapo uniform."

"Flattering."

"I tried to start him talking, but all I got was a grunt. By the time I gave up, Sahara was snoring.

"Fine, I thought, I'm spending the evening on my own. Too bad for me if it's Sahara's first night back—" She bites her lip, and I smell vulnerability.

"You spent a lot of time alone?"

She scowls. "At least this time I had a project. I figured . . . hoped the other Albert junk was magical too."

"You couldn't remember seeing any of it before?"

"Just the kaleidoscope. Anyway, I tried the lipstick on, and nothing happened. I hung the mermaid pendant around my neck. Nothing—or that's what I thought. The cat was scratching my door and I said something to her—Henna, bug off, go sleep with Jacks. She did, immediately. But I didn't think anything of it. As far as I was concerned, the mermaid was a dud. Strike two.

"Then I opened up the pocketknife. As my fingers touched the metal, I had another memory flash—Albert, telling me never to run with it. 'Don't run with knives, Bundle, and especially never run with this.'" Tears spill down her cheeks. "It didn't look dangerous: pocked with rust, blade almost eaten away. . . ."

I hand her a tissue. "Until then you hadn't remembered seeing this particular knife?"

She blows her nose. "I thought: It's a knife, so cut something with it. Reasonable, right?"

"Sounds logical."

"I reached for this suitcase full of clothes I hadn't unpacked yet—good stuff I never wore much. Nice slacks, the dress I wore to weddings, a couple jackets. I snagged a luggage tag and sliced it off."

The image flowers between us—a red leather case, packed to capacity, old but sturdy. Luggage purchased for a specific trip, perhaps, never used but once.

She flips the card over, and the same case is painted there, except now it is brown with age. The brass buckles are tarnished. Tattered, faded rags push through breaks in the zipper like puppies in the act of being born.

"It fell apart," Astrid says. "My clothes too. Everything smelled like it had been rotting in a wet basement for thirty years. I nearly spewed my dinner."

"There was no salvaging it?"

"It was totaled. Just like your aircraft carrier."

"Did you try cutting anything else?"

"Well . . ." A rueful smile. "I scooped up the suitcase and hauled it out back so it wouldn't stink up the house. And I found myself looking at Mark's car. Thinking it wouldn't be a tragedy if it crumbled into a pile. . . ."

"You were angry with Mark for cheating on Sahara?"

She blinks. "I didn't want Sahara taking off."

Of course. "But you didn't do it."

"It wouldn't keep her around, losing the car."

"True enough. What happened next?"

"I was tired, woozy. And I saw . . . I'd washed my hands at dinner, but there were smudges on my fingers, from the oily stuff that had been on the broken chantment."

"The perfume atomizer," I remember, touching a card that shows the pewter bauble in grimy, blue-slimed pieces.

"In the moonlight, the smudges almost glowed. And I had an idea: I wanted to start on the garden."

"Pardon?" I glance up from the picture.

"It was this . . . urge, like someone whispering in my ear. Go, sink your hands into the flower bed. My fingers itched with it. But I was exhausted. So instead I went upstairs and picked up the watch."

"Was this a pocketwatch?"

"Wrist." She shakes her head. "Dad's taste in jewelry ran to shiny stuff, but this was plain, with a black band and wide white face. He'd put a piece of masking tape on the back and written Jacks's name there. Everything he wrote ended in a scrawl. Always a scrawl. Bad checks, bad handwriting . . ." Her voice trails off, and I see the label: *For Jackson*, barely legible, painted on a card.

"It's funny," I say. "The things that remind us of people we've lost."

She stares into her tea. "Underneath Jacks's name, Dad had scrawled two words."

I squint at the card. " 'Perfect . . .' "

Her voice wobbles, then steadies. " 'Perfect timing.' "

An image of Jacks Glade etches itself onto a new card. Slender, serious, he leans into his easel. Dark curls hang in his face. His hands are familiar. They are wide and pale, and the little finger of the left hand has a peculiar twist.

"It was a fire," Astrid says.

"A fire?"

She whitens another card and creates a close-up of the hand, with its twisted, scarred finger. "At a coffee shop. One of the firefighters got trapped. Jacks pulls him out. The Chief is so proud of him that day. . . ."

"Astrid, do you know where Jacks is?"

Cringing, she raises her arms in front of her face, as if warding off a blow. The paintbrush-bristles of her fingernails glisten in the light.

"Astrid? It is Jacks making these cards, isn't it?"

She answers from behind her fingers, voice breathy. "He's reaching through, trying to help. Holding me up."

"Reaching through from where?"

"No. No, I can't—we're not talking about that now."

"Astrid, what happened to him?"

She shakes her head violently and speaks, voice falsely cheerful. "The pencil sharpener—now that was cool. It was a bulb of blue plastic shaped like an old-fashioned inkwell. The sharpener was built into the lid. The pencil shavings ended up in the bulb, you see?"

Too soon to push her on Jacks, clearly. I go with the change of subject. "Did you try sharpening a pencil?"

"As soon as the blade bit into the wood, the sharpener started spinning. It ate the whole pencil, even the eraser."

"It was a magic pencil-eater?"

"No. See, in the bottom of the sharpener instead of wood shavings—see the card?—there were flakes of gold."

"Gold?"

"About a tablespoon," she says. "They were so heavy!"

"This sharpener . . . ," I say.

"Sahara calls it the Crucible. Lead into gold, like a fairy tale about alchemy. She names them all, you know."

Many of the alchemized items Roche's teams have found have mythic antecedents. There is a sewing needle that makes people sleep if you prick them, a working pair of ruby slippers, a voodoo doll, a flute that lures rats.

"This Crucible wasn't recovered from your house."

She sighs. "The pencil sharpener and knife are gone by the time I get arrested."

"Gone where?"

"With Sahara." With visible effort, she lowers the hand hiding her face. "After the sharpener, I thought again of gardening. But it was late. I could hear Jacks washing paintbrushes, and I didn't want to pass him in the kitchen. My head hurt, and the wooziness had gotten worse." She twists a curl of hair around her index finger. "If I'd gone out right then, maybe it would have gone different."

"Different how?"

Her answer is a dark, bitter grunt. She leans back, and I catch another glimpse of the bright blue fluid. It is bubbling in the well of her damaged ear. Rounded with surface tension, it shivers with her pulse, moving with a liquid weight that reminds me of blood.

I've seen this fluid on TV, at the heart of a swarm of deadly alchemized wasps and flowers.

"I went to bed," Astrid says. "I lay there with the kaleidoscope and stared into other people's houses. I spied on my next-door neighbor, Mrs. Skye, who was scrubbing her kitchen floor. She was crying, completely freaking out. I thought about the gold flakes and whether money could help her. I thought about Ma and Olive and how much Albert had cost them over the years. Magic, turning lead into gold . . . I could help everyone. . . ."

"Your first thought was helping Mrs. Skye?"

She shrugs: according to the psych profile, Astrid rarely admits to being altruistic. "I wouldn't have wanted to end up like that. Alone, half-crazy. Watching her, I remembered I wanted a real home, a family. Kids, husband—"

"A husband specifically? You've had female lovers."

"Anyone," she insists, coloring. "The point is I hoped to use the chantments to pull my budding family together. Keep Sahara in town, mollify Jacks, y'know?

"Soon enough I got my hands into a garden, and learned what the chantments were, that they had to be a secret."

"But by then you'd already told Sahara and Jacks."

"It was my first big mistake." The bead of blue liquid in her ear seems to strain upward, reaching skyward. Then it sucks back down, out of sight.

CHAPTER FOUR

NEXT MORNING ASTRID CRAWLED out of bed, fighting unchar-
acteristic grogginess, and was startled to see the magic toys on the
dresser.

She had forgotten them.

Snatching up the watch, she tracked Jacks to the back steps. He
was basking in the sun, wearing only a pair of old jeans, an electric
razor beside his hip. Henna lay beside him, snoozing, as he
browsed the *Indigo Dispatch*'s crime report and obituaries.

It was a perfect spring day. Breezes ruffled the new-green leaves
of the birch trees in the ravine beyond the back alley. The air was
laced with a scent of lilacs.

A cloud scrolled over the sun, changing the light and render-
ing Jacks's skin colorless. Suddenly he resembled a statue, muscles sculpted in marble rose and dusty shadow. The scar on his
finger stood out as the lone burst of color, a twisting line the
pink of young earthworms. Smudges of paint edged his fingernails.

The cloud moved on, resurrecting him.

Astrid asked, "Can I join you?"

"You're the landlady." His voice was neutral.

She swallowed. "Normally I'd have no problem parking in the
doghouse. But I have something to say. So tell me what I've done
and get it over with."

Jaw clenched, Jacks looked up.

The scowl vanished. Scrambling to his feet, he gave her a
strained grin.

"Jacks?"

"Ah . . . good morning?"

"Good morning," Astrid said. "Hi. Hello also. Now spill. What's wrong?"

He held out his newspaper, seemed to remember she hadn't asked for it, and snatched it back. "I'm . . . what?"

"Aren't you mad at me?"

"What?" He shoved the paper at her again, and Astrid yanked it away. The back page tore off in his hand. "Mad?"

"Jacks, you're killing me. You sulk for two days and now when I'm brimming with news, you're acting like someone hit you with a shovel."

That seemed to penetrate. He cleared his throat, favoring her with a gaze so intense, she felt as if he were staring straight into her heart. "I'm fine. And I'm sorry about yesterday."

"Thanks. Now, I wanted—"

"It was a long couple days," he interrupted. "Moving here. Then Sahara showing up suddenly . . ."

"You knew she was coming."

"She was late . . ."

"And you hoped she wouldn't come?"

He dipped his head. "Sorry."

"Please stop apologizing." She took the paper inside and dumped it on the counter before checking the coffeepot. All she found was a half inch of scorched sludge. Jacks followed her, still staring.

"Is there dirt on my face?"

He gave her the smile that made Springer women go weak at the knees. "You look great."

"Great, sure. Listen, once Sahara's awake—"

"She's up."

"Really?" She raised her voice. "Sahara, come down here, okay?"

There was an inarticulate response from upstairs.

"Maybe we should go out for breakfast. I'm starving."

"It's too late," Jacks said.

"Late? It's not late."

"It's ten thirty—you slept in."

"I never sleep in."

"There's nothing wrong with sleeping in, particularly if you're up late having fun. . . ."

"It wasn't fun exactly."

"Maybe next time it will be." His tone was barely suggestive, but there was a wolfish glint in his eye.

"Brunch, then. We'll go to brunch." The intensity of his stare was making her itchy. "Jacks? Okay?"

"Yeah, fine. Brunch and talk." He blinked. "Talk?"

"Sahara, come downstairs! Yes, Jacks, talk. Remember the stuff you found in the pantry?"

"Stuff."

"The Albert junk?"

No reaction. She had brought the watch downstairs with her; now she dangled it in front of him.

"I saw it last night. So?"

"Dad wanted you to have it."

He squinted at the masking tape. "Perfect tigers?"

"Maybe you shouldn't put it on yet—" But he had slipped it on, snapping the buckle shut.

"Probably doesn't work," he said. "What time is it?"

Astrid's grip on the counter tightened, but nothing happened. "Ten thirty-two."

He set it. His eyes came up, and the playful light surfaced again.

"So . . . brunch?"

He brushed a curl off her forehead. Then Sahara burst into the room, trembling and on the verge of tears.

"What's wrong?" Astrid said.

"Mark's locked me out of my blog."

"Pardon?"

"He's put new content in my 'Ask Suzu' column." She ran both hands through her hair, tugging at the butchered hanks.

"Did he have your password?" Jacks asked.

"I changed it. But the site host is one of his jerk-off friends—"

"Sahara—"

"Eleven hundred hits a week, Astrid! I had ad revenue! I was getting kickbacks from this bookstore for recommending self-help books, I had my own mouse pads. . . ."

"Sahara," she said, more loudly. "Mark can't deprive you of a source of income. I'm positive that's illegal. That's illegal, Jacks, right?"

"Probably." He glanced at Albert's watch, gave her one more smile, and trotted outdoors.

"Look at me," Sahara muttered. "I'm so mad, I'm shaking. How does this happen to me?"

"Take it easy, Princess." Astrid gave her a quick hug. Her skin was ice-cold. Another lost memory flashed through her mind: Albert, playing hide-and-seek with the two of them. "Along with the house, my dad had this lawyer—"

"I can't pay a lawyer!"

"Shhh." She thought of the gold dust. "I'll scrape up the cash."

Sahara stuck out her lower lip in an exaggerated pout. "What good's a lawyer?"

"We'll get a . . . you know—to make Mark stop?"

"Injunction?"

"Injunction, sure, and we'll make the computer guy give you back your . . ."

"God, Astrid. Access. Restore my access."

"Then you write an article explaining that an impostor hijacked your blog."

"Forget it," Sahara said, pacing to the fridge. "We get into wrangling and Mark'll claim he helped develop it."

Feeling whiplashed, Astrid said: "I thought he did."

"Knave—whose side are you on?" She fell into a chair. "I can't do it. Write him and tell him to back off. Threaten to face him in court. Just the thought of him makes my skin burn. Does that make sense?"

"Like there's a fire just inches away, and the fuel is how you can't believe he lied," Astrid murmured.

"Is this how being dumped feels?"

"It gets better," Astrid said.

Sahara blinked, then turned away almost guiltily. Then she brightened. "Know what? I was using my radio show to promote the blog, and Mark never kept up with the fan forums on the station website. He won't know that password. I'll plant a rumor that the site's changed hands."

"Fan club? You have fans?"

"Bunch of women who think Suzu's terribly insightful. Very gratifying to my ego, even if they are a bunch of flakes who love being in crisis."

"You're heartless."

"Oh, some of them are nice enough. They'll be ripe for conquest after I drive 'Ask Suzu' into the hole."

"You're going to start from scratch?"

"Suzu is tainted," Sahara said. "Hey, weren't you bellowing my name a minute ago?"

"Yes. I want to take you guys out for brunch. I have something to tell you."

"It's not another speech about getting along, is it?"

"No."

"You haven't signed us up to dig ditches or pick litter or give horsie rides to disabled babies? I know you groove on that kind of thing, but—"

"It's news. Important spine-tingling, eye-popping—"

"Fabulous. I am all ears."

"I want to tell you at the same time."

"So tell Eligible to get his ass in here."

"Right. Don't move." She stepped through the porch door, expecting to find her stepbrother spread out in the sunshine again. But Jacks wasn't there.

Her hand dropped to the porch rail as she scanned the yard

and alley. The backyard was in sharp focus—each leaf on every tree diamond sharp, the lilac scent gentle and mouthwateringly sweet. She felt as if she could taste the moisture levels in the soil. I've been here before, with Dad, she thought. Right on this spot.

That's impossible . . . the first time I came here was after I inherited the place. . . .

"Is Jacks coming? Astrid?"

"No." Disappointment broke the spell. She gazed at the lawn, wondering if its fading clarity had anything to do with Jacks and the magic watch.

"We can't go off to lunch, can we? I thought your mom was coming over."

Astrid sighed, rubbing her temples. "I forgot."

Something glinted at her from an upturned pile of soil near the demolished blackberry brambles. She nudged it with the toe of her boot to shift the softly piled dirt. It was an aluminum hand-rake.

"Where'd he go?" Sahara's voice made her jump.

"No idea." She peered between the garden shed and the fence. Instead of Jacks she saw Henna exploring the crawlspace, eyes gleaming.

Sahara strode barefoot to the edge of the alley. "Is he communing with the ghost of the ravine?"

"You see him?"

"No, just being frivolous. Now, what's the news flash?"

"Not without Jacks."

"Spoilsport. Are you pregnant?"

"I wish."

"Please. You don't need a miracle to get knocked up. That only takes a drunk trucker and fifteen minutes." Producing a small camera, she clicked at a tree swallow that was sitting in Astrid's bird feeder.

"What are you doing?"

"Bucolic images for a new blog." Wheeling, she aimed at Astrid, focused, and clicked. "Aimed at New Age and Green-types."

"Don't."

"Too late." Electronic chatter warbled from the machine. "See? You look wonderful."

"I look like a wild animal." Astrid scrutinized the proffered camera. Orange lipstick from Albert's junk bag was smeared around her mouth. Clearly ill at ease, she was standing against the garden shed like a prisoner awaiting a firing squad.

Still, there was something . . . scrubbing her orange-streaked mouth, she frowned at the camera screen.

Sahara crowed. "Told you."

"You are not putting pictures of me on the Internet."

"This is just for me. In ten years, you've sent one picture of yourself. For the blog, I want nature stuff. Flowers. Animals. Fluffy bunnies. A shot of the creek if we can find one that doesn't look like a swamp. Earth mother fodder for my web groupies, you know?"

"There's a spot half a mile along the trail," Astrid said. Pleasure over the fact that Sahara wanted her portrait warred with odd discomfort; she hated being photographed. "The stream widens, willows overhang the bank, cattails—"

"Perfect," Sahara said, then glowered at the camera. "I doubt this shitty digital will do it justice."

Astrid pursed her lips. "Does that mean you stole the camera from Mark?"

"I'll replace it as soon as I'm working," Sahara said. "You want it?"

"That means yes?"

"Yes, it's the Unfaithful Prick's camera. Hey, maybe we can think of some way to ruin him."

"I came up with a lawsuit."

"Can't, I told you."

"Then—" Astrid frowned. The scent of the garden shed, of its rain-wet cedar planks drying in the sun, momentarily overwhelmed her. She turned, and the hexagonal paving stones half buried at the edge of the flower bed took on an illusory significance—as if they were grave markers, or clues on a treasure map. "You see that?"

"What?" Sahara scanned the yard.

"Never mind." Tingles crawled up Astrid's arm. She bent to pick up the hand-rake. It was sun-warm, and as her fingers closed on it she flashed on Albert.

Daddy, smoking a pipe and using a magic toy—a plastic net— to lure in a cloud of butterflies.

Wait—they're called chantments, not magic toys.

"Astrid, are you listening?"

"Just tell people the truth, Sahara. You broke up and Mark took over your Web thing."

"Blog. And nobody takes advice from a romantic loser."

"Mark's the loser," she said with automatic loyalty.

"Oh, Mark's gonna be the loser."

Dad taught me about the chantments, Astrid thought. Her head was starting to hurt again.

"Mark'll lose his shorts. I just have to figure out how."

She spoke slowly, trying to concentrate. "Basically you want to stop people looking at the Suzu net site?"

"Blog, blog, blog. Where've you been living, a cave?"

"Could you use a computer virus?"

"That only works in movies."

"I'm not a technology person, Sahara."

"Who said the revenge has to be high-tech?"

"Can't you just have a normal breakup?"

"Astrid. Most beloved, dearest friend." Sahara threw an arm around her shoulder. "Mark cheated on me. As the wronged party, I'm allowed some vindictive behavior, which he's supposed to suck up without retaliation. But here on the moral high ground, I'm pursuing my life without any payback—"

"Unless you count stealing his car."

"Which I bought in repair bills." Sahara plucked the aluminum rake out of Astrid's hand. "Stop undressing the garden with your eyes and give me your attention."

"Give it back," she said, reaching for the rake.

Sahara tossed it away. It bounced off the cedar tree, scudding through the grass. "Where was I?"

"The moral high ground."

Beneath them, the lawn jolted.

Astrid stepped in front of Sahara, putting her body between her friend and the lurching sod. There was a noise like a burp—a froggy, resonant croak. Long cedar-colored tendrils emerged from underground, knotting between the tines of the rake. Daisies and buttercups burst from the lawn, blooming, then fell onto the writhing cedar strands, which wove themselves into a flat surface.

Finally wordless, Sahara gaped, openmouthed.

The cedar strands twisted out and up, growing three feet high before weaving themselves into a basket. The motion stopped when the handle was completed and the basket was filled with yellow blooms.

Wiping a sudden sheen of perspiration from her brow, Sahara reached for the basket.

"Don't touch—," Astrid said, but she had already picked it up, stroking its curves in disbelief.

"How did you do that? Did you do that?"

"I—"

"It happened." She stared at Astrid. "You saw it, right?"

Astrid snatched the rake off the ground. "I saw it."

Sahara grabbed her shoulders. "This is what you wanted to talk about? Why didn't you say?"

"When? Every time I open my mouth you—I mean, somebody interrupts me."

"Ohmigod." Sahara kissed her on the forehead. "You aren't really going to make me wait until Jacks turns up?"

Astrid's heart hammered. The excitement returned.

"Astrid, he could've gone anywhere!"

"Okay—," she began, and Sahara beamed. But before she could go on, the front gate squeaked.

"That's Ma." Panic swamped her excitement. "It'll have to wait."

"Astrid!"

"Listen to me. There are more of these chantments."

"More what—more magic things?" Sahara said.

"Yes, on my dresser. Get them out of sight, okay? I don't want Ma seeing a pile of Albert's crap—"

"Upstairs," Sahara said. "Got it."

Brisk knocks sounded at the front door.

"Tell you all about it as soon as we're alone," Astrid promised. Tearing free, she sprinted out front.

CHAPTER FIVE

ONE MAY AFTERNOON WHEN Astrid was six, Albert had taken her to visit one of the flea markets he toured so compulsively. It was a long, hot drive, over a series of diminishing roadways. The highway shrank to two lanes, then turned off onto a paved road running between tall stands of cedar and spruce. This withered into a gravel alley that, in time, faded away entirely.

Aside from an exit sign for Hell's Canyon, there was no clue to their destination. They jounced along cross-country, singing with the radio, while Astrid wondered if Dad really knew where they were going and—if they got there—whether she dared hope there'd be a bathroom.

They broke out into a clearing near the banks of the Grande Ronde River. A warehouse hunched up against the water, surrounded by battered, dusty cars. Nearby a motorboat, its hull slapping the water, was tied to a ramshackle dock.

The market inside was packed with tables, all piled high with old curtains, hand-knitted potholders, and quilted tea cozies. One vendor had porcelain figurines—little girls, green lambs, obscene sailors, and nude Kewpie dolls. Antique coins, bedding, cutlery, scratched silver platters—all of it reeked with a faint odor of sweat, motor oil, and dust. The used-goods scent, the lingering ghost of past usage, was as familiar to Astrid as skunk or frying hamburgers. It was a smell that came home with Albert on his junking trips; she had never been to the source before.

"Have a party, Bundle." Handing her a dollar, Albert vanished into the crowd.

She braved the outhouse first, breathing through her mouth as she peed, afraid of the wasps circling the roof. Back inside the market, she let the crowd wash her around until she fetched up at a pair of creaking bookshelves. The vendor, glad for a break in the tedium, showed Astrid all the kids' books.

Astrid had been about to purchase a copy of *Jack and the Beanstalk* when a cover illustration caught her eye—a figure who could have been her mother, wearing the blue uniform of the postal service.

"What's that?" she asked, pointing.

"*Postal Mortem*. A mystery, sweetums. See the mailman?"

Close up, she could see that the figure was male, but he still looked like Ma: solid, cheery, and blond.

" 'Everett Burke, the hyperobservant mailman,' " the woman read. " 'Delivering justice with a smile.' "

"My mom's name is Ev," Astrid said, handing *Jack and the Beanstalk* back. "She delivers mail, too."

When Dad finally reappeared, clutching a white umbrella in his thin hand, she showed him her find. "You think Ma will like it?"

His smile was forced. "Course she will, Bundle."

Astrid's spirits dropped. She was silent on the long drive back, and when they got home, she buried the paperback between her mattress and box spring. At night she could feel it beneath her, and it left her anxious and troubled.

It was the first time she had considered her mother's tastes, had wondered about the preferences of another human being. The realization, partial though it was, was terrifying: Ma had likes and dislikes, was mistress of an interior world her daughter might never know.

After a week, she threw the book away.

A couple of summers later, Astrid looked up from the vegetable garden to see her mother settling on the porch with a brand-new Everett Burke hardcover in hand.

"I didn't know you liked those," she said sharply.

"They're my favorite," Ev said, already absorbed in the prologue.

Astrid shot her father an accusing glance through the wall of young corn stalks. He stood, dusting his hands, and meandered over to where she was weeding.

"I didn't want her to know we'd been junking," he whispered.

That had been another first: the keen pang of disappointment in him that Astrid felt as he walked away.

The memories played through her mind as she raced around the house, a fleeting recollection of childhood betrayal that gave way to more immediate worries. When Dad died, Ma had started acting as if *she* were the hyperobservant mailman from the Burke books— and pretending Astrid was Petey, Everett's crime-solving sidekick.

Had Astrid's moving out made her worse? It had been Ma's idea that she go, but if Ev had now decided that Sahara was Cindilou Mortone, or that Jacks was Petey's nemesis, Motormouth Cain . . .

But it wasn't Ma pounding on the front door.

That didn't make it good news. Jacks's father was on the porch, hammering hard enough to break the door down.

Lee Glade was brawny and blond, with a look of permanent sunburn and dust-brown eyes. Chief Lee, everyone called him— he had run the Fire Department for twenty-five years, since his own father had retired from the post. The Lee men had been fire chiefs for five generations. Before that, the town was barely settled, still Indian land in fact as well as on paper.

He had the biggest hands Astrid had ever seen, hands like pizza tins—red and wide, with the flat fingers he had passed on to his son.

"Hey, Astie," he said. "My boy here?"

"Sorry. You just missed him."

"When'll he be back?"

"He didn't say."

"You're sure he's not around?"

She put her hands on her hips and glared, but the brightness of the sun kept her from winning the staring contest. "You want to search the place, Chief?"

"No need." He beamed, happy he'd scored a point. "Tell him to call."

"Okay," she said, blinking sunspots out of her eyes. As he turned to go, the gate squeaked again.

This time it *was* Ma.

Ev was dressed in Everett Burke's civvies—shirt, slacks, homburg, and a bow tie. Her breasts hung loose under the shirt, pushed sideways, just slightly, by the blue suspenders that held her pants up. In recent years the hair on her cheeks and chin had begun coming in coarse. Ev plucked the offending follicles every evening, but this morning they were untouched, forming a stringy beard. She held a quart jar of fat homemade gherkins.

"Lee," she said. "How're the boys making out here?"

"Boys? Oh, Jacks and . . ." He smirked at Astrid. "The young fellas are just terrific, Ev. How you keeping?"

"Thanking God every day the politicians don't control the weather."

"Uh, yeah." He gave Astrid a broad wink, amusement and mock sympathy mixing in his expression, making her wish she could nail him between the eyes with a rock. "Tell Jacks I was here, will you—Sonny?"

"Sure. He'll be thrilled to hear you stopped by."

Point for her. Lee's mouth tightened, and he stomped away.

Ev held the gate as he bulldozed past, then strode into handshake range and stuck out a mitt. "Petey."

Astrid shook. "Hey, Pop." The word—a compromise they had reached with some pain—didn't stick in Astrid's throat the way it did when she had tried to humor Ev with "Dad."

"Chief bring you a housewarming gift?"

"Just the everlasting joy of his company."

Ev hefted the pickle jar. "I brought you something from the farmer's market. Hope Sahara still likes 'em."

Sahara. Not Cindilou. Ma's fantasy world was holding at a population of two. "They're her favorite," she said, hoping it was true. Her stomach rumbled—she was ravenous again. "What do you think of the house?"

"Doesn't look any different."

"Even in daylight?" The executor of Dad's will had brought them to view the place twice, both times at night.

"Seen it by day, too. My route used to take me here." Ma hitched her suspenders. "Well . . . exterior's nice enough. Paint job's sloppy."

Astrid nodded. The house had been painted the cobalt blue that some townspeople claimed as the signature Indigo Springs color. Whoever had done the job had painted over the bricks of the chimney. It was blue up to the eaves, with just a stub of red brick jutting up above the roof.

"Albert never could lay paint."

"It's quirky, Pop, but it looks okay."

"How's the plumbing?"

"Good plumbing, good wiring, good—"

"Doesn't look like he did anything with the garden."

"I don't know if he was here much," Astrid said. "He was living with Olive, remember?"

"The second wife," Ma said distantly, as if she had not been the first. "No garden . . . interesting. Indicative of his state of mind, maybe."

"State of—?" A fist closed around Astrid's stomach.

"At the time of his murder."

Astrid swallowed. "Daddy wasn't . . . His liver failed."

"Albert wasn't a drinking man. He didn't have hepatitis, no family history of liver disease—"

"That doesn't mean he was killed!"

"Cirrhosis is slow, Petey, and he'd had a physical prior to his death. The second wife had him applying for jobs as a truck driver."

"How do you learn these things?"

Ma hooked her thumbs into her pants, rocking back on her heels.

Astrid lowered her voice. "The real Everett Burke would never read somebody else's mail."

"Desperate times, Petey," Ma said serenely. "You gonna show me around the place?"

"You said it hadn't changed."

"House is always different when it's occupied." Ev trooped up the front stairs, noting Lee's dusty footprints before stepping indoors. "Something wrong, son?"

"No." Astrid followed reluctantly. What if there were more chantments—the rake *had* to be one—lying out in plain sight?

The living room was empty but for a painting Jacks had left leaning against the wall; they'd been looking for something that might match with a plush rose carpet and an eyesore of a fireplace. Like the exterior of the house, the hearth and mantel of the fireplace were painted blue.

"Now that is odd," Ma said, and Astrid was forced to nod, like a good sidekick. "Kind of empty in here, isn't it?"

Astrid scowled. Ev had been pushing her to move into this place of Albert's for months, and had offered to give her an old couch and chair that had been sitting in her basement. But the day Astrid agreed to move, Ev called the local Goodwill store and gave them the furniture instead.

The only thing in the room besides the paintings was the aspen urn containing Dad's ashes, a tall cylinder with copper inlay that had ended up on the mantel.

She decided to ignore the jab. "So, Pop, is it nice having the house to yourself?"

"I'm keeping up." Plucking up the urn, Ma weighed it against the jar of pickles. "Looks comfortable, son. More room than you had at home. You'll be happier."

"I wasn't unhappy, Ma . . . Pop."

"Nicer than the apartment where you shacked up with that basketball player, Jennifer, Jessica . . ."

"Jemmy. Jemmy Burlein."

"Right, Jemmy." Ev cracked open the door leading to the basement, listening.

"Pop?"

"Coast's clear, Petey. Let's snoop around a bit."

A protest came to Astrid's lips . . . and then died. She followed Ev into the laundry room.

Where Victorian order held sway above, chaos nested below-stairs. The basement was a warren of narrow rooms, some the size of cubicles, all arranged in a puzzlework that barely came out square. At the hallway's end, Jacks's studio jutted up six inches above floor level. Its corner walls were covered in windows that be-gan at Astrid's hip and rose to the ceiling. The room might have been an enclosed porch, if only it had a door leading outside. In-stead, it extended oddly into the yard like the bridge of a small ship. Paints and brushes were spread over a small table in one corner. On the easel, a portrait of Lee Glade glowered out from a background of dense black smoke.

Ma clucked. "Not much to guess about the state of that boy's mind."

"Jacks and Lee have been having a tough time."

"Chief's remarkably high-strung for a man of action, but he means well."

"He pretends to, anyway."

Ma shot her a sidelong glance. "It's not like you to be nasty, Petey. Any idea why Jackson quit the Fire Department?"

She wasn't going to open that can of worms. "No."

Ma moved on to the bedrooms, tapping on the walls, squint-ing at the breaks in the layers of floral wallpaper. "Your father kept scrapbooks of news clippings, son—hard-luck stories. Man loses son in car wreck. Woman with amnesia found in Tucson. He got papers from everywhere, remember? Collected phone books. And he mailed packages, lots of packages."

"You're looking into Dad's . . . peculiarities?"

"Don't you wonder, Petey? Five years of marriage and then one day, all at once, he came over strange."

She shrugged. "It must have been before I was born."

"Know why he drove to Wallowa every month?"

"To hit the flea markets."

"To ship out his mail. He was afraid I'd learn what he was up to."

Astrid licked her lips. Dad had done crazy things to feed his junking habit: shoplifting, cheating at cards. He had gone to prison for fraud once—he'd pretended to be renting out an apartment, so he could collect damage deposits from ten sets of unwitting would-be tenants.

He was trying to buy an old tureen, he told her later.

Hiding his outgoing mail from Ev. Had Albert been delivering drugs?

No. Drug dealers made money. Besides, Dad had magic on his side. "He bought junk in Wallowa."

"Now we've finally got you inside this place, Petey, we can discover what happened to its former owner."

"That's why you wanted me to move? Pop, I am not helping you solve some nonexistent mystery. I'm going to meet someone, settle down, maybe have you a grandkid. . . ."

Ma crossed her arms over her chest, glowering.

"I'm going to have a life. I'm going to call the friends I stopped seeing when I dropped out of school—"

"Right. All of a sudden you're a different person."

Stung, Astrid sucked her lips between her teeth. Sahara was here. Things would change.

"You can't run away from Albert's murder, Petey."

"There was no murder! Albert got sick. Ma, this charade of yours has got to stop."

Ma's voice chilled. "It's no charade, son."

"You stopped caring what Albert did when you divorced him. He was your ex, and in case you've forgotten, Everett Burke isn't gay."

"Petey . . ."

"Ma, if you're my father, and Albert was my father too, how do you think—?"

The jar of pickles hurtled across the room and shattered, striking the wall an inch from Astrid's ear. Pickles hit the floor with splashy thuds. Bits of glass rebounded from the plaster, pricking her neck.

Astrid froze. Vinegar fumes burned her nostrils.

"You want your head rattled, boy?" Ev snarled.

Shaking, Astrid knelt to pick up the brine-doused shards of glass.

CHAPTER SIX

THE REAL EVERETT BURKE would never scare his kid senseless. Astrid swayed, tempted by an urge to sit down where she was, and never get up. Why not? Dad was compulsive and now Ma's not only delusional but violent. Catatonia could round out the freak show nicely.

The glass fragments on the floor shone slickly. Vinegar ran down the wall, spreading from the baseboard. A blue tint—paint? dye?—bled narrow streaks into the puddle. Astrid's stomach—by now she was so hungry, she was verging on nausea—flipped.

Ma was pacing. "It was murder, Petey, it was killing, he was killed-poisoned-stabbed . . ."

Leave the cleanup. Astrid tried to stiffen her nerveless knees.

". . . shot-banged up, he was banged up, baby. Bigbang, smallbang, bangbang!"

"You have to listen." Her voice shook; she was barely intelligible. "Ma . . ."

Then Sahara skipped into the room.

She was radiant. No, more than radiant—she was blinding. She had put on a sundress and sandals, too little clothing for the cool spring weather. Her breasts strained against the fabric, and her dark eyes sparkled. Her lips were orange, like mangoes.

The lipstick. Astrid put out a hand to steady herself and nearly drove pickle jar shards into her palm. With an effort she focused on Ma, shifting Sahara into her peripheral vision. It seemed to help.

"There you are, young lady." Red-faced but suddenly calm, Ev tipped her hat. "Welcome home."

Sahara dropped a curtsy. "I was going to explore the attic, Ev."

As she said Ev's name, her voice deepened, filling the air with mystery vibrations. "Care to join me?"

"There's an attic?"

She's wearing the mermaid pendant, Astrid thought dizzily.

"You bet there is."

"What are we waiting for?" Ma said.

"Come on, then." Sahara whirled out of the room. Ma trotted after, leaving Astrid to bring up the rear, her hands full of pickle wreckage and reeking of vinegar.

The kitchen's chaotic jumble of unpacked boxes was gone, probably—knowing Sahara—shoved into the pantry. Cups and spoons were set out on the table along with an open sack of sugar. The kettle murmured on the stove.

Sahara nudged Astrid toward the sink. "Let's get rid of these." She pried the glass shards out of her grip. "Ev, you take milk in your tea, don't you? I don't think Jacks bought any."

"Boy's a vegan," Ev grumbled.

"Sorry about that."

"I drink it black anyway."

"Since when?" She set the tea to steeping, then produced a flashlight and a short stepladder from the back porch. "Okay, we've got a few minutes. After you, Ev." Ma led the way upstairs, shoving the ladder up through the attic trapdoor and climbing it energetically.

"What if there are chantments up there?" Astrid hissed in Sahara's ear.

"She won't know what they are."

"Sahara—"

"Astrid, trust me," Sahara said, and she felt herself giving way. It was impossible to say no to this glowing, glamorous apparition.

"You two coming up?" Ev called.

"Right behind you." Skirt swaying, Sahara followed. Astrid climbed up last, steadying herself by laying a hand on the attic floor . . .

. . . and suddenly she was overcome with a mixed sense of nostalgia and dread.

Albert brought her up here once. It had been winter, and . . .

She jerked free and it stopped.

Touch, she realized. The flashes come when I touch . . . what? Things Albert owned?

The attic was a single room with a low-slanted roof, with dormer windows in front and back through which shone weak, grit-filtered sunlight. Ev, taking out a handkerchief, spat on the cotton and began scrubbing at the glass. Sahara shone the flashlight to and fro, swiping at cobwebs. Astrid just watched from halfway up the ladder.

"Not much in here," Ev grunted, kicking at a roll of old carpet. A stack of metal pails leaned against the wall next to some blue-splashed paint trays and one weathered brush.

She's calming down, Sahara mouthed. Then, bending to pick a small hunk of glass out of Astrid's hair, she raised her voice again: "How's work been, Ev?"

"Fine, young lady. Neither rain nor sleet, you know."

From screaming and throwing things to small talk, Astrid thought. What am I going to do?

The ladder trembled beneath her. She couldn't bring herself to touch the attic floor again.

"Good, good. And your friend Cherry Lugan, how's she?"

"She's dead, Sahara. Stroke."

"Oh. Sorry. Was it sudden?"

"I'll say. Her nephew was visiting at the time. He took her dogs back to Vermont with him after the funeral."

Astrid squelched a groan.

"Valuable dogs," Ev added suggestively.

"Do you think he should've let them starve, Ev?" The vibrato in Sahara's voice intensified, the mermaid flickering as if it was living flesh instead of metal.

Ma licked her lips. "I expect you're right."

Sahara gave Astrid a furtive thumbs-up.

Right. Jump in, try again. "Ma, have you seen your doctor lately? Maybe you should get a referral. You could talk to someone about how you're feeling."

Menace returned to Ev's expression. "I'm fit as they come."

"She means a therapist, Ev," Sahara said, and Ma's glare softened. "When Albert died—"

"Albert had a therapist? That'd make . . . make a good lead on his murder."

Sahara shook her head. "We're talking about you seeing a therapist, Ev."

Astrid's heart revved and she tried to guess what Ma might hurl next. But Ev frowned, mouth working silently.

"Okay, Ev? You'll call around and find a doctor?"

"You have my word, young lady," Ev said.

"Soon, Ma?"

Eyes flashing, Ev shoved the window open. Fresh air gusted into the room and dust swirled. "Don't *nag*, son."

"She's right," Sahara said. "You've got to do it right away."

"Right away." Ma tucked away her handkerchief and straightened her hat. "Absolutely."

Sahara coughed. "Uh, what I meant . . . I mean, are you going now?"

"Right away." Ma strode across the attic, each footfall echoing, her anger gone. "Sorry I upset you, son."

"It's okay, Pop." The words came out in a whisper. Astrid stepped down to the hallway floor, getting out of the way. Ma reverse-marched down the ladder just as the teapot began to whistle.

With another hat-tip, Ev turned on her heel and trotted downstairs. Astrid followed as far as the kitchen, flinching as her mother slammed the door on her way out.

"Jeezisgawd, are you okay?" Sahara snatched up a rag from the kitchen sink. She soaked it in hot water, wrung it out briskly, and began wiping vinegar off Astrid's limp hands. Even after they were clean she didn't let go, turning the wash into an impromptu massage.

Astrid had to close her eyes to keep back a surge of emotion. Sahara, looking so polished and assured, made her feel grubby and clumsy. It felt like an eternity since anyone, even a friend, had touched her.

The hand-massage brought back other things, too—Sahara in a ballgown, kissing her, hinting that maybe there was a chance for the two of them; discovering, the next day, that she and Mark had left town. . . .

"Breathe," Sahara said. "It's okay."

"She's eccentric," Astrid said. "That's what I've been telling myself."

"Why didn't you say she was so bad?"

"She was never like that before." She shook her head wearily. "I asked you to get the chantments out of sight."

"Sorry. I was trying, but I couldn't think of a safe place and I heard things getting nasty downstairs—"

"Whenever I've tried to talk to Ma about her Everett Burke charade—"

"No euphemisms!" Sahara tossed the rag away and kept kneading Astrid's hands, wringing tension away. Her hands, damp and warm, slowly pinched into the heel of Astrid's hand, easing numbness she hadn't known was there. Despite everything, she began to relax.

"When I brought up Ma's delusion, she glossed over it. Acted like it was a joke. There was the Petey and Pop thing, the clothes, but she seemed to be getting better. Faking. She wanted me here so she could snoop on Dad—"

"She ever get physical with you before?"

"I'd never have moved if she'd been losing it, Sahara."

"Yeah, you'd hang in to the bitter end," Sahara said. "I was trying to help—you know that, right?"

"I think you did help. But how did you know? The mermaid, it—"

"Darling!" With a flourish Sahara produced a crinkled yellow page from her sleeve. Flattening it, she cleared her throat dramatically. "I read as follows: 'Buy seedlings, call greenhouse at Wallowa . . .'"

"Sahara . . ."

"Oops, wrong side. Here, we go. 'Kaleidoscope—sees through walls. Lipstick . . .' what's this word here?"

" 'Dud.' "

"Oh." Sahara scrubbed at her lips, smearing the orange onto her sleeve. Her hair and skin dimmed to normal luster, and Astrid could look her friend square in the face again. "At least it looks good on you. 'Mermaid—made cat mind me' . . . you've written 'Miraculous!' "

"I was joking."

"I heard you say it. 'Henna, go bother Jacks,' in a ringing 'don't mess with me' voice."

"You were asleep."

"I woke up. You sounded contentious."

"Hmmm," Astrid said. "It changed your voice, too, whenever you said Ma's name."

"Well, Henna spent the night with Picasso. Which not only means the mermaid works, but the cat speaks English."

"That's disturbing."

"Let's hope the subtleties elude her." Sahara referred to the note again. " 'Knife dangerous'—that's a bit vague. 'Pencil sharpener . . .' and there the note peters out."

She tried again. "You were playing with the chantments. I asked you to hide them."

"I couldn't help myself." Sahara leaned close, rubbing Astrid's nose with her own. "I'm a spoiled brat, you know."

"You can't flirt your way out of this, Princess." Astrid snatched the page.

Sahara sighed, deflating as she pulled the mermaid pendant off her neck. "Do I sound normal now?"

"Yeah." She cupped a hand over the necklace; it was skin-warm.

"Okay," Sahara said. "Tell me everything."

The back door slammed. They jumped; Sahara tipped the sugar bag, spraying crystals across the table and floor as Jacks burst into the room.

"What kind of weirdo mystic crap was Albert into?" he demanded.

The women burst into nervous laughter.

"Well?" he said.

"Great," Astrid said. "I wait all night and morning to share my news and now you both know."

There was nothing left to do but demonstrate the chantments. She started with the kaleidoscope, explained about the pocketknife, then brought out the pencil sharpener and her bag full of gold flakes.

As the show-and-tell continued, she realized her fatigue the night before wasn't coincidental. Working magic this way—one small miracle after another—was draining.

She pointed this out and Sahara nodded. "Yeah. I'm starving *and* ready for a nap."

"I could eat," Jacks agreed, reaching for a bunch of bananas. They peeled the fruit in silence; Sahara dipped hers in the spilled sugar. After a second, the others followed her example.

"Are you guys . . . okay with this?" Astrid said between bites. "I mean, magic. It's not supposed to . . ."

Jacks shrugged. "We saw what we saw, and we aren't crazy, so . . . yeah. I'm okay."

"I'd be ecstatic if I wasn't so tired," Sahara said.

Astrid said. "You're tired from using the mermaid on Ma."

Jacks raised his eyebrows in query and they filled him in on Ev's visit. Then Sahara said, "What about you, Eligible? You disappear, then when you turn up, you want to know about Albert."

Jacks held up his wrist, showing off the watch. "Earlier when you came downstairs, Sahara, I got an urge to trot over to the fire hall and pick up my final paycheck. You were upset; I figured it would take Astrid a while to calm you down."

"You spun on your heel and walked out," Astrid remembered.

"Yeah," he said. "It was a strong urge. Go. Do it. One less errand. So I started walking and, and suddenly there's a kid dangling off the balcony of one of the houses."

"Did he fall?" Sahara asked.

"I caught him. Gave me a scare, though, and getting away from his mother—"

"Shouldn't you have hung around to see if somebody'd give you a medal or a cash reward?"

"We're not all glory hogs, Sahara."

"Bullshit."

He held up his hand, displaying the burnt and broken finger. "I did the hero thing before, when I pulled Rick out of the Volcano Café fire."

"Ah, yes. Astrid sent me clippings. 'Shucks, ma'am, I was just doing my job.'"

"It's not as gratifying as you'd think."

"I guess you can take the boy out of the Fire Department, but you can't take the Fire Department out of the boy."

"Are you saying people can't change?" There was a challenge in his gray-green eyes. Sudden tension crackled between them, like electricity.

"Do people change?" Sahara said, rolling it over.

"Once a jerk, always a jerk? Once a diva . . ."

Sahara colored and looked away, fluffing her ravaged hair. "I hope not, Jacks."

"I hope so too."

"Speaking of firefighting," Astrid interrupted. "Lee came by."

"When?" Jacks asked. "After I left?"

"Pretty much right after." She crunched sugar crystals under the heel of her hand, mashing them to powder on the table before peeling another banana. "Good timing."

"Perfect," he said. "I felt compelled to jog onward, so I headed down Striken Road, and there's Reggie Fitzwilliam. He asks if I want to run some white-water rafting groups through Mistico Park this summer."

"You got a new job?" Astrid asked.

"Just like that," Jacks said. "Reggie was paging through his mobile phone directory, wondering who to interview, when I came by. Then I'm hurrying back here and I knock over the new man in town," Jacks said smugly.

"What do you need with a man, Eligible?" Sahara asked.

"He's middle-aged, dapperish, in a recovering hippie kind of way. Name of Thunder Kim. I dust him off, and he asks if there's a bookstore. I walk him over to my mother's shop. She comes out to say hi and voilà! Instant chemistry."

Astrid's throat closed. "Already? Dad's only been dead . . ."

"Albert's been gone a year, Astrid," Sahara said. "That's long enough if Olive likes the guy."

"There you go," Jacks said. "The expert speaks. Anyway, I took off the watch to wash my hands and saw Albert's note, and I started thinking it couldn't be a coincidence."

"That was the end of the run of luck?" Astrid asked.

"Unless you count my missing the scene with Ev." He was glowing, and she knew why—bad luck had kept him out of art school for years.

And he showed up just when I was going to tell Sahara everything, Astrid thought, staring at their excited, awestruck faces.

"Anyone else still hungry?" Jacks asked.

"Me," Sahara said. "Let's grab some grub and plan our next move."

CHAPTER SEVEN

"YOU THREW A PARTY?" I shouldn't be shocked, I know. It is only in hindsight that their discovery seems unworthy of celebration. Still, I feel outrage that Astrid was partying as my orderly world began to fray.

"Best night of my life," she says. "Sahara started coming up with names, people she wanted to see. 'Call this person. Call that person.' Mostly people from high school, because she and Mark left right after Grad. Jacks thought of people too—folks I'd gotten to know after I dropped out of school, my ex-girlfriend. He invited his gang, guys he played poker with, hiking buddies—"

"How did Sahara feel about his inviting people?"

She doesn't answer, but a painting of the three of them gathered says it all—the wary lines of Jacks's and Sahara's bodies show them clearly at odds. "We told everyone to meet us at a local bar, the Mixmeander. . . ."

"Did they come?"

"Sure. It was Saturday night, and town's pretty dull. Eineke Glassen started giving me a song and dance about how she couldn't make it, so Sahara dropped the mermaid pendant around my neck. But it didn't work on the phone. Which was fine—forcing someone to come seemed . . ."

"Creepy?"

"Yeah. I took it off right away." She scratches her neck. "Sahara loved the mermaid. She named it Siren."

"She can't still have it?" Ever since Sahara escaped from Indigo Springs, she has been wooing people to her cause, not forcing them.

After fleeing Oregon, she'd appeared at a women's music festival in California, arriving on a flying carpet she'd purportedly woven herself. There she proclaimed an Age of Miracles and founded the Alchemite cult.

Audience members with camcorders filmed her as she worked magic for the incredulous crowd. She'd healed the sick and disabled, created baskets of fruit and flowers from thin air. She read minds, and immersed herself in the waters of a nearby lake for over an hour without drowning. Clumsily playing a harmonica along with the festival's headline band, she spread what witnesses described as "a feeling of safety, goodwill, and utter peace."

Sahara clinched her claim to godhood by bestowing mystic items upon her most zealous would-be worshippers. She gave a pair of shoes to a runner that helped her sprint at about sixty miles an hour—until they wore out, anyway. A midwife from Sacramento got a plastic pill bottle that relieved women's labor pains. Sahara gave a private investigator a book that helped her locate the bodies of long-lost murder victims. A musician got the harmonica. Indigo Springs's own Jemmy Burlein was there, and she got a set of tweezers that could short out anything electronic.

As the California State Police converged on Lake Shobogan, Jemmy killed their cars, computers, and communications equipment. Before the law could regroup, Sahara told her followers to scatter.

Within twenty-four hours, footage of Sahara's so-called miracle-working was spreading across the Internet. She was dropping in on raves, playing the harmonica, trancing out the crowds, and preaching. The private investigator was calling in tips on open murder cases to TV stations around the country.

A week later, people could download Alchemite podcasts, purchase T-shirts and philosophical tracts, and even get a CD of affirmations recorded by Sahara herself. Police arrested the Sacramento midwife when one of her patients was admitted to hospital with postnatal complications; they claimed the pain-relief chantment may have caused the bleeding. A mob almost broke her out of jail.

In early July, a month after Sahara's first appearance at the lake, pilgrims were headed in the thousands to the forest outside Indigo Springs, where a grove of trees near a sewer outfall had begun growing to a height of five hundred feet. They'd see Sahara there, it was rumored. So many people showed up looking for their goddess that police barricades couldn't contain them.

Savvy marketing: her success has been frightening. But if Sahara had the magic mermaid, she could simply force people to join her, couldn't she?

"Sahara doesn't have Siren anymore," Astrid confirms.

"What happened to it?"

"I'll get to that."

"What was *your* favorite chantment?"

"At that point? I'm not sure I had one."

"Did you wear the lipstick to the party?"

She blushes. "I wiped it off. It made Jacks babble."

"Did Sahara wear it?"

"She didn't know it was a chantment—I'd given her the impression it wasn't. Neither she nor Jacks knew."

"Didn't you tell them?"

Once again she chooses not to answer. "When we got to the Mixmeander, a yowl rose from the back. I saw two dozen people jammed in the booths across from the bar.

"Sahara was in her element. In ten minutes she'd weaseled us an invitation to a camping trip in August. She signed me up for a softball league. She had talk going about book clubs, dinner circles, movie outings. Penny Gonzales needed people to help with a fund-raiser for the hospital and we volunteered. I'd said I wanted a social life and she tossed one together like it was salad."

"And Jacks?"

"Surrounded by women, as usual. He was trying to avoid the pack, but gracefully."

"Was he avoiding Sahara too?"

Astrid flushes: the friction between Sahara and Jacks is clearly a sore point. "He'd run into the guy who owns the store next to the Mixmeander." She points to a photograph on her wall—herself at age seven or eight, standing with her parents beside a bicycle, posing in front of a concrete building. Its paint looks like it might once have been bright blue, but has faded to an uneven gray.

"And?"

"Once or twice a year some kid sprays dirty words on that wall. Then the *Dispatch* crime report carries on like that one act of vandalism means we're headed for a school shooting. Jacks had been wanting to paint a mural there, and he was making his pitch."

"He caught the owner in a receptive mood?"

"Perfect timing," she says. "Nathan was nodding and smiling and agreeing to buy him paint. People gathered around, telling them both how brilliant they were."

I scan the scattered cards with their painted images, but there is no picture here of the gathering Astrid describes. I wonder: If she lies to me, will the painted images back up her story, or reveal discrepancies?

Then I see a party scene on the card in her hands.

"Did your mother come?"

"Yes. She asked Jacks about those papers of Albert's—the clippings—but she did it without making a scene. And she talked to our next-door neighbor."

"You'd invited your neighbor?"

"Sort of. She had a job washing dishes in the Mix kitchen. She was this ancient Native woman . . . this must be in your files. Mrs. Skye?"

"Oh, of course."

"When Mrs. Skye's shift ended, Ma lured her out of the kitchen. She knew her, a little, because she used to deliver her mail. Ma had a gift for that—gallantly befriending old ladies."

"That was thoughtful of her."

"Ha! That's what I thought—and from what I'd seen, Mrs. Skye needed friends. But it was just Everett Burke playing games. Ma interrogated her about how much Albert was around Mascer Lane—whether he'd gardened at all."

"Mrs. Skye didn't find that strange?"

"She'd have been happy to have anyone to talk to. She was lonely, you know? I remember Sahara saying, later, she thrived on attention."

"What about you? What were you doing?"

"After Jacks had finished up his mural negotiations, he cajoled me into sitting up on the bar. We were telling stories about Olive and Albert's hand fasting. Everyone was laughing. I wasn't drinking, but I felt drunk, almost. Not sleepy—overstimulated, hyperaware. Edgy. Wired, y'know?"

I lean back. "You were in the spotlight."

"Nothing wrong with wanting that once in a while." Her eyes roam over the card.

"You usually avoid attention."

"It was a special night. And sitting there with Jacks, telling stories . . . it felt normal. Comfortable. Almost like being a couple."

"Did Sahara mind that it was you in the limelight?"

A stony glare. "She wasn't like that."

"Wasn't then? Or isn't now?"

"Wasn't then. Magic amplifies your flaws, Will."

"Is that what you call what's happening to your mother? Her *flaws* have been amplified?"

She rubs her eyes. "You want me to say Sahara was a saint before everything happened? She wasn't. But magic is a curse."

"Would you say you and Sahara are still friends?"

"Does it matter?"

"Do you think she cares now whether you live or die? Is she grateful you're taking responsibility for her crimes? That is what's happening here, isn't it?"

"Grateful, Sahara?" She presses her palms into the couch, chuckling bitterly. "You'll have to ask her."

"Astrid, do you want me to believe you're clairvoyant?"

"It'd help matters."

"Tell me where Sahara is."

She exhales, lips tight and bloodless, and my skin crawls as she flips over a card. It shows a familiar traffic exchange, darkened by a distinctive winged shadow. "On her way here."

I blink. It has to be a lie, a joke. There has never been any hint that she would consider ratting out her friend.

"Oh, it's true." Blue liquid rolls through her eyes.

I pick up the card and carry it to the nearest camera. "I'm looking at the interchange where the I-5 meets Helensville Junction. Sahara appears to be heading northwest. If this isn't clear, send someone in for the card. I can make out one of the Alchemite Primas in a car in the lower left corner of the image."

We wait, listening for the clank of the suite's steel door, but there is no response. At last I return to the couch. "Thank you, Astrid."

Smiling oddly, she lays her hands overtop of mine.

Suddenly I am sitting on a hump of soil the color of slate. Around me stretches a box canyon—azure walls hundreds of feet high, with rock formations of robin's-egg blue that look more like clumped wet snow than like stone.

"How's *this* for a parlor trick?" Astrid tilts her face up to a sky filled with azure clouds. "Welcome to the unreal, Will Forest."

Fuzzy dirt roils around me as I spring to my feet.

"Roach is checking my tip about Sahara," she says. "He won't notice if we flicker off his screens for a frame or two. Time's funny here."

"Time . . . is . . . funny," I repeat, and when she steps away I catch her arm. "Where are we?"

"You want me to trust you, right? So trust me. Come look around." She doesn't pull free, just starts walking. Curiosity gets the better of me; I fall in beside her.

We stroll off the dune and around a pillowy crag. Floating tumbleweeds the size of sparrows drift past, bobbing out of our way. The air tastes cool, almost minty, and there is a dripping sound.

We round the outcropping and I see a cord of blue fluid, blood-thick, twisting like a beheaded snake in an otherwise dry riverbed. Droplets splash off its flying ends, striking the rocks. They roll, slow and blood-heavy, to rejoin the writhing fluid.

"I've seen that flowing through your eyes." My heart is hammering, and my eyes strain against the perfectly adequate light, convinced by the palette of blue and gray that it must be too dark. "It's the alchemic contaminant that was on your roof this summer."

"It's called vitagua." Her shadow falls on the fluid and it congeals into an asymmetrical puddle, deeper and wider on our side of the creek bed. "Liquid magic."

"You're going too fast for me."

She peers into the rippling cobalt pool. "When Sahara, Jacks, and I found the chantments, it was clear they were magical. We should have been loony bin candidates. . . ."

"Because magic isn't supposed to be," I agree, but not because I've had any difficulty accepting the truth. The ease of it, the way the human backbrain embraces the fairy tales we learned as children, is just another peculiar aspect of the new reality.

Astrid nods. "But where had the chantments come from? Jacks and Sahara weren't thinking about that, but I'd mulled it over a bit. Dad spends his life chasing estate sales, flea markets, auctions. There was a phrase he uses when shopping: 'Gotta find a little sparkle.' My first theory was Albert was buying things that were already enchanted."

"Were you right?"

"No." She kicks a pebble into the vitagua and it vanishes without so much as a ripple.

"What was he doing, then? And what does it have to do with this?" I point at the lopsided puddle.

In response, she slides the wedding ring off my finger. "By 'sparkle,' Will, Dad meant an object that was receptive to spirit water."

"Astrid, before you do something we'll both regret—"

"Dad was making the chantments." Warming the ring between her hands, Astrid bites into her tongue.

"That's enough." My tone is sharp; I'm not about to let my witness start cutting herself.

"It's okay. Vitagua has to come through me—into the body, out through a break in the skin." As she speaks, blue liquid gushes from the bite, welling over her lips and drizzling down her chin. It drips into her palms, pooling in my wedding ring. The ring swells, like a sponge. There's a sucking sound and the vitagua vanishes.

Healthy color floods Astrid's normally pale face.

"What did you do?"

"I bonded the vitagua with a receptive object. It's a chantment now." She holds out the ring, which is dry and cool and properly sized again. "Go ahead, put it back on."

I don't move. "That belonged to my grandfather."

"I didn't damage it, and it won't hurt you."

"What is it?"

"Protection."

"You think I need protecting?"

"You're planning to go after Sahara's goons, right?"

I pick the ring off her palm, hold it up to the nonexistent sun. It looks normal.

For weeks now I have had nothing on my mind but retrieving my family. If that has meant finding the source of the magic and destroying it, so much the better. It is an attitude of which Roche heartily approves.

In her public statements, Sahara has said that alchemic contamination makes her better than ordinary people. She argues we should follow her because she knows what's best for humanity, for the world.

What do I say? Magic is even more undemocratic than technology. But now I think: Was all that just have-not resentment?

It's Granddad's wedding ring. What am I supposed to do, toss it? And if it can help me get the kids back . . .

I slide it onto my finger. The words inscribed by my wife—*Forever begins today*, plus our wedding date—feel as if they are raised on the metal. I read them through my skin, and as the lie of them sinks into my consciousness I flail, momentarily, against rage.

Nothing happens.

"I'm 'protected' now?" I ask.

"I'd have to attack you to prove it," she says, her voice almost playful.

"Never mind that." I stare at the pool. "So this is the source."

"Raw magic," she agrees.

"Vitagua makes the chantments. Vitagua made the monsters in the rivers and forests."

"Yes."

"How?"

"Simple contamination. See this poppy seed?" She holds up a speck of black, then spits a tiny droplet of blue onto it. The seed explodes in a profusion of unfurling stems, leaves, and roots. Red poppies bloom in Astrid's fist, and she drops the plant to the crumbly soil. Its roots grub downward. By the time I count to ten, the flower is as tall as I am.

"Hold your ring over the puddle," Astrid says. I do, and it quivers. "See how it's attracted to the chantment? Magic calls to magic."

I withdraw my hand and the puddle settles. "Like magnetism. Put the north and south poles of two magnets close to each other, and they pull together."

"Exactly."

"Magic is a tangible entity." This is certainly information Roche can use.

She produces a playing card from her pocket, leaching its color and then covering it in a painting of what looks like a blue amoeba. "Once upon a time, magic was an extremely rare living cell, just a component of the human organism. Magicules, they've been called. They had similarities to both plant cells and human blood cells."

"Cells," I parrot. A scientific explanation is the last thing I expected in this odd place. "And they did what exactly?"

"Responded to human will by bending or breaking the laws of nature. That's what magic is, when you get down to it. Flying is defiance of gravity. Lead transforming to gold, seeing through walls. Properly channeled, vitagua can do anything."

Her words hit like a hammer. "Anything?"

"If I can imagine it, I can make it happen."

"You're talking about power on a scale that's—"

"I'm no god, Will." She hands me the cell diagram and then holds both hands out over the vitagua. The fluid rises, as if to touch her hands . . . and then falls again.

"Unbelievable," I murmur.

"Magicules respond to collective will," Astrid continues. "In areas where most everybody believed in a given supernatural creature—say fairies—the particles made them come to be. They'd migrate into birds, or butterflies, and alter them. In Europe people believed in brownies, ghosts, werewolves, and demons. Magicules enter some female virgin's horse, it grows a horn—presto! Unicorn."

"What about this place you've brought me to?"

"People have always believed in invisible realms. Because they took their existence for granted, those realms came into being. We're standing in one."

"The unreal," I murmur.

"That's what Dad called it. Later, magic was driven out of normal people and the magicules came here."

"Driven?"

She presses the paintbrush to the stone wall of the gray cliff. Pictographs bloom on its surface like bruises, blue-black stick figures crowded in what looks like a stockade or a courtyard. Lines fill in the scene: an execution. In the center of the crowd a woman is bound to a stake. Ocher smudges at her feet suggest flames.

Making pictures. The same thing Astrid has been doing to the playing cards, but on a greater scale.

An image paints its way across another outcropping, a village of long houses and totem poles, its people beset by disease. They lie in attitudes that—despite the simplicity of their forms— suggest coughing. Elsewhere on the cliff, a mob watches as a man is drawn and quartered.

"Magicules were diffuse once, Will. Most everyone carried a few. Rare people had none, and others had extra, enough to make them mystics, prophets, healers. There was a time when they were honored for it. But eventually . . ." She gestures at the woman on the stake.

"You're saying that the Inquisition . . . that they were burning real witches."

"Sometimes, yes."

"Witches, unicorns, and . . ."

"And Fairyland."

I let out a breath. "You're saying we're in the land of the fairies?"

"I think that's what this realm was, at one time." She nods. "Then the witch burnings caused a shift in collective will, creating a fear of enchantment. People didn't want to be tainted, because they'd be murdered. Their native magicules migrated away, con- centrating in people who weren't scared. As the number of friendly hosts diminished, magic had to go somewhere else."

"To the unreal. To Fairyland," I repeat. The latter concept seems safer, like something out of my kids' books. "Are there fairies here?"

"No." The blue puddle is drizzling along behind us, following Astrid like a dog. "The fairies are dead."

"It's just you, me, and the vitagua?"

"Well, there aren't any fairies."

Begging the question. Every criminal has her own way of lying. Astrid's evasions seem disarmingly honest.

She gazes up at the painted cliff, voice dreamy. "Microscopic bits of magic, Will. They had to go somewhere. The witch-burners thought they were establishing a monopoly over enchantment. Instead, they drove it here. The physical pressure became im- mense. Magicules got concentrated, like crude oil." She points at the cobalt fluid. "One drop of that stuff contains as much magic as ten thousand people might carry. There are oceans of it here, seas of enchantment. Before this summer, it was trickling back into the world a drop at a time. Now, though, the dam's been blown."

"Sahara blew it." I stare at the blue hills, the puddle, the burning figures painted on the slate wall. It is too much—so I grope for something I can fasten on. Bad guys. Sahara. Caroline. And . . . "What people, Astrid? Who are these shadowy villains who pushed the magic out?"

She shakes her head. "Time's up."

Suddenly we are back in the apartment. I'm in my appointed place on the love seat. Astrid starts poking through the cards as though they are a collection of photos, pausing to admire images of Jacks and her mother. The portraits of Sahara she sets to one side. She selects a half-painted image, a tall man rendered in the style of the cliff paintings I just saw in the unreal. He is muscular and sur-rounded by clouds of smoke, a powerful, dangerous-looking figure.

"Nicely painted," I say.

"Someone's showing off," she says with a sigh. "We were talk-ing about the party at the Mixmeander."

"I remember." I suspect she wants to see if I'll terminate the interview, tell Roche about our escape to the unreal. But there's plenty of time for that. "You were telling jokes and your friends were—"

"Sahara was watching my mom," she says. "Everyone else . . . Well, word was spreading about Jacks rescuing that kid earlier in the afternoon."

"The one who fell off his balcony?"

She nods. "I found Aran—the *Indigo Dispatch* editor—trying to interview him."

"Trying?"

"Jacks wanted a trade—Aran was supposed to write some-thing about a famous fire that took place a couple hundred years back. Jacks believed local townspeople had burned out a Native potlach to settle some land dispute."

"This is what he'd been fighting with his father about."

"Yeah. Aran wasn't interested, so Jacks refused to give the interview."

"A journalist not interested in a story?"

"Aran's a chicken when it comes to controversy. Nobody ever talks about that potlatch fire."

"Not even descendants of the survivors?"

"Mrs. Skye and her niece are all that's left."

"I see. So Jacks was trying to enlist this . . . Aran, in his private fight with his father."

She frowns. "Not that I think the Chief read the *Dispatch*. He called it a rag. But he prided himself on knowing everything that happened in town. He talked to people. Gossiped. Town hero, y'know—everybody loved him."

"Everybody except you?"

She runs a hand over her eyes. "I guess if Aran had run the story, somebody would've told the Chief."

On another playing card, two tangled sets of arms and legs are knitted in a position that is distinctly carnal. The picture is unfinished, the invisible brush moving hesitantly, and I can't see the lovers' faces.

Clearing her throat, Astrid takes up the tale again.

CHAPTER EIGHT

THERE HAD BEEN A drip in the house from the beginning, a low gurgle in the walls, audible only in rare quiet moments. Astrid was faintly aware of the sound as she lay in her bedroom with the kaleidoscope, guiltily spying on the next-door neighbor. Tonight Mrs. Skye was pacing through her house, talking out loud to nobody. Once she paused, head tilted as if she heard a response.

We'll invite her for dinner, Astrid thought. I can ask Ma if she has any family. We could get her a pet. . . .

The stuttering rhythm of falling droplets prickled her consciousness.

New house, new noises, she thought—get used to it. Burrowing into her blankets, she let her mind drift. It was good to have a place of her own, good that life was finally moving forward. Mostly it was good to have Sahara back. . . .

She was dozing when Sahara's radio, next door, shut down with a click, filling the house with cottony silence. Astrid's legs twitched and she was awake again.

She drew a breath in, let it out slowly. No problem, she thought. Bad timing, that's all. Outside, an ambulance wailed briefly, probably heading up Boundary Lane to the hospital. She sipped air, smothering growing dismay. Insomnia had filled her nights too often in the year since her father's death.

On the other side of the hall, bedsprings squeaked—Sahara, rolling over.

Now Astrid could hear a whole nighttime orchestra: cats yowling beyond the yard, the distant murmur of a conversation outside, wind rattling the willow next door . . . and the drip. Trying to hang on to the vestiges of sleepiness, she rose and slid the window shut.

Ignore the noise. Idly, she picked up the kaleidoscope again. Downstairs, she found Jacks haloed by the amber glow of the streetlight outside his window. His chin was dark, stubbly. Jealousy tickled her: he was fast asleep.

Plan the garden, she thought, watching his chest rise and fall. She hadn't had her hands in dirt since Sahara arrived. Now she pictured the yard of her new home. Start under the fig tree. Bedding plants for the summer, and in the fall I'll load it with bulbs—crocuses, daffodils, tulips to go with the hyacinths already flourishing there. There are iris bulbs in the shed. . . .

She squeezed her eyes shut as Sahara rolled out of bed, tried not to hear the footsteps padding down the hall.

I'm tired, honest. Sweet peas by the fence . . .

She heard the squeak of weight on a soft part of the kitchen floor.

Don't listen. Relax. Think about honeysuckle, about where to plant a clematis.

In the kitchen, water ran in the sink and stopped. Silence. Then the drip sounded again, and Sahara cursed.

Climbing out of bed, Astrid scrambled down to the kitchen. She found Sahara on hands and knees, with her head in the cupboard under the sink. Her panty-clad bottom peeked out from under an orange T-shirt as she ran her hands along the pipes.

"You're blocking my light," she said, and Astrid dutifully moved. "*This* is why you're not charging me rent."

"You can pay someone to fix the taps if it'll make you feel better."

"You know Mrs. Skye said the house is haunted?"

"No. She didn't say this to Ma, did she?"

"'Fraid so. According to her, the previous tenants hanged themselves. The owner before that killed his twin daughters and is institutionalized—in Switzerland."

"Just what I needed. Ma's probably halfway to Geneva."

"Don't be hard on Mrs. Skye, Astrid. Her niece is paying some doctor to come certify she's too deaf and senile to live alone anymore."

Astrid thought of the old lady wandering the house, muttering. "You don't think she's that bad?"

"Just overtired. She lost her driver's license, so she's walking to work. She just needs a ride, basically, but the niece is taking advantage. . . ."

"We could help with that, right? Find a carpool."

"Yeah. People are such assholes." Backing out of the cupboard, Sahara blinked at Astrid with reddened eyes.

Crying over Mark again. "You okay?"

Sniffing, Sahara nodded. "Pipe's dry. Bottom of the cupboard too. I don't think our leak is down here."

"Doesn't sound like it." The drip spoke up obligingly and they canted their heads.

"Bathroom?" Sahara jerked a thumb in the direction opposite the sound's apparent source.

"Shhh." Listening hard, Astrid turned to face the cavernous living room. "Maybe the chimney?"

Sahara sprang up, bounding past Astrid to the massive blue-painted fireplace. In the curtain-filtered glow from the Mascer Lane streetlights, it looked less blue, less like an artifact from the honeymoon suite of a tacky hotel. The copper inlay on Dad's urn glinted in the dim light.

Stopping in front of the hearth, Sahara traced the mortar seams before laying her ear against the stone.

Drip-drip.

"You're right—it's louder. Put your head here."

Astrid set the kaleidoscope next to her father's urn and reached up the chimney, tinkering with the flue. "Rainwater maybe, trapped up there?"

"Could be. We could light a fire, steam it out." Sahara's eyes danced—she loved a good blaze.

"If the water's falling, where's it ending up?" She ran a finger along the inside of the fireplace, coming up sooty but dry; then she laid her hand flat under the grate.

Drip-drop. Faint vibrations buzzed her palm.

"What is it?" Sahara crowded in beside her.

"Someone's sealed the bottom of the fireplace." *Drip-drip* and she felt it again, minute impacts under her hand. Like someone was tapping from beneath the sealed surface.

Sahara pulled the grate free, sprinkling grit and ash everywhere, streaking her T-shirt. Henna, who had been about to squeeze between them, hopped sideways, sniffing as Sahara leaned the grate up on the hearth. She brushed away soot, revealing a grid of bricks grouted against the bottom of the fireplace. It was an odd but solid job, thick mortar sealing the stone into place. It raised the level of the hearth by almost an inch.

"Must you stomp on my ceiling?" Jacks appeared in the basement doorway, wearing nothing but a pair of shorts and his magic watch. He looked sleepy and harassed.

"Underwear model look suits you, Eligible."

"Shut up, Sahara."

"Sorry, Jacks," Astrid broke in. "There's a drip—"

"It can wait until morning."

"But look at this." She tapped the bricks.

He sighed. "Another inept Albert repair job. Maybe the hearth was cracked."

Sahara laid a cheek on the smudged brickwork. "What about the sound? It's coming from underneath."

"You're never going to get down there," Jacks said. "Let it go. Bad pipes, bad tiles . . ."

Drip-drop, agreed the house.

"This brick's attached funny," Sahara said, tugging at the edge of the hearth. "I might work it loose—"

"To what end? Sahara, leave the property damage for daytime."

"Do we have a screwdriver?"

"I don't think so," Astrid said.

"We could try the Crumbler," Sahara said.

"What?"

"You know. The magic pocketknife."

"You want the roof to collapse?" Jacks said.

"Right, bad idea. But this brick's loose, I swear."

He pointed at the kaleidoscope. "Look down and see what it is."

"Hmmm," Sahara agreed, still worrying at the brick. "I just need some leverage."

"It's probably too dark. . . ." Astrid reached for the kaleidoscope.

There was a scrape of stone on stone and a deep liquid belch from under the floor. Sahara's cry of triumph was cut off as a rush of something bright and blue splashed out of the hole, driving the hunk of brick into her forehead. She fell, Astrid catching her awkwardly as the stuff geysered out. Warm, syrup-thick, redolent with lilac and strawberry perfume, the gout of liquid sprayed them both. The remainder hit the ceiling with a wet *splud*.

Astrid flinched as the fluid soaked her hand and face. Her eye was tingling and the room was filmed with a faint blue haze. She saw a splatter of blue on Sahara's throat, centered around the mermaid pendant. A red mark in the middle of her forehead showed where the brick had struck her; its corner had gouged a tiny slice of skin loose. Blood welled from the center of the injury.

The smell . . . cloying, flowery . . . somehow familiar.

Astrid remembered the broken perfume atomizer from Albert's sack of junk. It had been oil-wet, slick with an unidentifiable fluid. . . .

. . . her head, already achy, began to pound. And suddenly there were whispers, a rhythmic, almost singsong grumble she couldn't make out. . . .

Looking faintly scalded, Henna licked a glob of blue off her belly. Only Jacks was untouched—he had stepped away from the hearth just in time. Had the watch moved him? Did that mean the liquid was dangerous?

He reached out to steady Astrid. "You okay?"

"I think so." She blinked hard, and the tingles in her eye became needle sharp. She turned her hand over. It was stained blue, colored by the fluid but already dry.

"Look." Sahara pointed at the ceiling.

Astrid expected to see the rest of the strange blue fluid pooled up there, about to dribble back down on them. But its drops were flat and mobile, sliding together near the light fixture to form one big pool.

Sahara giggled nervously. "Well, I think we're ahead. I don't hear the drip anymore, do you?"

"Not funny," Jacks said. "What is this stuff?"

Astrid's stomach did a slow roll, as if she were upside down. She ground a fist against her throbbing temple, and the pain spread across the right side of her face.

Grabbing an ash-shovel from the fireplace, Sahara scooped at the puddle. As she neared it, the puddle stretched in her direction, and she scooped a few spoonfuls into the shovel.

"Maybe it's a chemical spill. We should call a hospital. God, Astrid, it's all over you."

"This isn't pollution, Eligible, relax." Sahara brought it down, flipping the shovel so they could peer at the stuff. The fluid immediately launched itself at her neck, spattering the mermaid before sinking into her skin.

"Sahara!"

She peered up at it. "Do you think it's attracted to the magical objects?"

"If so, why's it up there?" Jacks demanded.

"Because . . ." She jittered up and down on her toes. "Because Astrid's room is above this part of the ceiling, and there's a bunch of them in her desk!"

"Great. You've got the answers, tell us what it is."

"What do you think it is, dummy?"

"Frankly, I don't care," Jacks said. "A handful of weird luck charms was one thing. Flying blue . . . whatever that is . . . that's too much."

Sahara's eyes sparkled within her blue-stained face. "Maybe we can get it into a jar. Hold the mermaid underneath the glass, pull it in?"

"And what if it's carcinogenic?" Jacks said.

"Magic carcinogens? Come on, Astrid and I have both been splashed and we're not dead."

"If that's supposed to be a rationale for more exposure—"

"It is, yeah."

"That's like saying you want to swim in radioactive waste because you survived a chest X-ray!"

"I didn't say it was a good argument," Sahara said. "This stuff is magic, guys. Like the widgets."

"Chantments," Astrid corrected, wincing as their voices rose.

"It may be magical, but that doesn't make it safe."

"If it is dangerous, that's all the more reason to bottle it. Come on, Astrid, can you really say no?"

And of course she couldn't; she never could.

"No more touching it," she ordered, trying to placate Jacks and instead sending him into a low fume.

"Sure, no touching." Sahara snatched a jar of nails from the windowsill, dumping them onto the hearth.

"Give it to me." Jacks took the jar.

"Why, 'cause you're the boy?"

"I'm taller and I'm more careful."

"Fine." Sahara was watching the blue puddle. Then Jacks reached for the mermaid and she stepped back, startled. She opened her mouth to object, but he put a finger to her lips.

"You shouldn't be wearing it anyway. Not around us."

Sahara looked to Astrid for support.

"He's right, Sahara."

"I fell asleep with it on, that's all." Yanking the pendant over her head, she slapped it into his palm. "I would never use it on you."

"That's good," Jacks said. "Because if you ever so much as try, I'll take a blowtorch to it." He clapped the mermaid underneath the jar and raised it to the ceiling.

"Nothing's happening," he said.

"Come on," Astrid muttered.

Rippling with miniature waves, the large pool flowed obediently into the glass container, leaving a big blue stain on the ceiling.

CHAPTER NINE

THE FOLLOWING MORNING ASTRID awoke to the sound of tapping at her door. "You in there?" It was Jacks.

"Yeah, come in." She sat, making sure her T-shirt was pulled down, before rubbing her ringing head. It was bright outside—too bright—she had slept in again.

He slipped inside. "You're lucky I wandered past. I thought you were up at dawn and gone as usual."

"I have to get an alarm." She yawned, mentally ticking through her client list. "I can't keep sleeping in."

"You need to eat more," he said. "Besides tired, how are you feeling?"

"My head hurts."

He peered into her eyes, expression friendly but detached: his rescue-worker face. "No sign of the blue goo on your face." He turned her hand over, searching.

Blue goo. The chantments, Jacks's watch, the fireplace, and the odd fluid. Astrid had forgotten completely.

"What is it?" He was still assessing her. "You okay?"

"Maybe I need some air."

He opened her balcony doors. Dew covered the lawns of Mascer Lane in glittering silver beads. Two months into the growing season, the rhododendrons were fading. She could see hints of color among the rosebushes as they prepared to bring in the next wave of blooms.

A trio of local kids dressed in blue baseball uniforms was walking through the alley. One of them waved, an ordinary gesture that made her feel inexplicably teary.

"Hey," she called, waving back.

Taking a deep breath of the morning air, she looked at her hand, searching for any sign of the blue stain. Bruisy color seemed to puddle under her fingers, then vanished.

Maybe the magic was gone.

Jacks had followed her outside. "You're not okay."

"I am. I was just . . . thinking of Dad," she lied, and he folded her into a hug. She leaned her aching head against his chest, smothering guilt. Saying it was grief would keep him from dragging her to a doctor.

"I'll be fine," she said, suddenly awkward. She remembered dancing with him at Dad and Olive's wedding. They'd been the same height then; now he towered over her.

"You sure?"

"Yeah. I have to get to work. Thanks for waking me."

He locked glances with her, still assessing, and she tried to look even-keel. "Call my cell if you need to."

"I will."

"Good. And no playing with the blue goo until we're all home tonight."

"I promise." She saluted.

Once he was gone she lurched over to the dresser, trying on the lipstick and staring at her reflection anxiously. Rumpled, worried Astrid became a picture of tousled glamour; she sighed, reassured, and opened her drawer. If the blue fluid had disappeared from her skin . . .

But no—it was there, caught in a sealed pint jar.

Relieved, she donned her gardening uniform—a layer of sunblock, boots and jeans, T-shirt and a ball cap.

"Ssst!" Sahara's hiss drew her across the hall.

"You rang, milady?"

Sahara was preening in front of her mirror, clad only in a bra and panties, an outfit in each hand. "Interview clothes," she said. "The suit too much for rural America?"

The suit was a straw-colored two-piece, slacks and a jacket with a pale green blouse. "Let's see you in it."

"Lecher."

"You have an interview?"

Sahara jerked her head in the direction of her laptop. "Local radio station needs a nighttime host."

"You're looking for work in Indigo Springs?"

"I have this addiction to money. Without it I get all hungry and strung out. The withdrawal's awful."

"What happened to 'This is a stopover on the way to Los Angeles'?" Astrid asked. "Or 'you'd better keep me entertained if I'm going to last three weeks—'?"

Sahara winked. "Believe me, I'm entertained."

"You're staying?"

"Don't you want me?"

Astrid blushed. "Is your interview with Matt Goode?"

"Yeah."

"Wear the skirt, then. And act like you're glad to be out of the big bad city."

"Shucks, sir, I always was a country girl at heart."

"Lay it on half that thick and you're a shoo-in."

Tossing the suit aside, Sahara pulled the dress over her head. "I could just mermaid him into hiring me."

"You need magic to get a job in your own field?" Astrid asked.

"Of course not," Sahara said. "How do I look?"

The dress was cream-colored linen, stylish but reasonably conservative. "Perfect," Astrid said.

Sahara unrolled a pair of nylons and slid into them, every move graceful. "Hey, were you serious about wanting to fall in love?"

"Why?"

"Classifieds. Same webpage as the job listings. 'Shy guy, thirty, just discharged from army, loves hiking, fishing, watersports . . .'"

"I am not answering a personals ad. Anyway, that would be David Crane."

"The guy who used to spit on people's desk chairs at school?"

"Exactly."

"Then how are you going to get yourself a man?"

"I'll think of something."

"Want a makeover?" Turning to the profusion of bottles and brushes on her dresser, Sahara selected a comb and began working on her hacked-up hair.

"Thanks, no."

"Let me help you find some new clothes, at least. Your good stuff got trashed by the Crumbler, didn't it?"

"The what—oh, the magic pocketknife." Astrid tilted her head. "I might agree to clothes shopping."

"I bet you and Jacks can tell me exactly how many available men are in town."

"Just men? Are we shopping for you or for me?"

"Well, I am on the market too. Besides, if there were any single lesbians in town besides Jemmy, you'd have made your move." To Astrid's surprise, the hair was taking shape, curling around Sahara's face as obediently as if it had been professionally styled. She spritzed it with something that smelled of pineapples and chocolate.

She fiddled with the mermaid pendant. "Maybe this isn't a good time for an Astrid romance project."

"There's never a good time. Love is by definition a vast inconvenience."

"Cynic."

"We'll just make a list of candidates, okay?"

"Not now—I'm running late."

"Wait, don't go! There's something else."

"What?"

Reaching for the laptop, Sahara clacked keys. "I've been surfing for references to magic on the Web."

Astrid sank to the bed. "Find any?"

"About what you'd expect. Fake psychics, UFO nuts."

"Anything about the blue goo?"

"Not yet. But that word you keep using—*chantment*—I found it in one discussion thread." She began reading: " 'I have a stickpin that makes people feel happy, but whenever I use it, I have to eat big meals over the next few days. It burns me up like fire-wood.'"

"Firewood," Astrid repeated.

"Then another poster, Eldergodz, answers, 'I'm always hungry and exhausted, I'm losing weight like crazy.' That leads to a bunch of off-topic stuff about dieting, but after *that* a third person—Marlowe she calls herself—says she has a bookmark that can answer tough questions."

"What kind of questions?" Astrid asked. "Does it say?"

"Yeah." Sahara flipped ahead. "How can my brother keep from losing his house, where did my neighbor's missing cat get to, what do I tell the IRS when they audit me? . . ."

"Wish we had that one," Astrid said.

"Yes, except Marlowe says she was wasting away from helping her friends with their various problems. She was having fainting spells and seizures. She couldn't eat enough to keep up. It sucked the life right out of her."

"Makes sense."

"Happypill—the one who has the magic stickpin—seems to know the most. She's the one using the word *chantment*, and she refers once to an 'angel' who gave her the pin."

"Great. Does that mean Dad was getting the chantments from angels?"

"I don't know," Sahara said. "Hopefully we'll find out. This Happypill person seems to think there's another way to power the chantments."

"Is that something the angel said?"

"It doesn't say." Sahara scowled. "Doesn't it seem unfair that magic takes energy? Always a catch, huh?"

"It's why I'm sleeping in," Astrid said.

"I'd hoped I was so hungry because of Jacks—the crappy food, you know? But it must be my little mermaid." Brushing on blush and eye shadow, Sahara selected a plum lipstick a shade darker than her own lips, and completed her transformation into a polished job seeker.

"I'll keep reading the thread," she said. "Information is power, right?"

"Definitely. The more we know, the better."

Turning to the mirror again, Sahara nodded in satisfaction and reached for the mermaid.

Astrid caught her hand. "Seizures and fainting fits, remember? Matt will give you the job."

"It's not for him. I'm going to sell the gold dust to a jeweler today."

"But—"

"How else can we launder it here in the boonies?"

Launder, Astrid thought uneasily. A crime word. "You'll be careful?"

"Soul of discretion, I swear."

"Don't you think you'd better check on Ma first?"

"What—make sure I haven't fried her brain before I do someone else?"

"Exactly." Astrid searched her friend's face, to see if she was offended by the insinuation, but Sahara nodded.

"Right. Ev first, then—if she's okay—the jeweler."

Astrid hugged her. "Thanks. Tell Ma I'll call, okay?"

"I'm just keeping busy. Jacks made me swear I'd leave the blue goo alone until after you're both off work—"

"Work! Dammit, now I'm late."

"Then get out of here," Sahara said, smacking Astrid lightly on the backside to send her on her way.

The gardening business, like much of her life, was something she had fallen into. Dad had been a high school dropout too, unemployed and unemployable until he got married. Ev was widely pitied for having saddled herself with him. As soon as she fell pregnant, goodwilled Springers began trying to redeem Albert with job offers.

By the time Astrid was old enough to crawl, her father was tending a handful of lawns and yards around town. He had been little more than an odd-job man at first, a mower and weeder, a clearer of debris. Then he'd discovered a natural flair for land-scaping. From cursory gardening for old ladies who couldn't keep up with their yards, he slowly built up a client base.

Albert's real break in the direction of legitimacy came when he landed a caretaker's job for a row of cottages at Great Blue Reservoir. When he began, the sad row of weather-beaten cabins looked half-ready to collapse into the scrubby meadows of long grass and dandelions that surrounded them. Albert slapped a careless layer of paint on the structures and got to work. A few years later they were flower-strewn and verdant. The abundant blooms and greenery gave the cottages an air of noble fatigue.

By then Astrid was sixteen and working for Albert part-time, mowing lawns in town and helping with the gardening. But some-thing was already nibbling at Albert's marginal success—his mania for antiques had worsened. Junking devoured his time, drawing him farther from town and clients. Astrid raced to keep up with his workload, cutting classes to hang on to jobs. Her B grades dropped to C's, then shivered on the edge of a real nosedive.

The idea that she had to preserve the business—that Dad would come to his senses one day—kept her going. But then Ma realized Albert had stopped paying Astrid's wages, and their mar-riage finally died.

Astrid dropped out of school then, splitting her time between her divided parents and the business. She managed to hang on to most of Dad's garden contracts, preserving his business for the day he recovered from his compulsive antique collecting. She couldn't accept the permanence of his change, even when he got himself jailed. Prison will turn him around, she promised herself.

But when he got out, Albert didn't even try. He got into debt instead, borrowing every cent Astrid could give. When she was tapped out, he'd married Jacks's mother.

Her father vanished into junking, leaving her his vocation as a warped consolation prize.

Astrid's first client today was one of the town matriarchs, a woman who had hired Dad in the early years and never ditched him, even in bad times. Leeda Flint had five acres of land just off the highway to Wallowa. Most of that was pasture for her horses. Expensive warmbloods, seven of them: Leeda loved those horses so much, she kept a donkey too, so none of her precious babies would be at the bottom of the equine pecking order. She was sixty-two, and rode every single day.

Her yard was simple, with beds of flowers bordering the property and walkways. The rest was lawn, an expanse of green wide enough to accommodate trench warfare and—thanks to Astrid—meticulously groomed as a golf course.

Astrid unlocked the lawn mower and began working careful circles around the grass, keeping an eye out for weeds or other blemishes and returning to check suspect areas after she mowed. Two precocious dandelions were scouting out the territory near the driveway; Astrid, wielding a long plucking fork, ripped them out by the roots.

As she picked them off the fork and tossed them into a bucket, another Albert memory tickled her consciousness. Vitagua, Astrid thought, stopping short. The blue goo is called vitagua.

She closed her eyes, trying to remember. Her and Dad, here . . . when?

Nothing.

"Now who's going nuts?" She fetched some border plants from the truck and knelt at the edge of the flower beds, reaching out to pluck a chickweed that had stretched into the sunlight from its nest underneath the tulips.

As her fingers closed over the stem of the plant, brushing the topsoil, words slid through her mind like oil: chantments, vitagua, the unreal, the Spring.

She placed her hand flat on the ground and a string of memories unspooled:

Dad had been showing her how to weed a stand of foxgloves and dahlias. Working her fingers down to the shaft of the unwelcome plants, tugging to gauge how loose the soil was before the slow progressive pull . . .

She'd plucked her first dandelion successfully, bringing up the whole root, sprinkling dirt everywhere.

"Let's take a break," Dad said, holding out a cupped hand.

Astrid bent, peering into his palm and seeing a drop of vitagua there. She reached for it, but Dad pushed her fingers aside.

"Don't touch it," he said. "Not until you're ready to chant it into something."

"Is it poison?" she asked, glancing at the foxgloves—she knew they were toxic.

"Sort of. Could make you sick." Dad tapped his skull.

"Head sick?"

"Worse. You know how, in stories, princes get turned to frogs?"

Shivering, Astrid lifted her hands from the ground so she could rub her forearms. The flow of memory faded. How could she have forgotten?

Magic, of course.

Deliberately this time, she began to garden again, sinking her hands into the soil. The memories were waiting.

· · ·

"Don't be afraid," Dad said. "Vitagua is just like bug spray, camp-fires, gasoline, or anything dangerous. Nothing to be afraid of, if—"

"If you're sensible," Astrid said.

"You got it." He poured the blue droplet from his palm into a small glass vial, sealing it carefully before handing it over. "I'll initi-ate you soon."

Astrid flipped the vial over, watched the fluid slide around. "What is it?"

"Spirit blood," he said. "Liquid magic. Vitagua. I used it to make your kaleidoscope."

"Vitagua," she said, savoring it. She liked grown-up words—she had a collection of them. Oscillate, idiosyncrasy, germane, igni-tion, propagate, iridescent . . .

Dad tucked the vial into his toolkit. "Astrid, this is a big secret, okay? Nobody can know. Not your mother, not your friends . . ."

"Secrets are bad," she said, quoting Ma.

"Magic grows best in the shade, Bun. Only way to keep it safe is to hide it from daylight. . . ."

.   .   .

The whinny of a horse broke Astrid's reverie. She straightened, briefly disoriented as Leeda, grinning cheerily, came up beside her, her white hair loose and wind-tangled.

"Been here long, Astrid? Garden looks beautiful."

"Um, not long."

"Come inside," Leeda said. "You wanted to jaw over what you're buying from the greenhouse for me, didn't you?"

She nodded, stunned. Don't touch the fluid, Dad had said. She and Sahara had splashed it all over themselves.

Princes into frogs . . .

"I've got a check for you too," Leeda said, offering her a hand up.

Astrid drew away, as if she might infect the older woman by touching her. "I'm dirty," she said by way of explanation as she scrambled to her feet.

"Hell, girl, I've got horse spit all over me." Crooking a finger, Leeda sauntered back to the house.

Astrid followed, struggling to find a place for this latest piece in the puzzle that was her father's life.

CHAPTER TEN

"I GOT AWAY FROM Leeda as fast as I could," Astrid tells me. "Even as we talked, I was thinking about my client list, trying to figure out who'd been around longest. To remember, I'd need to work in gardens where Albert and I had been together."

"You wanted to know more," I say.

"I *had* to know more. All I'd learned was that you weren't supposed to touch vitagua."

"But Sahara had gotten a pint of it in the face."

"Exactly. I had to find a way to clean her up."

"You were exposed too. Weren't you worried?"

"Not as scared as I was of having my best friend go crazy."

"You always worry about others first, or just her?"

She hunches over the coffee table and does not answer.

"Don't you know? Or is it that you don't want to say?"

"What do you want, Will? I give you one answer, I'm some kind of saint. The other, I'm obsessed with Sahara."

"Aren't you?"

She looks down, face sulky. A jumble of containers has been brushed onto one playing card. I see the jar of magical blue fluid and a plastic tub full of gold flakes. There's a bottle of plant fertilizer too, and tubes of acrylic paint. Water surrounds this stash: tin cans, buckets, teacups, and brimming pots. The picture's shadows are tinged bloodred.

"Watch this." She lays out the completed cards in a block and they begin to form a mural in miniature, a series of illustrations that flow into one another. The greater image has a grandness to it; it ought to be enlarged a thousand times, not confined to scraps of paper.

"Jackson Glade is very talented, isn't he?" I say.

Her tone is sad. "He should've left town, gone to art school. Staying in Indigo Springs . . ."

"Why didn't he leave? I'd have thought, given his relationship with his father, he'd be dying to get away."

"He was attached to his friends."

"His friends? Or one friend in particular?"

"You're asking if he stayed because of me." It wasn't a question.

"Yes. Are you the reason he never left town?"

"No." Her tone is certain. "Jacks tried to leave, but stuff kept getting in the way. Colleges losing his applications, funding drying up. Olive got hit by a car one year, and needed him to run her bookstore."

"Bad luck."

She grunts. "Finally Jacks struck a deal with his dad. He'd give the Fire Department a try and after a year if he still wanted to paint, the Chief would pay for school."

"Seems fair."

"Funny thing was, *my* dad was always after Jacks to go—spread his wings, he'd say. I think that's why he gave him the watch, to see if he could save him. . . ."

"Save him from what exactly?" Was Albert Lethewood the sort of father who hates competing for a daughter's love?

Covering her mouth, Astrid takes a shuddering breath. "Jacks wasn't bitter. He had his painting, his buddies—"

"And you."

"No rush, he'd say, the world wasn't going anywhere, and he'd always come back to the Springs anyway."

"Didn't that seem odd?"

"Indigo Springs is home for us both." Her hands clench. "You can get up and stretch if you want, Will."

"Pardon?" I realize my neck is sore, that one of my feet is nearly asleep. The furniture is too hard.

I decide to take her up on the suggestion, walking slow circles around the room, swiveling my head to get the kinks out. I half expect her to yank me back to the unreal. But she doesn't grow fur or sing an aria or even squirt vitagua through the whites of her eyes again.

Instead, she tilts her head, speaking wistfully. "Patience must be in a TV station by now. Holding court."

"Probably." Patience's cult smacks of the sort of devoted fandom celebrities have always garnered. She preaches common sense: Don't panic about the magic, don't take everything Sahara says at face value. Along with her overwhelming loveliness, the wisdom and authority with which she speaks makes people take her seriously.

An electronic shriek issues from the foyer.

"That's for you," Astrid says. She is watching the latest card—the picture of the containers. Crimson paint flows between the bottles, pooling underneath them.

"I'd forgotten you have a phone."

"My own personal hotline. Why should Roach come all the way down to my cage for a two-minute conversation?"

I follow the sound to the foyer. I must have seen the phone when I came in, but its normalcy made it invisible.

"Yes?"

"Like the lady says, it's me," Roche says. Reminding me, none too subtly, that he's listening in.

Arthur Roche and I met in college, around the same time I met Caroline; the three of us took a few psychology courses together. For a time we were close; we'd hung out, gone skiing and camping. We'd stayed in touch, a little, after he was posted overseas. I'd e-mailed him when he was caught in an explosion in Afghanistan; he'd sent a card when Carson was born.

"We missed Sahara at the highway." Arthur was always a bit terse, but his hearing was damaged when he was wounded. Ever since, he has spoken in clipped sentences, with precise diction. A hearing aid adequately compensates for what he has lost, but he seems to have a dread of seeming, in any way, disabled. "No idea where she is now."

He seems to want an answer, so I say, "Astrid said Sahara was headed here."

"We scared her off. Got one of the followers, though. The one you saw in the car. Burlein."

"Good."

"You should tell Astrid we've captured Sahara."

"You must be joking."

"Give it a try. If she thinks we don't need her, she'll be more forthcoming."

"She's showing signs of prescience," I murmur.

"If she laughs it off, blame me and go on with the interview. I want a better sense of her capabilities."

"She's capable of hearing my half of this conversation from the living room."

"She's in the bathroom," he says. "Maybe she hasn't seen that Sahara's escaped. Maybe she won't know for a couple days we haven't captured the little psycho."

"Maybe she's known for weeks. I'm not going to lie, Arthur—it'll alienate her, and she's finally cooperating."

"Relax, Will. It's just a suggestion." Backpedaling, I think. Good. "We have an advantage; I want to exploit it."

"What you have is another prisoner. Go exploit her. Don't ask me to jeopardize the relationship I'm building."

I wait out a long silence.

"The braincrackers up here say Astrid's encouraging you to think I'm stupid, Will."

"Please. Give me a little credit."

"There's got to be a reason she's opening up now."

"There is—I know what I'm doing."

"She wants your sympathy."

"She's a murderer," I say—though I am not sure I believe it. We don't know the whole story yet. "My sympathy is more limited than you think."

"You said you thought Sahara did all the killing."

"It's a tactic," I murmur. Is she truly out of earshot? "Arthur, lying to her—"

"You've never hesitated to lie to a subject before." Frustration burns in his voice.

"Except when it's likely they'd catch me out," I say. "Arthur, what's the sudden rush? You did run Sahara off, didn't you?"

"Hardly matters—she'd never get in here," he scoffs. "This facility is secure."

"Then let's stick with the plan."

"We almost had them, Will. Sahara, that second-in-command of hers, Passion, maybe Caroline too."

Caro . . . now I'm the one struggling for control.

"Until Astrid gives me a preliminary statement, we're playing a guessing game. And we're getting somewhere here. We thought she'd be raving, remember?"

"Okay," Roche says. "It's your show, I guess—sing your heart out. Just come home with good reviews."

"It'll be just like St. Louis." I interviewed a kid there, a young man convicted of killing his sixteen-year-old girlfriend. He'd been up for release after six months in minimum security. He was a clean-cut boy from a well-off family, a model prisoner showing model displays of remorse. If he's sorry, the victim's parents said, let him go.

But he wasn't, and I sank him.

Sahara's Primas—her high priestesses—may have fished the aircraft carrier crew out of the Pacific, but the Alchemite cult has plenty of blood on its hands. Women resembling Sahara and Astrid have been shot in twenty cities across the country. Sahara has taken responsibility for two major earthquakes, the epicenters of which were near Indigo Springs, quakes that have taken over ninety lives. Alchemized animals—crows, mostly—have caused horrific traffic accidents. A Wiccan who disputed Sahara's claims to godhood was beaten to death by an Alchemite mob.

Poor Roche. The calls he must be fielding!

"Prisoner's headed your way," Roche says. "Showtime."

"I'll get results," I promise, and he hangs up.

I put the receiver down, turn . . . and almost jump out of my skin. Astrid is right behind me.

"Ever fire a gun?" she asks.

"I'm a policeman," I say, "I go to the target range."

"You didn't ever point a gun at someone? Never went hunting? Ever see someone get shot?"

"Have you?"

"What about hitting someone? Fighting?"

"We're talking about you, not me." I gesture down the corridor toward the couches.

She closes her eyes, seeming to listen. "I'm sorry you're caught between us. Me and Roach."

It is easy to see this comment of hers as a stratagem, a means of driving a wedge between me and Arthur. "What makes you think it's like that?"

"He wants me dissected. You're the knife."

"What do you want?"

"To get through Will day."

"That's not much of a goal if you know how everything's going to play out."

"Do you think seeing a train wreck before it happens makes it easier to live through?"

Train wreck? "Doesn't it?"

"There's the cutting edge now," she whispers.

"Astrid, nobody is here to dissect you."

"Roach wants you to take me apart. That's what you do, isn't it?" When I open my mouth, she adds, "Don't lie."

"Sometimes."

"But you can't help liking me. This was all harder than I thought it would be. . . ."

Was harder—her sense of time is slipping again. "You're worrying about me?"

Her hands have become entangled in the phone cord, twisting its coils as she presses her ear to the fake white door of her prison. "Keep them out, right? It's all about keeping them out, just long enough to hide the spill. Daddy knew I was going to blow it. . . . He avoided initiating me, looked for another apprentice, anyone, anyone, marry Olive, get money, any alternative—"

"Shhh." I pry the cord out of her hands before she can break the telephone. "Astrid, it's okay."

"Did you call my father a hypocrite once?"

"I never met him. And why would I say something like that?"

"Which part is this? Patience?" Her voice rises to a scream.

"Astrid, listen to me." Glancing around, I see a laminated picture on the wall, a square board with an image of a country cottage on it. I pull it off the wall and the fastener comes with it, harmless plastic hook and a chunk of plaster. "Listen to me. You can't live like this, can you? It must be painful—"

"Of course it hurts." Thick fury in her voice now, and tears are running down her cheeks.

I offer her the picture. "I can help. You talk of me dissecting you, Astrid, but what if I could cut away some of the hurt?"

"Confession is good for the soul, is that it?" Her voice is still raw, but I'm on the right track. It is so obvious she longs for peace of mind.

"Stay with me." I lay the picture on her trembling palms. Immediately it fades to blankness. "Show me how I can help."

She pants shallowly. "Right. Okay."

I give her a nudge and she shuffles back in the direction of the couch, eyes locked on the picture. Paint begins to color in the interior of Albert Lethewood's house: wood and wallpaper, old tile and worn carpets. All vastly different from this elaborate, modern prison cell.

I glance around, struck by how colorless the room is.

Inhaling raggedly, Astrid begins to speak. "That afternoon in Leeda's garden, I learned the basics. The magic fluid trapped beneath my fireplace—the vitagua—was the source of the chantments—"

"I know—" Then I remember she told me this in the unreal,

where Roche could not hear. "Did you learn how to deal with your and Sahara's alchemic exposure?"

"No." She regards me soberly. "And I had other reasons for wanting to learn more."

"Such as?"

She reaches for one of the scattered playing cards, poking it with a finger. All its color seems to flow toward her skin, shrinking to a black dot. Then small drops of ink ooze up from beneath, as if the card is mesh lying just above a sea of paint. She raises her hand and the multicolored seepage resolves into an image of her father's face.

"In Springer eyes, my father was a deadbeat. He took care of me while Ma brought in the bacon. When he started doing odd jobs . . . then he became the guy—every town has one—who paints your fence every other year, hauls your dead leaves to the dump for ten bucks. Dad was the town drunk, except he didn't drink."

"Instead he shopped for junk, is that it?"

"It destroyed him," she says. "He lost Ma, he nearly lost Olive, he was always broke. Whenever something odd happened in town, the police questioned him. Most Springers thought he did drink, or gambled.

"When Dad cheated those people out of their damage deposits, when he actually went to jail—I was ashamed of him." Her face colors, and I see strong emotion straining to break the dams of her self-control. "But suddenly, it looked as if there was a reason for it. The junking, the money he spent on things that vanished afterwards—"

"He wasn't a deadbeat, so you could love him?"

"I always loved him," she snaps.

Point for me, Roche, I think. You happy?

"I wanted to look up to him, like I did when I was little."

Time to push. "You weren't concerned about the fact that you and Sahara had been exposed to the vitagua, were you? Or that you'd told Albert's secret to the least discreet person in the world.

He spent all those years playing the buffoon, and you had tossed it away."

"It's not—"

"He gave up everything, and now you were encamped in that house with someone who was giving the chantments cute little names as if they were toys or—"

"Stop it!"

"Pets—"

"That's unfair."

"And—let's not forget—she was playing with your mother's mind."

"Shut up!" Her voice rises. "I didn't know what was at stake, I didn't realize there was so much vitagua coming out of the unreal. My head hurt all the time, I was exhausted and forgetful. I couldn't believe the chantments were dangerous. . . ."

"Or that Sahara was?"

Blue is flooding the whites of her eyes. "Sahara wasn't dangerous."

"Please. She led hundreds of her followers to a contaminated area outside of Indigo Springs. Are you saying you don't know this, Astrid? Your psychic powers didn't tell you three people got shot rushing police barricades?"

"Your guys got trigger happy." Her voice is angry.

"We lost people too. The retrieval team sent to get the Alchemites out of the woods didn't come back."

She shrugs.

"After the government burned out the alchemized trees, Sahara returned to Mascer Lane with all her followers. She caused a six-point-two-Richter earthquake there. Do you know how many people died, Astrid?"

"She can't help herself. You can't blame—"

"Who should we blame?" I say, and Astrid's head rears back, like a snake about to strike. "You can't pretend Sahara isn't reckless, morally corrupt—"

"Quiet!" She slams her hands down on mine, on either side of the table. The brushtips at the ends of her fingernails are bright blue, seeping vitagua. The fluid is a quarter inch from my skin—a bizarre threat, but a real one.

It is a shock, but I can't afford to show fear. I resist the urge to yank free, even as I think of Mark Clumber's obvious paranoia, and of the wet sound he makes whenever he tries to speak.

Astrid clings with ferocious strength. Unnaturally blue veins throb in her face. Her skin is ice-cold. "The vitagua has made Sahara insane."

I refuse to look at my hands, the drops of blue welling so close to my skin. I keep my voice even. "Has it made you insane too, Astrid?"

"I'm different." She releases me and lolls onto the couch. The blue fluid pulls back out of sight, leaving her so pale that each freckle stands out on her skin.

The phone shrieks again in the foyer.

"Roach is worried about your safety," Astrid says.

"I'm not in danger," I say. It stops in midring.

"Can we go back to talking about gardening now?" she asks wearily.

"Fine. I've got all day, don't I?" I keep my voice light, as though she hasn't just attacked me. "The gardening. It triggered your memory flashes."

"Touching things was triggering the flashes. At first it was contact with objects Albert and I had both touched."

"I understand. Leeda's garden was a place you'd been together. Digging in the garden brought on the memories of your father."

"Right. As time passed, I got better at it." Her anger seems to ease. "Remembering wasn't quite like seeing Dad again. The memories were vivid, but old."

"Did you leave Leeda's? Go on to your next client?"

"Shamro Moore. Yes."

"And did you learn anything else?"

"Plenty," she said. "How to make a chantment, where the vitagua came from, why Dad had lived his life letting everyone think he was the village idiot. What he'd done with the things he'd bought and chanted over the years."

I look at the painted image of Albert Lethewood. He is kindly and guileless, with childlike eyes. He reminds me of an alcoholic I used to arrest twice a month, back when I was new to the force. A sweet drunk's face. It is easy to see how the people of Indigo Springs made assumptions.

Harmless, invisible. A perfect mask for his activities.

I look at the daughter who has thrust Albert's mystery into my world. She has the same chin, the same wiry red eyebrows. But the innocence that suffuses his face is gone from hers. Maybe that's a game, and this half-crazed exterior is all she wants Roche to see. Is there more to Astrid, or is this all that has survived Sahara?

She didn't expose me to the vitagua just now, I think, and I certainly made her furious.

Despite my denials to Roche I wonder again: Did Astrid really commit the crimes she has all but confessed to, or is she covering for the friend she so obviously loves?

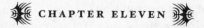

CHAPTER ELEVEN

JACKS WAS HOME WHEN she returned from work, pulling hot corn bread out of the oven while a thick mass of curried potatoes and chickpeas bubbled on the stove.

As soon as Astrid walked through the door, he set a plate in front of her. She didn't bother to sit, pulling apart the bread and taking a bite. It was thick, grainy, and fragrant.

She dunked a piece into the curry. "You can't keep cooking all the time—you'll get resentful eventually."

"Mom made this. I stopped by the bookstore and she dumped a housewarming package on us."

"Oh. Good. And how was your day?"

He beamed. "I ran into a woman who'd blown her radiator on the highway. She spotted the sketches for the mural while I was calling the mechanic and it turns out she works at an art gallery in Eugene. Probably nothing will come of it, but she liked the sketch. Oh, and Dad stopped by the tour office twice and missed me both times."

"You're gonna have to talk to him one day, you know." Curried potatoes sang on her taste buds. The spice was intense enough to make her sweat.

"All in good time." Jacks brandished the magic wristwatch playfully.

She thought about pushing the issue, only to decide not to break his good mood. The choice brought a faint pang of sadness. She and Albert hadn't been getting along at the end. She didn't want Jacks to end up with regrets.

There's time, she thought—the Chief is healthy enough. "I found out some stuff about Albert and the chantments today."

"You promised to stay away from the blue goo."

"It's called vitagua, and I have. Dad told me everything a long time ago."

"You've been holding out?"

"Course not. I forgot, somehow."

" 'Somehow'? I love the sound of that." He glowered.

"Well, I'm remembering now. Where's Sahara?"

"Can't you give me the ABC's without Her Majesty present?"

"Don't snark. *A* is for Albert. He was making chantments out of the crap he bought at flea markets."

"Making them?"

"Yeah. *B* is for the blue goo in the fireplace."

"Vitagua," Jacks said.

"Yes, vitagua, which is what he used to pull it off. You infuse vitagua into an object and it becomes magical."

"Okay. And what's *C*?"

"Uh . . . confidential. He was pretty firm about it being a bad idea to tell people about this stuff."

"Damn. I just sent out a press release." With a teasing smile, he popped a clump of hot bread into her mouth.

Momentarily flustered, she swallowed. "Be serious. There's also *D* for danger. Apparently one day there will be too many chantments gathered together in one place—"

"What's that . . . a prophecy?"

"I guess. If they pile up, people can sense them."

"What people?"

"Chantment collectors—thieves, really. And Albert hinted some people would destroy them if they could."

"Why? They seem pretty benign."

"He was vague." Now that she wasn't hands-deep in a garden, her recollection was getting fuzzy, as if the conversations with Albert had been dreams. Pain ground into her skull. "Know that face he used to pull when he didn't want to admit some ugly truth? A thing he'd done, money he'd spent?"

"Oh, don't I just. But if Albert was making chantments but couldn't stockpile them, where are they?"

"He sent them away."

"To who?"

"People in trouble, or in need. All that junk he bought, Jacks—he chanted it and then gave the stuff away. That's where his money went."

"Mom's money," he said. Then, grudgingly: "Ev's too."

"Yeah."

"That ol' drunk Al Lethewood," he said, doing a fair imitation of his father before bursting into laughter. "He conned the whole town."

Catching her hand, he tangoed her around the kitchen, twirling her into the hall.

Astrid concentrated on not tripping over her boots as he reeled her back against him. He smelled of aftershave and hot bread. "Chief'd bust a gut if he knew, huh?"

"To say the least. Why didn't Albert sell the things?"

"It would have made it easy to trace him?"

"Would have kept him solvent too," Jacks said ruefully.

"He found hard-luck cases in the newspapers and mailed them the chantments anonymously."

Still dancing, he dipped her. "Magical gifts."

"Exactly," Astrid said as she came up again.

"And we're supposed to do this—be an unregistered charity? Become Santa Claus?"

"It'll be fun, Jacks."

"Screw charity." Sahara chose that moment to appear, drifting through the back door in a high-necked black dress and new shoes. The mermaid hung over her collar and her arms were full of bags. "We're funded," she announced. "The jeweler was putty in Siren's hands."

"Take that thing off now," Jacks said. Astrid stepped away from him, flustered.

Sahara removed the mermaid and dropped it into a new purse. Throwing herself into a chair, she grabbed a hunk of bread. "I'm starving."

"What's this about a jeweler—you zapped someone else?"

"Only a little, Eligible. What's with the bread?"

"Olive made it, it's delicious, and we are grateful," Astrid said, rubbing her temples as Jacks bristled.

"Don't encourage him, Astrid. We've been running ourselves ragged all day and he's feeding us health food." Sahara fished in one of the bags. "I bought champagne."

"*C* is for conspicuous," Jacks grumbled.

"Flashy by nature, that's me."

"We have to keep a low profile, Sahara," Astrid said.

Sahara tossed her head. "Astrid, my dear, unless you plan to become your father—bad reputation, bad finances, bad liver, and all—"

"It's not that simple, Your Majesty," Jacks said.

"Did Albert tell you how to make new chantments?"

"We have to send them away, Sahara. We can't let them or the vitagua concentrate."

"Fine. Did he tell you how?"

"She means it, Sahara. We can't keep them."

"I'm not deaf." Sahara picked at the potato curry. "Speaking of people with crappy hearing, I sent that life-skills evaluator of Mrs. Skye's packing. She's safe from the machinations of the niece, at least for a while."

"You're going to use that thing on everyone you meet."

"I should've let him pack the old lady off to a home?"

"How do you know she doesn't need assistance?"

"Jacks, there's nothing wrong with her I can't mend. She needed new batteries for her hearing aid and a ride to work every day."

"Mend her. She's not a busted tap."

"She's not a busted anything. Astrid, we're gonna go over Saturday and clean up her house and garden, okay?"

"Fine," Astrid said, wondering if she and Albert had ever worked Mrs. Skye's yard. "Thanks for looking out for her, Sahara. I was worried."

"You worry about everyone."

"You can count me out of your little rehab project—I'm going rock climbing with Saje and Kevin," Jacks said.

"I didn't invite you, Eligible."

"How was Ev?" he asked pointedly.

"Okay. She was playing amateur detective again, but I got her to focus on her shrink appointment. Whatever I did to her, it was wearing off. I don't think I'm that good with our Siren yet."

"What about the jeweler?" Astrid said. "Doesn't that mean he'll spill the beans about the gold dust?"

"I convinced him he needed me to build him a webpage. Nobody will wonder if I'm at his store a lot." Sahara fiddled with the collar of her new dress. "I ran into Eineke Glassen on the way home. Gave her a hard time about skipping our party at the Mixmeander."

"How'd she take it?" Jacks said.

"I never realized before that she hates me."

"She's jealous," Jacks said. "She has a thing for our girl."

"Doesn't everyone?" Sahara leaned over the counter, her expression sly.

"Don't I wish," Astrid said.

"Ooh, you're blushing. You date her, Astrid?"

"I went out with her brother."

"They dated for eight weeks," Jacks said, grinning.

"And what was wrong with him?"

"He was lovely," Astrid said. "But he wanted to move to Florida."

Sahara laughed. "I guess the homebodies win. A rolling stone gathers no Astrid." She and Jacks were still eye to eye, not quite glaring. "Home team advantage."

A quiet thump at the front door broke the staring contest: all three of them jumped.

"Could be your dad," Astrid said.

Glancing at his magic watch, Jacks shook his head. "I don't think so."

"Chickenshit," Sahara said.

Jacks's gray-green eyes narrowed just a little, glinting with anger. Astrid put a hand on his, intending it as support—and suddenly she sensed how deep the anger ran. Jacks was furious with his father.

"Hey, Sahara," he said. "Since you're mending everyone else in the Springs, you want to take him on?"

"No can do," Sahara said. "Chief's a force of nature."

"Ah. Still shying away from the tough jobs."

"You saying I'm lazy?"

The thump at the door came again.

"I'll go," Astrid said, crossing the still-vacant living room and tugging open the door. Nobody was there.

She glanced down. Henna was stretched out on the porch, washing one bloody paw with slow licks of a crimson tongue. On the doorjamb at Astrid's feet lay a dead rabbit. It was—thankfully—only minimally mangled.

"What is it?" Sahara called.

"The great fluffy hunter got . . . lucky."

"Oh gross, dead mouse. It's my cat, I'll clean it up."

"No, I got it." Astrid knelt beside the furry corpse. Then she froze. Dark certainty flooded her, knowledge as familiar as her name or hair color. She would follow someone out onto this porch one day, into a glare of artificial brightness, light so blinding, it baked her skin.

Lights—TV cameras? A haze of strangers' voices would greet her. "Where's Mrs. Skye?" they would shout. "Is anyone still in there?"

Bile scorched the back of her throat. It's the vitagua exposure, she thought. Dad said it can make you crazy.

The panic ebbed, leaving her with the smug cat and rabbit corpse.

"Head sick," she murmured to Henna. Astrid thought of the

splash of vitagua across Sahara's face, the stain on her own hand. The cat was exposed too. . . .

Got to get it out of us, she thought. Fetching the shovel, she scooped up the rabbit quickly and took it out back to the garden. She quickly dug a hole.

Voices floated through the open door: "Basically you're hiking out to the middle of nowhere to climb rocks with the same guys you've been camping with ever since high school. Sounds exhilarating."

Jacks's reply was frosty. "I could spice it up by seducing one of them, then running off to the other side of the country with someone else."

"And your shiny new day job is also hiking, am I right? Could you be more one-dimensional, Eligible?"

"Why did you come back, Sahara?"

"Am I interfering with some plan of yours?"

Hastily Astrid pushed the corpse into the hole and kicked dirt over it, trotting loudly up the steps and silencing the argument. "What else did you buy today?"

Cheeks pink, Sahara upended a bag on the table. Household necessities tumbled out—boxes of pencils, a tape measure, a red towel, a picture frame, batteries, an icepick, plastic drinking glasses, a soapdish, a deck of cards, CD-ROMs, fruit-shaped fridge magnets, lightbulbs, a screwdriver, duct tape, shower curtain and hooks, scissors, a memo board, a cutting board, hard candy, a windup mouse for the cat, and an egg timer.

Astrid poked through the pile, looking for Albert's sparkle. There . . . "Want to see me make a chantment?"

"Are you kidding?" The edge in Jacks's voice softened into curiosity.

"Nope." She reached for the soapdish, a ladybug-shaped disc of rubber bristling with flexible nubs designed to keep the soap raised and dry. She gripped it in her left hand. The nubs pressed against her palm.

"Assuming we can make chantments, who would we send them to?" Sahara asked.

"We'll work it out," Astrid said. She scratched the point of the icepick across the back of her hand. Vitagua bubbled from the cut, spilling off her wrist and vanishing into the soapdish, which sucked it up thirstily.

It was just as Albert had said—strength filled her, buoying up muscles tired from hours of digging, filling her with vitality she could barely contain. The headache spread across her right temple, but the surge of energy made it less significant, suddenly bearable despite the tears dribbling down her cheek.

"You okay?" Jacks said.

"Yes." The scratch began to sting and blood came to the surface.

Sahara leapt up, digging a box of bandages out of another shopping bag. "Can I learn to do that?"

Astrid shook her head. Her awareness of the vitagua within her body—a diminished presence now—was keener. "It's just me."

Jacks was staring at the soapdish. "This is a chantment now? What do you think it does?"

Astrid already knew. She set it on the kitchen counter, squeezing the tiniest drop of liquid soap onto it. Bubbles foamed from between its nubs, a drift of soap that churned across the curry-splashed counter. Then it withdrew, leaving the tiled surface bright and clean.

"Sorcerer's apprentice." Sahara clapped her hands, and Astrid chilled. *She's going to say we need to keep it,* she thought, *and I'll have to change her mind. Are we going to fight now?*

But her friend scooped up the ladybug. "I know who to send this to."

"Who?"

"One of my crisis junkies."

"Pardon?" Jacks said.

"She means her fan club," Astrid said.

"Woman with three kids," Sahara said. "Grubby apartment.

No money, no time. She mentioned once she can't keep up with cleaning their place."

"Couldn't someone trace that?" Jacks objected. "We're trying to be sneaky, and this is someone you know—"

"That's just it: I don't know her. She posted her address in a newsgroup so one of the others could mail her something . . . astrological charts for her kids, I think. I'll scoop it out of the archives. We write some basic instructions in an anonymous note, wrap up the package, ship it—"

"We can't mail it from town," Astrid said. "Ma."

"With luck, Ev won't be opening people's mail for much longer," Sahara said.

"I can't take the chance." She cradled her throbbing head in her hands, feeling hunted. "I'm going the same route as Albert. I'm never going to have a normal life."

Jacks rubbed her shoulders. "You can do Albert's job, if you want to call it that, without making his sacrifices."

"Job," she said, easing into the massage. "It was his job, wasn't it? All those years."

"Some job. No thanks, no money, no benefits," Sahara said. "Astrid, you are *not* going to turn into your father. There are three of us, we'll use the gold dust to get money when we need it and we'll spread out the labor."

"Share the load," Jacks agreed. "You won't be alone with it the way Albert was."

"Lord, when you think of it!" Sahara's voice was reverent. "All that secrecy, all that trouble—for his entire life. It's . . . heroic."

Tears pricked Astrid's eyes. She felt lighter, knowing things hadn't been Dad's fault. Sad too—that she hadn't thought well enough of him to see through his charade.

But I did know, once. And then forgot. Why?

"With the three of us on the job, it'll be more discreet. Does this thing do floors?" Tossing the ladybug onto the linoleum, Sahara squirted out dish soap.

"Not too much," Astrid cautioned, but it was too late. Suds

boiled outward like a swarm of ants. Before any of them could move, it was knee deep and rising.

Sahara stepped toward the back door.

"No," Astrid said urgently. "We can't let anyone see the foam."

"What did someone say about discretion?" Jacks lunged at the kitchen window, losing his balance and then catching himself on the counter. Pulling himself upright, he shut the curtains with a clatter.

"You okay, Monet?"

"Yeah." The soap bubbles were as high as his hips. "Floor's slick, that's all. Let's retreat."

"Hold hands," Astrid said, reaching out. Sahara's hand—small, dry, and warm—folded into her right. Jacks took the left. The soapy tide had risen to her chest. Below its surface, a million small scrub brushes scraped her exposed skin. Her shoes squeaked over the ice-slippery surface of the kitchen floor.

Hand in hand, they inched toward the living room.

Sahara said, "Did I say I'm sorry yet?"

"Do you ever?" Jacks replied.

"Peace," Astrid warned. She lifted her chin, prepared to gulp air like a swimmer going underwater. But before the soap could rise over her neck, the suds sucked back into the ladybug with an echoing slurp. The three of them were left at the edge of the gleaming kitchen.

"Whew," Sahara said, wobbling. "Sorry, Astrid."

"Forget it."

Sahara collapsed on the rug in the empty living room, dragging first Astrid and then Jacks down beside her. As one, they flopped onto their backs.

"I feel about how I would if I'd really just scrubbed the kitchen from floor to ceiling," Sahara announced.

"Those guys on the discussion group weren't kidding about chantments draining your energy," Astrid agreed.

"It's too bad," Jacks said. "We could've tried cleaning in here."

"Why?" Sahara asked.

"Because if magic is a huge secret, maybe we shouldn't have a big blue stain on the ceiling."

"If it won't scrub off, I'll paint it," Sahara said.

"Okay, I'll get paint," Jacks said. "I'm buying for the mural anyway."

"Thanks, guys," Astrid said.

"See?" Sahara squeezed her. "We're a team!"

"I'll mail the ladybug from Wallowa," Jacks said. "The rafting group I'm leading tomorrow meets there."

"Will the Chief hear about that?" Sahara asked. "We don't want anyone thinking *you're* turning into Albert, either."

"We'll have to rely on my sense of timing—" He raised the hand wearing the watch; they were still holding hands, and he shook Astrid's arm like a noodle. "This'll keep me from running into any of the county busybodies."

"I guess you're the obvious choice," Astrid said.

"Don't worry." He blew a hair from her forehead. "It'll be fine."

"I know." It was at once scary and a relief to hand off the responsibility.

"Please. He's offering to mail a package, not defuse a nuclear warhead."

"We have to take this seriously, Sahara," Jacks said.

"What makes you think I don't?"

Astrid giggled. "You don't take anything seriously."

"I'll be good as gold dust, I promise. Know why? Because once a secret like this gets loose, there's no reeling it in. You lose control, and I *love* these things."

"I do believe that," Jacks said.

"That doesn't mean I'm convinced there's a magic Geiger counter out there that's gonna lead a bunch of would-be thieves to our door."

"Albert said we disperse the things, we disperse them," Jacks said. "Especially until we know more."

"I'm not saying we keep everything. Did I say that?"

"Stop fishing for wiggle room. Once Astrid learns more, we'll know if it's safe to hang on to a few things. A few, Sahara."

"Albert kept stuff."

"Things that were too dangerous to give away," he said. "The knife, for example. It would certainly be easy to misuse the mermaid, wouldn't it?"

She flushed at his pointed tone. "Do you honestly think there's some bogeyman out there looking for us?"

Astrid remembered her moment of terror out on the front porch. The certainty of it—the media at her door—was unshakeable. But now as she lay on the rug with Sahara on one side, Jacks on the other, their bodies warm against hers and her heart singing with joy at discovering that Albert hadn't been a deadbeat—it was easy to discount the fear, to chalk it up to vitagua-induced paranoia. "Probably not," she said. "But let's do it Dad's way until we know it's safe to do something different."

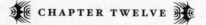

CHAPTER TWELVE

THE NEXT TIME SHE was alone in the house, Astrid climbed up to the attic. Remembering the flash of memory that struck when she'd been there earlier, she paced from corner to corner, fingers trailing the walls.

Lost memories tickled her like stray hairs, but nothing came through. Finally she knelt near the hatch, laying her hands flat where she'd touched the floor before.

. . .

Albert had initiated her here when she was eight years old.

They had slipped away from Ma that day, as they so often did, supposedly to pick up shoes for school. She'd felt guilty about that, Astrid remembered now—the secrecy. Each lie made it worse. She had even asked Dad: What if I didn't become the chanter? What if you picked someone else?

It was about to be too late.

"Ready, Bundle?" Albert said, and young Astrid had nodded. Astrid herself, caught up in reliving the experience—it seemed at once like new information and a very old part of herself—remembered fear and reluctance, mixed with a need to please.

"Okay," said her father, taking a bundle of cloth from his shirt pocket. Inside was a scarred glass bead.

"Is that a chantment?" Astrid had asked.

"It's sea-glass. It'll show me if you've ever been contaminated with vitagua."

"How?"

"Just take it, Bundle."

She picked it up. It was warm and dry.

"Does it sting at all?" Albert asked.

"It's supposed to sting?"

"Only if you're contaminated."

She rolled the bead on her palm. "No stings. Don't feel anything."

"Okay, that means you're clean." Albert caught the bead in the piece of fabric again. Next he produced a golden bowl, and an eye-dropper full of vitagua. Astrid tipped her face up, and he put one tiny drop of liquid magic into each of her eyes.

Pain jolted her. She pitched forward, and Dad caught her, drawing her hands away from her face as her eyes welled up. A sobless cascade of vitagua-laced tears had fallen into the gold bowl.

"Ow," Astrid had complained. "This hurts!"

"Half-over," Albert crooned. "It's okay, Bundle, you're very brave and we're half-done."

"No, stop!"

"We can't," he said, and Astrid remembered the pain on her father's face. Like an animal in a trap, she thought now—back then she had been too young and scared to understand. "We stop here, you're cursed."

"I don't care," Astrid whispered, then and now.

"You would care," Dad said grimly, and as the flow of tears stopped he sat her up. Dipping a comb into the bowl, he ran it through her hair. Her curls snagged in the comb, even though he had trimmed her hair the week before.

"Ow," Astrid said again, but this time it was subdued, a protest almost for form's sake.

"You know, initiation is the most dangerous moment of life as a spring-tapper," he said. Astrid, who had been about to yank loose, stilled. "Usually you do only one initiation, see, when you pick your apprentice. And the first time you do anything with magic, with vitagua, that's when you're most like to mess it up."

"But you did this before," she mumbled.

"That's right. I initiated my cousin Ron, years ago."

"And he died of that sick thing."

"I thought becoming a spring-tapper might cure his leukemia. No such luck, though. I tried another fellow too, but he had a bad accident. I'd been hoping my little sister . . . well, she ran off East with that fellow."

"That's why it has to be me," Astrid said.

"But, see, I'm better at initiating . . . better than my grandmother, than anyone." Dad stroked her cheek. "It's gonna be fine, Bundle. Third time's the charm."

She shuddered. Dad was careful not to touch her scalp with the mixture of vitagua and tears, simply drawing it through her hair. The combing brought with it a sense of hollowness, awareness of unfilled spaces inside her body, vaults of room between her molecules.

She heard ice groaning, a sound of dripping . . . and below that a murmur that sounded like her name.

The fear dissolved. "Can I make a chantment now?"

"I'm not quite finished, Bun." Taking the nail clippers, Dad chopped off a few strands of her hair, laying them on the kerchief. He took a fingernail clipping too, then handed her a small pin.

Astrid poked her finger. A single drop of blood welled out; she dribbled it on the fabric.

"When you've done something once, you get ideas for next time." Digging in his pocket, he produced two white nubs.

"Are those my baby teeth?"

She must have scowled, for her father grinned. "I paid the Tooth Fairy good money for 'em, I promise."

She giggled. Dad added the teeth, poured the last of the tears onto the kerchief, and pulled its corners up into a bundle. He wound another strand of Astrid's hair around a strong piece of twine, using it to bind the kerchief shut. Then he pierced his own finger. Vitagua flowed out.

"Watch," he said. The fabric folded in on itself as he chanted it, becoming hard and blue like stone, a lump as wrinkled as a walnut or a brain. "Now we get rid of it."

"Where?"

"In the creek."

      .   .   .

The memory cut off there, cleanly truncated upon the two of them leaving the attic. Astrid ran out back to the edge of the ravine, looking for a path. When she found it, she pushed both hands down through twigs and weeds, groping for soil.

There—she remembered eight-year-old Astrid walking solemnly to a sheer edge of the path.

      .   .   .

It had been cold and snowy; her breath hung in the air. She had thrown the bundle, underhand. It arced up, maybe five feet, and then tumbled down the incline, leaving small dents in the snow-pack. When it reached the iced-over thread of the creek, it punched down, like a fist going through drywall. A tremor ran through the ground. A fall of slush from the snowbank tumbled down, covering the small hole in the ice.

"You're done." Albert sighed, clearly relieved, and wrapped her in a hug. "Thank you, Bundle."

"Can I make a chantment now?" The distant grumbles were friendly; she wanted to please them and Dad too.

"First things first—let's see if the spirit water will mind you." Young Astrid watched as he squeezed a drop of vitagua into the golden bowl. "Hold your hand over it."

Staring at the blue droplet so hard her eyes hurt, Astrid obeyed. Her fingers tingled, and she felt as if the bead of vitagua was all but in her grasp, like a watermelon seed sheathed in slippery fruit juice.

"Push it around inside the bowl," Albert said. "Don't worry too much if it won't go the first time."

Easy, so easy, one of the grumbles whispered. Imagine the spaces inside yourself compressing.

"Hop, hop," Astrid crooned. The bead of vitagua shot up, over the lip of the bowl, and struck a nodding, snow-covered daffodil.

"Um, okay." Albert laughed, looking for the droplet and seeming only slowly to realize how far it had gone. He darted to rip up the

flower. Its dirty roots protruded from the bulb, writhing like worms, tinged with blue and growing longer in his grip. "What'd I say about first times?"

. . .

He was uneasy, the adult Astrid thought, remembering his expression. A hand on her shoulder drew her still further from the mystic reverie. She wobbled, off balance, and Jacks steadied her.

"What are you doing?"

"Touching things," she said. "Remembering."

"Get anything useful?"

She beamed. "Nice things . . . about Dad."

He tweaked her nose. "I'm glad. Listen, I had an urge to roust you and . . . maybe go somewhere?"

"Where?"

"I dunno." Jacks held the watch to his ear, as if listening to it tick. "Hiking? Biking? I'm still getting the hang of this thing."

"There's a hang? I thought it dragged you around like a dog on a leash."

"Woof. You want to come, or not?"

She glanced at the house.

"Come on, Sahara's helping Mrs. Skye sort out the garbage in her basement. Fixing her, you might say."

"I might say helping her out, being neighborly."

"Whatever. Let's go up Yellowtail Trail."

"My bike brakes are shot."

"I fixed 'em." He raised his hands, showing off smudges of oil and dust. "You're tuned and ready to go."

Minutes later they were pedaling down Main Street, driving past the brick façade of the courthouse. The building was undergoing reconstruction, an earthquake-prevention measure mandated, despite local disapproval, by the State. Beds of flowers were blooming along the streets. People everywhere looked happy to be outdoors.

"Look, there's Mrs. Kale." She waved to the history teacher who had taught them both during Astrid's abortive attempt to return to high school. "Reader, reader?"

Jacks laughed—it was a game they hadn't played in years. "Olive mostly sells her true crime books."

Astrid scanned the square for someone else they knew, finally pointing at the aging dentist.

"Doc Liam? He reads novels about animals. *Call of the Wild,* that sort of thing."

"That's right, we've done him before. Amy Burkette?"

"Magazines only. Makeup, celebrities, diet fads."

They stopped at the lights and Astrid's gaze fell on a woman who was crossing in front of the truck. "Her?"

"Newcomer. If she's been to Olive's, it's since I stopped working in the bookstore." Jacks leaned sharply to one side, stamping a foot down. His boot came down on the leash of a terrier on the run from its owner.

"Guess the magic watch has done its good deed for the day," Astrid said, after he'd handed back the dog. "Is that all it wanted? Should we go home?"

He shook his head. "Turn right at the Grand Hotel."

"I thought you said Yellowtail Trail?"

"Change of plan." They crossed onto a secondary highway, starting uphill. With every mile the trees crept closer to the ditch, while fences, power poles, and other signs of human occupation— everything but the road itself—began to thin out. They were well out of town when Astrid saw the bottle-factory sign.

Jacks's body bunched, as if he was going to put on a burst of speed and pass the turnoff. Then his tire slid, and he had to brake.

Astrid stopped beside him. "I guess we're here?"

"I guess," Jacks grunted. They pushed the bikes to the gate and he punched a code into its electronic lock. The latch clunked.

"Chief gave you a code?" Astrid asked.

"Last time he started in on me about coming to work here." He frowned at the two-story brick factory. "I keep telling him to sell the place and retire."

Stubbornness is a family trait, Astrid thought. "Aren't you afraid we'll bump into him?"

"Doesn't seem likely, the way my luck's running." Even so, he didn't object when Astrid chose to push her bike all the way around to the back, out of sight of the road.

Peeling off her helmet, she eyed the building. OREGON BOT-TLEWORKS, EST. 1812, was painted on a sign hung at roof level; the letters looked newly retouched.

"We going in?"

"That I don't have a key for, but there's a ladder to the roof. Want to see?" He trotted to the corner, peeking around in a way that suggested he was more spooked than he'd admit by the prospect of seeing his father.

Astrid followed, expecting to find a fire escape. Instead Jacks was halfway up an aluminum ladder with I.S.F.D. painted on every other rung. Up top, she found a tar-and-gravel roof punctuated by humps of moss. Rain-bleached playing cards, beer bottles, and poker chips were scattered among the rocks. Jacks lifted a blue tarp that lay flat in a corner, revealing a card table underneath.

"Dad has poker games up here in the summer sometimes."

"That's funny," she said. "I knew you played, but I didn't know he does."

"Dad was the one who taught me. Manly arts are required learning for the Glade men."

"Poker's manly, huh? But you don't play together, you and him."

"Not in ages," he agreed, letting the tarp fall.

Astrid nudged a beer bottle with her toe. Much of what Jacks did was an obvious reaction to the Chief's values: embracing his mother's peacenik politics, refusing to hunt or fish. A natural ath-lete, he had shunned team sports, depriving his father of a football or baseball star to brag about. Instead he favored uncompetitive pursuits like hiking and rock climbing. His friends were all good guys, but they too might have been handpicked to annoy the Chief. Unemployed stoners, Lee had called them once.

Unemployed stoners. She was suddenly angry. Woolly-headed nature freaks. That ol' drunk Al Lethewood.

"What do you think of the view?" Jacks said.

"We're on the Bluffs," she answered, surprised. A stand of wood sheltered the factory road. It hid the near side of town, the part that was tucked against the low edge of Indigo Creek and the ravine. Across the ravine the land rose again, and Astrid could see the steeples of the Catholic and Baptist churches, the courthouse with its scaffold-encrusted dome, the beige-and-yellow block of the high school. A tall rocket-shaped slide poked up above a line of maple trees, marking a playground where Albert had taken her as a kid. Flags drooped from poles here and there; the breeze was too gentle to unfurl them. Blue mail trucks hunkered around Ev's post office, which in turn was dwarfed by the fire hall's four-story training tower.

"Why did you quit the Fire Department, Jacks?"

He kicked a bottle over the edge of the roof. "You ever wonder how the town can afford six firefighters and a truck? The Sheriff's Department has two deputies."

"Never considered it," she admitted.

"I wondered. I was in the fire hall, where the records live, so I had a look. I found out the building was bequeathed to the volunteer fire squad of the day—not the town, as you'd expect—in the eighteen hundreds."

"So?"

"That was right after their chief dropped the investigation into the fire at that Native potlatch."

He was watching her face carefully, trying to look neutral, but Astrid could sense his tension.

"Okay, I admit it's suspicious. Who did the bequeathing?"

Right answer—he relaxed a hair. "The name on the records was Lionel Sparks."

"Never heard of him."

He pointed up at the fire hall. "He owned that hill and all the timber rights for fifty miles in every direction. Pillar of the community. The sort of founding father libraries and highways get named after."

"Like I said, never heard of him."

"I went to Kettle Falls and Wallowa. He's all over their histori-cal records. Ran a lumber mill, hired hundreds, blah blah blah. Union-buster too—he had this crew of thugs who burned out a labor meeting once."

"Burned out. You think they set the potlatch fire?"

"It's suggestive, isn't it?"

"Jacks, I'm having trouble seeing why the Chief would care about any of this. It can't affect the department's reputation now."

"The story goes that twenty years after the potlatch fire, one of the survivors started making trouble. Said she could prove the fire was arson. She disappeared."

"Which still sounds like ancient history."

"My great-great-great-grandfather Glade gave Lionel and his firebugs an alibi for the night this witness vanished. Sparks prob-ably had her killed—"

"Or maybe just run out of town," Astrid said.

"Either way. The great-Grandchief lied, and ten years later Lionel died and left the department an endowment."

"Endowment?"

"Enough to run the department pretty much forever, salaries and all . . . as long as they invested well and raised money to keep up with inflation and capital costs."

"It was a payoff?" Astrid asked.

"Huge payoff."

"That is awfully ugly." She scratched her head. "Still, Jacks—"

"What?" His voice was sharp.

"You know your dad isn't my favorite person, right?"

"Yeah."

"And I understand why you'd be mad—"

"Try sickened, Astrid."

"Sickened, then, if your ancestors covered up a bunch of mur-ders and got paid for it."

"Are you saying that's not the logical conclusion?"

"I'm saying what could the Chief do about it now? It's over a century ago."

"He's damned well making sure it stays buried in the past, that's what."

She slipped an arm around him and squeezed. "Albert and I weren't speaking much before he died. I don't know what happened—"

"Maybe if you keep gardening, you'll find out."

"Maybe. My point is that if anything happens to Lee, you could find yourself wishing—"

"Dad's indestructible."

"He runs into burning buildings for a living."

"For fun," he grunted.

"As for the bottle factory, if he wants you to have it, so what? You could turn the place into studios. The view . . . I had no idea you could see so far."

"You sure you haven't been out here before? Your amnesia . . ."

"It's not amnesia," she said, letting her hands rest on the roof. She felt no sense of her past, but as the metal flashing warmed under her skin, she did feel a thread of something else. "It's an old building. . . ."

"You can tell that just by looking," Jacks said, and the sensation faded.

She brushed dust off her palms. "This is neat, Jacks, but I don't see anything lucky around here. Are you sure it was the magic watch that brought us?"

"Must've—I hate this place." Picking up a weathered tree branch, he staggered around the rooftop, pretending to dowse for water. "Did you ever want to move away?"

"Leave Indigo Springs? No."

"I don't either, you know. Want to leave."

"What about school?"

"My scholarship applications keep going astray," he said. "Maybe school's not meant to be."

"Meant to be," she echoed skeptically.

"If you believe in magic, why not destiny?"

"You make your destiny," she said.

"Is that your philosophy or did Sahara give it to you?" Avoiding her sharp glance, Jacks hurled the stick, bouncing it off the factory flagpole. "Sorry."

"What is your problem with her?"

"She dumped you," he said.

"We weren't ever—"

"I saw you kissing," he interrupted, "before she left."

Astrid shut her eyes, letting the memory in just for an instant. Sahara in her Alpine Princess dress, the tiara on her head. The first kiss nothing more than a triumphant smack aimed at Astrid's cheek and coming square on the lips instead. Shared glee at Sahara's having won the crown, nothing more.

Mischief had risen in Sahara's eyes. She'd kissed Astrid again . . . and suddenly they were making out. All her hopeless fantasies about necking with her best friend had come true. Her hands wrapped around Sahara's waist and their tongues slid together. Astrid's imagination leapt to the end of her favorite daydream, the one about the two of them living together. The rest of her body stayed closer to the moment, singing with desire as her hands inched up the bodice of the ballgown dress, toward her breasts. . . .

But Mark Clumber's voice had rumbled up the hallway, and when Astrid tried to pull Sahara away, to flee in the opposite direction, the mood passed.

Sahara had straightened her crown. "Wanna pick this up tomorrow?" she'd said. "I ought to give someone his walking papers."

"Yes," Astrid had said. "Oh, yes."

But the next day Sahara was gone.

"She didn't mean anything by it," was all she could say now.

"Actually, Astrid, that's my point," Jacks said. "People were like toys to her even before she could use the magic mermaid to make them into her little puppets."

"I don't see you complaining about the lucky watch."

"I'm not using the watch to warp people's brains."

"Jacks, the mermaid may be the only thing standing between Ma and a nervous breakdown. And it burns energy, just like the other chantments. Sahara won't . . ."

Won't what—start a cult? The grumbles mocked her.

"She's not going to start a religion with it," she said, feeling shivery and untruthful.

"I suppose you think she won't split town either."

"Sahara went to college, Jacks. It's not a crime, it's what's you do. Grow up, go to school. She's back now—"

"She came because she had nowhere to go. She'd be gone if not for the magic."

"She's been hurt. She needs to feel safe."

"She needs to feel like the center of someone's universe, Astrid, and you indulge her. Sooner or later she'll find someone else to worship her, and then . . ."

"What?"

"She'll fuck you over and leave again." He hurled a stone, again hitting the pole.

Natural athlete, Astrid thought irrelevantly, shocked by his vehemence. The silence stretched, until finally she made herself laugh lightly. "You're trying to distract me, Jacks. Did the watch bring us out here or not?"

"Maybe this is my idea of a cool date." He kissed her hand, bowing extravagantly.

"Goof," she said. "Come on, Jacks, perfect timing. Produce."

He put a hand to his ear, as if listening for guidance . . . then pulled her from the edge, out of sight.

"Is it your dad?"

"Garbage truck." He was speaking right into her ear, his voice low. He'd pulled her into a crouch, and one of his arms was over her shoulders.

"Jacks?"

"Yeah?"

"You basically own the place, right? We're not trespassing."

"Yes."

"So why are we hiding?"

"Good point." He didn't let go, though, just looked at her steadily until she felt a little weak-kneed.

"Cut it out, Eligible," she said, giving him a playful shove. They straightened up as the truck pulled in to collect the plant's trash. Astrid raised a hand, trying to look less furtive, but the driver didn't look up. The loader grabbed the glass factory's Dumpster and flipped it, emptying the week's trash with a bang.

"Look." Jack pointed. A box had fallen out of the Dumpster, hitting the ground as the truck rumbled away down the factory road.

"Let's go." They descended the ladder, Astrid first. The box had tipped and spilled, revealing a collection of faded toys: action figures, a six-gun, a plastic box full of polished stones, and a rusty tractor. "Dad kept the toys around for when he had to bring me to work. He must've tossed them."

"Maybe he's given up on you taking over."

"Never." He was looking at her expectantly.

"What?" she said.

"Are they chantments?"

"Oh." She touched them one at a time, dropping one of the stones with a hiss of indrawn breath when it turned out to be sea-glass.

"Cut yourself?"

"No. Vitagua doesn't like sea-glass. Don't ask me why. Albert didn't tell me yet."

"Should I throw it out?" He picked it up, brushing away a caked-on bit of grit.

"No, it could be useful. Maybe it's why the watch brought us here." He's uncontaminated, she thought as Jacks rolled it on his palm. Dad had checked her for contamination before making her his apprentice. Maybe . . .

She felt a twinge of unease at even considering Jacks as her apprentice. What would Sahara say?

No. It wasn't fair to ask, not with Lee trying to stick Jacks with the Fire Department.

"Some treasure." He stuck it in his shirt pocket. "Rubble that hurts you and no magic toys."

She shook her head. "Albert used sea-glass in my initiation. Maybe it means I should get an apprentice."

"Figure out what you're doing before you go teaching anyone else, okay?" Her fingertips were burn-reddened where she had touched the piece of glass; Jacks took her hand, examining them professionally.

"Albert and I played poker sometimes, you know? Just penny stakes, but—"

"Was he any good?"

He kissed the burns and released her. "So-so. His luck was terrible, but the man could definitely bluff."

She hugged him then, blushing, before tossing the remaining toys back in the garbage.

CHAPTER THIRTEEN

THEY WERE ALMOST BACK to the highway when Astrid's mobile rang.

It was Sahara. "Where are you guys?"

"Nowhere much," Astrid answered, and as Jacks braked and shot her a look of inquiry she mouthed, *The Princess.*

"Can you meet me somewhere?"

"We're headed home."

"Not the house." Sahara's voice was taut with excitement . . . or tension? "Get Jacks to pick a site."

"She wants us to meet her out in the middle of nowhere," Astrid said.

He pointed to a gravel lane branching north. "Tell her we just reached the exit for Tishvale."

"Sahara, you remember where Tishvale is?"

"The ghost town? Did the magic watch bring you there?"

"We just hit the exit when you called."

"I'd say that's a yes."

Astrid said: "Do you remember how to get here?"

"Yeah, I'm on it."

Jacks asked: "Has someone found out about us?"

Astrid's heart pounded. "Sahara, are we busted?"

"Not by a long shot. Tell you everything when I get there." With that, Sahara hung up.

Tishvale lay on the banks of Teale Creek, a fast-running stream that had hosted a momentary 1850s gold rush. Panners headed to California tried their luck up and down the creek, with enough initial success that a few cabins sprang up on the riverbank, along with a saloon and general store. The would-be founding father of the town, one Ernie Tish, had been raising money for a church when the gold vein they were mining was tapped out.

Astrid and Jacks parked the bikes and took a leisurely poke through the remains of the cabins. Overgrown and rotten, they were encrusted with the remnants of high school bush parties: bottles, cigarette butts, litter from spent fireworks, and even the occasional shotgun shell.

"What if we are busted?" Jacks said.

"Sahara said we weren't."

"If it happens one day, then."

Astrid shuddered. "Dad got away with it his whole life. Why shouldn't we?"

He didn't answer, just glanced down the road, where Sahara was pulling up in Mark's car.

"Well?" Jacks demanded as she parked and darted to her trunk, yanking out her laptop bag.

Sparkle from the backseat drew Astrid to the car. Cardboard boxes were jammed in the backseat, all brimming with garage sale junk—toys, old books, shoes, cassette tapes, dishes, a set of wax fruit, and clothes.

"What's all this?" she said.

"Crap from Mrs. Skye's basement," Sahara said. "Guys, I've just been chatting online with Marlowe."

Jack sat on the stump, frowning. "The woman from the newsgroup? The one whose chantment almost killed her?"

Sahara nodded. "Remember the posts dried up just as they got interesting?"

"How could we forget?" said Astrid. The trio of chantment-users had been discussing ways to use their chantments without draining a user's "life force"—as Happypill had put it—when Eldergodz stopped posting. After that, the others agreed to move their conversation offlist.

"I've been surfing around looking for Marlowe and Happypill," said Sahara. "I found an e-mail address, dropped her a message. She sent me back a Web address."

"Let me guess," Jacks said. "Chantments-dot-com."

"Nah. It was one of those free pages with about five billion pop-up ads."

"What did the page say?" Jacks asked.

"First it said Eldergodz was dead. That he stopped posting because he roasted to death in a fire at his pub. . . . I guess he was a bartender."

"Dead?" Astrid said. Jacks's hand tightened on hers.

"Yeah. Marlowe had autopsy photos." Sahara grimaced. "Said if I was smart, I'd stop asking questions."

"But of course, you weren't smart," Jacks said. "Why are we talking about this way out here?"

"After I blew off her suggestion to turn off my machine and walk away, Marlowe sent a link so we could chat directly. She told me the guys who got to Eldergodz got to her too. Her gas pipes blew up and the magic bookmark burned. She's been homeless ever since. She's totally paranoid . . . thinks whoever did it is still after her."

"Witch-burners and chantment thieves," Astrid said, quoting Albert. She pulled a ceramic sailboat out of one of Mrs. Skye's boxes. "Maybe it's true."

"You didn't tell her where we are?" Jacks said.

"No. No names, no locations, nothing," Sahara said. "I did promise we'd mail a chantment to a friend of hers."

"You promised what?"

Astrid dug at a scab on her knuckle, bringing vitagua to the surface of her skin and chanting the tacky sailboat statuette. Her headache diminished.

"Hey, Wizard, you with us here or are you just playing with the sparkly things?"

"I'm listening, Princess," Astrid said.

"How could you make a promise like that?" Jacks demanded. "Without consulting us?"

"You weren't around. Marlowe had fifteen minutes in some Internet café. She's convinced Albert's bad guys are chasing her, she lost everything she owns, and she wants some magic that'll help her keep from getting murdered. Pardon me for making a judgment call."

"It wasn't your call to make," he said. "Astrid?"

She sighed, not wanting to referee a fight, and examined the newly made chantment. The grumbles had whispered something about Aladdin's lamp when she made it. You got a genie from that lamp if you cleaned it, she thought, rubbing a smear of dust off its sails.

She immediately felt her memory sharpening: every idea she'd had lately about work, the house, and the chantments fell into order, neat as books organized in a library. She knew who owed her money and how much, she thought of four more gardens where she and Dad had worked together in the past. The Albert memories came together like a jigsaw puzzle: there were still holes and gaps, things she didn't know, but fresh details shone out.

Trivial facts—phone numbers, gardening articles she'd read, even years-old conversations—were all dusted off, handily at her command.

So was everything she knew about how Sahara's mind worked. "Let's hear her out," she said to Jacks. "We aren't out here in the middle of nowhere for no reason."

"Right you are." Sahara grinned. "I didn't offer Marlowe a chantment for free."

"No? What did we get besides a stranger who knows we can provide her with chantments?" Jacks asked.

"Marlowe was hoping these Internet buddies of hers could help her figure out how to run her chantment without frying herself. When they disappeared, she decided to take a risk. She bought a nice thick journal, stuck her bookmark in it, and asked it to cough up the answers on magic. She had a massive seizure, and ended up in hospital for a week. When she finally made it home, she found the journal had been filled with information about chantments."

"There's a book?" Jacks said.

"Magic lore," Sahara said. "Instructions."

"So . . . we get the book, she gets a chantment?" Astrid said hopefully.

"Ha," Sahara said. "Don't I wish. Marlowe scanned me one page as a sign of good faith. If we send a chantment care of her friend, she might send more."

"Fantastic," said Jacks. "Why not give her our address and ask her to move in?"

"Stow it, Eligible. Don't you want to see the page?"

"Of course," Astrid said.

"Good." Sahara popped open her laptop and started booting. "Did I just see you make a chantment, Astrid?"

"I don't think the sailboat uses much juice."

"I brought the stash from home."

"Let me try again." She reached for another sparkly object— a beaded purse this time—from the boxes in the backseat. She chanted it, enjoying the rush of energy.

By now the computer was up and running. Sahara double-clicked on an icon and an image filled the screen—a primitive line drawing. Nonsense words were scrawled beneath it. Beneath those, typed text read "Phonetically spelled-out cantation for converting heat to magic."

"Are those waves?" Astrid asked, flipping the purse chantment in her hand as she looked at the picture.

"Sand dunes, I think," Jacks said. "See the curl here? It's more evocative of sand. Is this a Native petroglyph?"

"Maybe if my risky little business arrangement works out with Marlowe, you'll find out." Sahara scrolled down, revealing more in-structions. "First I hold the chantment in both hands and recite the text below the picture. Did you make something exciting, darling?"

Astrid handed it over. Sahara read the syllables, a mishmash of baby talk and Latin-toned phrases. The rhythms had the singsong lilt of the vitagua grumbles. As she finished, the air seemed to crackle, hazing ever so slightly and then clearing again.

"Okay," she said. "What does this thing do?"

Astrid plucked a feather out of a tattered pillow resting atop one of Mrs. Skye's other boxes. "Put the feather inside, close the purse, and then open it again."

Sahara obeyed. As its clasp snapped shut, the purse bulged. When she opened it a sequined egg rolled out, bursting apart to reveal a full-grown goose sitting amid a pile of gold glitter.

Sahara flinched, startled, and the bird flew away, honking. "Geese and golden eggs. Very useful."

"Do you feel tired?" Jacks turned from the petroglyphs on the laptop to close observation of Sahara as she transformed two more feathers, dumping the eggs on the hood of the car so the birds could hatch there.

"Nope," she said. "Not tired, not hungry."

He felt her forehead, then laid a finger on her throat. "Your temperature's fine. Pulse seems normal."

"Supposedly it converts ambient heat to magic," Sahara said, tapping the laptop. "Does it seem any cooler?"

"Maybe," said Astrid. "Do a few more?"

"Always happy to work a little sorcery," Sahara said.

Astrid took a stone pestle from the box. Would it be safe to make three chantments if they shipped them out of town right away?

Sahara shoved another three feathers in the purse. Three more geese hatched and then flapped away. She reached for the pillow again, but Jacks stopped her.

"I feel fine, Eligible."

"It is getting cold," he said. And it was—they were exhaling clouds of mist, as if it was midwinter.

"Look," Astrid said, pointing. Frost was spreading in a circle from Sahara's feet. Water had condensed on the bumper of the car, and the air was noticeably chilled, as if the sun had slipped behind a cloud.

"It is drawing heat," Sahara said, closing the laptop and tucking it into its bag. She grabbed a handful of feathers, then glanced at Jacks. "What do you think?"

"Sure," he said. "Push it a little further."

She did, closing the feathers into the purse and then opening it on an eruption of geese. They flapped out of the open mouth of the purse, flying in every direction, honking loudly as gold sequins pooled at her feet. The circle of frost on the ground spread, climbing up the tree trunks and silvering the log cabin walls. Astrid, Jacks, and Sahara began to shiver as a patch of Teale Creek froze over.

"I bet this is how Marlowe got discovered," Jacks said. "If our yard starts freezing in June—"

"So maybe it's not the most useful thing we ever learned—," Sahara began.

"Maybe your Web buddy wants us to get caught."

"She's got a book, Astrid," Sahara said. "A whole book. Think about how much we don't know. Isn't that worth a bit of risk?"

"Albert wouldn't have thought so," Astrid said, chanting the pestle. The circle of ice was still spreading, even though Sahara had stopped making geese. A breeze ruffled her hair.

"Maybe the next trick she teaches us will be more discreet," Sahara said.

"Jacks?" Astrid said.

He pinched up a frozen chunk of moss. "It is risky. But I'd like to know more about what we're doing."

"So we'll send her a chantment?" Sahara asked. "We'll talk to her some more?"

"We'll be very very careful," Jacks said. "Nothing about who we are or where we live, nothing about Astrid making chantments."

"Careful is my middle name," Sahara said solemnly, and when both Jacks and Astrid laughed she looked hurt, just for a second, before joining in.

The ice on Teale Creek crackled; the air was warming.

"I guess the purse took all the heat it needed," Jacks said.

"At least we know how to do something big, if we need to," Sahara said.

"Let's hope we never need to," Astrid replied, gazing skyward. Far above them, the flock of geese had stopped its confused circling, forming a large *V* and following its leader north.

CHAPTER FOURTEEN

"OVER THE WEEKS THAT followed, we learned many things," Astrid tells me. "Some from Albert through the memory flashes, some from Sahara's Internet friend, but most by trial and error. It was a crash course in learning about the invisible world, an exercise in giving up the things we'd always known with certainty.

"Sahara put it this way: Suddenly, after a lifetime, gravity was optional. Momentum and inertia were just ideas—stronger than myths like the Tooth Fairy, but still just recommended guidelines for being normal."

Her words ring true. Since Astrid's arrest, the world has been dealing with this same paradigm shift. We are in the grip of a collective nervous breakdown, complete with riots, skyrocketing drug use, and mad swings in church attendance. No amount of hysteria, prayer, or government action has stopped the spread of magic . . . or of fear. The spiritually rootless are flocking to Sahara's cult to the dismay of sincere pagans.

"There have to be some rules . . . some limitations."

"Sometimes it depends on the chantment," Astrid says. "For the mermaid pendant to work, you had to say the name of the person you were . . . persuading to do something."

I nod. "And this need chantments have for energy?"

"Ah, yes," she said. "Magic needs power. Most chantments fed off the person controlling them."

"That explains Patience's appetite and her sugar cube habit," I say. "But the energy required for some of the things Sahara has done—"

"Marlowe taught us cantations for drawing energy from other sources," Astrid says. Pictures emerge on cards, smears of blue ink on slate. She holds up the sand dune. Nonsense syllables—the cantation, presumably—are etched beneath it. "This is the one that converts heat to magic."

Heat. The ocean had frozen around the shattered aircraft carrier, catching its wreckage in icebergs. The air had been below freezing for hours after the confrontation between the Alchemites and the Navy.

The next cantation card shows a crudely drawn cluster of human figures. "This one pulls the life from other people. Vamping, Sahara called it," Astrid says. "Chantments can draw light out of sunshine, static out of the air, electricity out of the power grid. There's a cantation for drawing power 'from the earth itself'—that's what a page Marlowe sent us said—"

"Let me guess. That's the one that caused the earthquakes and volcanic eruptions."

"We didn't know that yet. All we knew was the first cantation, which would've made the house and yard all frosty if we'd used it. So we kept eating like pigs and sleeping late."

I fish a third card out of the pile, one with a sun on it. "Is this the one for light?"

"Yes. Use a powerful enough chantment, the area around it will go dark."

"That's rather conspicuous, isn't it?"

"Everything Marlowe told us was conspicuous. The more so because chantments can't be turned off. Once you stick a feather in that goose purse, it makes a goose. It draws whatever power it needs until it's done."

I look at the cards unhappily. Cutting the mystics off from their source of power is going to be problematic.

Setting the cantation cards aside, Astrid changes the subject. "We learned that some things wouldn't be chanted."

"What things?"

"Glass wouldn't work, ever. It could contain vitagua but not absorb it. Or electronics—you can't make a chanted TV, or a calculator."

"And everything had to be receptive, to have what your father called 'sparkle,' isn't that right?"

"At first. As I continued making chantments, more objects started to call to me."

"You improved."

"Yes."

"Why didn't Albert improve?"

"He did . . . just not as fast as me. I was remembering stuff about that. He'd been nervous about how quick I picked up skills, things that took him years. Now and then I'd improvise too—try something new. That panicked him."

"Why were you improvising?"

"When you're initiated as a spring-tapper, you start hearing voices coming from the vitagua. Grumbles . . ."

"I remember. They guide you, make suggestions. Why didn't your father hear them?"

"He'd been told not to trust the grumblers."

"By who?"

"His grandmother," Astrid says. "Let's see . . . I learned to move the vitagua within my body, to hide it inside, deep, or push it to the surface." She does that now, looking up at one of the ill-concealed cameras with a suddenly blue face. Then she lets a drop ooze from her bitten tongue. It floats above her hands, bouncing in midair twice before sinking into her palm.

"Sahara was exposed too. Could she—?"

"No. Albert had wired me into the spring. I was the designated chanter—no others need apply."

"But you and Albert could both make chantments after you were initiated. What would have happened if you initiated Sahara?"

"I couldn't. She'd been exposed—she was already cursed."

"Did you tell Sahara what Albert said about contamination, about it making her ill?"

"Head sick," she murmurs. Her face tightens. "I didn't want her to worry. I thought I'd dig up a memory of Albert telling me how to get the vitagua out of her body, or that Marlowe's book would have a solution. I went everywhere Albert and I had ever been, looking for places where he'd taught me things. There was one problem, though—"

"The headaches?"

"Yes. It hurt all the time. Most mornings when I awoke, I'd forgotten everything. Everything, Will. Seeing a chantment would bring all it back, but part of me kept wanting to bury everything I knew about magic."

"Instead you kept touching things and having flashes."

"Yes. That's another thing I got better at. I started out getting images from things like the kaleidoscope. Then it was scenes, whole memories caught within items Albert and I had both touched. Then I started learning unrelated stuff. Remember when we met?"

"Of course." She had known about our dog, my car accident, the divorce.

"Was that just a few hours ago?" She shakes her head, sifting through cards.

I consult my watch. "We had that conversation about three and a half hours ago."

"So today is finally today?"

"It's early afternoon, Astrid, on what you've called Will day—does that help?" I lean back, examining her. She is so different from the Astrid I expected to be dealing with, the one who has been under observation for ten weeks. She knows past from future, can put together a sentence.

I wonder how much she learned when she shook my hand.

It was just after the napalming of Sahara's so-called Sacred Grove that Caroline left me. The Alchemites had gathered outside of Indigo Springs, at a spot along Teale Creek where the trees were rapidly growing to fantastic heights. The police tried to keep them out, but thousands of worshippers got through the barricades before the National Guard secured the area.

I was on a team of negotiators assigned to call the mobile phones of Alchemites who'd entered the grove, to try to talk them back out. I got lucky with two—and that, more than our past friendship, was what had brought me to Roche's attention.

Nobody else came out of the contaminated grove, and the Air Force carried out the planned operation against the alchemized trees, hitting the site with napalm to stop the runaway growth.

A massive earthquake followed the bombing. I'd been evacuated with the rest of the nonessential personnel.

Everyone assumed Sahara and all her pilgrims had died with the trees. But when I got home, six scorched-looking Alchemites were hiding out in my basement.

Caro and I had managed not to argue about the magical outbreak and the Alchemites until then, but now a screaming fight was inevitable. We'd gotten incoherent and irrational, keeping it up until we were finally reduced to name-calling and swearing at one another.

Finally Caro had scooped up her keys: it was time to fetch Carson and Ellie from school.

"We'll sort it out," she croaked, and despite the hours of recriminations and fury it never occurred to me not to trust her. "We always do."

She never came back.

"Will?"

I drag myself into the present: it is nine weeks and one day since I've seen my children. And apparently it's Will day. "What were we talking about?"

Astrid touches the cards for reassurance. "It was early summer. I was still learning things from gardens where Albert and I worked together. The things I did, Will! My work roster had changed over the years, so suddenly I was going back to Albert's original clients, people who'd fired him. I begged, worked for free, whatever it took."

There's a picture of her on a playing card, wearing jeans and a dirty shirt, wrestling weeds, clearly happy.

"How did the others feel?"

"We were having the time of our lives. Knowing about Albert's secret life was a joy. I believed things could work out. My misgivings were all low-key."

"And yet they proved valid," I murmur.

She glowers. "We sent Marlowe the sailboat that helped you notice and remember things. Brain-sharpener, Sahara called it. Marlowe sent us the cantation for vamping energy out of groups of people."

"Another one you didn't dare use, I'm guessing."

"Not a chance. Next we let her have a rubber cockroach that worked out sneaky routes for getting places—ways to avoid people. I wanted to give her things that would help her hide without making her dangerous."

"Good tactical thinking on your part."

She seems pleased. "Sahara started keeping the mermaid with her all the time. She'd drop in on the jeweler every few days, to remind him to keep quiet about the gold dust we were laundering. Every morning she checked on Ma, keeping her sane, keeping her in therapy. She was as good as she had promised: discreet and reliable."

"How did that work for Ev?"

"Okay." She laughs. "When I first started living with Jemmy I'd thought the town would freak out about us being gay . . . but it was only a few people who couldn't shut up about it. Now suddenly Ma was talking about 'gender dysphoria,' about going on testosterone."

"That must've been strange."

"Strange, yeah, but it explained a lot too."

"What about Sahara?"

Astrid touches a card, and an image of Sahara streaks across it, vibrant and happy, her long legs flying. "She seemed like a better person than the one who had bugged out of Indigo Springs so many years before."

"You resented her leaving?"

She shrugs. "It grew out of what was happening at the time. I dropped out of school, she started spending time with Mark.

Boom! They were dating, they were graduating, they were gone. That's what you do when you're eighteen."

"Unless you're you, I suppose." Needling her now, just to see if I can find a nerve.

"Unless you're me," she agrees serenely. "Anyway, I thought I knew her. I wasn't worried."

"Except about the contamination."

"Yeah, there was that. I gardened constantly. It was something I could do without attracting attention, and I wanted to remember the old times with Dad."

Another card forms an image, showing the yard of Astrid's blue house, now reordered from chaos into glorious splendor.

"As I worked, Albert memories played through my mind. He described the unreal, told me about the witch burnings, said there were prophecies about the burners coming back. He warned me, always, to stay in the shade, out of sight."

"About the memories," I ask. "How did they work? Were they interactive?"

"You mean could I ask questions?"

"That's right."

"No. And I couldn't pick and choose what I would remember next. It just played out, a bit of knowledge here, a fact there. Like opening a book to random pages."

"So you couldn't ask your father what to do about the vitagua inside Sahara."

"No."

"Or in yourself."

"That was less of an issue. Every time I made a chantment, the amount of liquid magic in my body decreased and the grumbles got quieter. The premonition I'd had—of being out on my porch surrounded by reporters—dimmed. I watched Sahara for signs of madness, this supposed curse. But she seemed okay. I wasn't as worried as I had been."

"No," I agree. Sahara may be insane, but she's an organized maniac. She triggered the earthquake that shattered National

Guard barricades around Indigo Springs, then led her followers out of the napalmed grove. Having identified those among her flock faithful enough to brave the fire, Sahara bestowed still more "powers" upon them, naming them Primas and sending them out with chantments to work "miracles" and recruit more followers.

It worked. The Alchemites' survival of the bombing was national news. Primas brought rain to the drought-stricken Midwest, healed highway accident victims, opened bank vaults and dispensed cash to the poor. Simple acts in a confusing time; the cult's numbers swelled.

I pick up a card Astrid has pushed off to the side, a portrait of Sahara's former lover, Mark Clumber. It is a current picture; he's profoundly alchemized. Under the influence of magical contamination, his hair has fallen out and his skin is damp and slimy, covered in black and red spots. Froggy eyes bulge over a still-human nose; his hands have salamander fingers. His mouth is so altered, he cannot form human words, and his glasses no longer fit. "Did Albert tell you the contamination could be this bad?"

She shook her head. "I don't think he ever saw anything like this."

"Were there any signs of it in Sahara?"

"I couldn't decide. Sometimes I'd think she was getting more selfish, but . . ."

"She'd always been selfish?"

She nods.

"That's her weakness?" I wonder what use might be made of this.

"One of them."

"Tell me more."

She sighs. "Sahara likes to fix people. She's a performer, manipulative—"

"But she wasn't any worse than before?"

"How could I tell? I thought she and Jacks might be fighting, but they saved it for when I wasn't there."

"Why didn't you do something?"

"I'd wonder if I was being paranoid. Then I'd promise myself Jacks and I could handle it—handle her—be responsible enough for all three of us. My biggest worry about the contamination was actually Henna."

"The cat?"

"Remember how she killed that dead rabbit?"

I nod.

"Well, she was still doing it. Bringing home pigeons, rats, rabbits. Once in a while it'd be a barn owl, a fox."

"A fox?" I whistle incredulously.

"I know. Plus the vitagua was still flowing from the fissure in the mantel. Once a day we'd pop the hollow brick out of the hearth and siphon the droplets into a jar. We got a few drops a day, sometimes less."

"So little?"

"Yes. The big splash that first day had built up over the year since Albert's death."

How much vitagua had Astrid poured into my wedding ring? A half cup? "If the flow was so modest, you ought to have been able to catch up."

"You'd think so, wouldn't you?" She laughs bitterly. "We'd constructed our whole lives around the vitagua spring. A couple drops a day. It should have been easy."

CHAPTER FIFTEEN

MANAGING THE MAGIC WAS simplicity itself.

Sahara had a gift for secrecy and intrigue. She was the one who suggested Astrid take up driving as a volunteer for the local secondhand store, picking up unwanted junk from big-hearted Springers and searching the castoffs for chantable items before delivering the rest. It was Sahara who found hard-luck cases in news stories on the Internet, who tracked down their addresses and matched chantments to their needs. Jacks dumped packages in post offices all over the county. Nobody was the wiser.

"We're getting behind," Dad had told her.

The memory came back to her as Astrid was thinning foxgloves at Percy Heath's, pulling up just enough to make the flowers look— as the old farmer put it—"like they come up wild." In the memory flash, she had been about thirteen and achy with cramps from one of her first menstrual periods.

. . .

"Behind?" she'd said, feeling disaffected, resentful.

"Too much vitagua, not enough sparkly things. I gotta find more— or risk making a few biggies. Pressure's increasing, see?" He rubbed dirty hands through his hair. "I can't keep up, Bundle. Even if I make two chantments a week instead of one, I have to find 'em homes. Your ma's starting to think I'm shooting her paycheck up my arm. . . ."

They were alone in a big commercial greenhouse, facing each other across flats of newly sprouted garden vegetables—broccoli, cabbage, dill, glossy plants with leaves unmarred by age, dust, or insects. Albert was wearing a grubby white-and-red T-shirt, looking the part of town derelict. Astrid wore the uniform of her early teens— rugby pants, tank top, and ball cap.

"Tell her the truth," Astrid said.

"She'd be in danger . . . she'd be a danger. We don't know how the witch-burners find chanters, Astrid. Everyone my granny ever told died, but for me. My other two apprentices too." He paced, anguished. "We're the mice hiding in the corner, Bun. Nobody notices us."

"If you tell Ma, she'll stop being so mad at you."

"And if someone notices that, and wonders why?" He shook his head. "We can't risk it, baby."

"Let me talk to the vitagua. Maybe there's a way."

"I don't want you carrying too much spirit water."

"If you won't let me be a chanter, we might as well both quit."

He sighed; she'd said this before. "Bun . . ."

"Why?"

"You gotta learn to be careful." He stroked a spinach leaf. "You'd tell Ma, let someone get contaminated—"

"I have not!"

"We got to keep people away from the raw magic. Even before it got pressed together and concentrated, a little spirit water went a long way. A little splash to make a medicine woman, shaman, prophet, whatever you call her. Even then it drove them mad sometimes. . . ."

Astrid sighed, bored.

"Listen, Bun. With the crude stuff, even a drop's too much. Granny told of people growing horns, killing people with just a thought, bringing down hurricanes—an' all of them became lunatics before the witch-burners got them."

"Say I do contaminate someone," she broke in. "Couldn't I just fix 'em?"

Albert led her behind the greenhouse to a couple of outdoor sinks, washing the dirt off his hands. He was thinking about it, Astrid could see, thinking hard. Would he finally let her show him something?

Hope rose in her—and then was dashed as he filled a glass with water. He drank half in three gulps. Then he upended it, spilling out the rest.

"Look," he said. "Water's gone, but the glass is still wet."

"Use a rag and dry it."

"There'd still be a bit of water on the glass," he said. "Residue. Only way to really dry it off—to get all the liquid off it—is to let it evaporate naturally. That's something a person can't do. Understand?"

She shook her head.

"Vitagua, it lies in your bones. If we can't dry water off a cup . . ."

"Dad, let me experiment."

"No. Please, kid, do things the way Granny taught me."

"I could change the rules," she said, grabbing his arm. "Make it evaporate—make everything different, Dad."

Albert had gone pale. His voice, when his mouth stopped flapping, was terrified. "Don't hope for that, Astrid. You don't want to live through that, I mean it."

. . .

The recollection ended there, leaving Astrid headachy and morose.

That night Jacks was out playing poker while Astrid and Sahara hosted a dinner for Sahara's old school pals. The following evening they all went to a movie with Olive and her new boyfriend, a Korean-American hippie named Thunder. She crawled through both evenings in a haze of headachy pain.

That Saturday morning, she found the cat dragging a mangled Scottish terrier up the steps.

"Oh Henna, no," she said, horrified. She looked both ways for witnesses before she took up the cat, stroking her until she was relaxed and purring. Gingerly she edged the magic pocketknife out of her jeans, nicking the dog before anyone could come by and spot the corpse. It crumbled to a smelly pile of dust and bones.

"Come on inside," she said wearily, cuddling the triumphant cat all the way to her room. Henna's legs were unusually long; the pads of her toes elongated into proto-fingers that curled amid fur mittens.

Astrid, her stomach churning, laid the purring animal on the bed. Time to improvise.

"This'll work, Dad," she murmured. Listening hard, she picked a suggestion out of the musical, grumbling hum inside her head, pulling on the magic within her. Vitagua welled up her throat like a wet fist, cutting off air. Fluid bubbled around her tongue, a cold stew aboil, blue and frothy, behind her teeth.

She gagged. Vitagua was in her sinuses, popping as if it were carbonated. Her ear was ringing, her right eye leaking tears again. A muscle in her cheek twitched.

Sorry, cat, she thought. She tried to be subtle as she pinned Henna's legs down. But feline danger sense had kicked in; the tabby yowled and struggled with more than animal strength. Her back leg scissored through bedclothes and jeans to lay open Astrid's leg above the knee. Astrid tried to adjust her grip, and a swinging forepaw tore one of the pillows into foamy shreds.

Bite her, the grumbles urged. Astrid pressed her blue, boiling mouth against the body of the struggling cat. Her teeth—was it illusion, or were they sharper?—combed through the fur even as the fluid clogged against her lips. Her canines found flesh, and while Astrid had imagined struggling even to pierce the cat's skin, her jaws reacted instinctively, squeezing hard.

Draw it, came the grumble. She imagined vitagua pouring through the cuts and pulled—too hard.

Henna yowled and Astrid felt something tearing. Then a bolt of cold unflavor hit her throat. Neither blood nor water, it punched her backwards. Her aching head smacked the wall, crunching the dragon earring against the plaster.

As Henna darted free, Astrid was overtaken by another rush of paranoia. Sahara would abandon her . . . soon.

Fluffed out and haughtily furious, Henna balked at the closed door of the bedroom. Sobbing, Astrid crept forward and caught the animal. She writhed furiously, just a cat again, easily held. Four seeping blue-lined punctures . . .

. . . the residue, Astrid thought . . .

. . . lined the cat's back, buried under the thick fur, the only evidence of the bite.

"But you're better," she wept, examining Henna's apparently normal paws.

From her glare, Henna had a different opinion.

"It doesn't have to fall apart," she told the cat. "If I know it's going to happen, I can change it."

The door banged. "Yoo hoo, Sleeping Beauty, busy day ahead! I've brought contraband!"

"Contraband?" Dashing the tears away, Astrid gave herself a mental shake. Sahara wasn't leaving. The grumbles were just playing games with her insecurities.

She's going, they replied. She's practically gone.

The door flew open. Sahara pranced in, bearing a long platter piled high with meat and cheese: sliced salami, steaming sausages, dolmades, olives, and Swiss cheese. "His Vegan Holiness is off getting a start on the Sistine Mural and we're going to eat animal flesh."

"Jacks never said you couldn't bring meat home."

"True." Sahara waved the platter. "He just exploits my inborn laziness by cooking all the time."

"Fiendish." Astrid took a slice of salami, turned away, and shoved the vitagua deep into her body. She flashed her teeth at the mirror to confirm the blue stains were gone; only then could she bite into the meat.

"Shall we go over our agenda for the day, milady?"

Astrid nodded, setting down the tray on a bloodstain she had only just noticed. Her lacerated leg burned, and she flipped the torn pillow to cover the tear in her jeans.

"First, you and I go on the weekly junk run, acquiring resellable crap for the community's underprivileged shoppers." Sahara reached out, twisting the dragon earring so its coils lined up. The ear burned; Astrid blushed.

"After we fish out anything you want to chant, we take Mrs. Skye to her doctor's on Spirit Valley Road. While she's getting poked and prodded, we go stroke the Ego known as Jacks Glade by admiring his masterpiece in progress."

"Doctor's appointment?"

"If Mrs. Skye doesn't see her doctor once a month, Lilla the wicked stepniece sweeps in and takes her house."

"I thought you got her a carpool."

"To work, yes." Sahara waved a slice of salami under her nose, and Astrid glommed on to it. Her teeth clicked shut over the meat, just missing Sahara's finger. "We'll also make sure she has her hearing aid."

"She's deaf?"

"Deafish."

"I didn't know."

"She gets vain and leaves it at home."

"Okay. What next?"

"We come home, you make chantments, I do the requisite Web surfing to find them new owners. Maybe we find another good one for Marlowe, maybe not."

"I want useful information from Marlowe this time," Astrid said. "She's stringing us along."

"Agreed," Sahara said, nibbling an olive. "Either way, we package up the goodies and we're free. Plus you'll be buzzed from the chanting and we can stay up late watching Indian musicals on my laptop. Sound like an agenda?"

"Mmmm," Astrid said casually. Eating felt good; she could feel the meat and cheese replenishing the strength she had used when she'd destroyed the terrier's body with the pocketknife. "There's one other thing. I know how to siphon the vitagua out of your body."

"Get it out?" Her friend's gaze skittered away. "It's not doing any harm."

"It is." She clasped Sahara's hand, and was struck by an image—Sahara, with iridescent hair and black, inhuman eyes. She turned her friend to face the mirror, pointing out the odd gold highlights in her hair. "It's cursed. Albert said people who are contaminated are doomed—"

"That's melodramatic."

"Doomed to self-destruct, Sahara. That what you want?"

"Can't you enjoy this?" Sahara waved a hand at the chantments. "You're working yourself to the bone to recover those memories . . . and I know you feel sick all the time."

"It's my responsibility."

"Just slack off a little."

"Sahara, the vitagua inside you is dangerous."

Sahara said, "It could be dangerous to take it out."

"I tried already." She nodded at Henna, who was snoozing in a patch of sun. "Behold our test subject."

Sahara grasped her hands. "I don't want you to. When I talk to people now, I know what they need to hear. I always wanted to help people sort out their lives, and now I can. Do you know how rare that kind of sensitivity is?"

Uncomfortable, Astrid extracted her hands from Sahara's grip. "It'll make you nuts."

"It's harmless."

"We can't let it concentrate—" She stopped, paralyzed by the grumbles' insistence that Sahara would leave. Was this what sent her away? She fumbled with a cracker and salami, stacking them, cramming them into her mouth, and chewing woodenly. Only after she'd swallowed did she speak again. "If you don't agree, we can ask Jacks—"

"He'll agree with you. He always agrees with you." Sahara's voice was surprisingly free of rancor, her manner, suddenly, almost meek. "Do you have to do it now?"

"Yes, now." Before you change your mind, Astrid thought.

"Okay. How?"

Blushing, she explained what she had done to Henna.

"You *bit* my cat?"

"It seemed . . . right," she mumbled, and her face was hot. "I was improvising. But with you . . ."

"Yes?" Maddening furled eyebrow—Sahara amused, the same expression she'd worn before kissing Astrid so many years ago. "You don't want to bite me?"

"Dammit, don't tease." She ruffled Henna's fur and showed her the bite marks, which had turned a bright bloody red. Henna growled halfheartedly, dozing.

Sahara said, "I wonder if they'll scar?"

"You can't see them through the fur. But I did think . . . what if we tried breaking the skin with a needle? It'd leave less of a mark."

"Worth a try," Sahara said. She reached for a pair of fingernail scissors. "Astrid, please don't do this."

"Sahara, we have to."

A full-body sigh from Sahara. She offered up her hand.

Summoning the choking well of vitagua into her throat again, Astrid sat on the bed. Sahara raised her wrist to her mouth. Astrid's teeth pulled toward the skin of their own volition.

"Ready?" she tried to say, but the vitagua got in the way—it came out a gargle.

"Just do it," Sahara said.

The clovey scent of Sahara's hair, so close, wafted through her. Astrid took her friend's hand and pulled on the vitagua inside her body, ever so carefully this time. There it was, a thin cold vein under the skin, a blue patch on Sahara's hand. Wincing, Astrid pressed down with the scissors, only to find she couldn't make the cut.

"Wimp." Sahara took them from her briskly and drove the blade home. A bead of blue welled from the puncture.

Holding her gaze, Sahara raised her wrist to Astrid's lips.

There was a passing warmth . . . and then the cold liquid moved. Astrid pulled more gently than she had with Henna, and vitagua—so much, too much!—eased over her lips. Imaginary knives cut through her skull, and the vitagua grumbles got louder.

"Ow." Hands trembling, Astrid gathered her friend into an awkward, unrequited hug. She won't go anywhere, she thought: she loves the magic. It's just blue-goo inspired craziness. Delusions. "How do you feel?"

"Normal," Sahara said, bursting into tears.

Astrid held her in stunned disbelief. Sobs racked Sahara's body, shocks intense as hammer blows. The fabric of Astrid's shirt got damp, then soaked. Quiet miserable wails: they couldn't all be about a little lost insight, could they?

"Shhh, shhh," she murmured, thinking of glasses and spilled water and residual contamination as Sahara keened, butting her head against Astrid's shoulder.

"It's not the goo," she managed finally.

"It doesn't matter."

"It's, it's . . . Mark."

"It's okay, Sahara. Shush."

Eventually she did, running down and sniffling. "I can't go out like this."

"You look fine."

"You have low standards."

"You always look fine to me," she said, and Sahara tensed up. She added, "It's okay. I'll do the junk run."

"Mrs. Skye?"

"I'll pick her up."

Sahara squeezed Astrid tighter, holding her close. "You won't go yet, will you?"

"Not until you're ready."

"I'm such a pillowcase. You'd think nobody on earth ever got dumped before. It makes me so . . ."

"Depressed?"

"Mad. I should've spit in Mark's face. Cutting off my hair and taking his car, some revenge."

"Call up a pizza joint in Boston and send him a hundred Hawaiian extra cheese—"

"Well . . . I did that too," Sahara said. "Sort of."

"Then you're ahead. You got the karmic last word."

"I'm gonna end up an unloved old hag like Mrs. Skye—"

"It won't happen."

"No?"

"I love you, Sahara."

Sahara punched her lightly. "We'll see how long that lasts once you've shacked up with a nice sperm donor."

"Just because you vanished the second you had a boyfriend . . ." Sahara's eyes brimmed again and Astrid found herself holding her friend through another bout of crying. This time the contact, skin to skin, brought a crawling sensation of dread. Sahara was already regretting that she'd let Astrid drain out the vitagua. But there was always more magic in the fireplace. . . .

Sahara shoved her away. "G'wan. Git on the road."

She's got the greeds, one of the grumbles singsonged.

She quashed the voice. The vitagua was out, most of it anyway. Sahara would behave reasonably. And Astrid could make sure there was no more contamination available. Sooner or later she'd find a way to truly uncurse Sahara.

You're gonna contaminate someone, Dad had said. He'd known it would happen. But she could still make it right.

"I'll bring some cream for your coffee," Astrid promised. The warmth of Sahara's body tingled on her skin as she fled.

CHAPTER SIXTEEN

FROM THE FIRST MRS. SKYE had reminded Astrid of a honey-bee—she kept her salt-and-pepper hair shorn close to her scalp, and was always digging in her purse as if it were a pollen-rich chrysanthemum. She wore two tarnished silver bracelets around her skinny wrists, two-inch bands with native designs on them—a frog on the left arm, an eagle on the right. When she rooted around in her bag, the bracelets jiggled, the stylized faces of the creatures drawing Astrid's gaze. They had lots of what Dad had called sparkle, those bracelets.

But if she chanted them, they'd have to be sent away. Sahara had offered to polish them once and Mrs. Skye refused. "Shine 'em up, someone might take 'em," she'd explained.

Now here was Astrid, topped full of vitagua and half contemplating the same theft.

They had never been alone together. Whenever Astrid was working on the old woman's garden, Sahara came along, chatting with Mrs. Skye, helping make plans to keep the old woman's predatory niece at bay. The attention seemed to pull Mrs. Skye out of her blur of fatigue, to bring her into focus. She told Sahara about dead friends and old town gossip as she fed her tea on her broken-down porch. They competed, arguing over who'd had more boyfriends, who was prettier at age seventeen, who was smarter, funnier.

Mrs. Skye swore that, like Sahara, she'd been an Alpine Princess.

Astrid had doubted the old lady's tales, but today as she chauffeured her through town Mrs. Skye raised her hand, time and again, to greet various white-haired Springers. They waved back with unfeigned enthusiasm.

"That's Penny Flayer—I fixed her up with her second husband," Mrs. Skye said. "And the old gent there, I helped his wife rebuild an antique crib for their granddaughter."

"My grandfather made furniture," Astrid said.

"That'd be Ev's dad, Struan MacTavish?"

"Yeah. He wasn't very good."

"Played the pipes like a dream come true, though. I did okay with the woodworking," Mrs. Skye mused. "Sahara found my tools in the basement."

"Could you still? Are your hands wrecked or anything?"

"I got nothing to build," the old lady said.

They were jouncing along in the truck, two people who'd thought themselves acquaintances, suddenly realizing they were little more than strangers. The set of Mrs. Skye's jaw was tense. Nerves about her doctor's appointment?

Sahara would know how to calm her, Astrid thought, or would have known before I leached the vitagua out of her.

No. That was silly. Sahara was plenty sensitive before she got contaminated. She hadn't needed magic.

What *did* you say? You offered reassurance, right? You said everything would be okay.

She'd opened her mouth to say it when Mrs. Skye broke out in a crooked-toothed smile, grinning with approval at the hardware store wall and the outlines of Jacks's mural.

"Thought he was the quiet one." She fumbled with her hearing aid.

"I don't see the joke," Astrid said.

"Who's he got it in for? The Mayor? Indigo Springs Historical Society?"

"The only ax Jacks has to grind is with his father."

"Chief Lee? Sure he's got a big enough stone?" Mrs. Skye chuckled as Astrid parked at the doctor's office. "I'll be half an hour, sweetie."

"Okay." Backtracking to Nathan's hardware store, Astrid

found Jacks squatting beside the road, poring over his mural sketch and a stack of paint color cards.

Crouching beside him, Astrid looked at the roughed-in mural. It showed the interior of the shop as it might have been at the end of the nineteenth century. Women in long dresses waited as aproned shopkeepers weighed salt and flour on old-fashioned scales. Children ogled glass jars of candy and cooed over hair ribbons.

She frowned—then hastily tried to assume a neutral expression.

"Go on," Jacks chuckled. "Critique."

"Well . . . isn't this a little conventional?"

"It is a public mural."

"Jacks, it's practically an advertisement."

"You think?" Face innocent, he examined a paint sample the color of vitagua, Indigo Springs blue.

"Mrs. Skye thinks it's hilarious." Astrid looked over the wall, looking for changes, areas where he'd worked hardest.

"Does she? Good."

There. Across the scene, at the far end of the store, was a window. A little Native girl peered through the glass, watching a shopkeeper sell a carved necklace to a white man. Her face was familiar. . . .

"No," she said. "This isn't about the potlatch fire?"

"Massacre."

"Nobody proved it was arson."

"Nobody tried." He tossed her a thin book—*The History of Indigo Springs.*

"Jacks, you've got to forget about that girl."

"I've learned her name—Elizabeth Walks-in-Shadow."

Sighing, Astrid opened the book to the marked page and found a black-and-white picture of a Native woman in a dress and bonnet. THE GHOST OF INDIGO CREEK? read its caption.

Jacks read over her shoulder: " 'After the flames died down, frantic villagers searched the smoking remains of the Indian settlement. The results were a grim reminder of the frailty of the human body. Nineteen souls were lost in the blaze. . . .'" He looked at her expectantly.

"'Its origin was never determined,'" Astrid finished.

"Never. Determined. 'What is known is the deaths effectively ended the dispute over the town's desire to extend its boundaries beyond Gibraltar Lane.'"

"Jacks, someone's gonna hear you."

He raised his voice. "'After the burials, a young girl named Elizabeth Almore began to insist the fire was set deliberately. Elizabeth was a half-breed—' Charming term."

"It's an old book written by an old bigot, Jacks."

"'Elizabeth's grandfather was Godfrey Walks-in-Shadow, hereditary chief of the immolated tribe. Though only eleven at the time and fully integrated into the God-fearing white community of her father, Elizabeth insisted that any objects or relics recovered from the fire belonged to her. She brought the matter to court when she reached adulthood, but by then the artifacts had been dispersed. Elizabeth herself vanished before the case could be heard. Local legend has it that she was murdered, and that her spirit haunts the ravine where Indigo Creek flows.'"

"Jacks." Her heart was pounding. "Say your great-grandfather was totally corrupt and covered up the cause of the fire. It's nothing to do with you."

"Is that what you think?"

"You're doing this to annoy your father."

"You of all people should be happy about that."

"You can't pick a fight with everyone in town."

"They'll be too chicken to mention it, trust me."

"They'll complain to the Chief."

"No!" He opened his mouth, aping shock.

She rubbed her temples. "Jacks, remember about keeping a low profile? Being invisible, all that?"

"If people are pissed at me, who's going to notice you?" He bumped his forehead against hers.

"Nobody proved anything," she insisted. Jacks paced the wall, scrutinizing his work. As he reached the corner, a woman on Rollerblades almost slid into the traffic on the highway. He lunged out and caught her.

"Good thing you were there," Astrid heard the woman say as he steadied her.

"Johnny-on-the-spot, that's me." He glanced fondly at his watch.

Astrid kept her voice low as he strolled back. "Do you think we got used to the chantments too easily? We use them all the time."

"Mark of our generation. Get a gadget, use a gadget. We've got no fear of the unknown . . . as long as it's plastic and fits in your hand."

"There's a cost, though." She thought of the waves of fatigue that came when she used the pocketknife on the dead animals Henna was bringing home. She thought of Marlowe. They needed a power cantation that could be used safely.

And nothing Astrid had remembered so far explained the headaches. Magic never caused her pain when she was a kid.

Jacks held her gaze. "Yes, it's weird and yes, there's a lot we don't understand. But we're on top of it."

"I'm not so sure."

"That's the vitagua talking. You said it was making you paranoid?"

"Yeah."

"When you make a chantment, you feel better?"

"Yes. When there's less magic in my body, the grumbles quiet."

He gave her forehead a quick kiss. "So fight off the heebie-jeebies until we get that crap out of your system."

"Right." She conjured up a smile and found it rested more easily on her face. "I'll go pick up Mrs. Skye."

The sense of relief was short-lived. As she crossed the highway, she tripped on a crack in the pavement. She would have pitched facefirst into the curb, but strong hands caught her from behind, arresting her plunge.

"Whoa there, Astie." It was Chief Lee. " 'Bout time you learned to walk, isn't it?"

"Seems like." Her face flushed; she could see Jacks's mural a hundred yards past him, and the image of Elizabeth made her feel like a kid caught breaking school windows. "Thanks for catching me."

"Sure thing." He patted her arm, looming over her with an air of uncertainty.

"Something I can do for you, Chief? Or are you checking my gait?"

"Peace, girl. I know we got off on the wrong foot way back whenever—"

"You called my father a perverted souse." Dad was a hero, she wanted to add; she blazed with a desire to bellow Albert's true story from the top of the fire tower.

"I'm not saying it ain't my fault."

That was a change. "What do you want, Chief?"

He shifted from foot to foot. "You kids making out all right in the new place? Jacks all right?"

This was about Jacks—he wasn't haranguing her for fun. Astrid relaxed a fraction. "He's feeding us a lot of sprouts."

"Goddamn Olive and all her Wicca bull." His face pinched. "I ought to send you girls a side of beef. And . . . Jacks and your pretty friend . . . they're an item?"

"Jacks and Sahara?" She laughed. "They're getting along, barely, for my sake."

"Oh." Clearly this wasn't the answer he'd expected, and he foundered. "Hear your mother's better."

She nodded.

"That's good," he said. "Listen, Astie . . . Astrid. Could you tell Jacks something for me?"

Anything to get out of this conversation. "Sure."

"Could you—oh! There he is." The Chief took a step toward the department store. Then traffic bunched up, forcing him to stop. Astrid edged toward the truck, but the Chief swiveled. "I gotta see him."

"Go to it," she said, gesturing across the street.

"I want to say: Whatever he's got to tell me, I mean to listen. He'll open up if he knows I'm listening, right?"

"You'll have to take that up with him." She thought: Jacks thinks the potlatch fire was arson. He thinks your great-great-grandfather was paid to cover up a massacre.

The Chief made another attempt to jaywalk, nearly getting clipped by a red SUV. Then his radio squawked. "Astie, one other thing."

She had almost escaped. "Yes?"

"I heard Jemmy Burlein was bitching about how Albert owed her money when he passed away. If you've got anything extra . . ." He looked embarrassed. "It's none of my business, I know you two are quits—but she's not doing too good with that hippie bike store."

"You there, Chief?" the radio barked.

He snatched it up, pivoting away from Main Street and Jacks, loping in the direction of the fire hall. Raising a hand good-bye, Astrid fled. The grumbles chattered at her. It was a relief when Mrs. Skye reappeared.

"How'd it go with the doctor?" she asked.

The old lady shrugged. "Not sure. Lilla—that's my niece—phoned him, asked him to send the assessor back. Says he needs to know there's food in my fridge and cleansers under the sink—signs I'm keeping up with home life, you know?"

"We'll go pick up whatever you need," Astrid said. "Sahara and I will help clean."

Playing chauffeur for the old woman took the afternoon: fetching groceries, hearing aid batteries, a mop and pail. Then, desperately hoping to rid herself of some of the vitagua she was carrying, she took Mrs. Skye into the antique store, one of Albert's old haunts. "Let's get you a rocking chair or something. If you can't rebuild it yourself, you can teach me to help you."

"Fair enough," Mrs. Skye agreed, but Astrid's eye had moved on; an old tripod glinted at her from the murky depths of the store. She bought it, mumbling something about giving it to a friend before bundling it into the truck like a thief. The allure of the thing was impossible to resist—with the added reservoir of vitagua she'd absorbed in draining Sahara and the cat, it was all she could do to keep from chanting it right there in the shop.

Dour inner voices gnawed at her: It won't matter, it's all going to fall apart. . . .

Mrs. Skye picked up a chair and a couple of picture frames. "Sahara says my walls are too bare. Lilla had me thinking I needed to move into one of those geezer farms. You girls hadn't helped me . . ."

Astrid flushed, pleased. "It's okay. Did we get everything you need?"

Mrs. Skye flapped a hand at the local shoe store. "Doc was eye-balling my beat-up sneakers. You mind?"

"Go ahead." The bike store was on the corner anyway. "I'll be next door talking to Jemmy."

Jemmy Burlein was a fragile-seeming nymph with Irish color-ing and long limbs. She had been an all-star basketball center in high school, the undisputed goddess of the court, queen of a cir-cle of horny boys and admiring, jealous girls.

She and Astrid had lived together for two years. It had been a sensation, that relationship—Jemmy was supposed to have stolen Astrid from an engineer named Stew Murphy. Town gossip had Astrid and Stew on the brink of marriage; in truth, they'd split up well before Jemmy came along.

When Albert died, things with Jemmy had fallen apart in their turn. Astrid had moved back home, hoping to keep Ma's growing oddness in check. Jemmy had opened the bike store and begun a long-distance relationship with a homeopath from Seattle.

Astrid found her onetime girlfriend just completing a sale, sending a young boy and his mother out of the store with a bright orange bike.

"Hi," she said, faintly awkward. "I heard a rumor today—Dad owed you money?"

Jemmy colored. "I shouldn't have told anyone. I was having a bad week . . . June Field told you?"

"Chief Lee."

She winced. "Sorry. I guess it's all over town."

"What's it gonna do, ruin Dad's reputation?" As she said the words, Astrid found herself smiling. Dad had everyone fooled.

"It'll give people an excuse to hash over our torrid affair again."

"I don't care if you don't. What happened?"

Jemmy set to work assembling a pile of bike components. "Albert came over one night, looking for you. He said it was an emergency."

"Where was I?"

"Spokane, at that garden show. He wanted to try catching up with you, so I lent him the car."

"When was this?"

"Just before he got sick."

"He never showed up. He wreck the car or something?"

"He never told you?" Jemmy raised her eyebrows. "Someone took a shot at him."

"What?" She reached for the counter to steady herself, only to discover it was out of reach.

"It's okay—they missed." Dropping her tools, Jemmy nudged Astrid over to a crate, urging her to sit. "He came back late that night with the windshield blasted in."

Ma's ravings echoed through Astrid's mind: He was killed. . . . Banged up, baby . . . bangbang!

"How do you know Dad wasn't inside?"

"From the holes. He'd have been splattered all over the driver's seat. Sorry—I just mean there was shot all over the upholstery." Jemmy cranked a pedal onto the bike frame, shaking her head. "Thing was, Albert insisted on fixing it right away. He'd only returned to talk me into giving him my credit card. He wanted to go to Portland and get the windshield replaced—"

"You *didn't* give my father your credit card."

"Crazy, huh?" Jemmy colored. "There was something in his voice . . ."

Astrid swallowed. Sahara's mermaid.

"He was gone for a day. When he got back the car looked . . ."

"New?"

"No. He'd gone out of his way to dirty it up. New windshield, new seat, new paint job, but the car looked just like it always had. He gave back the credit card and promised he'd pay me before the charges went through. And he begged me not to tell anyone."

"Didn't that make you suspicious?"

"Of course. Oh, Astrid, I figured he'd gotten into something shady. A drug deal maybe. I told myself if anything popped up on the news: somebody heard the shot, police looking for a car—I'd tell you. But then Albert was in the hospital, doctors said he had less than a week . . ."

Astrid flashed back to those days, the two of them sitting in the hospital, bleak and shell-shocked. Had it only been a year ago? Here was a memory she wished she could lose: sitting at Dad's bedside while he slapped at the side of her head. Holding his hands down, saying it was okay when it wasn't . . .

She fought a rush of tears. "Did you guys talk again?"

"No," Jemmy said. "A few days later . . ."

A few days later he was gone. Astrid swallowed thickly. "You never told anyone what happened?"

"It felt like a last request."

"And when the credit card bill came?"

Jemmy ducked her head. "It wasn't just the windshield. He'd gone to some pawnshops."

"Tell me how much," Astrid said.

"I feel rotten about this."

"Don't. I'm looking to keep it quiet too. How much did you tell June Field?"

"Only that he died owing me money. I couldn't admit I'd given Albert my MasterCard."

"You tell anyone else?"

"No, but June obviously told the Chief."

"A few thousand, am I right? More?" From Jemmy's eyes, she had it about right. "It'll take me some time, but—"

"I can't take money from you, Astrid—"

Equally embarrassed, they haggled until Mrs. Skye turned up, chatting away amid a trio of other old ladies but wearing a tired expression that let Astrid lay down a check for some of the damage and escape with the last word.

CHAPTER SEVENTEEN

"I DREW THE VITAGUA from Sahara and Henna on a Saturday," Astrid tells me. She expertly shuffles a pack of gaming cards covered in trolls and flame demons. "Some of the grumbles said Sahara would leave me. Others said it was me who'd be leaving. I'd be taken away from them all—Jacks, Ma . . ."

"Even Mrs. Skye?"

Her eyes crinkle fondly. "They didn't mention her."

"I see."

"I had maybe a pint of vitagua soaked in my body, Will. A fraction of what I carry now, but even so the grumbles had so much to say about my future: handcuffs, jail cells, cameras watching my every move. They said I would cut my leg—" She tugs up her jeans, revealing a pink scar on her ankle. "—on a rough edge of a bedframe, it turned out—and there'd be a hue and cry. They said Arthur Roche would think I'd attempted suicide."

"Why didn't you try to change the outcome?"

"How? Stop making chantments? Perhaps that would send Sahara away. Magic was pulling us together, Will. The secret made us so close; nothing could break us up. I had to believe the grumbles' predictions could be avoided: that the premonitions weren't set in stone."

I bend close. "Astrid, this is important. *Have* the grumbles been wrong?" I need to know if there is a window for free will in her worldview, if she believes the things she predicts are inevitable.

Suddenly we are plunged into darkness. The artificial sunlight vanishes from the windowscreens, and the overhead lights die.

"I don't know if they're always right." Astrid's voice is a thread in the blackness. "The real problem is they have an agenda. They told me just enough to get me in trouble."

She takes my hands. A trickling sensation, like blood flowing, spreads across my palms. I can feel the paint rolling over the cards, as if my skin is made of their paper surface.

Fear edges through me like a razor blade. I pull free and the sensation fades. "What's happening up there?"

"It was . . . is Jemmy," she says. "She's one of Sahara's Primas now, remember? Roach's men grabbed her, and now she's shut down the power in this cage. Sahara taught her a cantation that converts electricity to magic. It'll pull power from any nearby source of electricity."

"Enough electricity to black us out?"

"Looks that way. If she needs more, we might get lightning strikes. It's something to see."

"Is Jemmy trying to escape?"

"No. This is a message."

"To whom?"

"To the Roach, and I'm not about to translate it."

The darkness is beginning to get to me. The sense that my eyes would have adjusted by now, had there been any light at all, is strong. Where are the backups?

Astrid continues her story: "On Sunday, Sahara was sleepy and surly both. Every time we touched, I sensed how much she resented my pulling the vitagua out of her. She wanted to recontaminate herself, so I made sure there was no magic to be had— none pooled anywhere, none coming up through the fireplace. She thought I didn't trust her."

"Which you didn't."

"We pretended everything was okay." Pain thickens her voice. "I made chantments: a Christmas tree ornament that helped sick people get well. A cigar box that always had a little present in it, every time it was opened: neat rocks, a mounted butterfly, a fish skull. A snowglobe that, when you shook it, made you think you were on the beach."

"Bet you wish every day for that one," I say.

"Now you mention it, we did send it to a convict. I also chanted the tripod."

"Four chantments. How did you feel afterwards?"

"Better. Less . . . doomed."

"What did the tripod do?"

"Made violins out of dust," she says. "Ridiculous, huh? But that's what it does. Beautiful old violins."

I sit in the dark and imagine it, an old-fashioned camera platform weaving dust into wood and strings.

"While Sahara sulked, she surfed the Web. I think she was looking for proof that vitagua contamination was safe. Evidence, to change my mind. Instead, she must have typed a new combination of words into her . . ."

"Search engine?" I suggest.

"That's it. She found another newsgroup thread, much like the first one . . . but it was years older. Marlowe was in that group too. She was using another name but the messages she sent were identical. The people in the group, the ones who had chantments— vanished one by one."

"What did you think it meant?"

"Sahara tracked down a few of the people who stopped posting, figured out who they really were. They'd all been murdered or had fatal accidents."

"Murdered by Marlowe?"

"Who else? She had to be one of the chantment thieves Albert told us about. She'd look for people with magic, earn their trust, figure out who they were." She shudders.

"Good thing you found out the truth."

"Yes. Still, we'd mailed chantments to a murderer. And without her, our only source of cantations was gone."

"You didn't know she was a bad guy," I say.

"I was almost glad to have a reason to stop talking to Marlowe. It was risky. But Sahara was devastated. She'd found Marlowe, remember? First I'd drained her vitagua reserves, then her big discovery turned out badly."

"It's understandable," I say.

"Yeah. I decided I had to cheer Sahara up. I took her and Jacks out hiking, brought a picnic. When we were thinking of heading home, Jacks found someone's Dalmatian knotted up in an old fishing line. He untangled it, and the owner was so grateful he took us out onto Great Blue Reservoir on his boat.

"I found another sparkly object there—a lantern. I chanted it when nobody was looking. I figured if it did anything conspicuous, I'd toss it overboard."

"Did it?"

"Sat there not making a peep and lured in all the big fish. Sahara and the boat's owner hauled in whopping bass while Jacks pretended he wasn't reminded of fishing with his dad. The dog ran around and we barbecued and the sun set over the lake so beautifully. . . ."

Her voice breaks. Her hand tightens on mine.

"I left the lantern on the boat. The couple was from out of state. They could tow the thing home and nobody would know."

The emergency lights cut in suddenly, blinding me. When my eyes adjust I see Patience, embracing Astrid, as she so often does, and whispering in her ear. Patience is a new sort of goddess now—short, South Asian in appearance. Her hair is waist-long and thick, and her fingers, curled around Astrid's arms, are inexplicably compelling.

"It isn't time for that," Astrid's voice rises.

Patience coaxes her toward the hallway. "You should call Roche, Lawman. Tell him Astrid didn't speak in tongues during the blackout."

I do as she suggests, halfheartedly placating Arthur while I wonder what the two of them are up to. Astrid's voice is teary; Patience's soothing.

She's vulnerable, I think. I have always been good at sensing people in despair. Caroline saw this as predatory. opportunistic; she hated that part of me passionately.

Roche is eager to confirm that Astrid is under control, and just as eager to get off the line.

"Jemmy Burlein is barricaded in the infirmary—with hostages," he says. "We're locked down. You'll stay there for the duration of the emergency. It's perfectly safe."

"Fine," I reply.

"We've got cameras and mikes running, so just keep working on Astrid."

"Okay." Good-cop time, I think. Hanging up, I head for the kitchen. By the time Astrid appears, I've made tuna sandwiches.

"I thought we'd take a break." Making food is a deliberate attempt to remind her of Jacks, and it works—her eyes brim. She takes up a sandwich, blinking.

She asks: "How bad is it out there, in the world?"

"You don't know?"

"I'm not omniscient."

I ponder my response. After a moment, I say: "About fifty people from Indigo Springs have been alchemized and are turning to animals. The rest seem fine, though some are still quarantined. The town has been the epicenter of three large earthquakes, and the government has burned out several acres of wilderness to keep the contamination from spreading."

"It isn't working," she says.

"No." I shake my head. "Some of it is in the rivers."

She runs a hand over the table and a painted sea monster takes shape on its surface. "Sahara claims she created the monsters?"

"Yes."

"They're just contaminated fish. What else?"

"A lot of people are missing. Economy's in the tank, and seventeen countries have banned Americans from traveling within their borders."

"Sounds bad."

"The government needs to get a handle on the situation, Astrid. Sahara's going out of her way to make us look helpless."

"She's very in-your-face that way."

"For every person who has a chantment and some genuine magical power, there are ten fakes. People are shooting women who resemble Sahara." I gesture with a carrot stick. "If we catch her, Astrid, everyone will calm down. We'll be able to fight the contamination, establish order."

"You can't turn back the clock, Will. Magic's here to stay. Capturing Sahara won't change that."

"Do you mind if we try?"

She tilts her head, as if listening. "The rate of contamination will accelerate."

"Is that what the grumbles say?"

"Yes." She flips through the growing pile of painted cards. I examine the pictures as they flash by. Astrid lingers on a picture of a fishing boat, then digs out a picture of a bookstore. "The day after we were out on the boat, one of my gardening clients came out of her house, yelling that there was an emergency at Olive's shop.

"I thought something had happened to Jacks—he'd gone off to mail some chantments. I was so stressed, I was shaking—thinking of Albert getting shot in Jemmy's car, dying a week later . . ."

"Was Jacks okay?"

She nods. "The emergency was Ma."

Ev Lethewood appears on a card, postal uniform rumpled, rage contorting her fair features, a book in each hand.

"She was pacing up and down Olive's shop, swearing, tossing books, pushing over shelves. She said Olive murdered Dad, I was in on it, we were going to jail . . .

" 'Killers, killers, killers,' she was screaming."

"What did you do?"

"Called Sahara, what else? She showed up with the mermaid, and I coaxed Olive out of earshot. Sahara got Ma calmed and we took her home. Then . . ."

"What?" I have to go gently now. There's something here, details Astrid doesn't mean to share.

"Nothing. We nearly argued, that's all. The day before, Sahara forgot to check on Ma. I asked how she could forget and she said she wasn't feeling well. I said she'd been well enough to go fishing—"

"She was punishing you for siphoning the magic out of her body."

"Maybe. Anyway, we couldn't fight in front of Ma, and when we got to her place, the argument petered out."

"Just like that?"

"Something else happened—Ma had torn her house apart. Carpets, furniture, clothes, pictures—all of it busted up or chopped to rags. And on the wall in the bathroom where she'd been keeping a big poster of a Picasso print . . ."

"Yes?"

"There was a blue stain, like the one on our ceiling."

"Vitagua? At Ev's?"

Astrid nods. "Using the mermaid, Sahara found out that when Dad was in the hospital, Ma ended up with some of his things. She'd gone with me to visit, and the nurse gave the stuff to her instead of Olive. One thing she got was this ratty coat of his—"

"Let me guess—it was a chantment?"

"Yes. It disguised him—made him hard to identify when he was out working magic. Anyway, Ma was pacing around her house, waiting for me to call from the hospital. She didn't feel welcome there—the ex-wife, you know? Awkward."

I think of Caroline. Would she come, if I was hospitalized? "Ev must have been very concerned about you," I say. Still calm, sympathetic.

"Sure, and Albert. She lived with him all those years, and she never stopped loving him."

I nod. "Ev said something to me the other day in an interview. She said Lethewood women have loyal hearts."

Astrid swallows, seeming to struggle for equilibrium. "Ma was pacing, and she had the coat, and she saw it was full of holes, right around the belly. She filled the bathroom sink with water and dunked the coat. The water in the sink turned red—"

"The coat was soaked with blood. Albert did get shot?"

"Yes. Then Ma pulls the coat out of the sink and wrings it out . . . and she finds Dad's little glass vial in the pocket. There's vitagua in it, just a drop. She pulls out the stopper and it comes spurting out. Some hits the wall . . ."

"The rest struck your mother."

"Right. Ma was contaminated, Albert was gone, and I had forgotten the chantments. She covered up the stain on her bathroom wall with a picture, and nobody knew."

"And right after Albert's death Ev began acting strangely."

Astrid rubs at her eyes. "Ma told Sahara that a week or so after she got splashed, she picked up a sealed envelope at work and knew what was inside. Who it was for, what it said, everything."

"Ev was never opening people's mail at all?"

"Will, Ma didn't know about magic. But she knew what was in every envelope she touched. It was impossible. So she developed the Everett Burke delusion, told herself she was *deducing* what was in the mail."

"How did these revelations make you feel?"

"Excited. I figured I could siphon the contamination out. If Dad was right, there'd be a trace of vitagua left in Ma, but maybe she'd improve—be her old self."

"Did you do it?"

"Sahara said we couldn't." Astrid sucks on her lips. "I thought she was angry, because I'd taken away her vitagua, but she insisted she had to show me something."

"What was that?"

Astrid brushes a tear off her cheek. "The night before, while we were out on the tourists' boat, Henna had curled up on Sahara's bed and died."

CHAPTER EIGHTEEN

THEY BURIED HENNA IN the ravine behind the house, following a sketchy trail down to the banks of Indigo Creek. It was the first real day of summer, bright and hot, with a breeze that air-dried the sweat from Astrid's body without leaving her any cooler. The perfume of scorching cedar bark hung in the air.

Sahara led the procession, holding the aluminum hand-rake. Jacks had the corpse, a bundle wrapped in an old T-shirt. Astrid, in the rear, bore the shovel.

They descended in silence until Jacks said, "If we go any farther, we'll end up on Settlement Road."

He was right—they'd reached the middle of the ravine, a small clearing encircled by trees and bisected by the muddy green-brown line of the creek.

Shaking herself out of a daze, Sahara pointed at a spot beneath a willow. Astrid began digging. It was good to have a task—it kept her from thinking about Ma contaminated with vitagua, about Henna's withered body, tongue hanging loose, the festering gashes where Astrid's teeth had broken its flesh . . .

Her gaze fell on Sahara's hand for the twentieth time that day. The puncture where she had drawn the vitagua was healing cleanly. I did it right the second time, Astrid thought. She'll be okay.

Sahara said the cat's death meant it was unsafe to drain Ev. But, Astrid thought, fear of experimenting had always been Albert's problem. If she was careful, Ma might be okay.

"Deep enough," Jacks said. She'd dug a two-foot pit.

Sahara knelt beside the creek, clutching the hand-rake. She muttered the heat cantation, then drew the points of the rake through the grass. There was an explosion of movement—reeds growing and knotting, a churning of roots. A basket came together on the surface of the creek, filled with cattails and pinecones. The air grew chilly.

Sahara held the basket out and Jacks unwrapped the furry body, laying it on the greenery. Together they arranged the reeds. Solemnly, Sahara set the basket in the grave Astrid had dug.

"You want to say a couple words?" Astrid asked.

"Just cover it up." Sahara put her face in her hands, and Astrid saw the healing puncture again.

"Let me." Taking the shovel, Jacks set to work.

"Sahara," she said. "I'm so sorry."

"Don't be. It's Albert's fault. You didn't know extraction was dangerous."

"He said the first time you try anything magical you'll probably screw up. I should have remembered."

Sahara turned from the grave. "It was Mark's cat."

"If I'd hurt you . . ."

"It's for the best." Sahara's expression became bleak, just for a second, before the mask fell back into place.

Jacks had been about to speak but at Sahara's words he winced expressively and kicked at a sun-baked lump of moss, tearing it from the base of a tree root. "We've got to get a grip on this contamination thing."

"Yeah," Astrid sighed. Ma, exposed for a year now. Sahara, tainted by magical residue. Would she have to watch Sahara fall apart, as Ev had? By fall she could . . .

By autumn Sahara will be profoundly contaminated, her grumbles insisted.

"What are you gonna do about Ev?" Jacks asked. "If Sahara takes a day off again—"

"Who knew she couldn't go one day without a check-in?"

"Can we save this until we get home?" Astrid said.

"Why? Jacks has killer timing. Nobody will overhear."

"Astrid, if we're going to keep your secret, we can't have Ev going ballistic twice a week."

"It's not my fault, Eligible."

"Guys! Peace!" Astrid waved her arms. Jacks glowered and kicked at the moss again. "Jacks, a few days ago you said we had everything under control."

"A few days ago your mother wasn't hurling the annotated *War and Peace* at my mother's head. We weren't having a kitty funeral."

With a struggle, she unclenched her fists. "Let's go home, have some lemonade, and figure out what to do."

"I'm getting better at using Siren," Sahara said. "I'll get Ev under control—"

"Control." Jack's voice dripped sarcasm. "That's your specialty, isn't it?"

Astrid lifted her face skyward, letting the sunlight melt out vision, frying her cheeks and forehead. She had to stop this. Move them from arguing to cooperation . . .

Move, a grumble agreed, its tone dark and mirthful. The vitagua inside seemed to gurgle, and Astrid felt a deep internal wrench, a spear of cold deep in her diaphragm. Tightness made her clutch her gut. . . .

"Astrid?" Hands on her shoulders suddenly—Jacks. The light on her face dimmed and the air temperature plummeted.

The grumble was laughing.

"What the hell's going on?" Sahara said.

Gritting her teeth against a sharp new onset of pain, Astrid opened her eyes.

The ravine was gone. In its place were great glaciers of vitagua, mountain ranges of frozen blue, crags that extended to the horizon in every direction.

The three of them stood on a butte of cobalt ice, a sloping wedge that extended maybe thirty feet up from the ice flats around them. There was no breeze—just a deep cold that bit into Astrid's flesh—and no sun. What light there was seemed to be coming from the spirit water itself, a blue glow that caught the frozen cracks and facets.

"People," whispered Jacks, spreading his arms protectively in front of her. Impossibly tall trees were frozen within the icebergs towering above them, and nested in their branches was a building that looked like a longhouse, stretched out on a hammock of netted foliage.

"I don't see anyone," Sahara said.

"There." Astrid pointed at a figure—a young woman caught in the act of climbing to the building. She had bear paws for hands. Her claws dug into the lumpy tree trunk.

Beyond the first house, Astrid could see other buildings, and other half-human, half-animal figures.

A hunk of ice twenty feet long cracked loose from the berg, falling to shatter on the frozen vitagua below.

"Yeah," Jack said, voice breathy. "We've got everything under control. Where are we?"

"I'll find out." Bending, Astrid placed her hand on the ice. Information blasted through her, scattershot, and she yanked her fingers back. She was stuttering random words, in languages she didn't speak.

"Astrid!" Sahara shook her. "Astrid, stay with us."

She leaned on them, panting and staring at her hand. The warmth of her body hadn't melted the ice—her skin was a chapped and frozen-looking red. "We're in the unreal."

"Where?" Jacks asked.

"Fairyland," she said. "The spirit realm. A world within our world, where magical beings used to . . . live, I guess. To hide from the real world."

"Wow," Sahara said. Her eyes were gleaming.

The vitagua was trying to tell her a thousand things at once. There was much more to chanting than Albert ever guessed, said a grumble. Tricks and loopholes, ways to sequester magic within someone safely, endless possibilities. Spring-tappers had been making chantments for centuries, siphoning magic through the vitagua wells, but each generation got weaker, less knowledgeable. Nobody dared improvise, nobody listened to the voices of the unreal. . . .

Power was all around her, intoxicating knowledge, and Astrid sensed it had been this way when she was young. But she'd let it go to her head, the way Sahara did with Siren.

She looked at her friends. Can we keep each other honest?

Without discussing it, they edged down the slope, clinging to each other for warmth. The ice, fortunately, wasn't slick: it had the sticky consistency of tar. They shuffled in a huddle, letting Jacks lead the way.

"The witch-burners wanted to control magic," Astrid told them, isolating a grumble. "They drove it out of people all across Europe—killed fairies and witches. But not everyone sat around waiting to get fried. Some came here."

"Sounds okay," Jacks said. "Wizards and magic and mythical creatures were hidden here while in the real world the bad guys thought they were winning."

"Yeah," Astrid said. "The real became more safe, predictable. The witch-burners succeeded in creating a near-monopoly on magic. Unfortunately, they weren't content. They wanted it all."

"What happened?" Jacks demanded.

"A battle, I think." She rubbed her temple. If she touched the ice floe again . . .

"No, you don't," Jacks said, catching her hand.

They reached the edge of a glassine stretch of ice, where the air was misty and marginally warmer. Stalagmites of vitagua jutted upward from the mirror surface of the ice, forming a forest of widely spaced columns. Some were only pencil-thick, thin poles of blue that came to pinpoints at waist height. Others towered hundreds of feet tall, their bases as wide as the trunks of ancient redwoods.

"We need ice skates," Sahara laughed.

"Why are we going this way?" Jacks asked.

Astrid pointed. The spaces between the stalagmites were alight . . . and the light wasn't blue. It was gold. "We need to learn all we can."

They skated into the glow, Astrid leading until she rounded

a wide stalagmite and almost slipped. Jacks caught her before she could fall.

She had nearly bumped into an ice statue of Albert.

He was ten feet tall, dressed as usual in jeans and a T-shirt. Hair shagged around his face in a mane. One empty hand curved outward in a gesture of offering. Instead of his habitually weary expression, he was smiling.

"Daddy," Astrid said. Albert looking happy . . . so bright and heroic.

A half-dozen birds were frozen in the ice at his feet, gawking accusingly at her with dead eyes. Her face warmed with a rush of fresh tears. She looked away from the disturbing reproach she sensed within the small corpses.

Dad. She had been his apprentice, and she had forgotten. . . .

She touched his leg, and the thoughts of the frozen people of the unreal grumbled through her. The ever-present pain in her head hummed back, trying to drown it out.

Back in the real, nobody remembered Dad. If they thought of him at all, it was as a bum, a petty crook, a burden on his family. Here, where nobody could see it, he had a monument.

"Magic exists in the shade, Bundle," she mumbled, only stepping back when her tears ate into the chiseled ice of his leg.

"Come on, honey," Sahara said at last. "Come on, there's more to explore and we're getting cold. You got here once, you'll figure out how to return."

Jacks agreed. "You can bring flowers next time, okay?"

Astrid rubbed her nose, smiling weakly. They moved on, and behind a stalagmite of blue ice they found another statue, a woman Astrid recognized from old photos—Albert's grandmother. Farther still was a man who might have been Granny's father. After that it was strangers. . . .

"Who are they?" Sahara asked.

"The other spring-tappers," Astrid said, quoting yet another grumble. "Everyone ever initiated into the mysteries of the Spring."

They slid on in silence, briefly looking over each statue until

Jacks stopped short before a statue of a woman with long braids, clad in an old-fashioned dress.

"Elizabeth Walks-in-Shadow," he said.

The sculpture of Elizabeth was different from the others . . . darker. Flecks of red were dispersed through its icy body like poppy seeds in a cake, and instead of radiating goodwill, her face was tired and severe.

Jacks's mouth hung open. "I was sure she'd been murdered to shut her up about the potlatch fire."

Astrid brushed her fingers across the surface of Elizabeth's statue. Another rush of information jolted through her. "She was attacked. Instead of dying . . . Jacks, she's *in* there."

"Alive?"

"Half alive, like the birds," she whispered. Her heart was hammering. She clutched his hand. Something wrong, something bad . . . the grumbler was laughing again.

"Alive," Sahara scoffed. "She'd be two hundred."

"She's sleeping," Astrid insisted. "Vitagua isn't water. If you're submerged, you don't drown. Your spirit mixes into the spirit water. If you're frozen . . ."

"What?"

"Frozen," she stammered. "Get the body into ice before it cools. Only way to save—"

"Astrid!"

She fought to anchor herself in the present, gulping air, fighting back horror. Words battered her eardrums, shrieking: basement, window, snipers, blood. She pressed her fists to her ears.

Jacks asked, "Do the grumbles say who killed Elizabeth?"

Elizabeth. She mouthed the name and the din quieted. "Her . . . apprentice found her as she was dying and . . ."

"Put the body into ice to save her, you said," Jacks said. "Save her—can she get out of there?"

"Get out," Astrid whispered, pushing the words past a throat-clenching mixture of terror and hope.

"Let her be, Jacks." Sahara's voice cut through the hubbub. "Can't you see you're upsetting her?"

"She'd just . . . be able to say what happened," Jacks said. He stared up at Elizabeth's face, amazed. "She could tell me."

"You and your obsessions," said Sahara. "Astrid, we're almost there. Can you keep going?"

"Yes." Taking their hands, Astrid slid closer to the blazing golden light. They were near enough now that it was almost blinding, a hot wash that outshone the blue light emanating from the largest stalagmites.

Frozen inside another column was the source of the glow—a man blazing gold from head to toe. He was clad in peculiar armor, translucent plates that covered his body. His hair was red, and a fiery, transparent sword blazed in his grip. His left hand, its fingers twisted, clawed for the open air. He was encased in frozen vitagua, all but the tip of one fingernail. That had melted free and was stuttering with sparks that melted whatever they touched, leaving a thin ribbon of vitagua twisting against the bottom of a deep pothole.

Gazing down, Astrid spotted something dull and red.

"What is it?" Sahara crowded close.

"It's our house," Astrid said. "The bottom of our fireplace. See the red? It's the bricks Albert used to seal off the bottom of the hearth."

"Why? I thought he wanted chantments disseminated to the masses."

"To slow it down?" She peered into the crude hole, an icy bowl with a groove where the melted vitagua ran. The thread of spirit water wiggled like a tongue working at a loose tooth.

"This is where our drip comes from?" Sahara said. Her hand stole toward the melted spirit water, but Jacks pulled her back. "You said we'd never find it, Jacks."

He tugged Sahara beyond reach of the stream. "Not funny."

"It would be if you had a sense of humor."

"No quarreling." Astrid blew on the exposed fingertip of the frozen man and the candleflick of flame died. "Let's see what this guy has to tell us."

"Your head is going to explode if you keep that up," Jacks said.

"Just a touch," Astrid said. She reached up, brushing the nub of a finger.

And began to burn.

CHAPTER NINETEEN

SHE WAS A WITCH, that's what she was. A witch in need of burning, her and her unholy relics and all her allies. Anyone contaminated, anyone who knew—they would all die.

Astrid was seeing through the witch-burner's eyes, absorbing bursts of knowledge as her body heated, cooking. His name is Patterflam, she thought, or maybe she said it aloud. "He is the last great leader of the—"

He was a witch-burner.

People put to the torch—a dozen memories of executions, a hundred. She saw him scouring the Colonies for magic, seeking to bring the world under control, under the hand of his brethren. They thought when the New World was subjugated the battle would end, but the savages and their magic wielders had been crafty. Patterflam grew old, and even as the Brigade furthered its power, as they learned to contain enchantment within crosses and potions, he grew increasingly sure that their success was incomplete.

The burn was spreading from her hand. Distantly, Astrid felt her friends trying to separate her from the point of contact.

"Astrid, he's killing you!" Faraway worried voice.

"Don't leave me, Sahara . . . ," she mumbled.

"Can't get her off—"

"She's burning up!"

Fighting pain, Astrid pressed her other hand to the wall of vitagua. Now there was even more information, all of it confusing, and he was killing her, torching her, and she had no apprentice. The well would close and the unreal would be worse off than before.

"Vitagua has the following qualities," she heard herself say through chattering teeth: "It's fire-averse, cohesive, can be contained in glass, and tends to freeze unless heat is available to keep it warm. It's drawn to living tissue. Vitagua is as dense as crude oil or blood and cannot be mixed with water. It expresses, to some extent, the collective will of the people of the unreal."

"Tell them to get you out of this!"

She blinked, saw her clothes were smoking, knew Sahara was yanking on her belt, that Jacks's hand was burnt and blistering as he tried to pry her from the ice floe.

"Patterflam was trying to burn the unreal," she said. "That's when magic changed from mist to liquid. He and his men were using heat against us, so we fought back with cold. Magicules were everywhere, a fog. The air was blue. The fog condensed to a vitagua sea; the sea froze. Chill fought heat, ice fought fire."

One of the grumbles made a suggestion. "Break my skin," Astrid said.

Sahara dug in her fingernails, cutting into the flesh of Astrid's arm. Eyes streaming, Astrid pulled vitagua up from within herself. It shot from the small crescent-shaped wound, splattering the icy wall and her hands.

Freeze it. She had to freeze it.

"Cold," Astrid said. "Cold, cold, all of it. Chilly, chill it, make it cold, everything freezes . . ."

Vitagua flowed between her and the witch-burner, its movement sluggish as it turned to slush. And suddenly the burning sensation was gone; a layer of liquid magic broke the contact between her fingers and Patterflam. Jacks and Sahara tore her free.

Shivering, Astrid looked up. Patterflam's hand was covered in a layer of blue ice. The exposed, burning fingertip was wholly encased.

"Are you okay?"

"I tried too hard." She could feel the liquid inside her cooling.

"Overcompensated. Panic, you know. Sahara, did the vitagua touch you?"

"No," Sahara snapped.

"Overcompensated how, Astrid?" Jacks demanded.

It was hard to breathe. The interior chill was spreading and her guts felt icy. "Needed to freeze Patterflam . . . froze everything."

"We have to get home," Jacks said. "Astrid?"

"I can try."

"Is that safe?" Sahara asked. "You screw up now—"

"Who can know?" She felt dreamy; the only thing keeping her awake was the ache in her head.

"That's not good enough." The edge in Jacks's voice brought her focus back.

Her right eye throbbed, bringing more tears. Cerulean snowflake-shapes etched over her vision. The coils of her dragon earring were painfully cold. There was a distant groan from one of the larger ice formations, followed by a crack so sharp, they felt a shock through the air.

Sahara was rubbing her arms. Jacks's palm was burnt.

"You're wheezing," Sahara said, her voice an accusation. Her hand closed over Astrid's elbow, extending the arm. For Jacks to see, Astrid realized. On her wrist was a blister of frozen vitagua.

"I'm okay," she tried to say, though her voice sounded harsh and the left side of her face wouldn't move. Frozen vitagua had congealed between her back molars, and she couldn't close her mouth.

"Astrid." Jacks moved into her narrowing field of vision. His hands, burning hot, cupped her face. "You brought us here, sweetheart? You have to take us back."

"I'll try." She imagined the ravine, the tree that sheltered Henna's grave . . . go home, no place like . . .

There. A twist of muscle, and was that a hint of warmth? Astrid opened her eyes, certain she'd see the ravine again. But they were still surrounded by creaking stalagmites of blue ice.

"Try again," Jacks said. His teeth were chattering. "Think about picking blueberries in the summer, the wildflowers. Remember when we were out hiking the creek and that eagle splashed down in front of us?"

"Young eagle," Astrid said through numb lips.

"It flapped up, clumsy, a fish in its talons—"

"You painted it."

"Take us there," he urged.

"I need a second," she interrupted, mushing away from the glowing body of Patterflam and forcing them to follow. Her legs gave out at Elizabeth's statue.

"Astrid, we have to get you out of here."

He's right. I can't stay here. I should try to move. But it was so hard to breathe. Her friends' voices were rising even as they got farther away.

Oceans of frozen vitagua, she thought. She could stay here with it, wait for the thaw. If they all stayed—if they froze—neither Jacks nor Sahara could leave her.

No, the grumbles said. And for the barest of instants, their voice seemed familiar. You'll pull yourself into the real any second now. There's so much that hasn't happened yet—the flood, the fight with the witch-burner, the standoff with the police—

Sahara leaving.

Astrid's heart slammed; her body jerked. Terror flooded adrenaline through her system.

She was alone in the backyard, freezing despite the scorching sun overhead. Her hands were soaked in vitagua, stained to the elbows.

She stood. Her lungs were full of ice, and she couldn't draw a proper breath of the hot summer air.

Her friends . . .

Jacks appeared, sliding into the real almost weightless, like a balloon. Sahara was heavier. She was turned away, facing the icebergs.

Astrid coughed, her body painfully cold. Jacks closed in, taking her into his arms as the world darkened.

CHAPTER TWENTY

ASTRID DIDN'T REMEMBER THEM putting her to bed. Her awareness blurred as she hit the lawn, face tickled by the sharp blades of new-cut grass in the backyard. When she sharpened again, the world itself had gone fuzzy, all dimness, close air, and blankets.

The vitagua within her had pooled into a mass of slush around her lungs. It hurt to cough, and she couldn't draw air to speak. She tried to use her affinity with the stuff to push it out to her extremities, but it was too solid. Trying to move it was agonizing; it wouldn't flow.

Jacks held her hand, his skin unbearably hot, hanging on even when she tried to yank loose. Sahara piled blankets and chattered stories, making Astrid sip glass after glass of lukewarm tea. It didn't help; her teeth rattled and she shivered constantly.

Words and phrases bubbled through her mind, grumbles mumbling about vitagua and magicules. They were the voices of the frozen people of the unreal. Was she supposed to melt them all free?

No. Not just her. Dad said there were other springs.

He'd also said someone was closing them.

The Brigade. Patterflam called them a Brigade.

What if one day Astrid was the last remaining chanter? What if she was the only one now? Her fear grew; her mind circled the glowing blue icebergs as if tethered to them. All that ice. All those people.

Fragments of knowledge churned in her mind, solutions to problems she had never studied. Dad had rationed his store of information on magic. He'd give her a minuscule drop of vitagua and a sparkly object and let her chant one thing a month. Chanting takes something out of you, he'd told her once—I don't want it stunting your growth.

"Coffee stunts your growth and I drink that, Daddy." Saying it set her to coughing.

She'd make a chantment; he'd send it away. She hungered for more. The tiny drops of vitagua murmured like a kettle on the boil—she could sense secrets trapped within the spirit water, answers. It was all connected, all alive, and it never forgot anything.

To this, Dad had only one answer: No.

One autumn morning she ditched school and went alone to Mascer Lane, slipping into the house through a basement window. The fireplace had not yet been bricked over; back then, the crack in the hearth was a hairline. Astrid laid a hand over the gap, pulling vitagua into herself.

"Teach me," she had whispered and the grumbles had gotten clearer. Most didn't speak English, but that made it easier to pick out the few that did.

Astrid coughed and thrashed in bed, lungs frozen and achy. "Sorry, Daddy," she croaked.

It was Sahara's and Jacks's voices that finally lured her away from the guilt and the memories. The customary sharpness eased out of their tones, fading into sober discussion, and then—blessedly— agreement. Burying the hatchet at long last? She strained to hear what they were saying, but cold fluid had clogged her ears.

She was distantly aware of moaning a protest when Jacks released his grip on her hand. Then Sahara's long fingers twined with her own, and Astrid finally slept.

Daylight woke her, needle sharp against her puffy eyelids. The ringing in her ears had quieted in the night, and the familiar burn of her constant headache was almost welcome. A soothing smell— cloves—permeated her senses.

Ma was there.

Ev was still dressed as a man, but she wasn't in suspenders.

Better yet, she had a bra on. Her chin was plucked, and her hair was free of pomade. Short blond curls framed her face.

"Yet another bender, kid?" she said, tugging the covers up over Astrid's arm.

Fear brimmed over. "Sahara isn't gone?"

"Don't move. Yes, she's gone—I sent them both for lunch."

"Lunch." She relaxed back into the pillows.

"They needed to get out," Ev said. "Looked like scarecrows. When'd you fall sick?"

"Saturday, I guess. The cat died." Her throat closed and she blinked away cold tears.

Ma stroked her hair. "It piles up sometimes."

"What day is it now?"

"Thursday."

Familiar, panicky tension from the Albert days made her rise again. "Work . . ."

"Jacks called your clients," Ev said. "Nobody's going to can you for breaking down this once."

Astrid didn't answer, just huffed faintly.

"He'd a lick of sense, he'd have taken you to the hospital."

"It's just a cold, Ma." The words came out a wheeze. She levered herself upright, trying to look healthy.

"You and your dad," Ev said. Not affectionately, but not angrily either. Awkward silence bled from that, until she said, "I brought something for you."

"What, Ma?"

"Back when you were . . ." She paused, her mouth working. "When I was pregnant with you, I was stuck in bed a month."

Ma, talking about pregnancy. Astrid's throat clogged. "I didn't know that."

"Blood pressure. Albert brought me this to pass the time." She handed Astrid a heavy bundle, wrapped in polka-dot tissue paper.

"What is it?"

"I'd have wrapped it if I wanted to tell you?"

Another chantment? Astrid tore the paper aside, dismayed by how exhausting the effort was. Inside was a wooden case, a pine box with brass hinges and a clasp. Ma handed her a key and she fitted it to the lock.

It was a small dulcimer, sized right to sit on the bed, with two small silvery mallets.

"Before I married, I played in the town pipe band."

"You? Bagpipes?"

"Lot of old Scots in this town. I was one of the first girls they let in the band. I'd half forgot, but the therapist has got me going on all sorts of nostalgic . . ."

"Yeah? You gonna start playing again?"

"Nah. Half the band's died off." Ev set the dulcimer on the bed. "And I don't have the wind for it now."

"You're talking like you're old, Ma. You're not old." She touched a mallet to one string. A chime sounded, high and—as far as she could tell—completely unmagical.

"Albert gave my pipes away."

He'd probably chanted them. "I'm sorry."

"He gave me this when I was laid up. Figured it would keep the boredom away if I could pick out a tune or two."

"We could get you new pipes."

"I spend my days walking around town with a mail sack. I'm not strapping on the bagpipes in my leisure." Ma grinned. "I did dig out my father's old camera. Thought maybe I'd start taking pictures again."

"I don't remember you doing that either." Then she flashed on the albums: shots of Indigo Springs in the seventies, wildlife in the ravine . . . There'd even been a group of older men in kilts.

"I had the camera out the other day when . . ." Pausing, Ma actually blushed.

"What?"

"When I was watching Olive."

"You were taking spy pictures of Jacks's mother?"

Ma fidgeted, embarrassed, and Astrid felt like she'd spoiled something. To smooth the moment, she asked: "Were any of them good?"

"Lord, I'm not about to develop them. Give me another week, I'll expose the film and toss it." Raising the mallets, Ma began playing, mixing silvery chords into a cheery Highland reel.

Astrid shut her eyes, trying to imagine her mother in a kilt, marching past the fire hall with a bunch of geezers, leading a parade, perhaps, a funeral procession. . . .

Morbid thought.

They'd gone to school together, Ev and Albert. Suddenly Astrid wondered: How had he charmed her? Her laid-back, lazy-seeming father, her serious, musical mother. He hadn't magic-mermaided her into loving him, had he?

No. Dad wouldn't. Besides, he hadn't become the chanter until after he was married.

The reel ended and Ev handed her the mallets. "You try."

"I don't know how."

"I'll point at strings, you hit them."

"Okay." Following Ma's fingers, she plunked out a creditable version of "Mary Had a Little Lamb."

"See? Easy."

She tinkled out random notes, pleased by the way the chords hung in the air. "You were in bed how long?"

"Five weeks. You came late, remember?"

"Right."

"First and only time you were. Perfect attendance at school . . ." Stretching, Ev opened the curtains, cracking the patio doors and letting in a blast of air that set Astrid to shivering. Then her hand came to rest on Astrid's bureau. "Did you find Albert's clippings after all?"

"What? . . ." Then she remembered—Ma's vitagua contamination. Sahara had printed out some news stories from the Web, about people in trouble they might send chantments to. They were in the top drawer, below Ev's palm. "Snoop."

"Hyperobservant," Ma countered, with a trace of her Everett Burke huffiness but no anger.

"They're for Sahara's self-help website."

"I had a tough time getting Jacks to leave," Ev said. "He's awfully fond, isn't he?"

"Ma, my love life . . ."

"None of my business, true. But I wouldn't sit around waiting for a better offer. I'd run her down."

She pulled the covers tight, her teeth chattering. "How did Dad catch your eye?"

"We told you this story a hundred times, kid."

"He won a track meet and you melted? You must have cut out something. I mean, Dad was . . ." She wheezed. Dad was a magician, a miracle worker. A hero. "Dad couldn't have been the Springs' most eligible bachelor."

"Ah, the shiftless Lethewood boys," Ma said musingly. "They were too. Wouldn't stir if they were boiling over. But when Albert was racing . . . it's like he was trying to catch something. He had a way of wanting things, Astrid."

"And he wanted you like that?"

"Like I was air and he was drowning," Ma said, half smiling. "When he caught me, he seemed to appreciate it too. But when his great-grandmother died he changed. Started running again, but to the flea markets. Grief does funny things."

Astrid took Ev's hand again, feeling the callused firmness of it, remembering holding it as a kid, little fingers swallowed in Ma's, safe in her strong grip.

"You cut yourself," she said, rubbing a small scab.

"Caught the rough edge of the Johnsons' gate latch."

Astrid let her hand fold over the scab, dropping her arm to the covers. Knowledge hummed in her. Third time's the charm, she thought, and she picked up one dulcimer mallet, plonked a note. Ev took up the other mallet.

Astrid tugged on the vitagua inside them both, pulling the little bit inside her mother ever so gently through the break in her skin. She watched Ma from the corner of her gaze as they improvised music together.

Vitagua flowed out of Ev bit by tiny bit. A tablespoon, maybe two. Unlike the iced slush in Astrid's body, it was warm and mobile. She pushed it against the cold places in her lungs.

Then there wasn't any more to draw, just the inevitable residue, a blue tinge around the picked scab.

A thumping sounded at the front door.

"I'll get that," Ma said.

"No, I need to get up." She tottered to her feet, discovering as she did so that she was wrapped in Sahara's pajama top. Clove oil wafted up as she buttoned it.

The banging stopped. Astrid headed downstairs anyway, struggling against a sense that the floor was rocking back and forth. Dizzily, she fixed her eyes on the upper corner of the hall and squeezed the banister.

The walls lurched—taking her frozen stomach along for the ride. Ma laid a hot hand on Astrid's shoulder. The room wobbled, and then froze in place.

"You okay, baby?"

"I'll make it." She shuffled across the unfurnished expanse of the living room, wrinkling up a white sheet that lay spread on the pink carpet. The doorknob was cool to the touch, setting off more shivers as she grasped it.

The porch was empty. Out of habit she glanced down.

"What are you doing?" Ev asked.

"Looking for a killed . . . bird. I forgot for a second about Henna being dead."

"Henna's what?" The voice was unexpected and shocked.

Wobbling, Astrid turned.

Sahara's ex, Mark Clumber, was at the edge of the living room, wearing smudged glasses and a stricken expression. Seeing him, Astrid lost her balance. She fell against the doorframe, openmouthed and gasping. Mark. Come to take Sahara away?

They might have stayed like that forever—or at least until Astrid collapsed—if Ma hadn't intervened.

"Your Henna passed last week, son," she said. Kicking the

sheet on the floor aside, she led Astrid to the stairs and nudged her so she sat. "I'm sorry to have to tell you."

"Dead," he repeated. "A car hit her?"

"Ah . . ." Ev paused. "She fell sick? Astrid?"

She nodded dumbly, distantly noting that Mark's hair was thinning. In high school he had dyed it a vivid tangerine. Now it was a collection of mottled blue and green swatches, mixed with hanks of his natural color, a light brown that implied blondness without achieving it. Behind the glasses, his eyes were two different shades of brown—one walnut, one cedar. His teeth had been rigorously straightened.

Sahara bullied him into getting braces, then complained about how dumb they looked, she thought.

Mark and Sahara had become close after Astrid dropped out of high school to save Dad's gardening business. He'd barely been on her radar until it was too late.

"It happens with animals, sometimes," Ev said. "One day they're good, the next . . ."

"Henna wasn't old," he said, cleaning his glasses with his shirt. "You did feed her?"

Astrid wiped her mouth, remembering her teeth in the cat's neck, fur bunched around her lips as she tore vitagua out of Henna's body.

She examined Mark critically, trying to disperse guilt with contempt. He was unshaven, and his pants hung on him like old banana peels. He wore a white tank top speckled with brown stains and his mismatched eyes were shadowed.

"Was there an autopsy?" he asked.

"For a cat?"

"Come to think of it," Ev said, "you did bury him awfully quickly. Whose idea—?"

"Ma—" Then she saw Ev's eyes were twinkling. "You're joking," she said, almost voiceless with surprise.

"Son, it's not a person. And it's a hundred degrees out. Of course they buried it fast," Ev said.

Mark shook himself. "Right. No autopsy."

Astrid buried her head in her hands. The room lurched, and she hissed uncomfortably. A tense silence fell.

"Where's Sahara?" Mark said at last.

"Shouldn't you be with your new girlfriend, Mark?"

"I don't have a new girlfriend, okay? I'm miserably single, unlike you two."

"Pardon?"

He sneered. "You finally get her on her back, or are you just borrowing her pajamas?"

"What do you care?" Astrid's stomach leapt again, but this time the room wasn't spinning.

"Fine. Be her exotic rebound fling. Just don't be surprised when she finds an excuse to toss you away."

"Excuse? You cheated on her."

"And I quote, what do you care? I just want the car and an apology, okay? Then I'm out of here."

"Apology for what?" Clapping a hand over her mouth, Astrid coughed. Blue ice sprayed her palm, melting into her skin. She put it behind her back.

Ev had bent to pick up the sheet on the living room floor. Now she straightened, folding the fabric. "Excuse me, son. Am I to understand you came all the way across the country to hear Sahara Knax say she's sorry for something?"

He scowled at Astrid. "Tell her."

"It's Mark's car, Ma. Sahara took it."

He was looking at her expectantly, tapping the toe of one dirty running shoe. "Tell her the rest."

"Rest of what?" She fought another cough.

"You help her do it? You bitch."

"Son, you're not staying if you can't be civil." Ev caught Mark by the shoulder and pushed him into a chair.

He started to rise. "I—"

"Young man." There was no Everett Burke in Ma's tone—just the old steel. Mark stayed put.

"Honestly, Mark," Astrid said. "I don't know what else you're talking about."

"She didn't gloat?"

She shook her head.

"Little Miss Busyfingers has a vengeful streak. She gets out here and decides she doesn't like the deal we made over the 'Ask Suzu' page. She goes on the Web, spreads rumors—an impostor's writing the advice column—"

Astrid interrupted. "You did put new columns up."

"Then she gets cute. She hints around the newsgroups that Suzu is missing. Suddenly Sahara's fans are calling Boston Homicide, claiming someone's killed their guru."

Ev frowned. "Surely the police could determine that Sahara wasn't dead."

"You'd think that, wouldn't you?" Mark said. "But guess what my neighbors told 'em? 'Mark had a fight with his girlfriend and nobody's seen her since.' 'Mark's car's missing and my dog found her hair in his trash.'"

"Why didn't you just have her call them?" Ev asked.

"She won't answer my e-mails," Mark said.

"She wouldn't do that," Astrid said.

"Then why are the cops convinced I'm Jack the Ripper?"

"Sounds like you should have gotten to know your neighbors," Ev said. "If they'd come to like you—"

"Why didn't you just call?" Astrid interrupted. The ache in her chest was getting worse.

"Because he's hooked on melodrama." Sahara stepped through the back door, a nasty gleam in her eyes that hinted she'd been eavesdropping for a while. "You blew town, huh? Way to convince them you're innocent, moron."

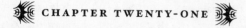

CHAPTER TWENTY-ONE

ALWAYS THE BIG ENTRANCE, Astrid thought tiredly as Sahara and Mark began to shout. Rising voices battered her eardrums, and all Astrid could do was wheeze.

Finally Mark began stamping his feet, drumming the floor with his boot heels until everyone shut up. "The cops think I killed you."

Sahara laughed. "Honey, you're in no danger. You're innocent, remember? They can trace my credit history."

Head sick. Astrid thought uneasily of the vitagua contamination. "Sahara, you didn't."

"Mark, as long as you don't confess or run, they'll work it out. Oh wait . . . you ran."

"I want the car."

"Too bad. I crashed it."

"What?"

"It's slag, Mark. Wrecked it on my way out West. Had to bus here from Chicago. Right, Astrid?"

No. The word rose to her lips. Then Sahara's amused mask slipped. Desperation flickered in its place—a plea for solidarity. "Yes," she said. "She hit a tree. She still had a shiner when she arrived."

Ma coughed, disappointment stamped on her face. Sometimes, Astrid thought, you couldn't win.

Mark's jaw worked furiously. "Wrecked. Sure."

Sahara spun abruptly, emptying her purse onto the counter. Her fist closed on the mermaid pendant.

"Wait," Astrid said. "We don't need to go crazy here."

But Sahara had already dropped the pendant over her head. "Mark, we're not going to argue." Her voice thrummed, and

Astrid's skin buzzed with vibrations. A glass beside the sink shivered and cracked. "Mark, go back to Elaine's for the night. Hang out, eat dinner at McMurdy's, do whatever, but keep your mouth shut."

Mark's chest jerked, shoulders rolling inward as if he'd been punched just below the throat. "Shut," he mumbled, pushing his glasses up on his face.

"Talk to anyone you want, just don't go whining about me," Sahara clarified. "Come back in the morning and we'll discuss the car. Okay?"

"'Kay." He lurched into the hall.

Astrid glanced at her mother, only to find her watching Sahara vacantly.

"Ev?" Sahara asked. The buzz in her tone lessened. "How you doing?"

"Fine," Ma said distantly.

"Listen, why don't you go too? Help Mark get home to his sister's. Then go about your day."

Ma followed Mark without another word.

"How could you let him in?" Sahara swooned against the counter. She pulled an energy shake from the fridge and struggled to open the can.

"Did you really set the police on him?" Astrid said.

"Don't change the subject."

"Sahara, you . . . zapped him. Zapped them both."

"Mark resigned from my life. Guest appearances are not allowed."

"But if the police think he killed you—"

"Cheating, fickle piece of . . . If I had any guts, I'd have set him on fire."

"You don't mean that."

"Don't I?"

"You framed him for murder!" She fought down a cough, pain sparking through her chest. She was freezing.

"It just worked out that way."

"That's . . ."

"Crazy? I'm not contaminated anymore, remember?"

Residue, Astrid thought, but the anger in her friend's eyes kept her from saying it.

"Maybe you just think I'm a bitch."

"Mark won't back off just because you used the mermaid on him. You have to talk to him every day now, remember?"

"Ah, sweet wizard." Drawing composure around herself like a shawl, Sahara kissed Astrid's head. "Our situation has improved since you fell into your enchanted sleep."

"Meaning?"

There was a thump from the direction of the bathroom.

Sahara groaned. "Idiot. He went the wrong way down the hall."

Mark and Ma emerged from the hallway before Astrid could intercept them. Ev had Mark by the arm, leading him back toward the kitchen and Sahara.

Astrid rushed to the front door. "This way, Ma," she wheezed.

She threw the door open . . . and was startled to catch Jacks's father out on the porch, his fist raised. He'd been about to knock.

She squeaked in surprise and Chief Lee jerked back a step. He hadn't been expecting her either, she guessed.

"Hey, Astie." He glared down at her, face red, as if she'd popped out just to scare him.

Before she could reply, Ev and Mark trooped past. Ev gave the Chief a quick and very sane smile as she guided her young charge down the steps. "We'll get you to your sister's," she said, and Mark grunted.

"Jacks isn't here, Chief," Astrid said. It was practically a reflex. The fireman was staring after Ma and Sahara's ex as they departed.

"That the Clumber boy?"

"Yes," she said. "He's visiting from out of town."

He nodded, visibly filing the gossip but suddenly far away.

"Chief? Jacks isn't here."

He glowered, then stepped through the doorway. "Late in the day for your pj's, innit?"

She blushed, realizing how tight and short the orange T-shirt was. Its buttons gapped at the front—she was broader across the shoulders than Sahara. "I've been sick."

"I heard. Where's your furniture?" He looked past her into the living room, taking in the tacky blue fireplace. Astrid couldn't help glancing at the ceiling, with its vitagua stain. What would he make of that?

But the stain was gone.

Sahara painted again while I was ill, she thought, remembering the sheet that had been laid out across the rug. It was hanging on the back of a chair now, folded and inconspicuous—Ma's doing.

She felt a glimmer of gratitude, relief that Sahara had covered up the blue stain, that she was working to keep the secret without Astrid's having to watch and nag.

"I have furniture everywhere else," she said. "It's just this room's empty. Want the grand tour?"

"No, I won't wear you out." He peered down at her. "So, what is it? The flu?"

"Guess so." Self-conscious, she crossed her arms over her chest.

"When's Jacks coming back?"

"I wasn't up when he left."

Sahara chose that moment to appear, a bathrobe in her arms and—thankfully—no mermaid pendant in sight. "You should go back to bed," she said. "Chief, Jacks ran into Lorry Hamilton downtown and got conned into taking him home. I don't figure he'll be back anytime soon."

The Chief's expression soured.

"You can wait in the kitchen if you like. I'll fix some tea." She slipped the robe over Astrid's shoulders. "I think we have some vegan muffins."

He sighed. "You don't want me around all afternoon."

"I doubt the town could do without you that long," Sahara said sweetly.

"I'll tell Jacks you came by," Astrid added.

"Right." With a curt nod, he jogged down the steps and was gone.

Sahara shut the door loudly, throwing the dead bolt. "I thought for a second he was gonna force his way in."

"And then you'd have zapped him?"

"Ha," she said. "Wonder how Jacks would take that?"

"Was it true?"

"What?"

"Where Jacks went."

"Yep. Lorry had a painting to show our resident artiste. Way Jacks's luck has been running, I figured it's probably a lost van Gogh. Plus he was drunk."

"Jacks?"

"Lorry. Jacks had to see he got home safe. Hey, you're awake!" She swept Astrid into a hug, setting off painful shivers in her midsection and triggering an inexplicable urge to cry.

Astrid pulled free. "Speaking of brainwashed elders—how come Ma's so improved?"

"Ta da," Sahara sang. "I've been practicing. You said the more you practice magic, the better you get?"

"Yeah," she said. "Speaking of which, I drained her. With luck we won't have to zap her very often now."

"Wonderful," Sahara said, but her expression clouded.

"What's wrong?"

"What if Ev likes knowing what's in the mail?"

"You ought to be glad," Astrid said. "The less you need to use Siren on her, the better."

"I don't mind."

She reached for Sahara's hand, but her friend pulled away. "I know you want to recontaminate yourself."

"If I did, I'd have jumped in that puddle in the unreal, wouldn't I?"

Jacks was watching you like a hawk, Astrid thought, but it wasn't worth arguing.

"Astrid, I've been thinking."

"Yeah?"

"You know I'm setting up a new advice column online, marketing myself as a psychic. I'll open an e-store, sell books, Tarot cards, crystals . . ."

"Did you make a lot from your old site?"

"No. But I was thinking—what if I did some public appearances? At psychic conferences, music festivals, Renaissance faires . . ."

"What—oh. Appearances with Siren?"

"I'd just use it here and there, on people with cash they're gonna spend anyway."

"No," she said. "It'll get noticed. We're supposed to be under everyone's radar, remember?"

"Please. Even with inflation, Web self-help gurus are still only a dollar a dozen. This could help people, Astrid, and we could use it to cover up our cash flow."

Sahara on the road with Siren. She tried to stand straighter, and was dismayed by the pain. Her stomach cramped.

"Your dad hid what he was doing by pretending to be a shiftless mooch. You can't do that."

"If anyone realizes you're using chantments to make people buy stuff, they'll trace the money here."

"So I'll move—"

"No!" It came out too loud, and Sahara's brows quirked in astonishment. Astrid folded her arms over her chest to keep from trembling.

"I'll move the company address," Sahara finished.

"Eventually the money comes here," Astrid said dully.

"We're not hiding from Homeland Security. An ancient cult of witch-burners, that's who Albert said to watch for."

"We can't," Astrid said. "Make things right with Mark and get rid of him, okay?"

"Make things right?" Sahara repeated scornfully.

She struggled to find the right words, gentle words. "He's suspected of murder, Sahara. I know he was unfaithful, but that's pretty mean."

"I didn't expect it to go so far—how could I? You've got to admit there's a funny side."

Astrid smiled, pretending she agreed it was funny. "Just now, the way you hit him with the mermaid—"

"Astrid, nobody is going to notice us."

Astrid winced. Maybe they'd be better off if Jacks made good on his threat to blowtorch the mermaid pendant. "Let's talk about this when Jacks gets home."

"Why? We're pretending this is a democracy, but you're the chantment maker, you own the house, you get the instructions from Dear Dead Dad. I'm your minion. If you're going to veto me, have the guts to admit it."

Astrid raised her gaze to the ceiling. Now that she looked again, the paint job wasn't perfect. A blue shadow was just barely visible through the white. She eyed the fireplace uneasily. Had Albert painted it to hide a vitagua stain? Was that why he'd painted the chimney?

The frozen expanse of the unreal rose in her memory, silent, waiting, and reproachful. The trapped tree-dwellers . . . how long were they supposed to wait to be freed?

"Astrid, where are you going?"

She hadn't realized she was moving. "I need to think."

"Think here! You're sick—you're not even dressed."

Tightening the bathrobe around her waist, she stepped into her sandals and shuffled out to her truck.

"Astrid, I wasn't trying to upset you, it's just . . . you *can't* go."

"Stop me," she rasped, getting in. The sun-baked cab of her truck was a furnace, and she felt the internal chills subside a little as she started the engine. Sahara's protests blew away in the wind as she drove off.

She turned onto Ravine Road, then right at Penance Way. Trees rolled by on either side of the road, blurring green in the windows.

Maybe if I just keep turning randomly, I'll find Albert's favorite old flea market. Then she was bouncing down the gravel maintenance road that ran behind the cottages at Great Blue Reservoir.

Astrid had been ten back when Albert started working as a gardener for the resort. In the summers he'd take her with him to work. Sometimes she found kids to play with on the beach, children whose parents had rented the cabins. Mostly, though, she roamed the woods around the Reservoir.

Parking at the back, she cinched the bathrobe again and staggered along a trail at the edge of the property, following it down a spruce-covered hill. Grass rubbed her exposed ankles, and she broke through cobwebs with every step. Twice she got so out of breath, she had to stop. The third time she succumbed to a coughing fit so severe that her vision fogged over.

The land had been bought at the turn of the century by an eccentric coal baron with ideas about building a castle on the riverbank. He'd left the place to a daughter with a more practical turn of mind, and in the fifties she had built the cabins, opening the lake to summer tourists. Astrid remembered her, a little—she taught grade school in town for over forty years. When she died, the cabins went to a cousin who hired a manager to handle the business.

Springers had always claimed Mrs. Voltone was a legendary pack rat, that she kept every student gift, every lesson plan, every program from school recitals. Astrid was probably the only one who knew this legend was true. The house the old teacher lived in—and the junk collection—had been untouched since she died.

The abandoned house looked the same as when she'd prowled it as a kid—guarded by garden gnomes with smashed-in faces, swaddled in overgrown hedges, its windows oily. Pushing on a cracked window frame to gain access to the latch, she found the gap was too small for her adult-sized hand. She had to knock out the glass with a rock instead.

Then she was reaching in to unlatch the rusted door, raising dustclouds as she pushed her way inside and stared at the shelves of school trophies and bric-a-brac—ceramic cats, child-crafted clay mushrooms, a coffee can that had been covered in glued-on macaroni and then spray-painted gold, wooden flutes, a lumpy plastic doll, a horseshoe, rubber flies—all of it on garish random display.

"A little sparkle," Astrid said, retrieving a shard of broken glass from the floor. She inched over to the nearest likely item, a necklace hanging on a crooked shelf. Then she sliced into the back of her hand with the shard.

Red blood and blinding pain. Vitagua pushed toward her arm, eager to bond with the necklace but too slushy to flow freely. It tried anyway, dragging—at least it felt that way—her internal organs with it.

Eyes streaming, hunched over and shivering, Astrid fumbled the buttons of Sahara's pajama top. A cold knob of shining blue skin bulged under her left breast, and she pressed the glass against it. Just a pinprick, she thought, but the skin tore open in a ragged line.

Secrecy forgotten, Astrid screamed. She heard a sound like pipes emptying: blue slush rocketing out of her chest. It struck the necklace of fake pearls, vanishing inside them and leaving them glistening. Then it changed direction, soaking a rag doll on the shelf nearest Astrid. A massive pinecone covered in silver glitter was next, followed by a plastic pony and a cast-iron griddle.

Strength flooded into her body, bringing warmth, a sense of safety. The dreadful sense of the future dulled. The certainty that Sahara would flee Indigo Springs diminished, and Astrid could finally breathe.

By now the force of the vitagua spray inside her chest was

diminishing. The stream washed over a wooden vinegar cruet next, and then an old photograph. A last drop spat over one of the horseshoes. Then she was bleeding—painlessly—from a gash under her breast.

"Exit wound," she gasped, and the dust seemed to rise slightly at her words before settling once more.

The vitagua, all but that last indelible trace, was gone. Her head cleared, pain receding for the first time since she'd found the vitagua in the fireplace. She touched the blue-tinged edges of the rupture in her skin.

The grumbles quieted to whispers. The knowledge she had gained in the unreal—the story of how vitagua had formed, Patterflam's history, all of it—seemed to dim, becoming dreamy, untrustworthy. At the same time, the room glowed. Astrid scanned Mrs. Voltone's carefully stored objects, and saw their chanting potential everywhere.

They all had sparkle now, not just the handful of items she had noticed when she first staggered inside. Only the glass knick-knacks and an old adding machine remained dull and magic-resistant.

"Getting better at it," she grunted.

How very like Albert she would seem if anybody caught her now—trespassing, half-dressed, looting the ancestral home of a venerable Springer family. Maybe Sahara was right, and they needed a better way to do things. If she didn't want sole responsibility for the magic, she had to let her friends make some of the rules.

With the pain and chill and pessimistic grumbles gone, Astrid found it easier to take hope in the future.

"And if Sahara left, whose fault would that be?" she said as she tucked the chantments she'd made into a canvas gym bag. "You can't expect someone to read your mind."

Putting a life together. That's what she was supposed to be doing. That's what Sahara was trying to help her with. This magic stuff of Dad's had to fit in, but it didn't have to be everything.

Humming Ma's Highland air, she skulked to her truck and found her first-aid kit. After bandaging her chest, she drove home.

As Astrid pulled up, Sahara came sprinting across the yard. The terror on her face was genuine, not at all the look of someone who would abandon her.

"I'm fine," Astrid said, before she could ask.

"I thought you'd passed out and had an accident!"

She shook her head. "I just had to decontaminate."

Sahara's voice dropped. "You chanted something?"

"Maybe too many somethings." Astrid handed her the bag. "We have to unload these fast."

Her friend barely glanced at the chantments, instead throwing an arm around her and squeezing.

She hugged back, inhaling the clove scent of Sahara's hair. "Let's go out somewhere tonight, you and me."

"I'm on the air," Sahara answered. "Early show."

"You're off at nine? We'll have supper late, like big-city girls. Somewhere fancy, my treat."

Sahara licked her lips. "What's the occasion?"

"Me not freezing . . . no. Me having a life."

"Astrid day," Sahara said.

"Say yes and I'll buy you a steak."

Sahara laughed. "Here I am trying to figure how to explain to Jacks that I let you run off and you're—"

Astrid hopped in place. "Say yes, Princess."

Sahara dropped a curtsy. "Why, Miz Wizard. It would be an honor and a pleasure."

Astrid bowed, and flourished her arms outward.

CHAPTER TWENTY-TWO

"MAGIC WANTS TO BE known," Astrid says, twirling a lock of hair on her fingers. Before her, old playing cards are being bleached white and repainted with new images almost faster than my eye can follow.

"What does that mean?"

"It means becoming a chanter is about opening yourself to the vitagua. Being initiated into a vitagua well gives you access to all the knowledge of the unreal. The more vitagua you take in, the more you hear the grumbles. But there's a downside. The more you hear, the more confused you get. Too many voices, each with its own agenda . . ."

I pick up a card that shows the young Astrid with her father, the two of them sitting with a single drop of vitagua between them in a golden bowl. "My impression is that your father never got terribly good at chanting."

"The grumbles scared Albert. He made small chantments and got rid of them fast."

"He kept his vitagua exposure low?"

"It kept the grumbles quiet," Astrid said. "Me, on the other hand—a year passed after his death before I found the well in the fireplace. There'd been buildup. I got a big blast of spirit water all at once. That—and the amount of chanting I had to do—taught me a lot. By the time I'd made all those chantments in the old Voltone house, tons of things had Dad's sparkle. He needed antiques, but I outgrew that. If I hadn't siphoned out my vitagua reserves, I could have chanted every piece of bric-a-brac in that old house."

"Except the glass and electronic gadgets." I rub my face. "So it wasn't that you had more natural ability to begin with?"

"No, my basic ability *was* stronger. Dad did a good job of initiating me. . . ." She looks—to see if I remember why.

"He'd done it before . . . some cousin who died?"

"Right. Cousin Ron and then some other guy. 'Third time's the charm,'" he said to me that day.

"What other guy?"

"Dad never said for sure, but he had been pals—in a quiet way—with this greenhouse operator's son."

"Why do you think it was him?"

"Because he died in a gas explosion."

"Ah."

"My point is that Albert had initiated people before. When my turn came, he was good at it. Then I got exposed to more vitagua than him, I made more chantments than he did, and I accidentally visited the unreal. Of course I was a better chanter."

"And it was your second time learning," I say. "How is it that you forgot what Albert taught you as a child?"

"I—" Her hand drifts upward, to her ravaged ear. "Jemmy's on the move." The change in her tone makes me tense up, even before the emergency lights flicker out. "I bet your recorder's dead now."

I do a rundown on my pager, phone, and recorder, looking for battery lights. "All dead," I report. The idea that we aren't being monitored comes as a relief. It is a bad sign: Astrid is engaging me, and I need to pull back.

"What's going on upstairs? Is Sahara here?"

Astrid utters a lyrical mishmash of nonsense words, and suddenly I can see again. She has chanted one of the teaspoons. Light blazes from it like a torch. "Yes, Will, Sahara's come."

She hands me the spoon. Its handle is chilly.

"She's here for you?"

She nods. "She wants me to make her followers into people like Patience."

"You knew about this? Why didn't you warn Roche?"

A flinty smile. "I'm the bad guy, remember?"

There is a sound of things breaking, muffled by the thick walls, and then gunfire.

"Oh," Astrid says. "*This* is the part where the guards start shooting."

"What's happening?"

"Sahara's Primas are holding off the troops."

"Primas, here?" I think of Caro, and my stomach burns. "What about Sahara?"

"She's with Ma. Will, your ring is a protective chantment. You're completely safe."

"Says the alleged bad guy."

"She won't keep us waiting long." Now she does rise, leaning against her grandfather's cabinet, breathing in its woody scent before licking the wood. Blue fluid seeps from her tongue and into its structure. The grain of the oak glimmers blue before the vitagua is absorbed.

"Another chantment? What does this one do?"

"Toughens things up." She lays both hands on the cabinet and sings the cantation again. Then she sets one of the empty teacups inside, closing it. Bringing it out, she invites me to smash it.

I clunk the delicate china against a wall and the jolt travels up my elbow. It feels diamond hard.

"Try again?"

"No." The floor trembles. Astrid could have walked out of here anytime, I think. Roche ought to forget about Jemmy Burlein and the others.

But there's no getting out, no warning him. All I can do is my job. I raise the spoon, noting the moonlight silver of its glow, and continue the interview. "You say after your experience at the Voltone house, you could chant a wider range of items."

"Yes."

"Albert could only chant antiques. Why antiques?"

She weighs her answer, her expression suddenly calculating. "Albert preferred things that had been loved."

"When did you get to the point where you could control what an item would become when you chanted it?"

"A couple days after the batch at Voltone's."

"Your learning process was accelerating." I touch the bright bowl of the spoon. It isn't hot; I can close my fingers over it. The blood within me glows red.

Astrid plucks a couple of her photographs off the wall and puts them in the cabinet, toughening them up.

I sort through the facts. "On your first trip to the unreal, the vitagua in your body froze. You became ill."

"Yes. I almost froze myself solid trying to contain Patterflam."

"And it was all ice, all of Fairyland."

"Yes."

"You took me to the unreal, and it was warm and dry."

She nods. "All the vitagua the witch-burners forced out of the real? It's thawing."

I don't like the sound of that. "The unreal is warming? What about the people frozen in the icebergs?"

"They're getting loose, of course." She puts the paintbrush handle inside the cabinet. "Luckily for the real, most of them are too busy celebrating to think about revenge."

"For how long?" A flutter in my gut. I flash on campouts from my Boy Scout days, remember that I always hated ghost stories, darkness, and freaky tales.

"Some big players are still stuck in those ice floes."

"Elves or something? Brownies?"

"The fairies and leprechauns are dead. The witch-burners did a thorough job on the Old World's magical ecosystem."

"Who then?"

She gives me a moment to come up with the answer, then shrugs. "Raven, maybe? Wendigo. Quetzalcoatl."

"You expect me to tell Roche a bunch of old Indian myths are going to rise from the grave—"

"And bite him on the ass? It's true."

"Why would Raven be around if the fairies are gone?"

She sighs. "Will, the witch-burners owned Europe when they started their crusade against enchantment. They had to *take* the Americas, inch by inch. There were people here—spirits, walking gods—and they weren't dumb. They saw what was happening and banked their power in the unreal. They hoped their shamans and medicine women could trickle magic back drop by drop, without doing any harm—"

"No *harm*? We've got a flood on our hands, and Sahara busted the dams."

"They're busted, it's true," she says, voice rising. "I don't know what I was doing."

She is panicking. With the paintbrush chantment locked in the cabinet, Astrid is losing track of past and present again. I open the cabinet and hand it to her.

She gulps air for a second. "Albert's great-great-grandmother Melissa was a proper white lady whose adopted sister happened to be Elizabeth Walks-in-Shadow. Melissa got Elizabeth's birthright because her tribe was dead. Maybe she stole it from her, I don't know. The Almore family—my family—got the chanting ability, but they never understood the magical well. Dad was hastily initiated and scared of its power. He didn't trust the grumbles, and never learned how things worked. A spill was inevitable."

"So it's fate? Fate's to blame?"

"I'm to blame," she says. "If I'd listened to Jacks about the potlatch massacre . . ."

"You can't expect to convince anyone that what's happening is payback for the past five hundred years. Sahara's not Native. She's not spearheading some anti-colonial Renaissance."

"Renaissance? Try Apocalypse." She raises her gaze to the ceiling. "Those five hundred years could get wiped off the board. It could all go, Will—elections, satellite TV, presweetened breakfast cereal. Sahara's no Renaissance. She's out to destroy the world she used to love."

I laugh. "People aren't going to give up centuries of democracy, freedom, and technology without a fight."

"You are fighting."

"You're saying we'll lose? Astrid?"

"I am the one with the sneak preview. You're just some guy who's afraid to grow flowers in his own backyard."

My face heats.

She plucks a silk begonia off one of the fake plants, chanting it. Once this crisis passes, we'll have to put her in a cell with nothing but glass objects. How will we keep Patience from slipping things to her?

Reciting a cantation with the fake blossom between her hands, Astrid brushes it over her wardrobe. The cabinet shrinks, becoming smaller and smaller, until it is less than an inch high. Bending to pick it off the floor, she puts it in the pocket of her shirt.

Packing up her treasures . . . I try to think of ways to raise an alarm amid a blackout. "Astrid . . ."

"The nice cultivated world is over with, Will. No amount of pruning or even firebombing is gonna keep the weeds from overrunning the petunias. The only questions are how long will it take and how ugly is it gonna get?"

Below the cuffs of her shirt and under her hair, she glows with dim blue light.

"I can't accept that. Sahara's not that powerful."

"It's okay to be sad." Our eyes meet and my inner criminal analyst sees how good Astrid is at engaging me. "I am. I liked the old world fine."

"There must be a way to stop her."

"Sahara? She's just riding the flood." She leans against the fake picture window, her breath fogging a circle on the dead, opaque glass. "Using magic to pull in the gullible, the weak—"

"Meaning what?"

Another bump and more shots—closer than before.

We're shut down tight, I remind myself.

The steel bolts bang open . . . and I am in the presence of Sahara Knax.

She is taller than I expected. Long-limbed, willowy, and terrifying, she glows blue. She has none of Astrid's control: the liquid roils randomly, squirting from one part of her body to another, raising her skin in bulges.

Sahara's long hair is mottled with the iridescent markings of starlings. Brown feathered wings sprout from her shoulder blades. Her leather coat—a blue sheath with dozens of bulging pockets—has been modified accordingly.

Sahara's eyes are dark and beady. Her fingers are shaped like talons, sharp-tipped and cruel. Her mouth is pursed, half a beak but still lip-pink. Necklaces dangle from her throat, bracelets from her wrists. Rings encrust her fingers.

Two of Sahara's so-called Primas are with her, similarly bedecked. Ev Lethewood stands between them, dressed as a man, fully bearded, ears pointed and bristling with white hairs, like a goat's. One of the women gripping Ev's forearm is Jemmy Burlein, Astrid's onetime lover.

Sahara is completely focused on Astrid.

Jemmy moves, stepping sideways so that I, like Astrid and Ev, am encircled by the three Alchemites.

"Time we struck a deal," Sahara says.

"No, it's not that time." Astrid smiles at her mother. "Hi, Pop."

"Petey," Ev Lethewood replies, back in the grip of delusion.

"Sahara wants me to work for her, Will. She brought Ev as a hostage. It's not just Patterflam's curse, you see. Albert would say she's got the greeds."

"Astrid," Sahara growls. "Stop talking to this drone and shut up about the curse."

"Take a person whose weakness is selfishness. Add vitagua and—"

Sahara raises an old-fashioned cigarette case and cracks it open. A thin stream of fire burns from its opening, crisping a line across the floor, through the couch. The singed upholstery reeks and burns as she plays the flame over Astrid's wall of photographs.

"So you're a firebug now?" Astrid says. Alarms ring and sprinklers chug, soaking us with chilly water. "Just like old times. Wait. When are we?" Her hand rises to her throat.

"I will hurt her, Astrid." Sahara glances at Ev with her dark avian eyes. "You think I won't?"

"Are you that far gone?"

Trilling laughter, Sahara turns, opening her magic flamethrower full-on.

In my face.

A furnace of heat blows past me, scorching the air. As I flinch, raising my hands over my face, flames play over my skin . . . but I do not burn. My hair doesn't so much as crisp. The heat is answered by a chilly gust from my ring. The fire goes out.

Heart pounding, suddenly famished, I start for Sahara. Her Primas grab for my arms, and as I shake them off, something moves through me.

It's Patience, using her unusual ability to go misty to pass through my body. "Boo!" she shouts. Sahara backpedals, startled. Jemmy Burlein releases Ev, groping for a chantment of her own.

And like that, we are in the unreal again—me, Astrid, Patience, and Evelyn Lethewood. Sahara and her Primas are left behind. There's the sound of starlings shrieking, far away. A white dust devil swirls up from the chalky soil underfoot.

"So this is Fairyland?" Ev says, and in the same instant Patience points at the twisting vortex of sand and asks, "What's that?"

"Sahara's trying to break through," Astrid says, wrapping her mother in a tight hug. I look away as mother and daughter cling to each other, laughing and crying.

Painted and unpainted playing cards are scattered at my feet, fluttering like windblown leaves. I bend to collect them as I ask: "Is this what I think it is?"

"It was a jail break." Astrid hands me a protein bar.

"I can't allow you to leave."

"You can't stop me. You must know that by now."

"You can't go," I say. "Astrid, there are people out there who want to kill you. Unless you plan to hide in the unreal forever, your safety is at risk."

"You'd rather Sahara got her?" Patience slays me with a reproachful frown. Her body changed when she slid through me. She is an Aztec goddess: copper-skinned, with coal-colored hair. Her hands are exquisitely symmetrical, and she smells of cocoa.

"What part is this?" Astrid melts into confusion and I pass over the cards. She sighs, almost petting them as she thumbs through the deck.

"Give her a minute," Patience murmurs to me. "Ev? Sweetie, you okay?"

"Damn glad to be out of that cell," Ev says. Her *a*'s are drawn out into goat-bleats: *da-a-am, gla-a-ad*. She peers at me suspiciously.

"Hello, Mr. Burke," I say. "I'm Will—I interviewed you Monday, remember?"

"Sure. Good cop to Artie Roche's bad. Been interrogating Petey? You won't get anything out of him."

"Will's okay, Pop," Astrid says. "You'll see."

"What does that mean?" I ask.

"Let's get going, shall we?" Ev offers Patience a gallant bow and her arm, and they set out.

Consulting her cards, Astrid looks at me. "Coming?"

What can I do but fall in beside her? "I thought you'd jump at the chance to be with Sahara again."

Looking tired, she rubs her throat. "She's no good for me."

"You love her."

"You said it yourself: She doesn't forgive. If you remember to tell Roche anything, it's that. I'm just another magic toy to her now."

"What do *you* want from *her*?"

She doesn't answer.

At the top of the canyon, the heat is less intense, the land less barren. Chalk-white grass fuzzes over a series of rolling hills, and man-sized jade formations jut upward through the sod like teeth cutting up from gums. Shivering puddles of vitagua lie in the shadows of the stones.

"We need to head east, Will? That's the fastest route out of the compound?"

"I couldn't say."

"East," Patience affirms.

"You don't have to come," Astrid says. "I'm no kidnapper."

"You've got to return to custody, Astrid."

"You're welcome to tag along and try to change my mind. Right, Patience?"

Patience nods, skipping in her pointy shoes.

"What was I talking about?" Astrid asks.

I look at her blankly.

She consults the card in her hand. "The Astrid day dinner. My big date with Sahara."

"What?" I see paint crawling over yet another card. Astrid is going on with her tale, as though we are all still locked away in the underground vault.

It takes me a second to switch gears. "Did you tell her you wanted a romantic relationship?"

"I didn't get a chance. She stood me up."

"Oh."

"Yeah. I got to the restaurant on time. I'd dressed up—she'd bought me this strapless blue sheath, Indian cotton, very pretty— and I put on a touch of the magic lipstick. But no Sahara. Finally she called. Said she had to work late.

"I drove to the station, turned on the radio. She was on the air all right, playing love songs for strangers."

"Did you go in?"

"No, just listened—sulked, really—then decided I didn't want to confront her in the parking lot. I drove around town until I was damn near out of gas."

"You were disappointed."

"Yeah. But then I decided that I'd wanted an answer from her—about us—and this was as good as any I'd get. I'd pretend dinner was no big deal. . . ."

"No big deal," I echo.

"I'd let it drop and we could stay friends."

"You thought that would be enough?"

"What else could I do? She didn't want me."

"Were you surprised?"

"Well, I'd got my hopes up. Ma was better and I'd learned so much about the vitagua. Everything seemed possible. But—"

"You'd allowed yourself to hope, then been crushed?"

"Yeah. What was wrong with me? I had to wonder. Wasn't I lovable?"

Fishing the painting of the lovers out of her deck of cards, she passes it over. The image is finally complete.

I can guess what Astrid will tell me next.

CHAPTER TWENTY-THREE

JACKS WAS OUT WASHING paintbrushes on the back porch when Astrid got home, pouring water from an antique bottle onto the bristles, letting the red-brown liquid spatter down onto a pile of stones. His expression was guarded.

"What are you doing?" She was so tired that the unfamiliar pumps she'd worn to the restaurant felt like leghold traps. Her purse weighed fifty pounds.

He set the bottle aside. "Working on a painting. The gallery thing looks like it might come through."

"But you're guiding tomorrow."

"I couldn't sleep if I wanted to. Sahara's careening around upstairs in a dither about where you got to."

"God." She slumped.

"You two fighting?"

"I'm the one who's going to be Mrs. Skye one day," Astrid said. "Old, broke, alone. Your kids will be wangling this house out from under me."

Jacks wiped his hands on his shirt. "You know better."

"I have to get cracking if I want a family."

"What's wrong with—?" He made a vague gesture encompassing the house.

"Sahara's only here until she finds someone interesting. Ma won't live forever and you . . ."

"What about me?"

"You'll marry some art promoter and move to Paris."

"Where I'll blend in perfectly with the intelligentsia, no doubt." He rubbed his nose, smearing it with paint-juice. "You're not doomed to solitude."

"When's my life gonna start, Jacks? Am I ever going to stop existing in bits of Albert's past?"

He kissed her.

There was nothing gentle or hesitant about it. His lips met hers with all of Jacks's characteristic directness. Crackling with the passion he kept bottled so tightly, the contact was sudden and startling.

She kissed back, barely knowing why. When they broke, they were forehead to forehead, gasping.

"We're brothers," she managed.

"Barely in-laws." He took her face in his hands.

And Astrid responded. She wanted Sahara, but as her hands twined in his hair she threw herself into the embrace. She clung to the solidity of Jacks, the unmoving never-leave-her presence of him. Heat burned up from her belly and she met his tongue with hers, pulling his shirt with tight fists. When he fastened his teeth on her earlobe, she groaned.

He reached back and up, accidentally catching her coiled earrings on his sleeve, tugging them for a quick painful instant as he unlatched the door.

"She'll hear us," she whispered.

A painful pause—they couldn't, not out here.

"Windows," Jacks said, leading her to his studio. They slid between the tall panes and into the basement.

Groping and necking, they worked their way down the hallway to Jacks's room, falling onto his thin mattress. Astrid was yanking his shirt, socks, wristwatch, scrabbling at the garments with her fingers and teeth. She had him half-stripped before he'd gotten a hand inside her dress.

"You're not gonna be alone," Jacks said hoarsely, his thumb brushing her nipple. Astrid felt tears threaten and raised herself to his mouth again.

Upstairs she could hear Sahara's tread bump-bumping on the wood floors as they fumbled with nylons and condoms.

Jacks's hands were everywhere, but it was his eyes that were feeding the flood inside Astrid, an intent gaze she had seen on him a thousand times since the days of Dad and Olive's whirlwind courtship. Jacks's face with nothing but Astrid in it, and why hadn't she taken him seriously? Now he was sliding against her, inside her, and she drew him deeper as with every thrust he whispered the things she needed to hear: "I'm here, I'm staying."

His love, naked at last and Astrid battered it against herself, driving onto Jacks, trying to shove him through the sealed door to her heart.

Then as quickly as it had begun it was ending, their breath coming short, the emotion discharging like bursts of lightning. Stifling a moan, Jacks fell beside her on the pillows, his breath warming her cheek.

"I love you," he said. His bones felt like knobs through his skin.

She kissed him hard, pulling him close.

She woke to find Jacks sitting up, nestled in pillows with one hand caught in hers. With his free hand, he was pushing a line of acrylic paint along the wall with the bristles of a worn-out paintbrush. Random patterns covered the wall in red and gold as far as his arm could reach.

She sighed and stretched, shifting her weight off his leg. "You must be squashed."

He nodded, kept painting.

"Whyn't you push me off? You have to go to work soon?"

Another swift affirmative jerk of the head.

He thinks I'll have regrets, she thought, and shook herself awake. "That's too bad," she said, and kissed him.

Gratified surprise broke across his face. The resistance in him gave like a breaking dam, and Astrid threw herself against his lips, telling herself how it could be: marriage and kids and trips to art galleries on the weekends . . .

. . . and chanting, of course, shared secrets.

Jacks lifted and turned her. She curled against him . . . and then he wobbled. Instead of joining they rolled off the bed, fetching up against the closet door. Astrid banged her head on the knob.

"What happened?"

"My leg's asleep. Couldn't take our weight." His face darkened. "This isn't what you want."

"Don't. I'm lucky to have you, Jacks. I'm *glad*."

He stood, rocking the pins and needles out of his leg. His face contorted, and his erection drew in on itself.

"Jacks . . ."

He grabbed up a bundle of clothes. "I can't be late."

"Jacks, it'll work out."

"Will it?" His voice was strained. "Is that what she'll say?"

"She?"

"Your romance consultant."

"Sahara doesn't care who I . . ." The words snagged in her throat like fishhooks. "Who I end up with."

"Who you love?" He vanished into the hall.

"Sahara won't care," Astrid repeated. It was true. Sahara wouldn't—didn't care.

Her sinuses tickled unexpectedly. Her eyes watered.

"I'm in love," she said slowly, trying it out. She kicked her legs free of Jacks's tumbled sheets—tried to anyway, but they wouldn't come loose. She grabbed the knob of the locked closet door, levering herself upright and triggering a sudden memory of Albert.

"If you ever have to run for it, Bundle, don't hesitate. Leave it all behind and go."

She'd answered: "I'll never run. Never leave Ma. You shouldn't have picked me. . . ."

She jerked away from it, as if burned, and the door bounced open.

"I'm in love, Sahara," she said, rehearsing the words. "I'm in love with . . . Sahara, I'm . . ." She stepped into the closet, breaking through cobwebs, shivering at the cold touch of the concrete floor. There was a small box on the floor in the back corner.

Another chantment? No. Astrid groped for it, struggling with its dusty latch. Inside were two piles of twenty-dollar bills.

Had Albert squirreled this away? She flipped through the bills, thinking there might be a note, an explanation. . . .

Nothing. Just more mystery.

"I'm in love with Sahara," Astrid whispered. In all these years she'd never said it aloud.

What was she going to do now?

"I love her," Astrid said, louder now, voice steady.

She grasped the closet door again and was peppered by re-membrances.

. . .

She had sneaked into the house and absorbed some extra vitagua from the fireplace. The new grumbles had contented her for a while . . . until they had told her everything they could. Hungry for more, she had gone back, working her hand into the fissure in the fireplace hearth, touching the ice on the unreal side, listening, learning.

Albert caught her there, crouched with her hand in the ice, mumbling to the glaciers. He yanked her away, and the vitagua in the unreal had heaved, chasing her. The hearth cracked, and spirit water splashed the inside of the chimney, the red bricks.

He'd been so angry, so afraid.

. . .

Astrid backed away from the memories, fumbling in the salad of blankets for her date dress, her date shoes. The stockings had runs in them; she left them on the floor. As she searched for her purse, her hand fell on Jacks's chanted watch. The piece of tape with Dad's handwriting was still there. The label was almost unreadable.

Perfect timing. Suddenly enraged, she wiggled her shoe on. After dropping the watch, she crushed it under her heel. Gears popped and vitagua oozed out of the broken clockwork. She wiped up the droplet with her hand and left the pieces on the floor.

There—her purse. Astrid found the lipstick. She applied it using

Jacks's grime-spattered shaving mirror. Her face changed, becoming smoother, glamorous.

She went to find Sahara.

At the foot of the basement steps she paused, seized by a mix of turbulent emotions—apprehension, determination, wretched affection.

What would Sahara think if she emerged from Jacks's domain? Instead, she slipped out through the studio, easing herself into the yard through the same window they'd used last night. Getting in had been easy, but this time she got her skirt tangled in plants: ivy mostly, and a rhododendron that seemed intent on invading the studio.

Blinded by the sun, she fumbled her way inside.

She got two steps before a sound in the living room—Sahara's humming, accompanied by a metallic tapping—rooted her to the floor.

"You're back!" Heavy things thumped on the carpet and her friend burst into the kitchen. "Where were you?"

"Where were you?"

"Frankie got sick at the last minute—had to have his stomach pumped." Sahara was uncharacteristically dressed down, clad in a sweatshirt with cut-off sleeves and a ratty pair of jeans. Both garments were smudged with white.

"Did you paint the ceiling again?"

"Astrid, did you hear what I said?"

"You did paint." She inhaled, smelling fumes. It was cold in here, chilly as the inside of a grocery store.

"Stop avoiding," Sahara said. "I couldn't make it to dinner, okay?"

"It's not important."

"No? You stay out all night and it doesn't matter?"

"We don't need to talk about this."

"I had to *work*," Sahara said. "Astrid, I came to this shitty town to be with you. You're my only friend—"

"Friend."

"—only one who gives a rat's ass if I live or die—"

"Don't sweet-talk me."

"I don't want you mad!"

Astrid searched her face, finding real anxiety. "You didn't ditch me?"

"I swear."

She swallowed. "There's something I need to tell you. Sahara, I love—"

A metallic clink from the next room interrupted her.

"Don't you dare vague out on me now, Astrid Lethewood," Sahara said. "You love someone?"

She looked into the dark eyes and her courage fled. "Jacks. I love Jacks."

A pause. Then Sahara threw her head back and laughed. "Jacks? You do not."

"Why?"

"You're too gay for him."

"I'm not gay, I'm bisexual." She blushed as she spoke; she had never said either word aloud before, not when speaking about herself. "What does that mean? 'Too' gay?"

"Jacks is all wrong for you. He's sulky and quiet, and he's got more food hang-ups than Gandhi. You need someone with some goddamn *joie de vivre*."

"I fucked Jacks last night."

Sahara's jaw dropped. "You did not!"

"We did."

"I'd have heard."

"We were *quiet*." She forced the words out.

"How passionate could it have been if the neighbors didn't have to call animal rescue?"

"You know how he feels about me—"

"Whole town knows! So? Just because the kid has a thing for you doesn't mean you've got to humor him—"

"Humor him?" She was starting to get angry. "I fucked him, I love him, it's . . ."

"What, a done deal?"

"Yes," she gritted.

"Jesus. This is what you wanted to say last night?"

She looked away. "It makes sense, Sahara. He knows about the vitagua, he's . . ."

"A good lay?" Sahara asked.

Astrid's face got hotter. She's leaving, she thought. Sahara leaves me; Jacks never will. It's the right choice. A normal life. Invisibility.

"Well . . ." She could almost see wheels turning in her friend's head. "I guess it could work. . . ."

"You just said he was all wrong." She tried to catch Sahara's hand in hers, but Sahara slipped out of reach. Their fingers brushed, overwhelming Astrid with a sense of Sahara's singular focus on the idea of magic, power. The issue of Astrid's love life was barely relevant, had diminished into an interesting distraction from . . . what?

"Jacks is wrong—but you're pigheaded enough to make it work. I can be nice about it, if that's what you want."

Tears threatened. "What I want, Sahara . . ."

"It'll work out. You and Jacks can make babies, I'll run the mystic end of things. You still want me to help?"

"What?"

"You don't want me to . . ."

"To what?"

"Bail. Three's a crowd, right?"

"Sahara." She closed her eyes. "I don't want you to leave." I couldn't bear it, she thought, but part of her insisted she would do just that—accept the necessity of doing without Sahara. Mournfully, in confusion, but . . .

It won't happen, she told herself. I'll figure out a way to stop it. "Don't go. Don't go, Sahara, I love you."

"Cool down, I'll stay. Just thought I should ask. The ravished look does suit you, I will say that."

"Thanks." Astrid swept her friend into a tight hug, catching her off guard. She'd try again. She'd tell the truth, make sure Sahara understood. . . .

"I—" Her fingertips brushed Sahara's neck and the knowledge came. "You're trying to reexpose yourself."

Sahara stiffened, pulling away, face dark with stubborn resolve. A tick sounded from beyond the doorway.

"Astrid . . ."

Conflicted and weary, she walked into the living room.

A chisel protruded from the crack in the hearth. Wedged between the bricks, its wooden handle was scarred with chips and dings. A small hammer lay beside it, haloed by red brick dust.

Astrid turned slowly.

"All that ice in the unreal," Sahara explained. "We could heat it up. Make things flow again."

"You're digging into the unreal?"

"Why not? You can chant anything now, right? We'll just buy things in malls."

"Sahara," she said, fighting a surge of anger. "Get that chisel out of there."

"Okay, but I want to talk about this," Sahara said, "really talk about it." She grasped the chisel handle, tugging it free. A few drops of vitagua came with it, speckling her hand with liquid magic.

"I'll have to siphon that," Astrid said woodenly.

"Don't start," Sahara said, rubbing the hand on her jeans and turning away. To hide a smile?

A deep glugging sound rumbled through the fireplace then, cutting off Astrid's reply.

CHAPTER TWENTY-FOUR

THE FOUR OF US aren't alone in the unreal for long. Patience leads Ev, Astrid, and me up an expanse of white plain, and as we crest the hill we come face-to-face with an assortment of alchemized people-creatures. Their skin runs the gamut of reds, from Aztec copper to sun-leathered tobacco brown. Everyone has animal features—turtle flippers where hands should be, fox tails, cats' eyes, and elongated muzzles in profusion. Ev, with her goatish features, fits right in.

They surround us without speaking, and Patience is the one who steps forward. "I've brought the spring-tapper," she says.

The hostility of the people eases slightly. Now they are less angry, more watchful.

"Patience knows these people?" I whisper to Astrid.

Patience throws me a smile but keeps speaking: "I was exposed to vitagua months ago—and I'm not alchemized."

A disbelieving rumble.

"You're still cursed!" someone accuses.

"She's been stabilized," Astrid says.

A shout from the back of the crowd, "Is that true?"

Patience spreads her hands. "Would I lie?"

The alchemized people begin to move, obliging us to walk with them. An escort? Or is this an abduction?

Unconcerned, Astrid and her mother stroll with the group, their heads together.

"You get any news of town after I surrendered, Ma?"

"It's a ghost town now."

"I figured they'd evacuate."

"Yeah. Elaine Clumber visits sometimes. She says most everyone who didn't get quarantined is bunking with family. Rest went to big cities, chasing jobs. Maybe a hundred folks insisted they wouldn't leave. No one knows what happened to them after the quake."

"I'll check up soon," Astrid says, but before I hear any more, Patience takes my arm, drawing me out of earshot.

"These people," I say. "They're all alchemized?"

"They were in the ice floes, exposed to pure vitagua."

"Why does spirit water turn people into animals?"

"The curse Patterflam laid upon magic. Part of the litany was 'lower nature overtakes higher, base animal urges overrule reason.' General idea was that enemies who are little more than animals are easier to defeat."

"I see."

Her eye falls on my magic ring. "A chantment allows you to possess magic—wield it—without touching vitagua directly. It's a barrier method."

"My wedding ring is a big magic condom?"

Patience winces beautifully. "I'm sorry."

"How do you fit in?"

"Around the time of the freeze, a prophet said a woman would break the curse."

"You, Patience?"

Her hand brushes the feathered shoulder of one of our escorts. "Could be me, I suppose."

"Or Sahara Knax?"

"Let's hope not." She shakes her head. "The likely messiah is Astrid Lethewood, don't you think? She can already draw vitagua from our bodies—"

"But the residue . . . ," I object.

She gives me a fond, indulgent look. "She'll find a real cure in time. She has a better knack for chanting than any spring-tapper before her."

"Because of Albert's gift for initiations."

"Poor kid. He made her into a force of nature."

"Are you suggesting we should pity her? At least chanters aren't cursed."

"Are you sure? Think of the lives they've led, the things they've given up."

I'm not inclined to sympathize with Astrid right now. "How did she do it? Make you . . . what you are?"

She shakes her head. "Albert and his grandmother knew how to fuse vitagua into objects to make chantments. What Astrid found is a way to fuse a chantment into a living person, to bind it to them."

"Of course." I look into her bewitching eyes. "The magic lipstick. She fused it into you."

"That and some other things—the chantment that lets me go misty, for example."

"And the one that alters your appearance. But what good is that?"

"All in good time." She winks.

Our escort pauses as we reach the high edge of a ridge. At the horizon lies a sea of vitagua, a blue expanse dotted with massive, luminous ice floes. On a plain, inland from the beach, is a lumpy mass of nests, an interweaving of colorful, irregularly shaped structures. The air around these lumps teems with dust; colored beams of light cut bands in the haze. I see ant-sized dots that must be alchemized people. Some are winged, and circle the nests.

"Is that a city? Do people really live in that?"

She shrugs. "They have to live somewhere, don't they?"

"Will we reach the city before Sahara catches us?"

"I'm not the prophet, Will."

Her words remind me I should be focusing on Astrid. I fall back a pace, and immediately Patience is surrounded by animal-people. They mob her gently, bearing her up to the broad shoulders of a man with grizzly bear fur.

Astrid and Ev catch up with me and there's a muddle as we work out my place within the procession. Astrid ends up between me and her mother.

"Ma and I were talking about the Blue Mountain Fair," Astrid says. "Every year they pick a Alpine Princess. Mrs. Skye was one. . . ."

I nod. "Sahara won in her senior year." I look back into the wind. The white twister is still following us. "And now she's fitting herself for another crown."

The Lethewood women, mother and daughter, exchange a glance I cannot read.

Then Astrid produces another card from her pocket. It shows an image of Sahara and Astrid, staring at the shattered fireplace. "When I hugged Sahara that day, I learned she'd been furious with herself for letting me siphon the vitagua from her. In the unreal she'd wanted to re-expose herself, but Jacks and I were watching too closely. When I froze all that vitagua onto Patterflam, it stopped the flow from the spring. I could have brought it back, but she wasn't about to ask, because she wanted—"

"To get the power back." I glance at Ev Lethewood's billy goat's beard, remembering Sahara's wings. "So she chiseled into the unreal through the hearth?"

"Yeah, and she softened the ice. Vitagua responds to the will of the unreal . . . the frozen people who want to be thawed out. They were hungry for heat . . . and they could feel Sahara, so close, wanting what they wanted."

"Were you angry?"

"Furious. It was then that I finally accepted that the spring was my responsibility. That no matter how much they helped, I was the one. I'd tried to divide up my destiny, give it away—"

"But Sahara wasn't content to be a helper."

"Girl always was an all-or-nothing type," Ev says.

"Isn't that the truth?" Astrid grimaces.

Ev squeezes her arm in sympathy, and we continue on toward the lumpy nest of the city.

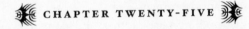

CHAPTER TWENTY-FIVE

THE RUMBLE IN THE fireplace had echoes, burps and belches that spread from the hearth until they were everywhere: walls, windows, staircases. The carpet vibrated underfoot; on the fridge, spice jars chattered.

Moving as if in a dream, Astrid rescued the urn with her father's ashes from the top of the mantel. Then she grabbed her friend's arm—getting a shot of Sahara's glee at having exposed herself to magic again, at last—and towed her away from the fireplace.

"Let go." Sahara jerked free and they fell. A tremor thrummed through the floor.

"Shit," Sahara whispered. Astrid was shaking. Disaster was imminent, she knew it, but all she could do was stare at Sahara, who was goggle-eyed with excitement. An orange smear of lipstick from Astrid's lips marked her neck.

The quivers in the house stilled, and the noise faded. Silence . . . and then vitagua began bleeding from the fireplace.

"No . . . ," Astrid murmured. The cobalt fluid dribbled off the edge of the hearth, forming a palm-sized—and spreading—puddle on the pink carpet.

Sahara took a half step toward it.

"Get back," Astrid ordered. Setting the urn aside, she snatched up the fitted brick that sealed the hearth and tried to force it into place. Ice-cold vitagua flowed over her fingers and wrist. Some seeped into her body, bringing the chill of the unreal with it. The rest continued to spill out into the house.

"Is it working?" Sahara asked.

"Too much pressure," she grunted. Sahara's chisel-work had deformed the opening. . . .

Hot air from outdoors was being sucked down through the chimney, was whisking in from the windows. She could hear the screen door in the kitchen creaking.

"Can I do anything, Astrid?"

"Try closing the windows." She twisted the brick ferociously and it slid into the groove. By now she was saturated with vitagua, more than she'd ever have guessed she could possibly absorb. A storm of things-that-were and things-to-come pelted her. She realized this was a bad idea, she should let go. . . .

Too late. She snapped the brick into position only to discover the seal couldn't hold the increased pressure. It was like sticking her thumb in a garden hose: with its point of escape tightened, the vitagua flow changed to a flat spray, wide and fast.

It caught Astrid in the face and chest, coating her open mouth and spilling down the front of her dress. Sahara was spattered too; a thick line splashed across her shoulders before striking the window.

With a scrape of stone on stone, the brick snapped. The spray dropped back to a gurgle. The miniature waterfall kept flowing over the edge of the mantel.

"I never meant—," Sahara stammered. "This is my fault."

Astrid sighed, resigned. "Forget about it."

"What are we going to do?"

"I don't know. Catch it in a bucket, I guess."

"What if we can't stop it, Astrid? The secret—"

"I do stop it," Astrid said. "I just don't know when."

Sahara held up her blue-spotted hands. "We're drenched. Look at your face."

Astrid touched her cheek. Her skin was cool, like polished marble, and she knew if she looked in a mirror, she'd see vitagua lying under the flesh like a birthmark. She closed her eyes, imagined it contracting around her innards, and pulled, chilling her belly.

Sahara said: "I can't get over the way you do that."

"Is it okay now?"

"Yes," she said. "You look normal."

"I'll go find something to hold it," Astrid said. "Don't get any more spirit water on you."

"I'm fine."

"The more you have in you, the more I have to siphon."

"I can't go through that again."

Instead of arguing, Astrid trotted down to the laundry room. Vitagua was leaking through the ceiling—the laundry was right below the fireplace—and running into the washer's overflow drain. Snatching up a bucket, she set it under the drip. It filled quickly—too quickly.

Magic in the sewer system. She shivered.

She threw open the big freezer, hauling out frozen food by armfuls and dropping the packages at her feet until the cube was empty. She unplugged the freezer, heaving it into the middle of the room until it was below the drip.

"Fill that," she grunted, praying the unreal wouldn't rise to the challenge.

Liquid magic spattered the bottom of the freezer, and Astrid found herself temporarily unmoored from time: she couldn't remember if the cat was dead or just contaminated. Visions of river fish changing into massive man-eating menaces wound through her mind. Trees, growing impossibly tall beside the sewer outflow, firebombs, giant hedges of blue brambles . . . she froze, trying to sort out where—no, not where, *when*—in time she actually was.

"It's the flood, we're at the flood," she murmured. "Lots of time, everyone's all right—"

Then she paused, cotton-mouthed. Who wouldn't be all right, and how soon?

Grumbles muttered, in their singsong way, of the basement flooding with vitagua, of Jacks's stuff bobbing in liquid magic, Astrid wading through the flow. . . . No, it isn't time for that yet, the basement floor is dry. She bent, pressing her palm on the concrete, trying to figure out what it was she was going to manage to save.

She picked up the paintbrush he'd used this morning, tucking it in her hair and then bursting into tears.

"This is when I think of the ice I just pulled out of the freezer," she said, fighting a sob.

Ice?

Oh. The heat in the living room, the way the unreal was drawing it in. There had been a big block of party ice in the freezer. Maybe if she set it on the hearth, the water would melt, cool things down. The idea of freezing all that vitagua was frightening. It would solidify within her body, making her sick, and Jacks and Sahara would take care of her until Ev . . .

No, that was a few days ago.

Ice. Focus on ice. She found a block of it on the floor in a plastic grocery bag. She closed her hand around the bag's handles, and another sob rose in her chest.

There was a series of crashes and thumps upstairs.

"What are you doing up there?" she shouted.

No answer.

She searched her clot of future memories, but her head reeled; it was too dense, insensible.

Clutching the bag with its block of ice, she crept upstairs to see what had gone wrong now.

CHAPTER TWENTY-SIX

THE DOOR TO THE living room was blocked.

"Hey!" Astrid yelled, thumping on the door with her free hand. Now what? Was Sahara rolling in the vitagua?

She ran to the studio, swinging the block of ice in its plastic bag, and, for the third time that day, scrambled through the windows. Moving fast and carelessly, she knocked a pane of glass loose, breaking it to shards as she tumbled out into the yard. She ran up the porch stairs to the kitchen entrance, and found the door unlocked.

No, not unlocked: forced open. Splinter marks marred the frame; the latch hung loose.

Jangling, thumps, and a strangled mew of distress emanated from the living room. Sahara.

Astrid tiptoed through the kitchen, the heavy block of ice dangling from her hand in its bag. The brightness of the yard had blinded her: now the kitchen was too dim. It took a moment to make out the short-handled ax on the kitchen table, the shotgun beside it.

She followed the noises: the wet squish of carpet, grunts, vitagua dripping, keys jingling.

It's Mark, Astrid thought. He came back. . . .

She stepped into the blue-splashed living room and saw a figure bent over the limp body of Sahara, a man, familiar somehow, hands locked around her throat, squeezing. Vitagua was boiling from Sahara's eyes, nostrils, ears . . .

. . . she wasn't breathing . . .

. . . and the man wasn't Mark at all, he was too big, and anyway Mark was standing by the hallway, eyes blank behind his dirty glasses, twirling Sahara's car keys around his index finger. But it was too late, and it didn't matter anyway: the man was strangling Sahara, and Astrid was already moving. Her arm swung the block of ice at the end of its plastic sling. . . .

It's Chief Lee, she thought, I figure that out right before I—

Contact.

Before I kill him.

The impact of ice against the Chief's skull was remarkably quiet. He slewed sideways, then caught himself—but Astrid was enraged now. The block dropped to the bottom of the bag, jerking her wrist before she swung it again, overhand this time. When it struck him there was a crack. The Chief fell facedown to the floor and she pushed him off her motionless friend with one blue-stained high heeled shoe.

Jacks's dad. He was dressed all in black: baggy pants and a turtleneck. He repelled the vitagua that was, by now, all over the room. As he tried to raise himself, Astrid saw the blue liquid bubbling and hissing, becoming floral-scented smoke, leaving pristine handprints on the pink carpet.

The Chief groped for the handle of a glass dagger that hung in a scabbard at his hip. Astrid grabbed his hand. Knowledge seared into her—memories of Lee Glade's grandfather teaching him to hunt well wizards. He'd developed the killer instinct, a calm righteousness that soothed his conscience. But it was time now for Lee to train someone, and Jacks kept trying to leave town. Shredding the boy's art school applications, funding requests. Even Olive's road accident, breaking his ex-wife's leg as she lay drugged in her car . . .

The sensation—touching the Chief—was like touching Patterflam. The magic within her boiled and died where her skin met his. Astrid clung anyway, savoring the Chief's frustration with Jacks. His perfect son, so much like his mother, refusing to go hunting, even to fish. . . .

The Chief jabbed at her, bringing her back to the present. Lightning ran up and down her arm, vitagua burning in a line up her wrist. A shard of white glass was embedded in the meaty part of her hand.

Shrieking, she kicked out, knocking the Chief down by good luck rather than by design as she staggered toward the mantel. Moaning, she pinched the hunk of glass out of the wound. It fried her finger and thumb when she grasped it, and she dropped it on the vitagua-soaked mantel, where it flared into a dancing, electrified ball. A sizzle annihilated the sliver and a good portion of the vitagua slick it had landed in. A smell of ozone filled the room.

"Sea-glass," Astrid choked. "We found sea-glass in the bottle factory."

The Chief was struggling to his knees. "Astie," he said, voice thick. "She has to be stopped. Sahara's into something that you don't want to see let loose. Water magic . . . dangerous stuff . . ."

"If you killed her . . ." She fisted her throbbing hand.

"Has to be done," he insisted. "Come away from the fireplace, kid. I gotta clean this up, burn out the spring. Everything'll be okay, I promise." He touched the back of his head, swaying. "Jacks here?"

"You're one of the witch-burners Albert talked about," Astrid said coldly.

Dismissal flickered in his bloodshot eyes. "What's Albert Lethewood got to do with anything?"

"You shot him. One night when he was moving chantments . . ." She had known it since she touched him. It felt like she had known it all along. "You were on the ridge, watching. Always watching, weren't you? On the bottle-factory roof, on the training tower at the fire hall. You fired that shotgun, without knowing whose car it was, who was inside. . . ."

"Albert?" This time he was incredulous. "Albert's liver pickled— he didn't have anything to do with—"

"He's wearing the magic coat; you don't recognize him. He gets away, but there's a piece of shot embedded in his liver. You spend weeks looking for a shot-up car, and you don't think anything of Albert dying. You shot at him blindly, with sea-glass."

"Crushed sea-glass in a shotgun shell." He lurched closer, one foot dragging. Pink footprints marked his path across the vitagua spill. "It's not Sahara."

Astrid bared her teeth, backing away, up onto the mantel. The Chief's fist closed around her throat.

"Albert Lethewood wasn't the ancient enemy of the Fyre Brigade," he hissed. "He was a rummy."

She pushed vitagua into her neck to counter the strangling pressure, gargling her answer as the fluid boiled against his touch. "He had you fooled, Chief."

He shoved her against the fireplace, grinding her earring against the bricks until her head rang. "Is my son cursed, witch?"

She surprised herself by laughing.

Glass sliced into her skin just below the collarbone. Vitagua fizzed throughout Astrid's body; her bones vibrated like tuning forks. Burning and boiling, she thought. Roasted Astrid, poached Astrid . . .

"Is Jacks infected?"

"He'll never become like you," she managed.

"Let him make his paintings," he said. His voice was guttural, his enunciation mushy. Or had the pain affected her hearing? "The magic well closes today, Astie."

"That's not how it goes." Biting her lip until the skin ruptured, she pulled the madly bubbling vitagua into her mouth, spitting it in a stream at his unprotected eyes. The Chief's grip on her broke.

With a crude, panicky movement, Astrid shoved. Her bare palms smacked against his chest, and more knowledge—memories of deaths, Lee learning the bloody history of his fathers, prophecies about Patterflam's eventual escape from the unreal—poured through her in a flood. Braced as she was against the hearth, the jolt added force to the push. The Chief rocketed backwards, slamming to the floor. His body slackened as vitagua burned out from under him, creating a man-shaped halo of singed pink carpet.

Astrid collapsed, falling into a crouch as she clawed the glass shards out of her arm and chest, only then crawling to his side.

She was shaking violently, and it was almost a minute before she could put her hand on his throat. She was expecting another shock, but nothing came from his bare skin as she felt for a pulse.

No heartbeat. He shuddered under her hand. Then the smell of urine merged with the oversweet flower-stench of burnt liquid magic in the room.

"Birds," she mumbled. "I froze the birds for this."

Weeping, she leaned over to listen to his chest, but heard nothing. She tried to pull vitagua to him, to pool it around his corpse, but there wasn't enough.

"This isn't the part where I freeze the body?" She listened intently, but the grumbles refused to help. Finally she crawled to Sahara, groping for a heartbeat, dully certain that it would do no good.

Unlike the Chief, Sahara's heart was fine. Her chest rose and fell in a steady rhythm. Blue-black marks smudged her throat. The mermaid hung on her neck.

In the corner, Mark was twirling the car keys as if nothing had happened.

"Mark?" Astrid said.

His face pinched up, and he gaped at her foggily.

"Help me," Astrid pleaded.

He plodded to her side, staring blankly down at Sahara. "What the hell?"

"She's hurt," Astrid said. "Can you carry her upstairs? Whatever you do, don't touch the blue fluid."

He lifted Sahara clumsily, and as Astrid caught her friend's lolling head, their hands met.

"Oh," she said, and Mark froze. "This is the part where I figure out why you're here."

Knowledge came in a rush. The Chief had gone to Mark's sister, asking about the confrontation with Sahara.

"He saw I was messed up, the other afternoon," he said, more alert now.

"Right. He came here just after Sahara zapped you."

"What the fuck is going on, Astrid?"

"Magic," she said. "Okay, take her upstairs."

"Magic, right," he repeated, but he carried her away.

Astrid picked up the block of ice with numb hands, dropping it onto the still-leaking hearth. It crackled, melting fast. She kept her back to the body.

The body. Oh god, I killed him.

She made a round of the first-floor windows, pulling curtains shut, closing up the house. When she was done, she stood in the kitchen, desperately trying to think. Mark returned, still handling the keys. She fought an urge to snatch them away.

He'd have killed us and let Mark take the blame, she thought. He needed someone to take responsibility because Jacks lives here, because Jacks might suspect . . .

Oh shit, I killed Jacks's father.

"I decided I could use the pocketknife on the . . . the corpse, Will," she said, remembering how she had crumbled the animals Henna had brought home. "If I move fast . . . I still think he doesn't have to know."

"Will?" Mark repeated. "Listen, I think Sahara needs an ambulance. Maybe you do too."

"I'll have a look at her. Could you check the Chief for more of that glass?" she said. "Take it off him. Then—I don't know . . . just wait here."

He stepped toward the body and she cringed.

"Don't touch the blue stuff."

"I heard you the first time," he said, a hint of the old whine returning to his voice.

Mark had taken Sahara to Astrid's bedroom by mistake. Her friend was tucked in like a doll, covers up to her shoulders and her arms laid straight at her sides.

Astrid kissed her forehead. No response.

She glanced around, finding a plastic saltshaker on the desk next to a dirty plate. Snatching it up, she dripped vitagua from her bitten tongue.

"Something to heal her," she muttered. "Please, no birds today, just fix her, make her better."

It worked. She turned the shaker over, and small white stars drifted out. Sahara's bruises faded. Her cuts closed.

I should have siphoned her first, Astrid thought, too late, as all the cuts healed and Sahara's eyes opened.

"Thought I was dead," she rasped. "God, look at you. I must be."

Astrid sniffled, shaking her head.

"Where's the Chief?"

"G-gone," she said.

"Mermaided him off, huh?"

"No. I hit him, Sahara."

"That he richly deserved." She rubbed her throat.

"No. I mean I hit him a lot . . . a couple times, uh— Hard. Sahara, he's . . ."

Sahara's face paled.

"H-he was attacking you," Astrid said. "He's . . ."

"You killed him," Sahara said. She looked, more than anything, astounded. After a second she opened her arms. They clung to each other, squeezing so hard, Astrid's ribs began to ache. "You killed someone for me."

"I love you, remember?" Astrid laughed bitterly.

"I broke this, Astrid," Sahara said. "I'll fix it."

"No, it's too late."

"Darling, it's never—"

She was interrupted by screams.

CHAPTER TWENTY-SEVEN

"JACKS HAD MARK UP against the wall when I got downstairs," Astrid says. "He was livid—given half an excuse, he'd have busted Mark's arm. But Mark wasn't struggling. He kept saying, 'It wasn't me, it wasn't me. . . . '"

"Astute of him," I say.

"Mrs. Skye was there too. She was on the phone, telling 911 that Chief Lee was hurt, that Mark had broken in and assaulted him."

In Astrid's hand is a fortune card, its paint still crawling. It bears a mini-portrait of an enraged Astrid in a blue dress, swinging the block of ice at the Chief.

So she did kill him after all. I hoped, for reasons I barely understand, that Sahara had done it, that Astrid was lying to protect her. But she has always been the logical suspect. She and Lee Glade have a history of antagonism, of conflicts over Jacks and Albert. It adds up.

I've talked to more than one killer whose actions, however spontaneous at the time, seemed inevitable when tallied against his relationship with the victim.

"How did you feel?"

"With Mrs. Skye talking to the cops, our options were melting away. Everything was covered in vitagua and I had to tell Jacks it was me who'd cracked his father's skull."

"But—"

"Don't ask again; I'm trying to remember. I was . . . panicky."

"Not remorseful?"

"Not right then."

"How about later?"

Her face fills with what looks, strangely, like sympathy. "Sometimes I'm sorry, sure. More often I remember the Chief had his hands on Sahara's neck, that he shot Dad. Or I think how stupid it was that he died. I hit him, yeah, but people are supposed to be tough. You hear about babies getting frozen solid in snowstorms and being saved. People crashing their cars in the middle of nowhere and surviving for days before they're found. You know?"

"Yes."

"Sometimes I can't believe someone so strong died from a few smacks to the head."

A few smacks. The autopsy report speaks of multiple cranial fractures and craniocerebral injury. The first blow fractured Lee Glade's skull in two places and in itself constituted a terminal wound, albeit one he might have survived—if he'd gotten immediate treatment. The second compounded the problem, expanding the fractures and creating a massive subdural hematoma.

"Astrid, suppose his general state of health had made him more resistant to 'a few smacks'—"

"Then he'd have lived."

"No. You'd have assaulted him more ferociously. You wanted him off Sahara, didn't you?"

She looks away.

"You were angry, and you hit him hard. You say he was groggy and confused after he got off the floor—"

"Don't—"

"Come back to the containment facility with me."

"I'm not sorry enough to consider that."

"How sorry are you?"

Her voice rises in frustration. "You don't think I've been over this a thousand times? One minute I was deciding to have a romance with Jacks—"

"Fucking him, Sahara would say."

". . . the next, I'd beaten up his father."

"Murdered him."

"Murdered him, fine, and the Sheriff was on his way. Vitagua was dribbling out of the fireplace, there was a body on the floor of Albert's house, Mark knew about magic, and Jacks was furious. . . ." She wipes away tears. "On top of that, Sahara had triggered this huge melt in the unreal. Patterflam was going to break out and burn everything."

I imagine the unreal burning. "Why did you do it?"

"I wanted him off Sahara, remember?"

"Not the murder. Why did you choose Jacks?"

She dries her eyes, carefully, one at a time. "What would you do? If you had to choose between having the person you wanted or being with someone who loved you?"

"I don't know."

"Picking Jacks was the only way to keep them both. I wanted Sahara . . . but she didn't love me; not romantically. Jacks could give me kids and a normal life. Sahara might stay because of the chantments . . . and if she left, I wouldn't be alone. We could all be mostly happy, and nobody would get hurt."

"Mostly happy."

"Pathetic, huh?" She laughs bitterly, kicking a spray of dirt over the weeds. A thin furred tendril whips out at me, as if in response. Then a pulse of cool air blows out from my wedding ring. The tendril drops away, lashing sulkily, and I feel a thread of fatigue.

"So the police were coming. What did you do next, Astrid?"

"I focused on Jacks. Took him aside, told him what happened. I said the Chief had shot Albert . . . I was covered in punctures from the sea-glass he'd stuck in me."

In the news footage when Astrid is coming out of the house with Patience, she is filthy, barefoot, covered in blood, and her ear is shredded. Now she shows me a picture from just after the murder. There are angry gashes in her forearm and shoulder, a cut on her hand that is a classic defense wound. Her ear is intact, though, the dragon earring scratched but in place.

"How did Jacks react?"

"You mustn't think badly of him. I had the lipstick on."

"You'd killed his father."

"Jacks loved me. And he was in shock."

"So he forgave you."

I see her struggling to keep tears back. "Just don't blame him for what happened next."

"The standoff."

She nods. We had paused but now, without discussion, we hurry down the bone-bleached dune after Ev and Patience.

"Sahara wanted to preserve your monopoly on magic, and Jacks wanted to keep you safe. What's your excuse?"

She sighs. "I wanted to keep the cops from getting contaminated."

We have arrived at the edge of the peculiar city. People stream around us, chatting in tongues I don't understand. Their voices are friendly. The smell of cooking food fills the air, and as I inhale, I begin to feel as though I am eating the best meal of my life. The banquet lasts for a single, intense moment, and then I am full.

The crowd around us grows until it is thousands strong. People dangle from oversized blades of grass, hover on butterfly wings. Heads on giraffe necks loom above us. They regard Patience with wonder and hope. Hands extended, she circles the space they have left us, letting them brush her fingers. She is speaking, softly, asking about their long years under the ice. Some call back, their voices tainted with animal barks and the trills of birds.

She turns to Astrid. "They want to see you fuse a chantment into someone. If anything happens to you, they won't know anything about fighting the curse. . . ."

Astrid, of course, is unsurprised. "Will?"

"You're not contaminating me," I say.

A weak smile. "I need something to chant. Something small, something you don't mind losing."

Licking my lips, I take stock. Small, disposable. After a second

I pop a button off my shirt. I hand it to her along with a couple coins from my pocket and a key from my keychain—Caroline's house key.

Astrid chants them all, dribbling vitagua from her much-bitten lips. Then she holds them up.

"Magic button," she says dreamily. "It lets you see things—as if you had a telescope and a microscope built into your eyes. The quarter keeps you from getting lost, and the dime . . . Well, the dime's for you, Pop. The key unlocks doors—any door you touch will open for you."

She offers the dime to her mother. "Volunteers?"

A woman with a beaver's tail takes the button. A man with the talons of a bald eagle indicates he wants the quarter. The key goes to a small red deer with long black hair and the eyes of a human being.

Pooling vitagua in her palm, Astrid paints a blue line across Ev's hand and sets the dime on the smear, pressing the coin into the meat of her hand.

"Vitagua is cohesive," she says, loud enough for all to hear as she repeats the process with the other volunteers. "The magic in the chantment calls to the vitagua in the affected individual. The chantment's molecules fold into the person's body."

Ev waves her hand for all to see. The dime is gone.

"If you X-rayed her, it'd be there in her hand. But you couldn't get it out surgically," Patience murmurs.

Ev Lethewood bows to the crowd as Astrid, surprisingly, gestures like an old-style sleight-of-hand magician. Down she bobs—and when she comes up, Ev's goatish features are less pronounced. I blink—in addition, Ev is now male. Taking out a handkerchief, he mops his brow, puffing like someone who has just run a marathon.

"You okay?" Astrid asks, and Ev nods wearily.

There's a gasp from the crowd as the deer girl's head changes, becoming fully human.

"Magic calls to magic. The embedded chantment will absorb

the vitagua residue in her body," Astrid says. "It will take time. She was submerged for centuries."

I ask: "She can use the powers in the chantment?"

"Yes. From now on she'll be able to unlock doors."

"Well?" Patience asks the crowd. They murmur, examining the three changed individuals. Then their voices rise in a musical, chord-packed babble. Cheers erupt around us. They raise the trio onto a platform of woven reeds.

"This is the part where they ask you to go preside over a celebration," Astrid tells Patience. "If you want."

Patience glides up to the platform. "I never say no to an adoring crowd."

Astrid says. "Pop, you want to go too?"

Ev scratches her—his—neck and speaks in a deep bass. "You've still got business, son. I'd like to help."

"You do. You will." She leans close, lowering her voice. "Figure out the city for me? Who's who, where things are, if anyone from Indigo Springs ended up here."

Ev considers this, yawning. "I can do that."

"Sure you can," Astrid says. "You're hyperobservant."

Her mother shakes his head. "I can walk around town for you anyway. You'll be back soon?"

"Yes."

Ev offers me a hand then, and I shake it. "Try not to worry, young man. My kid, she'll take care of you."

"I know."

"Thanks, Pop." Astrid blows Ev a kiss.

With a wave, Ev climbs onto the platform with the others. The crowd abandons us. The city hums with voices—conversations, animal calls, music. The nestlike buildings are resonating, forming tones that play my emotions like a harp, lifting me on a rising wave of joy.

Astrid chooses a path out of the city. "Your kids are young enough to learn the unreal tongues, Will."

"What?" I hide the jolt that accompanies the thought of my

son and daughter having a future here . . . or anywhere. I've become accustomed to thinking all their prospects were doomed. "Do you know where my children are?"

"I'd have said if I did." She tilts her head, listening. "The grumbles say you'll find them."

"When?"

"I'm not so good with when."

"Try." I hand Astrid the ace of hearts.

She drains the card to whiteness and creates a picture—the house again. The police are in the picture now—literally— uniformed men barricade off Mascer Lane. "Sorry. We're still focused on the standoff."

I sigh. "Fine. How did that play out?"

"When Mrs. Skye said she could see the Sheriff coming, we all froze."

"Everyone but Sahara?"

"Yes. She had the mermaid on, and she had Chief Lee's shotgun. She put the gun in Mark's hands and told him to fire a shot out through the front door, over their heads."

"One more step and I kill them all," I murmur.

"That's what Sahara forced Mark to say," Astrid agrees. "That's how the standoff began."

CHAPTER TWENTY-EIGHT

"ARE YOU INSANE?" THERE was no force behind Jacks's words.

"They already think he's a killer," Sahara said, tugging Mark inside. She called out, "Sheriff Lews? Pete?"

A muffled call came in response.

Sahara's voice was thick with Siren vibrations. "Mark says keep your distance and everyone will be fine." She slammed the door and, coaxing Mrs. Skye away from the window, shut the curtains with a snap. "That'll buy us some time to fix things."

The old woman curled out of her grip, lifting Sahara's fingers off her braceleted wrist with visible distaste. "By blaming him?" she said slowly.

Sahara ignored her. "Mark, go do some crazed gunman stuff. Make sure nobody can see inside. Block the back door. Don't get shot."

Wordlessly—eyes blank—Mark moved to comply.

"Kids," Mrs. Skye objected, physically interposing her frail-looking body into Sahara's path, "think about what you're doing. Mark didn't kill the Chief."

"She's right." Astrid's gut twisted as she watched Mark disappear upstairs. A smell of gunpowder hung in the air, and her ears rang from the sound of the shot. She was full of vitagua and the headache had returned full-force, gnawing at the right side of her head. "We can't make him out to be some hostage-taking stalker type...."

Sahara groaned. "It's just for a little while."

"We can't," Astrid insisted.

"So ... what? We let him go, he tells the truth, they bust in here and get contaminated by the spilled magic?"

"No . . . but when you say you think this is fixable . . . how? Jacks, what should we do?"

Jacks was staring at her, half-smiling, and Astrid remembered she was wearing the lipstick. She'd put it on before coming up to talk to Sahara. Had that only been an hour ago?

She rubbed her mouth fiercely, and Jacks looked around the room, taking in the spill and the body of his father.

"We do have to hide the magic before anyone else comes inside," he said. "Saving Mark's our second priority."

"But how? How do we keep him out of trouble?"

"Yeah, smart guy—how?" Mrs. Skye crossed her arms.

"All I know is we can't let half the town troop through this mess and get contaminated."

"Right," Sahara sneered. "Contamination's so awful."

Astrid shuddered. "We clean up, then I'll confess."

"No," Sahara objected.

Astrid paused, foundering on everything she knew, or would know. Confessing. When would that happen? And Sahara going away. She had to find out what triggered the departure—find out, and change things so she stayed. Jumbled knowledge assailed her, and she couldn't sort through it. "Is someone crying? Is it me? Blood on my dress, freezing the birds—"

"Hey, focus." Sahara snapped her fingers. Terrible knowledge shimmered, just within reach . . . then slipped away.

"More people," said Mrs. Skye as car doors slammed.

"I'll get the kaleidoscope," Sahara said, heading upstairs.

Astrid rushed to catch up, murmuring: "We ought to have Mark let Mrs. Skye go."

"And have her tell them *you* killed the Chief?"

"Ask her to keep quiet."

"Too risky. She's pissed at us, didn't you notice?"

"Use the mermaid—zap her."

"She's practically deaf." Sahara shook her head. "Siren doesn't work on her."

"What?"

"The hearing aid—she's partly deaf. Remember it didn't work through the phone, either? It doesn't work, I've tried."

Astrid felt a pang of disappointment—she'd believed Sahara had scruples about brainwashing the old woman.

"I'll fix it, Astrid. I promised, didn't I?"

"Don't bark at me. It's not my fault."

"So it's mine?" Sahara said.

Yes, she thought, and tension boiled between them until Astrid grabbed the kaleidoscope, leaving the question hanging. She peered through the house walls to the street. "Three squad cars," she reported. "The whole Sheriff's Department. Pete Lews is knocking on doors. Evacuating the neighborhood? I can't believe this is happening."

"Don't you know anything that will help clear away all the vitagua we've spilled?"

You spilled, Astrid thought, but anger wouldn't help. "It's been weeks since I remembered anything new."

"Okay. Let's think—oh! Is there anything of Albert's left in the house? Something you haven't already touched?"

"I doubt it," Astrid said. She started opening her dresser drawers, poking through her tools and treasures. As the items passed through her hands, pieces of insight came to her—thoughts about the objects' history, old memories of occasions when she'd worn them, ideas about what kind of chantments they'd make—

"Nothing?" Sahara asked.

"Not yet." She thumbed through the clothes in her closet, dragging her finger over the hangers. Nothing. "Where's that dulcimer Ev gave me?"

"Ahh." Sahara chewed her lip. "Jacks was playing with it on the back steps yesterday."

"Did he bring it inside?"

"Astrid, you already touched it."

"Gotta try." She thundered back downstairs, only to be brought up short by the sight of Mrs. Skye draping a paint-spattered sheet over Chief Lee's corpse. Shaking, she slipped into the kitchen, where

Mark was heaving the refrigerator up against the back door. He had taped black garbage bags over the windows, cutting them to fit precisely. The darkened room was already getting stuffy.

Astrid said, "Jacks, where's the dulcimer?"

He pointed, and Astrid snatched it up, squeezing both the mallets in one palm, straining. She had a brief sense of her mother, pregnant, bored, and bedridden.

"Jacks, do you have anything of Albert's?" Astrid asked. "Anyone? Patience, he ever give you anything?"

They shook their heads, but something flickered over Sahara's face.

"What?"

"Nothing."

"We're in trouble here, Princess. Give it up."

"I just thought . . ." She jerked a thumb in the direction of Albert's funeral urn.

"Oh," Astrid said, voice small.

"No," Jacks said. "You don't have to, Astrid."

But she did.

Face pallid, Jacks handed over the urn. Astrid knelt on the floor, unscrewing the top. The mouth of the aspen container was as wide as her wrist. She slid her fingers inside, straining to just brush the ashes, to disturb them as little as possible. Grit raked under her nails.

"Is it working?" Sahara asked.

"Hush," Astrid said, and then the past swept her away.

• • •

She was at Liv Celedine's place, planting petunias for an upcoming wedding. It was the day before Albert was sentenced for the house-renting swindle, the last time they ever tended a garden together.

They had been trying not to fight. Albert didn't want to leave Astrid in charge of the magical spring.

They were almost done when a tree swallow swooped out of the ravine and hit Liv's front window.

"And then you bleed out," Astrid had said, irrationally, scooping up the bird. The vitagua in the unreal grumbled a suggestion, and she scratched off a scab on her wrist. Pooling vitagua in her hands, she immersed the corpse. Blue steam rose from her cupped palms.

"What the hell?" Dad was at her side, eyes wild as he looked around for witnesses.

"He doesn't have to die," Astrid had mumbled as she chilled the vitagua-soaked bird. Now it was iced: a faceted lump the size of a bar of soap that threw sparkles of reflected blue light around the yard.

Dad threw a rag over her hand, hiding the lump of ice.

"Dammit, kid! What're we supposed to do with that? Stick it in the freezer for the witch-burners to find?"

"Dad—"

"That's it, Astrid. No more improvising."

She laughed. "Stop me."

He slapped her, hard, horror on his face mirroring the anger rising within her.

She had knelt, sweeping dust off the sidewalk.

"Bundle . . . ," Albert pleaded.

She pulled on the unreal. Vitagua seeped out of the concrete, a perfect circular puddle with a circumference just wider than the cube of iced bird. "Live," she said, and birdsong rang through the vitagua. She slid the cube into the pool and it vanished, leaving the circle of vitagua in the sidewalk.

"Astrid!"

"Okay, go back," she said.

The puddle glugged. The grumbles hummed and murmured. Nothing happened.

She put her hand on the puddle. "Go," she said again, and the grumbles disagreed. They'd waited so long. Their time was approaching, why wait, why wait? . . .

"Someone's coming," Dad said, voice desperate. Astrid pushed, trying to force the vitagua to vanish. And it did. There was a crackle and the puddle was gone, replaced by broken chunks of sidewalk.

Albert let out a long trembly breath.

Then the ground began to shake. The gazebo wobbled, tumbling roses to the ground. There was a low rumble that became a roar. Astrid and her father were thrown to the ground.

I did this, Astrid thought. Did I just get us both killed? But the quake stilled a moment later. Dad hobbled to her side, favoring his ankle.

"You okay?"

She felt tears threatening. "I'm sorry, Daddy."

"I'm gonna check on Miz Celedine," he said, staggering to the house.

Sirens began to wail across the ravine. How many people had been hurt by the earthquake . . . had she hurt?

A horn blared nearby and she sprinted to the road. What she saw there chilled her heart: a postal service van had struck a blue sedan.

Ma, Astrid thought, but she could see the drivers climbing out, one uniformed postman and old Reff Jundy. They were laughing, clearly okay.

It could have been Ma, she thought, and she turned back to the Celedine place. Albert was pressing a bloodied rag to Liv's forehead.

He'd been right all along. She wasn't careful enough.

"I have to quit," she murmured.

You can't quit, the grumbles said. She'd been initiated—there was no way to undo that. Till death do us part . . .

She was pacing when her father returned. "I have to quit."

"Calm down, Bundle," he'd said. "You just need to learn some caution."

"If I can hear the vitagua, I'll want to improvise," she said. "You never wanted me to be the chanter, Dad."

"Astie, Bundle—who would I find to take your place?"

"Maybe you'll meet someone in jail."

He sucked on his lips, coloring. When he spoke again, his voice was soft, infuriatingly reasonable. "If I found someone, and initiated them . . . what if they were more powerful than you? How scared would they be?"

"I don't care," Astrid said, thinking of the mangled mail truck. "I could've killed someone!"

"Don't panic on me," Albert said. "You just do things how I showed you—"

"I can't!"

"Bun, I'm scared too. Granny couldn't do half what you can with magic. And you're still young, still learning. How'm I supposed to teach you? But quitting—"

"I'll hurt someone." She wiped her nose.

"Bundle . . ."

"Stop calling me that!"

Albert put his dirty hands on her shoulders. "I been careful about the magic all my life. Never had more than a few drops of spirit blood in me at once. Granny Almore, she took in the stuff by the quart, and it made her peculiar. She knew things, Astrid. Told me once I'd die a-suffering . . . I never figured it was good to know so much."

"You'll be in terrible pain at the end," young Astrid agreed, and then moaned as she heard her own words. "Don't you see? I can't stop myself."

Dad's mouth worked soundlessly for a second. "I know it's going to be hard for you. I should've done better. Should have risked it maybe, peeked at what's to come . . ."

Her words came in bursts between dry sobs. "It doesn't—matter because I'm—quitting!"

"Bundle, I know you end up the well wizard. I know. You can't back out—"

"Stop me." She yanked free, backing up against the remains of the gazebo. With the nails of her right hand she scratched hard, digging into the flesh of her left arm. When the skin broke and the vitagua welled up, she grabbed the only thing she could think of, the thick gold twist of her three-part dragon earring. She pulled and vitagua flowed into its gold coils. "I'm forgetting it all, Dad."

"You can't hide from this."

She'd bellowed then. "Find someone else!"

"Okay," he said, putting up his free hand in surrender. "Okay, Astrid. I'll get someone. You don't—"

She hadn't listened. There was one way out. She finished making the chantment, feeding vitagua into it, then releasing the dragon from the pinch of her finger and thumb. As her hand dropped to her side, everything she knew about magic drained out, like water soaking into a washrag. She wiped her teary eyes, mumbling. "Magic magic, go away."

The last thing she'd forgotten was the stricken look on her father's face.

. . .

"It's the Chief, Dad . . . ," Astrid tried to say now, as pain burned down the side of her head and into the cords of her neck. "Watch out for Chief Lee."

"Astrid!" Sahara's shriek broke the reverie.

Astrid blinked, finding her face wet with tears. Her left hand was fisted deep in the urn, clenched around ash and lumps. The palm of her other hand ached, as if something was biting through the meat under her thumb. Her ear throbbed, but her headache was diminishing.

"Are you okay?" Jacks asked, dabbing at the right side of her face with a rag that came away bloody.

"I think so." She looked at her sore hand and saw the three pieces of her dragon earring. Magic magic, go away . . .

"You tore it out," Jacks explained unnecessarily.

Gulping, Astrid dropped the earring.

It fell soundlessly, three interlocked gold pieces slicked with blood, and as they dropped away the gnawing in her hand and the fatigue cleared too. The memories came back cleanly, as if they had never been gone: everything Albert had taught her, everything she had learned from the vitagua, all the time they'd spent together. Hiding it all from Ma, from everyone.

She'd been so impatient with him. He'd spent his life playing it safe, and she'd been sure she knew better, chafing and fighting as he showed her everything in his imperfectly learned bag of sorcerer's tricks.

She remembered him in the hospital, dying, reaching up to grab at her face. Trying to pull out the dragon.

"Guys," she whispered. "I remember everything."

She slid her left hand out of the urn. Her fingers and palm were streaked with black and for a second she didn't know what to do. She didn't want to rinse Albert down the sink, or wipe him off on the increasingly grubby dress.

Finally she let vitagua flow over her skin, washing him into itself. The black-flecked spirit water clung to her hand like a glove.

She scooped up the bloodied bits of the earring with a rag from the counter, wadding them up and pocketing them.

"Astrid, did you learn anything we can use to contain the spill?" Sahara said. "You know, the vitagua coming out of the chimney and dribbling into the downstairs freezer? The big problem?"

"Talk it into flowing back?" Astrid said.

"Don't joke," Jacks said.

"No joke." Astrid returned to the living room, letting her hand drift over the blue-stained carpet. She tugged, and all the vitagua within her body surged to her hand, dense and cold, pulling her fingers down like magnets, magic calling to magic.

"Wait," Jacks said, still holding the bloody cloth. "You should practice, right?"

"No, this is old hat," she said, reveling in the sense of control. This was how it had been when she was a kid, before the quake, before she'd scared herself. "Watch."

She pulled a single drop of vitagua out of the soaked carpet, raising it in midair and letting it fall. She envisioned it getting bigger, like she was rolling a snowball on a warm winter day.

Grow it did.

She heard Jacks's measured intake of breath as she pulled, hard but carefully, sucking liquid magic out of the rug. A perfectly spherical reservoir formed under her outstretched hand, growing to waist height.

Astrid pulled harder.

Droplets of blue wept through the layers of white paint on the ceiling, leaving pockmarks in the plaster. Vitagua burst from the bricks of the fireplace, rupturing the blue paint as it joined up with the rest. Spirit water threaded up from under the floor, drawn from the spill in the basement. Another miniature river came from the fireplace—the flow from the unreal that was still shoving itself into the house.

Grunting with effort, Astrid forced vitagua out of her body through the punctures the Chief had left in her shoulder and arm. She drove it out, adding to the pool hanging in the living room, and as the level of magic she was carrying dropped, the confusing swirl of knowledge about the future decreased.

The grumbles quieted.

She didn't purge completely. . . . You never knew when you might need a little foreknowledge.

"Okay, you've gathered it up. But how about getting it back into the unreal?" Jacks said.

"That's easy too," she said. Skirting the Chief's corpse, she set her hands on the hearth. The globe of liquid followed her, rolling onto the mantel as if it were solid. She shoved it into the fireplace, letting it flow a couple feet up the chimney.

"Stay," Astrid said, as if it were a dog, and the liquid magic undulated in place, clinging to the mantel as if dammed there.

Once she was sure it wouldn't move, she imagined it flowing back through the crack in the hearth. "Just for a while," she crooned. "Not for long."

Resistance from the other side—the great vitagua icebergs and their frozen inhabitants had sensed a chance, after so long, to melt themselves free.

"Please," Astrid begged. She gripped the mantel, clenching mentally. After a second a vortex formed in the pool of fluid, a miniature whirlpool that crept around the edges of the vitagua, which was draining back into the unreal a bit at a time. "It's going back," she said.

"Okay," Sahara said. "One problem solved."

Jacks let out a sigh. "What now? Figure out how to get Astrid out of here once it's gone?"

"All of us out of here, Jacks," Astrid insisted.

"Right. Us . . ." He scanned the spattered room, gaze stuttering over the shrouded body of his father. Then he turned, disappearing down the hall.

The sound of Jacks retching made her concentration lapse . . . and the vitagua flowing into the unreal slowed, just a bit. She clenched her fist—a concentration trick Albert had taught her—and pushed. The flow increased.

Okay. She could lock her attention there in her hand—by keeping the fist clenched, she could keep the flow going and still think about other things.

"How long will it take to drain it?" Sahara said.

"An hour, maybe?" One-handed, Astrid fumbled with the kaleidoscope. The Sheriff and his minions were scurrying about outside, waving their arms and pointing at the house. "They'll try to contact Mark. Isn't that how it goes in the movies—they contact the hostage-taker?"

"Sheriff did call," Sahara said, voice edgy. "I shouted at them through the window, with Siren on—told them to hold tight. It should be okay."

"Okay." Beyond the police line, the street was filling up with neighbors. Grim-faced firefighters were on the scene, setting up lines to keep the people at bay.

"Just another hour," she said again, not sure whether she was pleading with the police outside or the impatient reservoir of magic in the unreal.

CHAPTER TWENTY-NINE

QUIET SETTLED OVER THE living room as the magic continued to drain. Astrid leaned against a wall, pushing vitagua into the unreal and trying not to look at the Chief's corpse. Jacks returned from the bathroom and took up the kaleidoscope, tracking police activity outside.

Mark Clumber rocked on his heels at the threshold between living room and kitchen, staying well away from the windows. The shotgun dangled from his left hand; with his right, he toyed with his glasses.

When Sahara broke the silence it was like a pin jabbing through skin.

"I know you want to get out of here," she told Mrs. Skye. She and the old woman were seated on the steps that led upstairs. "I can tell you're scared. I can feel it. You don't have to be—you could walk out of here right now."

The older woman fiddled with her hearing aid. "I knew this house was haunted. Didn't figure you three were breaking out the ghosts. . . ."

"We didn't do a very good job," Astrid said dully.

"If you wanted them loose, girl, you've done fine."

"Pat, you're not helping," Sahara said. "We want to let you go. Promise you won't tell what's going on?"

"Sweetie." Mrs. Skye brushed away a lock of Sahara's hair. "I can't lie and tell 'em the boy's to blame."

"Could you act freaked out—too upset to talk?" Astrid suggested.

"I'm no actor. But listen, after you get this . . . vitagua, you called it?"

Astrid nodded.

"After it's hid, you can tell the truth, more or less. I saw the Chief break in here. He did attack Sahara."

"Yeah, but . . ."

"As for what happened after—is it true Astrid hit him to get him off you?"

"Yes," Astrid said slowly. "We've got the ax marks on the door—"

"And you're all banged up," Jacks added in a hoarse voice. "As long as nobody said anything about magic . . ."

"Please. My niece'd toss me in the psych ward," Mrs. Skye said. "But what about Mark?"

Sahara glowered. "Do we care?"

"Yes," Astrid answered firmly. "We absolutely do."

"Then maybe you ought to ask my opinion," Mark rasped.

Sahara's lip curled. Jacks scowled back, a warning.

"Go ahead," Astrid said.

Mark shook his head, as if to clear it. "First off, you all officially suck. Second, she—" He pointed at Sahara. "—stops zapping me, or whatever you call it."

"That seems reasonable," Mrs. Skye said. Jacks nodded.

"Why not take the mermaid off, Sahara?" Astrid said.

Face taut, Sahara stuck the pendant in her pocket. "Happy?"

"Third," Mark said. "Me and the old lady are now part of the gang. We vote on what to do, we get a share of the magic goodies—"

"No way," said Sahara, rising. "Not a chance."

He spread his hands. "I cooperate, nobody has to feel guilty. Everything gets simpler. Isn't that right?"

Mrs. Skye said, "I'm not sure I want a share. . . ."

"It's a deal," Astrid said.

"This is crazy," Sahara protested. "He's an untrustworthy piece of shit. He'll betray us."

"So we make him our puppet?" Astrid said.

"We can't do that, Sahara," said Jacks.

"Okay, I know. That would be wrong." Sahara bared her teeth in an insincere attempt at a smile, and Astrid saw that her lips were strangely stiff. "But tell me—what do we say to the cops when we come out?"

Mark said, "I'll tell them I panicked when Jacks blamed me for the Chief's death."

Astrid said: "Panicked . . . you freaked out?"

"I knew I was in trouble, I saw the shotgun. . . ."

"Yeah, I can work with this," Sahara said. "He was worked up, because of the prank I played in Boston—"

"Prank." He sneered. "You framed me for—"

"They'll still charge you for shooting at them, Mark." The skin under Jacks's eyes was gray; he looked decades older. "They aren't going to laugh and slap your wrist."

"Yes, but you've got that mermaid. If you gave it to me, I could convince them to let me go."

Sahara gave him a flat, venomous glance.

"Or you give me something just as . . ." He groped for a word, then beamed. "Powerful. Something powerful."

"You'd be taking a big chance," Astrid said uneasily.

"Clearly the rewards are gonna be worth the risk."

"There has to be another way," Sahara said. "Astrid, you can't let him blackmail us."

Jacks glared. "If you hadn't been playing with people's minds, Sahara, this would never have happened."

"We can fix this, Jacks."

"You can't fix him!" he bellowed, pointing at his father. "Your screwing around got someone killed."

"Why are you yelling at me? Am I in charge here? Did I bash Lee's head in? You want to be pissed at me so you don't have to face up to the fact that the love of your life killed your old man—" Jacks barely moved, but Sahara shut up suddenly, backing away.

"She's right," Astrid said, convinced he was about to deck her. "It is my fault, Jacks."

He stared at them, face bleak and furious, fists clenched.

"The point," Mark said, "is that if I cooperate, nobody's going to jail. Not me, not Astrid."

Sure, the grumbles laughed. She bit her lip, fighting the misgivings. "So the Chief attacks Sahara, I kill the Chief, Mark gets blamed, Mark freaks out. Isn't that kind of a feeble story?"

Sahara shook her head, still cat-tense and watching Jacks. "That's because it's practically true. The cops have heard dumber things than this, believe me."

Astrid touched the gash the Chief had made in her forearm. "Jacks?"

"It's all we've got," he muttered. "If nothing else, it might buy us some time to run."

Us. Astrid smiled wanly, thinking idly of jail cells and interrogations that hadn't happened yet.

"Pat?" Sahara asked Mrs. Skye.

Mrs. Skye gave Sahara a stern look. "You keep Mark out of jail and I'll keep quiet about the magic."

Pat, Astrid mused. She'd never known the old woman's first name.

"Mark will be okay, promise." Sahara patted her hand. "So—now there's a plan, how about you get out of here?"

Mrs. Skye took the kaleidoscope from Jacks, looking out at the street. "They've trampled those flowers you put in my garden."

"Pat?"

"I'm not leaving Mark in here with you three."

"Fine," Sahara said, flapping her arms in frustration. "Don't blame me if something happens. You could be out there right now sharing your ordeal with the reporters, selling your story to the highest bidder."

"Reporters?" Astrid said.

Wordlessly, Mrs. Skye passed over the kaleidoscope. Astrid squeezed her clenched fist tighter, ensuring she could still concentrate on pushing the liquid magic into the unreal. Then she peered at the mob outside her house.

The police were tense, alert, and numerous, in sharp contrast to the spectators wilting in the wretched heat. Townspeople were gathered behind yellow tape, some furtively munching convenience store goodies—potato chips, chocolate bars, and nuts. Sure enough, there was a news van out there, a battered-looking vehicle with a satellite dish on top and an excited camera crew.

How long since Mark had fired at the Sheriff—two hours?

This won't work, Astrid thought. The resistance from the unreal increased as her hope faltered—she had to push harder, to squeeze her fist until the knuckles were white.

"I can't sit in here with him anymore," Jacks said. Pushing past Sahara, he headed upstairs.

Astrid found him in Sahara's room, pacing and red with anger.

"I'm sorry, Jacks."

He kicked the bedframe, rattling it so hard, a screw fell out. "Dad killed Albert?"

"Yeah, but—"

"And he hurt Sahara. He hurt you."

"If we'd been more discreet, like you said . . ."

He kicked the bed again. "If he'd hurt you, I'd have killed him myself."

She was afraid to reach for him.

"All that 'follow in my path' stuff. Dad wanted me to be one of them."

"A Fyreman. Yeah."

"Witch-burners. He wanted me to murder people." He laughed, rubbing his eyes. "So why am I mad at you?"

"I'm still here?" She kicked off the high heels, tears running down her face. I didn't mean for this to happen, she wanted to say, but what kind of excuse was that? "I could go to jail, Jacks. Confess, not fight it."

He sat, head lowered. "Then the well closes, right? Dad wins, it was all for nothing, and you and I—"

Footsteps interrupted him. The others came in, settling around them: Sahara crowding next to Astrid, Mrs. Skye perching in a wicker chair. Mark hovered at the doorway.

The phone rang, an electronic shrill that made them jump. Mark took it from Sahara. "Hello?"

Low words bumbled from the receiver, inaudible. "Demands? Um, no," Mark said. "I'm hashing things out with my ex, that's all. I'll let everyone go real soon." With that, he hit the disconnect.

"You shouldn't incriminate yourself," Mrs. Skye said.

"What do you know about it, Pat?"

"It makes him look guiltier, Sahara."

"We're gonna get him off, how many times do I have to tell you? He'll have a wonderful life and we'll keep him out of prison. Okay?"

"It'll work out," Mark said, pocketing the phone. "I'm coming out ahead on this one way or another."

"See, he's not worried," Sahara said irritably. "Is anyone else hungry? We're going to pass out if we don't fuel up." With that, she flounced out of the room.

"She can't charm every cop in the state," Mrs. Skye said.

"No," Astrid said. "She probably can't."

The woman put her hands on Astrid's cheeks, peering deeply into her eyes. "You owe Mark. He's taking the blame for you."

"She's right," Jacks said. "And Sahara's never going to give him Siren."

Astrid nodded, looking at Mark. A chantment, then. Something the police wouldn't confiscate . . .

She clenched her fist again, concentrated. The vitagua downstairs was still moving out of the real. Carefully, she drew on the magic still pooled within her, bringing it through the cut the Chief had made in her arm. Vitagua flowed down her wrist to her index finger, and she reached out, touching the plastic frames of Mark's glasses. The fluid vanished into them, glowing bright blue and then dimming. When Astrid dropped her hand, they seemed brand-new, almost sparkling.

"The glasses will make people believe you," she said in a low voice. "When you say you're innocent—when you say anything that's true—they'll buy it."

Mark's eyes gleamed—with greed? "What good does that do me if the sharpshooters get trigger happy?"

Chilling thought. Grasping the barrel of the shotgun, Astrid chanted it too. "Point this at the window and pull the trigger," she said.

"You crazy?"

"It's okay."

Mark fired the rifle. It clicked softly, and then the windowsill stretched like taffy, growing up over the glass and creating a hardwood barrier.

"No bullet's getting through that," she said.

"So I can lock us in," Mark said. "What if we want out?"

"Smack the butt of the gun against the barricade," Astrid said.

He shot at the bedroom door, watching the wood grow over it before doing as she'd said. The barrier flaked to dust, leaving an ordinary door behind.

"I'm starving," he said.

"Magic takes energy," Astrid replied.

"Can I do the other windows without passing out?"

Should they tell Mark about the cantations? She looked at Jacks.

"As long as you eat and rest," he said. "Sahara's getting food."

"Cool." With that, Mark went out into the hall, pointing and clicking the trigger at every possible entry point into the house.

Astrid looked at Mrs. Skye. "Are we good now?"

"It's not going to be easy," the old woman said. She dabbed at Astrid's gashed arm with the edge of her shirtsleeve. "They'll break you up, girl. Separate you, ask what happened about a hundred times. Take your stories, chop 'em up. Finally one or another of you will slip and tell some kind of truth that can't be taken back."

"Sahara can keep that from happening," Astrid said.

"That girl." Mrs. Skye's tone was sad. "She's too pleased with the sound of her voice."

The statement sent ice crawling down Astrid's back.

"I should check on her." Jacks disappeared down the hall.

"This is a big damn mess," Mrs. Skye muttered.

"I'll make other things to help us." Astrid fumbled for the lipstick, one-handed. "Would you take this one? If we end up in jail, at least I'll have gotten a few chantments out."

"What's it do?"

Astrid blushed. "Makes you pretty."

"Isn't Sahara watching the inventory?"

"You're part of the gang, remember? Besides, she doesn't know about this one."

"Oh, kid." The old lady's face filled with sympathy. "Don't you see what you're saying? You don't trust her."

Astrid's eyes welled with tears; she almost lost her grip on the vitagua downstairs. "I have to help her."

"You won't help by dancing to her tune." Mrs. Skye leaned into the mirror, putting on the lipstick and blotting her lips with a cotton hankie. Together they watched her features become stronger, the weariness around her eyes vanishing as the salt-and-pepper hair thickened, leaving her looking both beautiful and formidable.

"Cute trick." With a sigh, she tucked the lipstick into her pocket. "What if you put that earring on her?"

"On Sahara?"

"It made you forget about magic, didn't it?"

"Yeah, but . . ."

"Hold her down, put it on, get Mark to send her out to the cops before she can make any more trouble."

Astrid opened her mouth to refuse but the others returned, Sahara and Jacks each carrying a tray piled with random foods: a big bowl of instant soup, crackers, a salad made of canned asparagus and a mixture of pickles.

"Things look good downstairs," Jacks said. "The vitagua is almost gone. We can go soon."

"Good," Astrid said fervently. It was taking more and more effort to keep the flow going.

With the windows sealed, the room seemed like a cave. The temperature had dropped but the air tasted close, stale. They all smelled of nerves and blood.

Jacks sat beside her, draping an arm around her shoulders.

She kissed his cheek, pleased. He was on her left side; Sahara was curled on the floor at her right. The three of them picked at the makeshift feast, and the phone did not ring again.

For that last half hour, Astrid could believe that it could stay this way, that she'd find a way to make the events of this terrible day recede without ripples, that the trouble would wash away and leave her with the two people she loved most.

CHAPTER THIRTY

"IT'S GOTTA BE TIME by now," Mrs. Skye said, as they neared the end of their meal. "Should we check?"

"I'll go." Draining the last drops of her lukewarm soup, Astrid rose.

"We'll all go." Sahara hopped up, brushing invisible dust from her slacks. She had eaten nothing but pickles. Her eyes were peculiar, dark and inhuman.

I should have drained her while she was unconscious.

Pushing on the vitagua to hold it out of the real, Astrid tried to see forward, to see if danger lay ahead.

Nothing. The grumbles were all but silent.

Good riddance, then. "Come on."

Leaving the dishes on the floor, they trooped downstairs, single file, to see if it was time to surrender.

It would be okay, Astrid thought. They had magic on their side, after all—Sahara would Siren the authorities, and with the evidence of magic hidden away . . .

It was a shock to come upon the body of the Chief again, the motionless hump on the living room floor, covered in the drop cloth. Astrid flashed on swinging the block of ice, hitting him—and cringed.

Jacks groped for her hand. "It was self-defense," he whispered, voice thready but firm, and she nodded fiercely.

They crept up to the fireplace, searching for any trace of blue. There was nothing. The vitagua was gone.

"We're done," Sahara said. "Quick, Astrid, freeze it and we'll tidy up."

"We're not done," Astrid said. "Sahara, I need to drain you."

"No way! Henna died—"

"You know it's safe. I've done it three times now."

"I need it," Sahara said. "To gauge the cops . . ." She looked at Jacks pleadingly.

"I'm with Astrid on this."

"And what a big surprise that is."

"Sahara . . ." Astrid grasped for a gentle way to induce her friend to allow the drain. "It's the best way."

"It's not best for me!"

Jacks gave her a sidelong glance, eyebrow raised in query. Offering to grab Sahara, perhaps, make her submit?

It might be the only way. Sahara had always been headstrong, selfish even, and the liquid magic was making her worse.

And it had to be done. It wasn't just her eyes that had changed— the skin of her hands was pink and rough, and the streaks in her hair were more apparent, light circles on glossy, almost green-tinted hair.

Hold her down, drain her, and use the earring to make her forget, as Mrs. Skye had suggested. But Sahara had been betrayed by everyone she'd ever loved.

No. Try reason. "Sahara, I'm in charge of the spring. You said so yourself."

"You're punishing me for causing the spill."

"Your eyes look strange. They'll notice."

"We mermaid them into ignoring it!"

"Sahara—"

"I said no." She threw out a hand in a *stop* gesture, and caught Astrid under the chin with her index finger.

The jolt of contact brought knowledge with it, a sense of how fast Sahara was falling—had fallen—into vitagua-induced madness. Their plight didn't matter—all that mattered was getting more magic. The grumbles were telling her things about all of them, intoxicating knowledge. . . .

Astrid jerked back, raising a hand to her neck. Her clamped-down concentration on the fireplace—on the vitagua flood—broke.

The house trembled, shivering at first and then bucking. They all fell, Jacks pitching toward the kitchen, Sahara and Astrid doing an involuntary dance near the front door. Mark caught Mrs. Skye before she could pitch down the steps, then tumbled onto the carpet.

Outside, they heard car horns and people shouting.

Vitagua geysered out of the fireplace in a rush, spraying the room, washing over Mark, crumbling the hearth. Hunks of brick and mortar bounced on the carpet as the floor around the fireplace caved in, revealing the basement, the open maw of the freezer. Astrid had pushed it under the first vitagua leak but it had been perfectly cleaned out, just like everything else. Now it overflowed as the vitagua poured out in a gush.

With a boom like shattering river ice, the wall behind the fireplace split. A blue vein of frozen vitagua glimmered in the crack. Liquid magic gouted into the real through the widening hole in the hearth.

"No," Astrid said. She stretched out a hand and froze the vitagua in the fireplace, sealing the entry point with magical ice. "Cold, cold, everything just freezes up." She was careful to think only of freezing the vitagua before her—not the stuff within.

"Oh, no. No. Now we're really screwed," Jacks said.

"Was anyone splashed?"

"Not me," said Mrs. Skye.

"Jacks?"

Shaking his head, he pointed at Mark, who was soaked from head to toe. His skin was damp and translucent.

"Gonna be God," he mumbled, "Siren can run for president, Siren could rule the world."

"Shut up, Mark," Sahara said. "You'll be okay."

"Lie still," Astrid said. She needed to break his skin. Pooling vitagua into his arm, she groped for a loose nail that lay on the shredded carpet.

"Here," said Sahara in the same instant, holding out a paring knife.

Seeing the blade, Mark panicked. "Get 'way," he bellowed, snatching up and swinging the rifle. The blow caught Astrid on the side of the head and Mark broke free, sprinting past Sahara to the kitchen. He dived into the enclosed back porch and they heard a series of clicks.

The rifle—he'd used it to seal himself in.

"What are you doing?" Mrs. Skye was staring at the knife.

"It's not how it looks," Astrid said. "We need to break his skin to draw out the contamination. We weren't going to hurt him."

The old lady sighed. "I'll talk to him."

"We have other problems," Jacks said, pointing down.

Mouth coppery, Astrid stared into the laundry room. Vitagua lapped at the walls, three or four feet deep. Things floated amid the flood—corks, bits of paper, food containers.

"I saw this. . . ."

Sahara made a sound that fell somewhere between a laugh and a moan. "All your stuff, Jacks."

"It's just stuff," he said.

"It was chantable," she said, and he frowned. "And we could have used your watch. Why'd you take it off?"

"Special occasion." He squeezed Astrid's hand. "Maybe it'll survive."

Astrid glanced away, remembering the feel of it snapping underfoot.

"Perfect tigers," Sahara sighed. "Astrid, how fast can you push this into the unreal?"

She shook her head. "It doesn't want to go."

"There's another way to get rid of it, isn't there?" Sahara said.

"What?" said Jacks.

Astrid leaned on him. "She wants me to chant things."

"Everything in the house, if that's what it takes," Sahara said. Her odd eyes were shining.

"We can't create pools of chantments," Jacks said.

"What does it matter now? We know who was hunting us, and he's dead."

"Mark was supposed to release us soon," Astrid said.

"Screw Mark," Sahara said bitterly. "He signed on to play gunman, he can play gunman until we're done."

"Sahara . . ."

"Come on, we can't give him a bunch of chantments and turn him loose. Too many people know already."

"Whose fault is that?" Jacks said.

She ignored him, letting her voice drop to a whisper. "As for Pat, I have an idea—put the earring on her."

The frozen vein of vitagua in the wall glimmered as Astrid fought for calm. "Sahara. We're the crazed gunmen. You and me. I'm the killer, Pat and Mark the hostages."

"But—"

"You can't blame Mrs. Skye for looking out for him."

Sahara glowered. "She's making everything harder."

"I'll make the chantments," Astrid said. "We have to hold off the police until that's done. Then we have to get everyone—and I mean everyone—out of here."

"Making chantments will not fix this," Jacks said.

Sahara laughed shrilly. "Tell him what you told me—how you're the boss and all."

She ignored the outburst. "Come up with an alternative, Jacks."

"There isn't one." He kicked a loose brick into the basement.

"Okay," Sahara said, suddenly pleased. "Same job, different time line. Hold down the fort, lovebirds. I'll go upstairs and collect some chantables."

"Lovebirds," Jacks said, as she trotted upstairs. "I didn't think you'd tell her."

"Of course I did." Astrid kissed him. "Jacks, your paintings."

"I have everything a guy could ever want," he said quietly, and she folded herself against his chest.

"Your dad . . ."

"Started it," he said, not without difficulty. Then they were kissing at the edge of the hole in the floor, and he was wiping tears off her cheeks as she fought back sobs.

"Come on," he said. "Hang together or hang separately, you know? We have to keep an eye on the mad mermaid."

"She'll be okay," Astrid said.

"She's off the deep end."

"If we fight, she leaves," Astrid said. "I can't do this alone—"

"What am I, invisible?" he said, and then his face grew grave. "Astrid, last night, when you were asleep—"

A floor above them, the phone rang.

She went into the kitchen, leaning her ear against the locked door. "Mark?"

No answer. The phone continued to ring.

"Mark, they're probably freaked out by the tremor," she said. "You've got to talk to them."

"Not coming out."

She reached for the kaleidoscope, looking in. Mark was on the floor, mumbling to himself. His skin was glistening and red spots were forming on the backs of his hands.

"Mark, you want to be part of the gang or not?"

No answer.

"You said you'd help us buy time with the police. We've got a big spill here—"

"Don't I know it." His tongue looked flat and his lips were stretching back to his ears, making his words mushy.

"I wouldn't have hurt you," she told him. "I was trying to drain out the contamination. Why don't you prick your finger on some glass or something and just slide the tip under the door?"

"Slip me another magical object, and I'll answer the phone next time they call," he said.

"Mark—"

"Am I in the gang or not?"

She reached out randomly, picking up a saucepan lid and chanting it. "It'll stop bullets," she said, sliding it under the door. "But Mark, about the contamination—"

"Piss off or I'll tell 'em everything."

With a sigh, she turned the kaleidoscope's gaze outside. Sunset was in full glorious swing. West through the back wall of the house, she could see gold and cream-tinged clouds, streaks like lash-marks striping the blue.

The block was cut off by now, sealed tight by the police line and patrolled by grim young men in khaki. The townspeople watching at the perimeter looked fatigued and anxious. Men were unloading black trucks at the edge of the police staging area.

"Why all this attention for a small-town gun standoff?" she murmured, tracking her neighbors' upturned faces, their pointing fingers.

What she saw hit like a punch to the gut. Vitagua had sprayed up through the chimney. Syrup-thick, it had drizzled over the edge of the bricks, contaminating the moss on the roof. Humps of green fuzz as big as rats were growing out of control. A dandelion that had somehow rooted itself in the eaves was blooming at high speed, producing first buds, then fist-sized yellow blooms, then clouds of white seed parachutes. Those seeds were taking root everywhere, compounding the problem as they too burst out, gold flowers turning white in seconds, hurling more seeds.

Within the crowd, Astrid could see people sneezing; the air must be full of pollen.

Around the blue-slicked chimney, a cloud of insects had gathered, probably attracted by the vitagua's floral scent. Some were caught in it, writhing in the fluid, growing in size and then falling to buzz drunkenly in the humps of moss.

The contamination was out.

The vitagua within her was a-throb, beating against her pulse, demanding that she split the world open and let the flood come.

Do it, the grumbles whispered. Tune in to that vein of vitagua pushing into the real, lay your hand on it and think of warmth. The town will be under a magical lake so fast . . .

The thought was enticing, hard to shake off.

At least she knew enough to tug the spirit water on the roof back to the brim of the chimney, then pull it down to the hearth.

"Jacks, do you know where Pat is?" Sahara sounded frustrated. "I can't keep track of everyone myself."

On the other side of the porch door, the phone rang.

This time Mark picked up. "I didn't kill Sahara Knax in Boston," he said, voice thin. "You know that now. I want assurances from the Boston police that I'm cleared. Then I'll let everyone go."

There was a pause. "Nobody leaves until I talk to the same detective I talked to before," he said. He hung up with a moist sigh. "You out there, Astrid?"

"Yes," she said.

"That should hold them a while."

She scanned the crowd again, picking out the soldier in charge, a spare graying man who was slamming down a telephone receiver. Under his direction, a team of workers was erecting a wall of stereo speakers near the front yard.

A scattering of pops: gunfire.

Upstairs, Mrs. Skye shrieked. "What is that?"

Astrid climbed to the second floor. "Police are shooting at a contaminated sparrow."

"The vitagua's out?" Jacks said.

"I pulled back as much as I could," she said.

Mrs. Skye looked at Astrid reproachfully. "Things getting crazy out of hand, huh?"

Astrid nodded. The contamination was out; their secret was all over TV. "We should give ourselves up."

"Smart girl," said Mrs. Skye.

"No chance," Sahara said.

"Nobody's getting sweet-talked into ignoring this now."

"Be quiet a minute, Pat. I need to think. . . ."

"Sahara, we can't bluff our way out of this anymore."

"Then we run," Sahara said. "Make some chantments we can use to escape and just take off."

"Leave . . . abandon the house?" The grumbles cried out, as if betrayed. The idea seemed impossible, like leaving an arm behind. "Leave Indigo Springs?"

"There's a whole planet out there. Expand your horizons, Astrid—of course we leave! It's the only way."

"Abandon ship," Jacks agreed. He pulled her against him, drawing a long shuddering breath. "She's right."

"We all leave," she said, trying it out. Sahara leaves, but we go with her. Maybe this was what the vitagua had been saying all along. "Make some chantments and run."

"As many as we can carry," Sahara said. "Things to help us hide. They'll be after us."

"There's an understatement," Mrs. Skye said.

"Pat, you're like a broken record. Could you—?"

"Sahara!" Jacks and Astrid barked simultaneously.

"Sorry," Sahara said insincerely. She pressed a brooch into Astrid's hands. "Chant this, come on."

"It doesn't work," Astrid said. She looked outside again, watching the bustle near the big speakers.

"Don't give up," Jacks said.

"It's true," Astrid said, feeling the weight of her words even as she absently chanted the pin. It would summon fog, she decided—maybe it would buy time if the house was harder for the police to see. She pinned it on Sahara's chest. "Sahara leaves, I—oh, no."

"What?"

"Ma," she said. "And Olive."

Soldiers were escorting Ev Lethewood and Jacks's mother onto a sheltered platform near the speakers. They set Ev up with a microphone. She leaned in, lips moving. No sound . . . then a technician flipped a switch.

"Now?" Ev asked. Her voice boomed through the walls.

Far away, the small figure—Artie Roche, bad cop to Will Forest's good, Astrid thought—nodded.

"Mark Clumber, this is Evelyn Lethewood. You've got my daughter Astrid in there."

Astrid sank to the floor, feet splayed in the remains of their last meal.

"Mark, I've been delivering mail to your sister Elaine for ten years. She's a good woman, and she wants you out of there safe and sound. That's what I want for Astrid. You get what you want from these men and I get my daughter back. Don't hurt her. Don't . . ."

Astrid sobbed as her mother paused.

"They're putting her back on script," Sahara said. "They'll figure Mark needs to hear your name a lot. See you as a person. This means they're still buying that it's Mark who's in charge here. This is good."

"Good," she echoed bleakly. "How do you know this?"

"The vitagua you want so desperately to suck out of me, Astrid," Sahara said. "My sensitivity?"

"Oh, you're a bundle of sensitivity, sweetie."

"Pat—ah, never mind. Plus, Astrid, I watch a lot of crime movies." Her eyes sparkled, as if it were funny.

"Astrid is twenty-seven," Ev boomed, and as she went on, it was as Sahara predicted: Astrid loves this, Astrid did that when she was young. Astrid is a good person.

Astrid wouldn't hurt a fly.

"You have to start chanting things," Sahara said.

"Leave me alone." She covered her face, listening to her mother's dusty-dry desperate voice begging for her life. Then it was Olive's turn to speak, Jacks's turn to hear. He leaned in the corner, watching his mother through the kaleidoscope, not saying a word.

"Suddenly I'm glad I have nobody," Sahara remarked.

Mrs. Skye snorted.

"Pat, shut up."

"You don't have nobody," Astrid managed. She extended a hand, but Sahara pulled away, out of reach.

"They won't let us sit here forever," Jacks said.

"No giving up," Sahara ordered. "Please, Astrid, start chanting. I can get us out of this if you just pitch in."

Was this it? There was an argument, and Sahara leaves. Or maybe we all go. Is that what happens now, Astrid thought, are we there?

She stood, sensing Jack's support, silent and strong. "Yes," she said aloud, answering herself. It was time.

Except it wasn't. The sound of ice cracking downstairs interrupted her before she could speak.

CHAPTER THIRTY-ONE

IT WAS PATTERFLAM. HE had thrust one flame-licked arm from the unreal straight into the house, breaking through the base of the fireplace mantel. Smoke and blue steam boiled off him. The living room floor was burning.

"Shit, oh shit," Sahara said. "What do we do?"

Jacks's face was stony. "Kill him."

Astrid swallowed. "I can't. Not again . . ."

"I'll do it."

"How?"

"The pocketknife that decays things," he said.

"It's here." Astrid unfolded the blade with shaking hands. "Use a cantation."

"Do you remember the words?" Sahara asked.

"Yes," he said. "Astrid, the knife?"

Before she could pass it over, the fire lunged out, licking her wrist. She reared back, and Jacks caught her.

Both smoke alarms went off at once, keening shrilly. Flames were spreading everywhere, streaking along the walls, dancing on the sealed windows. The living room brightened even as the air became smoky and rancid.

Astrid thought fleetingly of the police outside, wondered what they were seeing. The house aglow with firelight, smoke gouting from the chimney . . .

"Kid!" That was Mrs. Skye. She was pounding on the sealed front door—Mark had used the chanted rifle to barricade it. "Do something!"

Do something. Astrid yanked a geyser of vitagua up from the flooded basement, drawing it over the flames, smothering them.

The smoke got denser, and fire continued to pour off Patterflam's arm. Where it touched the vitagua the flames intensified, filling the air with a stench of scorched flowers.

Screams from the unreal howled within Astrid's mind. Right—it wasn't water. Vitagua was flammable.

"He's destroying the magic," Sahara shrieked.

No. Astrid snatched a plastic drinking cup off the floor, chanting it swiftly and tossing it to Sahara. "Point this at anything that's burning."

"Everything's burning," she coughed, struggling to utter a cantation. The air was getting thicker—wet, smoky, and filled with the smell of burnt things.

Another flame leapt to the back of Astrid's wrist, burning a blistering line across her skin. Astrid and Sahara shrieked as one; Sahara pointed the cup. Water came out of it in a firehose torrent, soaking them both.

"Just like old times," Astrid said, and then wondered what she meant.

"Focus," Jacks murmured in her ear, bracing her before she could slip. "Astrid, you want to suffocate?"

"No."

"We need to filter the air."

"Okay." She reached up with a tendril of vitagua, pouring it into a nearby cookbook. When it was chanted she put both hands on it, reciting a cantation. At least there was plenty of heat to power things.

The book began to flap open and shut, sucking the smoke into its pages. Clean air whooshed through the living room with every snap of its covers.

"We're running out of time," Jacks said as the air cleared. Sahara sprayed the room and then—as the fires went out—trained the spray directly on Patterflam's arm. He was working his way farther into the real.

"Keep the fire down while I think," Astrid said, panting.

"Tell *him* that," Sahara said. Patterflam's reddened fist began to dig at the fireplace, breaking it down. A blazing shoulder appeared as the gap between real and unreal widened.

"I can get him from beneath," Jacks whispered in Astrid's ear. "Get down under the hole in the floor, stick the knife in him from below."

She nodded. It made sense. But the basement was flooded. . . .

She dragged more vitagua up and through herself. She sent it around and upward, covering everything in the house in a thin layer of blue fluid.

One by one she isolated items, beginning with the chisel lying at her feet. It would draw the dust and grime from the ruptured fireplace into itself, she decided, clean up the scene. The more normal things looked in here when the police came, the better.

She chanted the wailing smoke detectors, drowning their electric cries in vitagua and making them into chantments that would encourage anyone who stepped inside the house to believe that everything was normal here, that there was nothing extraordinary going on.

She chanted an old marionette of Jacks's. It would dig tunnels, she decided, in case there's no other way out.

The house was beginning to cool. Now to deal with the flood. Astrid kept chanting things, one after another: Henna's stuffed spider would spin them a repaired floor, the kitchen chair would make anyone who sat in it feel relaxed and calm, the tweezers in the bathroom could shut down all those news trucks, the yellow rug in the laundry room could fly. . . .

Her eye fell on Mrs. Skye, her bracelets. Everyone in the house is going to be notorious, she thought. Pat might need to hide from the press. The left bracelet would let Pat disguise herself.

She imagined the old lady getting shot by police as she came out of the house. No, they don't hurt her, she remembered—the other bracelet makes her misty. The soldiers out there were getting trigger happy, but the bracelet will make bullets pass right through her. . . .

Toothbrushes, art supplies, pens, a box of paper clips, the broken clock in the pantry. Astrid chanted the silver in the kitchen drawers, spoons, forks, chanted the pots and pans, the ceramic teapot and plastic sugar bowl. The clothes hanging in the closets, the coats and shirts, the dress she was wearing, all the shoes under Sahara's bed, everything that wasn't made of glass or circuitry . . .

"Hurry," Jacks said. "Patterflam's getting loose."

"I'm done—the basement should be clear." Astrid peered through the broken floor into the basement. Patterflam was nearly free; she could see a torso and leg hanging in the basement. The leg was swinging wild; it had kicked the freezer door shut.

The house hummed with mystic energy.

A small pool of vitagua lay on the basement floor—she had run out of things to chant. Astrid dragged the liquid to the back wall and froze it there in stalagmites.

"Good," Jacks said.

"Burn, witch!" The shout came from far away, from another world. Water boiled off Patterflam's arm as Sahara doused him.

Something was about to go terribly wrong.

"Maybe I should do this . . . ," Astrid said through a rising sense of dread. The fiery legs scissored in midair, swimming.

"This guy is my problem," Jacks said.

"Pat can fight the blaze," Sahara said, handing the cup to Mrs. Skye.

Jacks started downstairs.

"Wait," Astrid said. But there was more cracking, the chimney breaking apart as Patterflam demolished his prison.

No time.

She tried to force out the knowledge of what came next, but the grumbles had told her all they were going to.

Jacks was already downstairs. She hurtled down the basement steps after him.

Every object in the basement had been chanted—Jacks's paintings, his clothes, the laundry baskets. The blue glow of magic settling into solid matter was already fading.

Patterflam's foot swung purposefully, groping for something, anything, to support his weight. Flames dribbled off his toes, melting the plastic lid of the freezer.

"Jacks, let me."

"You can't touch him, remember?" His eyes were locked on the blazing, swinging leg.

"He's right," Sahara said, plucking at her sleeve. "He'll poach you from the inside out—"

Patterflam roared. His head broke through the wall of crumbling bricks. With a snap, the Fyreman pulled himself fully into the real.

He dropped lightly onto the freezer, leaving footprint-shaped burns in its lid before springing down to the concrete floor.

His gaze found Astrid; he started toward her and looked amazed when Jacks stepped between them.

"Stand aside, brother," Patterflam boomed.

Jacks slugged him, lunging with the knife. Patterflam caught his wrist, tossing him aside effortlessly.

A line of flame ran through Jacks's hair as he struck the concrete basement wall. He batted at it and leapt up to tackle Patterflam, only to get caught in a spray of water from above—Mrs. Skye, fighting the fire. He darted sideways, swinging the pocketknife.

"Don't run with that," Astrid heard herself murmuring. It was a mistake. Alerted by her words, Patterflam dodged the blow, catching Jacks by the scruff of the neck and hurling him forward. Hands outstretched, Jacks ran into the wall, the knife, point-first preceding him, puncturing the plaster before he crumpled to the floor.

The house groaned like a tree about to fall.

Patterflam rounded on Astrid again, but now Sahara had the mermaid on. "Patterflam," she said, voice abuzz. "Stop."

The man of flame paused, just for a second. Frost spread up and down the steps, melting as quickly as it formed.

"You're not going to hurt anybody." Sweat was rolling down Sahara's face. "Just stand still."

Patterflam boomed laughter. "Befouled thing, you think to challenge me?"

"Listen—," Sahara said. Her voice broke and she swooned.

Jacks groaned. Patterflam glanced his way.

"Hey!" Astrid said. "I'm the chanter!"

It worked: he advanced on her. She backed down the hall, leading him away from the others.

"Think your day's come, witch?" Astrid didn't answer, just kept retreating into Jacks's studio. Maybe the others could escape—

Fresh air ruffled her hair as she retreated, and she remembered the studio window was still open, that she had knocked out a pane when she climbed through earlier today.

That fact seemed important somehow, important and frightening. She stopped where she was, steps from the window, lost in time again, trying to think. . . .

Then Patterflam was on her. Smoke dried her face. Her hair crisped and the torn cartilage of her ear burned. The thin cotton dress steamed.

But none of that mattered. Through the wall of black smoke, Astrid could see Jacks coming down the hall.

Terror seized her. She opened her mouth, but Jacks put a finger to his lips. If she spoke, Patterflam would turn around, nail him again, maybe kill him.

A crackling of amusement from the man of fire. He put his hands around her waist, burning and squeezing. Waves of heat curled the air around her.

"Stop . . ." Reaching back, Astrid grabbed the only thing she could reach—a plastic apple sitting on Jacks's worktable. It was already chanted, of course, everything was, and all it did was help a person learn to read music. There was nothing left that she could turn into a weapon.

"Pathetic little well wizard." Patterflam immolated the chantment with a glance. He continued to crush her midsection, molten fingers singeing her skin, so painful, she gave in and screamed, remembering poor Dad and the sounds he made as he died. "No witch will ever finish me—that was written long ago."

Jacks was behind him now. "How about me . . . brother?"

Now, too late, Astrid knew what would happen, just in time to watch it unfold. Jacks drove the chanted pocketknife into Patterflam—through him, almost, driving the blade deep into the flames.

Patterflam bellowed in surprise, gouting smoke from the wound. Thunder cracked outside and sizzles of electricity danced over Jacks's skin. Dropping Astrid, Patterflam turned, his body of golden flame blackening at the heart.

Astrid launched herself at Jacks, thinking just tackle him, don't grab, that's how it all goes wrong . . .

. . . but Jacks turned, reached out with one hand even as Patterflam, dying, yanked his other arm. The force of his pull brought Jacks upright in front of the open studio window and he had to, *had* to be knocked back down—what else could Astrid do?

Her reflexes were too slow; she couldn't pull back.

Jacks reached out to catch her, as he always did. His fingers wrapped around hers.

"Let go!" she howled, horrified, as Patterflam lifted Jacks by one arm and her own weight dragged him down. But Jacks hung on, and as Astrid hit the floor she bore him down with her, stretching him between her arm and Patterflam's rising fist like laundry on a line, like a kid dangling between Mom and Dad. Jacks was spread out in front of the wide-open studio window and the dying man of flame stomped her, making her screech as he ground her underfoot. Oh, Astrid thought, there's Sahara kneeling on the floor, gathering the pocketknife along with all the chantments she can carry. Looting while Rome burns, I knew she'd do that. And there's the pop of the sniper's rifle.

I thought it would be louder.

Here's Jacks letting go, falling, even as Patterflam flames out, as he finally dies and the unreal rejoices.

Jacks landed heavily atop Astrid, crushing the breath out of her. Between their bellies she could feel a spreading warmth.

"Don't die," she wheezed, and his eyes widened.

"Don't die?" Sahara said, uncomprehending. "He's toast, baby, gone and good riddance."

"Get the saltshaker from my room. Pat, Pat, do you hear? There's a saltshaker. . . ." Her shout was faint, almost a gasp. Jacks's weight made it hard to draw breath.

"You said that last night in your sleep," Jacks said. His tone was normal, strong. " 'Don't die, Jacks, don't—' "

"Wait," Sahara said, getting it. "Stop, wait."

He sucked on his lips, hard. His forehead was resting on hers. "Then he bleeds out, you said."

"Then he bleeds out?" Astrid repeated. He was already chalk-white. Rolling him off her, she pressed her hands against his stomach. "Jacks, I won't let you."

"Look," he said. "All this mess, but that painting I did of Dad is untouched."

"Jacks," she said. "Don't die."

"He's going into shock," Sahara said. "If we surrender—"

"It's too late," Astrid said. Her belly and legs were drenched with blood.

"I can't find any damn shell," Mrs. Skye called from one floor up.

"She said a saltshaker!" Sahara bellowed.

Jacks blinked a couple times, seeming to shrivel, and she pressed her lips against his. "Hold on, Jacks."

"It was their wedding," he said. "Albert and Olive's. You were dancing with your dad and neither of you . . ."

". . . we didn't know how to dance," she finished. "Jacks, what about it?"

"Clumsy thing," he said. The pain washed out of his face, leaving him smiling. His muscles relaxed, all at once, and he died.

"No," Sahara said.

Astrid tried to close his eyes and then pulled back, horrified, as she streaked blood over his face.

"Astrid, we have to get out of here."

"Jacks," she said, trying to shake him awake. Stupid skinny runner, she'd thought, when Albert first introduced them. He'd been on the track team. He'd been quiet and polite, hard to hate.

Jacks had taught her to ride and raft. He'd taken her out caving for her birthday last year. He'd driven her to Ev's house from the hospital the night Albert died. He'd helped her move into and then out of Jemmy's place.

"Albert keeps trying to get you to leave town," she murmured, brushing his forehead with the back of her hand. She felt like she was falling into a well of ice water. "He gives you the watch. He tries to save you."

She sobbed. "You were right about Elizabeth. It was important, Jacks, I just didn't see . . ."

"Astrid." Sahara shook her shoulder. "Snap out of it."

She jerked away, furious. "He loved me. He always—"

"Astrid, baby . . ."

"Don't call me that." Wiping her nose, she hunched over him, pressing her face to his, kissing his limp mouth. "I'm sorry, Jacks, don't go, please don't . . ." Her eyes snapped open.

"What is it?" Sahara said.

"Now's when I remembered the dead birds at Albert's feet," Astrid said.

"What?"

She got up hurriedly. "He's not quite gone."

"What? He is, honey, he's dead," Sahara said.

"Help me pick him up."

"Sweetheart—"

"Don't call me that!"

"There's no time," Sahara said. "The house is falling apart. We have to make a run for it."

"Pick him up!" Astrid shouted. She lifted Jacks under his shoulders, struggling to stand.

Dropping the pillowcase full of chantments, Sahara took his feet. "What're we supposed to do?"

"Remember Elizabeth?" They bore Jacks's body down the hall, back to the vitagua frozen in the corner of the laundry room. Laying him out on the floor, Astrid blew on the ice and it melted again. With a small come-hither twitch of her fingers she drew the vitagua under Jacks.

"Elizabeth Walks-in-Shadow? What about her?"

"She was enclosed in vitagua by her apprentice. She was dead, but she hadn't quite died."

"Astrid."

"I'll do anything," she begged.

"What are you doing?" Sahara said.

"I practiced on animals when I was a kid," she told Jacks. "The grumbles knew this would happen. . . ."

They wanted him to die. . . . They knew I'd do anything.

Yes . . . this was right. Jacks's arms flopped outward, and for a second he looked like a kid learning to float on his back. He sank into the liquid as Astrid brought the temperature of the magic down.

His eyes opened.

"It's going to be okay," she promised, and kissed him.

Jacks sighed, once, a long rattling exhalation, just as his face went under. Astrid froze the vitagua around him in an inch-thick layer. "Ice sculpture. Mixed media, vitagua and artist," she said, and giggled.

"Don't you go hysterical on me," Sahara warned.

Astrid pulled the paintbrush out of her hair. Laying her hand against the ice of his blue-cased fingers, she chanted it. "Something to connect us. Jacks, please, let me keep something of you."

Jacks did not react. As the vitagua surrounding him hardened from slush to ice it sparkled, diamond hard.

"Then I slide him into the unreal," Astrid murmured to the

floes. She pushed, hard, and the statue of Jacks slid to the crack in the wall, where all the frozen vitagua lay waiting to break through to the real. Ice stuck to ice as he made contact.

Astrid leaned a cheek against the ice. "If you stay exposed, they'll come and burn you. You waited so long to get loose; do you want to throw it away?"

Murmurs came back to her from the ice. Reluctance, anger. Jacks was a fyrechild, the enemy.

"I'll do anything," she begged. "Please, keep him safe. I'll bring the thaw. I'll melt it all."

After a second, the vein of ice vanished, taking Jacks with it. Broken bricks and cement were all that remained.

"Astrid?" Sahara's alchemized fingers fell on her shoulder.

Astrid worked her mouth open and shut. "Then I say what do you think Jacks was trying to tell me? About Albert's wedding? And you say—"

"It's when he fell in love with you, dope," Sahara said. Tears sparkled in her eyes but did not fall. "I guess it's just you and me now, huh?"

Squeezing her paintbrush chantment, Astrid sobbed.

CHAPTER THIRTY-TWO

THERE WAS NO TIME to mourn.

She had dropped her head onto Sahara's shoulder to weep, but within seconds Sahara pulled away. "Listen, we have to escape before they shoot someone else."

"Escape? But Jacks—"

"Honey, I know. But the house is falling. It's time to go."

It was true. Mildew bloomed across the walls as the pipes rusted and ruptured. Underfoot, chunks of concrete cracked through the linoleum.

"We need chantments," Sahara said.

Astrid gulped. Could she have foreseen Jacks being shot? If she could work out why Sahara was supposed to leave, she could do better, prevent it. . . .

I know we fight, she thought. All I have to do is not fight her. Go along with whatever she says, siphon her next time she's sleeping.

The grumbles howled with laughter.

"No fight, no breakup," she said. "No fight—"

"You say something?" Sahara was grabbing up random items, stuffing them in the pillowcase as she towed Astrid toward the stairs. They shuffled along, Sahara looting, Astrid in tears, and as they got to the foot of the steps a blast of water hammered them.

Mrs. Skye had coaxed Mark out of hiding. Eyes bulbous, his damp skin patterned in red and black, he played the firehose cup over the dying fires.

"I've got the saltshaker," said Mrs. Skye.

Astrid turned her face to the wall, shivering.

"It's okay, Pat—it's too late," Sahara said.

"Too late?" Mrs. Skye took in the bloodstains on them both. "Stupid kids. Is he dead?"

"It's not Astrid's fault," Sahara said.

"Whose is it, then—yours?"

"Can we focus on getting away? Come on, Astrid, you made things, right, for our escape?"

No fight, no breakup. Head lowered, Astrid pointed at a yellow throw rug. "It's a flying carpet."

"That's you and me, then." Sahara stepped on the carpet, pulling Astrid with her. "Pat, take Mark out the front door."

"Part of gang," Mark gurgled.

"Not on your life," Sahara said. The carpet rose off the floor—one inch, then two . . .

"There's vitagua here." Astrid stepped off. She could sense it nearby, calling. She pulled, and the freezer door flew open as if punched. Vitagua rose from within. Patterflam kicked it shut, she thought.

"Fabulous," Sahara groaned. "Can you absorb it?"

Astrid reached for the fluid, then quailed. "Fighting . . . can't . . ."

"We aren't fighting." Sahara took her by the shoulders. "Astrid, if you leave the vitagua here, people will get contaminated, right?"

No fight, no breakup. Even so: "You want to get away with as much magic as I can carry."

There was a crash upstairs. Mark flinched.

"Go on." Sahara brushed a curl off her smoke-streaked forehead. "You know you can't say no."

Stretching out her hands, Astrid drew in the vitagua. The grumbles became a riot of shouts. She kept on, drinking it in until liquid magic lay under her skin, within the folds of her brain, behind her toenails. Voices slashed at her and she screamed, flailing.

"I maxed out, Will," she wailed. "No more, don't make me."

"It's okay," Sahara said. "Nobody's forcing you."

"Liar." She tried to focus on the future, the next few minutes. The cacophony chattered about everything, too many things.

"No more," she moaned, covering her ears.

Sahara crawled to the freezer, thrusting her hands into the fluid.

"What are you doing?" Mrs. Skye demanded.

"Helping." Sahara's eyes darkened, and the patterns in her hair clarified. Her arms began to tuft, the hairs on her wrists fluffing into pinfeathers.

"Owwww," Sahara said happily.

No. Astrid froze the last of the vitagua solid, so it was too cold to flow through skin. She ended up holding an icicle the size of a baseball bat.

"Jesus, Astrid, I'm trying to help."

"Now's when I recognize the pattern," Astrid said. "It's turning you into a starling."

Throwing back her head, Sahara buzzed with birdy laughter. "It's for the best. I feel great."

Don't fight. "You're *changing*. This is the part where I remind you—"

"I don't care about some curse! Patterflam's dead, the Chief's dead. Astrid, this is magic. We'll fix the ozone layer, reforest the Amazon. Jacks would have wanted—"

"Leave Jacks out of this." Icy tears froze her eyelashes. She heard Jacks's voice among the grumbles, imagined him behind her, ready to catch her if she lost her balance. But he wasn't; if she fell, she'd end up on her butt. She moved without premeditation, tucking the paintbrush into her hair, wishing him back, wishing for help. Her fingernails changed to brushtips.

Images bloomed on the walls—Sahara, at the lip of a volcano. Half animal and half woman, she had mad eyes, starling wings, and red-tipped talons.

"This is what you become," Astrid said. The house creaked. Plaster rained down from above.

"Astrid," Sahara said soothingly. "I know this is my fault. I should have been more discreet. But if we get out of here with enough magic to protect ourselves, I'll make it all up to you."

"How could anything make up—?"

"It's just the two of us now." She stroked Astrid's cheek. "I know what you need, what you've always—"

"I need Daddy," she said. "I need Ma and Jacks."

"You need *me*." Sahara leaned close. "The important thing is us."

No fight, no breakup. Astrid trembled. "You, me, and the spirit water?"

"Darling, you've wanted me since grade school."

Since forever. "You're saying—you'll love me, right, if I need you to?"

"Oh, my euphemistic darling. I'll fuck you brainless." Sahara kissed her on the mouth with chilly, beak-hard lips. Their tongues met for an instant.

She pulled back with a gleeful inhuman wink.

Astrid straightened, stunned, sucking wind. Crashes sounded above them in the attic—termites were reducing the beams of the roof to powder.

Satisfied, Sahara put on Siren. "Mark?"

"No!" Mrs. Skye bellowed. "You said you wouldn't do this again!"

"Gotta hide this last bit of magic, Pat. Mark, come here."

Face slack, Mark marched forward. Mrs. Skye couldn't hold him. She looked at Astrid, pleading.

"And here's where it finally comes apart," Astrid said. She snatched the mermaid from Sahara's chest, snapping its chain with one jerk of her work-muscled arm.

"Run!" Astrid screamed, and Mark stumbled backwards.

Sahara gaped at Astrid, eyes brimming. She tore a fistful of hair—hair mixed with feathers—out of her scalp. A furious, buzzing *snnk-snnk* hummed in her throat.

"Sahara, I'm sorry, but—"

"Don't. You don't want me, that's your choice."

"Because you couldn't buy me off with sex? Sahara—"

"Give me the mermaid." Sahara grabbed, and Astrid pushed her away with the frozen club of vitagua.

"Sahara, stop it."

"Give me Siren!"

"I can't."

With a shriek Sahara pounced on the icicle instead, wresting it out of Astrid's hand. She smashed it into the banister, breaking off a sharp edge, and then drove the point into Mrs. Skye's chest. The old woman collapsed, and Sahara kept pushing.

"The mermaid, Astrid, now."

"Now's when I finally tell you no." Cold tears ran down her face as Astrid melted the icicle embedded in Mrs. Skye's chest. Blood and vitagua poured down the old lady's blouse. For a dreadful moment, Astrid thought she had a third death on her hands.

No, she thought, she's breathing. . . .

Sahara pounced on the magic saltshaker. "She doesn't have to die, Astrid."

Grumbles jabbered, making her head ache. "Is this where I take that from you?"

"It will heal her, right?" Sahara held it up. "Trade it for the mermaid."

"No, Sahara," Astrid repeated. It was just as hard the second time.

"Maybe you think she might as well die. She is cursed, after all."

"Nobody else dies." Astrid pulled on the vitagua in Sahara's wrist, upending the shaker over Mrs. Skye. Bright healing stars drifted downward from the chantment. The ugly blue wound in the old lady's chest closed itself.

Sahara hurled the saltshaker away. It fell against a smoldering pile of wood stakes and melted, filling the air with the smell of burnt lilacs.

I could hold you, Astrid thought, and what hurt the most was she suddenly didn't want to. She released the vitagua. Sahara rubbed her hand.

"Go," Astrid told her.

Mrs. Skye groaned, folding over onto herself.

"Another contaminated victim," Sahara huffed, stepping onto the magic carpet. "You saved her life? So what?"

"I save her?" Astrid asked. "Has that happened yet?"

Smirking, Sahara stamped on the carpet. It rose, lifting her up the stairs. She maneuvered it through a widening gap in the roof and was gone.

She didn't say good-bye.

"Cursed," Mrs. Skye rasped as Astrid watched Sahara fly away. Her face was growing whiskers, a snout. A black bear? "I'm cursed."

"No," Astrid whispered. "I fixed you. If I could . . . Jacks? Did I do something? Did I save her?"

Smudged paint ran over the freezer. Staring at the images, Astrid reached out to the spirit water on the floor as Mrs. Skye continued to change, her canines getting longer, her hands becoming paws.

She traced the vitagua around Mrs. Skye's bracelets.

"Astrid?"

"You'll be okay," she said, concentrating. It was like chanting anything—instead of binding magic into an object, though, she was sliding the chantments into the woman's flesh, joining them.

Mrs. Skye seemed to grow, her limbs stretching waxily. Then she melted. Suddenly her face was Chinese, delicate and young, with wide, wise eyes.

No whiskers, no fur. She appeared human.

"Mrs. Skye?"

The goddess gaped, touching her face. "What happened?"

"I meant to do your bracelets," Astrid said. "I forgot you had the lipstick."

Blinking, Patience became misty. She tumbled past the freezer, sliding through it as if it wasn't there. She solidified, and her features changed again. "I can't control it."

Astrid stared at the radiant woman beside her. "There was never a normal life, was there? Now was when I realized there was never any hope I'd be able to hide being the spring-tapper. I screwed up."

Patience tugged on her arm. "Let's get out of here."

"We ask you to leave us," Astrid said. "But you don't trust us to do the right thing, do you? You feel responsible."

"Kid, if you're going to run . . ."

"I don't run for months."

"We can't stay."

She had let Sahara go. Had wanted her to leave. Despair rose in her. "Let the house fall."

Patience grunted, sounding like a cranky old woman. "This is no time for suicide fantasies."

"Mark was gone. There wasn't anybody left for you to protect, Patience."

"I'm not leaving you here to get crushed, kid."

Astrid sighed. "I could go into the unreal; freeze over."

"That would be avoiding the problem."

"It's what I did all summer."

"Summer's over." Patience took her by the chin, holding her gaze as debris fell around them. "You think you lost everything? Think there's nothing left?"

"Jacks died. I let Sahara go."

"There's always something else."

Rubbing her face, Astrid nodded. "Ma. I have to go with her."

"So let's go," Patience said. "There's nothing else to do here, is there?"

"No," Astrid said. "You were right. Summer's over."

They crept up the buckling basement steps, making their way across the living room floor. Its once-pink carpet was gray with mold. The shredding wallpaper stank of old glue and the fireplace was breaking into dust. Plaster dropped from above and Astrid heard sizzling inside the walls.

"Bad wiring, bad plumbing." She stubbed her toe on a hunk of molding. "Bad Astrid."

"Keep going." Patience tugged her away from the stairwell. Was it yesterday that they'd moved in?

"When did Ma attack Olive?"

They reached the half-open front door, with its rotten, sagging frame. Patience pressed her against a wall.

"We're coming out!" she yelled. "Don't shoot!"

A nova of spotlights shone on the porch. Outside, soldiers were shouting. One of them—Roche probably—had a bullhorn. "Hold your fire, you morons, hold your fire!"

"Then we went to jail for a while," Astrid said. "Believe it or not, you're going to like it there."

As they stepped out into the media glare, the house collapsed behind them.

CHAPTER THIRTY-THREE

"SO YOU SURRENDERED," I say. Reaching the end of this tale has left me wanting a smoke, even though it has been fifteen years since I had a cigarette.

"Yes." Astrid's brown eyes shine. "Patience and I . . . stepped back into the world."

"I saw it on TV." The images are seared into my memory like third-degree burns. Mark staggering out first, his glasses glimmering and a rifle in his hands. He was already alchemized, so much a salamander man that his hair was falling out.

Caroline and my daughter were watching too. My wife's face burned with something I didn't understand. Now I think it was greed, the same hunger for power captured in these portraits of Mark and Sahara.

The cameras caught Sahara Knax as she flew through the broken roof on a flying carpet, zooming away from Mascer Lane and outpacing the helicopters in pursuit.

Next came Patience. She drew the attention of every camera operator away from Sahara, from the spectacle of a woman in flight. Patience, who made Astrid seem merely ordinary as she too crept out onto the porch of the house, barefoot, clad in a bloodstained blue dress. Her head was bowed, her hands raised as though she were a criminal. As though she were to blame.

Roche had rushed in, bellowing: "Who's this? Where's Patience Skye?"

Astrid, caught at the edge of Patience's close-up, said, "This was Mrs. Skye."

Watching, I suddenly knew the world was slipping beyond human understanding or control. I'd still believed, though, that we could change it back.

Now, I'm not so sure.

I shake off the memories and look at the fortune cards. Astrid hands over the deck and I thumb through. Here I see Patterflam, stabbed by poor, doomed Jacks; there I see blue bubbles welling from the crumbling fireplace. Tulips edge the picket fence in one springtime scene, the flowers foreground to the trio of housemates as they laugh together on the front porch. Flipping it over, I see policemen blockading Mascer Lane.

I linger over an image of a water serpent—some kind of alchemized aquatic life. I've seen video of these too. Sahara claimed she had created them: my wife and countless others were suitably impressed.

"Roche whisked us off to jail," Astrid says. "He dug Lee's body out of the ruins of the house and learned Mark had never shot him . . . that the Chief had never been shot."

"They tried to get answers out of Patience," I remember. "But she wasn't talking. Protecting you?"

"She is kinder than I deserve," Astrid says. "I was so overwhelmed by the vitagua, I could barely work out what was happening. I couldn't get things straight—what happened when. I was so sad. . . ."

"Grieving over Jacks," I say. "And Sahara's betrayal must have been like a death too. The person you thought you knew was gone. . . ."

"In her place was a hole, something raw," she murmurs.

"Like having a tooth pulled without anesthetic. Bloody, painful, and there's a gap—"

"Exit wound." She peers at me through windblown curls. "I didn't know you knew that, Will."

It is a relief, I find, that she hasn't seen into every corner of my soul.

Wind snaps my shirtsleeves like sails, raising plumes in the gritty sand at my feet. I should prod Astrid—I still have questions—but I can't bear the thought of digging at her. Earlier she said I'm not sentimental. Roche once claimed he hired me because I'm a heartless bastard. I want to prove—to anyone—that it isn't true.

"Unsentimental and heartless aren't the same." Astrid answers my unspoken thought. Turning over the next card, I see . . . myself.

I am wearing the clothes I have on now, sipping tea and wearing an expression I've never seen in the mirror. My listening face, I suppose—but there is something in it, something wistful, affectionate. The portrait shows emotions I don't remember feeling, but I glance up and see them again, doubled, reflected in Astrid's pupils.

It's a shock, a view of myself I never wanted, and when I snap my eyes down they find the painted image again. I release the card into the wind, send it sailing over the white sand dunes.

"What about Sahara and you?" I ask.

"Ah, Sahara," she says. "Without the mermaid, she's had to seduce her followers with flashy stunts. Taking credit for creating the alchemized forests, bribing her favorite Primas with chantments. Luckily she knew where we'd sent all the things I made. But—"

"But she needs more magical objects."

"Yes. Which is why she needs me."

"But you're going to hide?" The sound of starlings shrieking and buzzing, behind us, is louder.

"That wouldn't be responsible, would it? I've learned my lesson, Will." White grit swirls around the toes of Astrid's shoes. "Do you like the unreal? I remember you saying so . . . soon? Have you said it already?"

"Astrid . . ."

"Would you want to stay?"

Fear and desire pull me in two directions. "Roche'll have my ass for letting you escape. . . ."

"Like you could've stopped me, tough guy."

"There's my children."

"Don't decide right away," she says. "You have the ring, you're safe. Think it over."

"Why should I?"

She smiles. "Will, the world will be a better place after this flood has broken. Cleaner air, lower birthrate, less poverty. Your kids have a future—a good one."

The thought of retrieving my children from their kidnapper mother . . . "The unreal has day care, right?"

"Um. Not exactly."

"Medical benefits?"

"Ma knows first aid." The dimple appears on her cheek.

"Retirement package?"

"When you get old I'll give you the rocking chair my grandfather made. Set it up on a porch somewhere."

"This would be the rocker that Ev fell out of?"

"Well, I'll chant it. Or you can wear a helmet."

I'm grinning. Unbelievable. "What do you want with me, Astrid?"

"For starters, I need an apprentice." She returns my smile. "I know I've made it sound real appealing."

All I can manage in response is a nervous cough.

"Think it over," Astrid says. "It's time we moved on to the pyrotechnics. Ready?"

"No."

My belly lurches and suddenly we are back in the real.

We are beside a small lake fringed by fir trees. The wind is gone and I place us immediately . . . I drive past this spot every morning on my way to work. We're perhaps five miles from the secured compound.

Starlings crowd together on every branch of every tree, on the ground around us, shrieking. The sound is so loud, my ears hurt.

Sahara Knax is here.

She steps out of the trees, expression haughty as she looks us over and dismisses me. Her iridescent wings are tinted with brown spots. Her coat drags on the ground.

Mark Clumber follows, his salamander face helpless and afraid, his magic glasses clutched in one slimy hand.

"So you came out," Sahara says, addressing Astrid. "Afraid I'd break into the unreal?"

"You're not that powerful, Sahara."

"Right. You're the anointed one. I'm just some thief wielding powers I can't understand."

"That's the gist." Astrid regards her calmly. "You should agree to let me drain you."

"It's cute how you think you're still in charge." Sahara flicks out a strand of pearls. I don't feel anything, but Astrid is thrown backwards. She comes down hard on her butt with a splash in the shallow lake. Her nose is bleeding.

"You're going to come with me," Sahara says. "Whatever you did to Patience? You'll do it for my Primas. You're going to make chantments and keep your mouth shut. Do it, if you like, because you figure I'll snap out of it one day."

"I know better, Sahara."

"Then do it to keep people from getting hurt." She waves vaguely at Mark, at me.

"Sahara?"

"Yeah?"

"I was always in charge." Astrid climbs to her feet. Clutched in her fist is a clump of mud, gray silt, and dangling green algae that writhes in her fingers, clearly contaminated.

"Whatever power you think you had, you threw it away." Sahara produces a diaper pin from her jacket, brandishing it like a weapon. Astrid's clothes knot together, constricting at her wrists, her waist, her throat.

Astrid barely has time to choke before I've moved between the two of them. My clothes quiver. Then there's a gust from my ring. The fabric goes limp and I feel the fatigue setting in.

"Remember Will?" Astrid says. "Will doesn't like traitors."

"Don't care much for violence, either," I say.

"News flash, then—it's Astrid who's your murderer. You

think I killed that asshole Lee Glade, don't you? She let you think
that?"

"I know she killed him."

"He'll tell anyone who asks too," Astrid says. Our eyes meet
and for some reason it's funny—we laugh.

Sahara leaps skyward, wings displacing gusts of air as she rises
off the ground. She aims at Astrid with the diaper pin from over
my head.

Then Astrid raises her hands . . . and Sahara freezes in midair.

She lets out a surprised sound, a buzzing, distressed birdcall.
Her fingers splay; she drops the safety pin. It falls end over end,
bouncing as it hits the ground. I retrieve it carefully.

Astrid doesn't move as Sahara's hands turn bright blue. "What
are—?"

"I'm holding the vitagua inside you," Astrid says. "As long as
it's in there, I can manipulate your body. Don't you remember?
You might as well be a puppet. Should I make you pick your
nose?"

"You won't hurt me," Sahara snarls, thrashing.

Instead of answering, Astrid looks at Mark. He bites into his
lip, and she draws the vitagua out of him, pooling the liquid above
us, out of reach. Mark's features humanize enough for him to put
the glasses on. Ignoring Sahara as she scissor-kicks the air, Astrid
chants the glasses into Mark, pressing the frames and lenses into
his face. They vanish like a stick sinking into mud, and the red
spots on his skin fade.

"Your turn," Astrid says to Sahara. Opening her muck-filled
hand, she displays a bottle cap and a fishing lure. Litter scavenged
from the bottom of the lake, no doubt, things she picked up when
she landed.

She chants them both, face flushing with vitality, and tosses
the lure at Sahara. It twirls through the air, dragging one sharp
fishhook across the palm of Sahara's bright blue hand. The skin
breaks. Vitagua spurts out in a geyser, rising to join the sphere of
fluid extracted from Mark.

Sahara shrieks again, voice still inhuman, like a starling's call. The birds around us flutter. Their clamor lessens as Sahara's wings shrink, as her features become more human. She struggles against her magical puppet-strings, with increasing success: as the vitagua drains from her body, Astrid has less to hold on to.

Sahara sinks from her position in midair, falling to the forest floor, hands stretched up toward the liquid magic bled from her body. As her feet touch down I take her arms. She struggles, but her strength is no match for mine.

This is the woman we've been so afraid of?

A last few drops of vitagua well up out of her cut hand, and then the scratch begins to bleed red. The only blue left is in the edges of the torn skin.

"Residue," I murmur.

Caught in my arms, Sahara Knax bursts into tears.

"Get the chantments off her," Astrid orders, tossing the chanted bottle cap on her palm.

I ease the long coat off Sahara. Its pockets are heavy with chantments, and I pass them to a dazed and wary Mark Clumber. The two of us pat her down, looking for other items. Chains and baubles dangle from her throat, her wrists and ankles. We pull off rings and earrings, stripping her of all the jewelry as she flaps and fights.

"She harmless now?" Mark rasps when we're done. I glance up, startled—I've never heard him speak.

"Don't I wish." Astrid sets the newly chanted bottle cap against Sahara's chest, between her collarbones. Sahara tries to lunge away, but I hold her.

"What does that one do?" I ask.

"You'll see." A drop of vitagua falls from the pool still floating above us, landing on the spot where the chantment meets Sahara's skin.

Astrid presses on the cap with a fingertip and the metal disappears into Sahara's flesh, vanishing without leaving a mark. "Magic calls to magic," she says. "The chantment will draw the residue out of your body and into itself."

"It won't change anything." Sahara heaves with all her strength, and I lose my grip. She stumbles a half step . . . and then her knee buckles.

"The bottle cap keeps her from running," Astrid explains as her childhood friend pitches into the dirt.

Sahara screams in all-too-human frustration, and the gathered starlings fly away.

"It's for the best, Princess," Astrid tells her. "You're going back to Roche, Will?"

Am I? I imagine packing it all in, becoming a chanter. Living in the bizarre city I saw in the unreal. It's a surprisingly tempting fantasy . . . but it's preposterous. I can't do anything until I've located Carson and Ellie. And I'm not ready to let go of the real. If it is slipping away, that only makes it more precious. "I'm going back."

"Take Sahara with you."

"Are you serious?"

"Roche wants her, right?"

I am flabbergasted. "But—"

"Remember the point, Will," she says gently. "I can't waste energy on her."

"Just as Roche shouldn't have," I say, feeling as though I've only just caught on. "You were the one he needed to contain."

"He spent all those weeks searching for her—"

"While you spent them recovering from your grief."

"I needed time." She lays a finger on Sahara's cheek. Testing her resolve?

"You can't walk away from me," Sahara says, a charming half smile lighting her face. "Come on, I'm drained, you've won. What damage can I do now?"

"Cut my throat in the night? Eat at my peace of mind?"

"I could atone or some maudlin thing. Astrid, you can't leave me here with them. Not me."

"I want you to get better, Sahara," Astrid replies quietly. "I want you to be uncontaminated, to live a—"

"You *love* me," she insists fiercely.

"I always will," Astrid says. "But—"

"Don't say it."

"We'll never be friends again."

Sahara shakes her head, turning on the charm, wheedling. When Astrid shakes her head, eyes full of sympathy, she goes red with rage.

"Will," Astrid says, "take her to Roche."

She turns her back on Sahara, walking to the edge of the lake. The unreal fades into view before her, an expanse of white sand opening up near the water. A step takes her to the boundary between the worlds. One foot rests on the unreal dune; the other remains on broken cedar and moss.

I trot in her wake. I ought to try to arrest her, but the idea seems ridiculous. Instead I catch her hand and murmur, "That offer you made . . ."

"It'll be open whenever you're ready."

I squeeze, not wanting to let go, and paper scrapes my palm. Astrid is holding something. Gently, I pry her fingers open.

It is one last card, a portrait of the two women standing back to back. Astrid's painted face, confined as it is to one side of the image, seems to be looking for a way out. Everything she wanted is behind her: Sahara, looking skyward, ready to fly away.

The portrait is a bleak one. Astrid's view is blocked by prison bars. Jacks's blood stains her stomach and legs.

In this portrait Astrid's despair is so deep, I feel it running in my veins. I want to give her everything she has lost: be her rescuer, save the world for her. Give her that ordinary life she wanted.

I don't need an oracle to tell me that I'm not that man.

"It's okay, Will—it's old news," Astrid says. She turns over the picture and shows me another portrait. Her gaze is clear in this one, and she's wearing the same waterlogged jeans she's dressed in now. She has found a measure of peace. "Get your prisoner back to Roche, okay?"

"I will," I say. "I guess . . . I'll be seeing you?"

"Don't sweat the future—that's my problem. You're about to be a big hero. Enjoy it, okay?"

I nod. My next words are forced, pushed up from my belly through a dry throat. "And you? What now?"

Astrid Lethewood looks up, beaming.

"Now? Now's the part where I remake the world."

I must look alarmed, because she reaches for my hand. "It's the curse that makes the magic dangerous, Will. Once it's broken, we can release the magic, carefully. We'll free all the trapped people in the unreal . . . maybe even find Jacks."

"That's a tall order."

"I won't be alone." She glances at the pool of vitagua still hanging above us, liquid magic she drew out of her contaminated friends. It rises and expands, growing like a balloon and getting farther and farther away. With every second, it gets lighter, thinner, harder to see. Eventually it disappears.

The trees, dusted by a vapor-thin edge of magical contamination, begin to grow. Their leaves brighten, and out-of-season flowers bloom at our feet in a carpet.

"Mark," Astrid says. "You still want in the gang?"

Clutching Sahara's coat and the collection of chantments, Mark Clumber scuttles through the opening between worlds, kicking up clouds of unreal sand.

"Good-bye, Will," Astrid says.

I raise my hand in farewell.

An image of her burns on my retinas as the worlds between us pop apart like bubbles. Astrid is in the unreal, and I am left facing my reflection in the lake, warped by water into someone I no longer recognize. Left with a magic ring, a pack of cards, and the world's most wanted fugitive.

And I'm standing at the heart of an alchemical apocalypse.

But that's more than I can process. I decide to believe in Astrid's newfound confidence. What else can I do?

Tucking the cards into my coat, I take the wilted Sahara Knax by a forearm, nudging her in the direction of the compound. She limps dramatically; it's going to be a long walk.

"She's lying, you know," Sahara says. "She doesn't know shit."

"Caroline Forest, Sahara—where is she?"

"Screw you."

"Do you know where you're going? You think anyone is going to care what happens to you? You could use a friend."

"I know where your loyalties lie."

"Caro flew to San Francisco on the fourth of August. She stayed with our children at one of your Alchemite safe houses."

"Let me go and I'll tell you where she is."

"Do I look that stupid?"

She scoffs. "I could pass the word to my followers. She could kill herself. She could kill them—"

It's as far as she gets before I knock her onto the writhing grass. "You're powerless now, remember?"

"Just you keep believing that," she spits.

I'm saved from my temper by a young soldier who pounds up to me at a run. "Sir? Commander's searching for you. You okay?"

It's not a question I can answer honestly, so I yank Sahara to her feet. "I'd be better if you got us a car."

"Us?" He sees who I'm with and goes pale with shock. His jaw drops; then, as it registers that she's helpless, in *custody*, he reaches out, as if to touch her. Sahara glares and he recoils, looking at me in awe.

"It's over," he says, wonderingly.

It's just begun, I think. The ground shivers, and a ladybug the size of my fist flies past, carapace chattering. "How about that car, soldier?"

"Temporary command post's half a click due east," he replies.

There's nothing to do but hike down.

We start toward the command post, me assisting our notorious prisoner as our escort struts at my side, his hand resting on his weapon. His steps are light; I barely hear his shoes hitting the ground. The activity in the trees doesn't bother him: we've caught Sahara; he thinks this is the end.

Her arrest has renewed his faith in the future. He believes I'm holding the end of our troubles by her slender brown arm. They all will. Will they believe me if I tell them it's not true?

The ground jolts again, harder. Sahara stumbles, and as I catch her, our eyes meet. We are both scared.

The part where I remake the world, Astrid said.

We break out of the murmuring trees and below us I see an improvised square of official vehicles surrounded by armed soldiers. Within the square is a collection of salvaged equipment and satellite dishes.

Beyond the cars where the underground complex should be is a smoking crater. I take a long look: at the hole, the dead machines, the ruined concrete and steel walls. Millions of dollars of property scattered like trash, destroyed as surely as Astrid's house or the aircraft carrier yesterday. The air around us is icy.

Behind me, the trees are blue-green and growing fast, and nobody's paying attention. Roche must believe he can napalm them later, if he's noticed them at all.

"Laid waste to your big-ass fortress," Sahara boasts. "Not bad if I'm supposedly the warm-up act, huh?"

The soldier gives me a queer look, uncomprehending.

"Keep walking, Sahara." But though my voice is confident, my hands and feet grow icy as I look farther, beyond the burnt-out complex, beyond the smoke rising like a column above the trees. I look all the way to the horizon, where the midafternoon sun hangs above the mountains in a sky already aglow with alchemized radiance, drowning in purest blue light.

A. M. Dellamonica lives in Vancouver, British Columbia, with her wife, Kelly Robson, and two very spoiled cats. She has been publishing short fiction since the early nineties. Her work has appeared in *Asimov's Science Fiction, Realms of Fantasy, Sci Fiction*, and *Strange Horizons*, and also in numerous anthologies; her 2005 alternate history of Joan of Arc, "A Key to the Illuminated Heretic," was short-listed for the Sidewise Award and the Nebula Award. In 2006 she received a Canada Council Grant for Emerging Artists for a novel-in-progress called *The Wintergirls*. She also teaches writing courses through the UCLA Extension Writers' Program.

Dellamonica's website is at www.alyxdellamonica.com; she also has a blog, Planetalyx, at LiveJournal. She sings alto in a Vancouver community choir, has a blue belt in ki aikido, and is an avid digital photographer.

She is currently working on *Blue Magic*, the sequel to *Indigo Springs*.

FICTION

Dellamon
ica

Dellamonica, A. M.

Indigo Springs

DUE DATE   14.99
